NO GREATER LOVE

DANIELLE STEEL

NO GREATER LOVE

CORGI BOOKS

NO GREATER LOVE
A CORGI BOOK : 0 552 13523 2

Originally published in Great Britain by Bantam Press,
a division of Transworld Publishers

PRINTING HISTORY
Bantam Press edition published 1991
Corgi edition published 1992

9 10

Set in 10pt Plantin by
Cambridge Composing (UK) Ltd, Cambridge.

Corgi Books are published by Transworld Publishers,
61–63 Uxbridge Road, London W5 5SA,
a division of The Random House Group Ltd,
in Australia by Random House Australia (Pty) Ltd,
20 Alfred Street, Milsons Point, Sydney, NSW 2061, Australia,
and in New Zealand by Random House New Zealand Ltd,
18 Poland Road, Glenfield, Auckland 10, New Zealand
and in South Africa by Random House (Pty) Ltd,
Endulini, 5a Jubilee Road, Parktown 2193, South Africa.

Printed and bound in Germany by
Elsnerdruck, Berlin.

To Beatrix,
sweet, special girl,
you fill me with joy
and love and admiration.
Brave girl, may your life
be ever easy,
on calm seas,
with kind people,
gentle breezes, sunny days
and if a storm should ever come
one day,
remember how much we love you.

And to John,
for whom there never was,
never will be,
never could be . . .
a greater love than mine for you.
No greater love,
and all my heart and life,
forever.

          d.s.

NO GREATER LOVE

1

The only sound in the dining room was the ticking of the large, ornate clock on the mantelpiece, and the occasional muffled rustling of a heavy linen napkin. There were eleven people in the enormous dining room, and it was so cold that Edwina could barely move her fingers. She glanced down at them and caught the gleam of her engagement ring in the morning sunlight, and then smiled, as she glanced across the table at her parents. Even with his eyes cast down at his plate, she could see the mischief at the corner of her father's mouth. And she was sure that beneath the table, he was holding her mother's hand. Left to themselves, they were always teasing and laughing, and whispering playfully, and their friends liked to say that it was no wonder they had six children. At forty-one, Kate Winfield still looked like a girl. She had a lithe figure and a slim waist, and walking behind them at a distance, it was often difficult to discern Kate from her oldest child, Edwina, who was also tall and had shining dark hair and big blue eyes. They were very close, as the entire family was. It was a family in which people laughed and talked and cried and hugged and joked, and great mischief was conducted daily.

It was difficult now for Edwina to keep a straight face as she watched her brother George make clouds of vapor with his breath in the arctic dining room, which their uncle Rupert, Lord Hickham, liked to keep slightly colder than the North Pole. The Winfield children were used to none of this. They were used to the comforts of their American life in the warmer climate of California. They had come all the way from San Francisco a month before to stay with their aunt and uncle, and announce Edwina's engagement. Their ties to England seemed to be repeating themselves. Kate's sister, Elizabeth, had married Lord Rupert twenty-four years before, and she had come to England to be the second viscountess and the mistress of Havermoor Manor. At twenty-one, she had met the much older Lord Hickham when he had come to California with friends, and she'd been swept off her feet. More than two decades later, her nieces and nephews found it difficult to understand the attraction. Lord Hickham was distant and gruff, inhospitable in the extreme, he never seemed to laugh, and it was obvious to all of them that he found it extremely unpleasant having children in his house. It wasn't that he *disliked* them, Aunt Liz always explained, it was just that he wasn't *used* to them, never having had any of his own.

This by way of explanation for his being most unamused when George put several small tadpoles in his ale, after Uncle Rupert went duck hunting with their father. In truth, Rupert had long since stopped wanting children of his own. Long since, he had felt he needed an heir for Havermoor Manor, and his other large estates, but eventually it was obvious that that was not part of the Grand Plan. His first wife had suffered several miscarriages before dying in childbed some seventeen years before he married Liz. And he had always blamed Liz for not bearing him any children either, not that he would have wanted as many as Kate and Bertram had, and he would most assuredly have wanted his to be better behaved than theirs were. It was absolutely shocking, he assured his wife, what they let their children get away with. But

Americans were known for that. No sense of dignity or control, no education, no discipline whatsoever. He was, however, enormously relieved that Edwina was marrying young Charles Fitzgerald. Perhaps there was some hope for her after all, he had said grudgingly when Liz told him.

Lord Hickham was in his seventieth year, and he had been less than pleased when Kate wrote to her sister and asked if they could all come and stay. They were going to London to meet the Fitzgeralds and announce the engagement, but Rupert was aghast at the idea of all of them coming to Havermoor after that.

'What, with their entire brood?' He had looked horrified when Liz gently asked him the question over breakfast. It was almost Christmas then and they wanted to come in March. And Liz had hoped that with enough time to reassure him, Rupert might actually let them do it. Liz longed to have her sister come, and have the children brighten her dreary days. She had come to hate Havermoor in twenty-four years of living there with Rupert, and she missed her sister, and the happy girlhood they had shared in California.

Rupert was a difficult man to live with, and theirs had never become the marriage she had dreamed of. Early on, she had been impressed with his dignified airs, his title, his acute politeness with her, and his stories about the 'civilized life' they all led in England. They were twenty-five years apart in age, and when she had arrived at Havermoor she had been shocked to find the Manor dismally depressing and in shocking disrepair. Rupert had kept a house in London in those days as well, but within a very short time, Liz had discovered that he never used it. And after four years of never setting foot in it, he had sold it to a good friend. Children might have helped, she felt, and she was anxious to start a family and hear young, happy voices echoing in the somber halls. But year after year, it became more obvious that this was not to be her fate, and she lived only to see Kate's children on her rare visits back to San Francisco. And eventually, even those small pleasures were denied her, as Rupert became too ill to travel much of the time, and finally announced that he was too old. Rheumatism, gout, and just plain old age discouraged him from roaming the world anymore and as he needed his wife to wait on him night and day, Liz was trapped at Havermoor with him. More often than she liked to admit, she found herself dreaming of going back to San Francisco, but she hadn't been able to go there in years. All of which made Kate and the children's visit all the more important to her, and she was all the more grateful when Rupert finally said they could stay with them, as long as they didn't stay forever.

This proved to be even more wonderful than Liz had expected. It had been several years since they'd last come, and she was overjoyed. And her long walks in the garden with her sister were all that she had longed for in her years away. Once upon a time, the two had been almost like twins, and now Liz was amazed to see Kate still looking so youthful and so pretty. And she was obviously still very much in love with Bert. It made Liz regret again that she had ever married Rupert. Over the years, she had often wondered what life might have been like had she never become Lady Hickham and instead married someone in the States.

She and Kate had been so carefree as young girls, so happy at home with their doting parents. They had each been properly presented to Society at eighteen, and for a short time they had both had a wonderful time going to dinners and balls and parties, and then too quickly,

Rupert had appeared, and Liz had left for England with him. And somehow, although she had lived in England for more than half of her life now, Liz was never able to feel that she truly belonged here. She had never been able to alter the course of anything that Rupert had already established at Havermoor Manor before she arrived. She was almost like a guest here, a guest with no influence, no control, and one who was not even very welcome. Since she had failed to produce an heir, her very presence there seemed without purpose.

Her life seemed so totally in contrast to her sister Kate's. How could Kate possibly understand? With her handsome dark-haired young husband, and her six beautiful children who had come like gifts from heaven at regular intervals for most of the twenty-two happy years they'd been married. There were three sons and three daughters, all full of high spirits and good health, with their parents' beauty and intelligence, and lively sense of humor. And the odd thing was that although Kate and Bert seemed almost too blessed, when one saw them, one had absolutely no doubt that they deserved it. Although Liz had envied her sister for years, and often said as much, she could never allow herself to be jealous in an ugly sense. It all seemed so right, and Kate and Bert were such basically good and kind and decent people. They were all too well aware of the riches of joy they had, and often made a point of saying as much to the children. It made Liz nostalgic for what she had never known . . . the love of a child . . . and the obviously warm loving relationship that Kate shared with her husband. Living with Rupert had made Liz quiet over the years. There seemed so little to say anymore, and no one to whom to say it. Rupert was never particularly interested in her. He was interested in his estates and his ducks and his grouse and his pheasants and, when he was younger, his horses and his dogs, but a wife was of relatively little use to him, especially now with his gout bothering him so much of the time. She could bring him his wine, and ring for the servants, and help him up to bed, but his sleeping quarters were far, far down the hall from hers, and had been for many years, once he had understood that there would be no children from her. All they shared was regret, and a common home, and the chill loneliness that they shared there. All of which made a visit from the Winfields like throwing back the shutters, tearing down the curtains, and letting in the sunshine and fresh clean air of a California springtime.

There was a small hiccup, and then a stifled giggle at the other end of the table from where Liz and Kate sat on either side of Lord Rupert, who appeared not to have heard it. The two women exchanged a smile. Liz looked ten years younger than she had when they arrived. Seeing her sister and her nieces and nephews always seemed to revive her sagging spirits. It always broke Kate's heart to see how her sister had aged, and how lonely she was living here in the bleak countryside, in a house she hated, with a man who very clearly did not love her, and probably never had. And now she felt the anguish of their leaving. In less than an hour they'd be gone. And Lord only knew when they'd come back to England. Kate had invited her to come to San Francisco to prepare for Edwina's wedding, but Liz felt she couldn't leave Rupert for that long and promised to come in August for the wedding.

The hiccup at the other end of the table was almost a relief, as Kate glanced down at nearly-six-year-old Alexis. George was whispering something to her, and Alexis was about to erupt in gales of giggles.

'Shhh . . .' Kate whispered, smiling at them, and glancing at Rupert. Their own breakfast table usually sounded like a Fourth of July picnic, but here they had to behave, and the children had been very good about following Rupert's rules this time, and he seemed to have mellowed slightly with age. He had taken sixteen-year-old Phillip hunting several times, and although Phillip had admitted to his father that he hated it, he was always polite, and he had thanked his uncle and gone with him. But Phillip was like that, wanting to please everyone, he was always kind, gentlemanly, polite, and astonishingly thoughtful for a boy his age. It was difficult to believe he was just sixteen, and he was clearly the most responsible of all the Winfield children. Except for Edwina, of course, but she was twenty, and full grown, and in five months she would have a home and a husband of her own. And a year after that, she hoped perhaps even her own baby. It was hard to believe, Kate kept reminding herself, that her oldest child was old enough to be married and have children.

They were going home now to attend to all the preparations for the wedding and Charles was coming back to the States with them as well. He was twenty-five years old, and he was head over heels in love with Edwina. They had met, by chance, in San Francisco, and they had been courting since the summer before.

The wedding was going to be in August, and they were taking with them yards and yards of the exquisite ivory fabric that Kate and Edwina had bought in London for her dress. Kate was going to have her dressmaker in San Francisco embroider it with tiny pearls, and the veil was being made by a Frenchwoman who had just come to London from Paris. Lady Fitzgerald was going to bring it over with her, when they came to San Francisco in late July. And there would be lots to do in the meantime. Bertram Winfield was one of the most prominent men in

California. He and his family owned one of San Francisco's most established newspapers, and there were hundreds of people they had to invite to the wedding. Kate and Edwina had been working on the list for a month. And it was already well over five hundred people. But Charles had only laughed when Edwina warned him that there might even be more.

'It would have been far, far worse in London. There were seven hundred two years ago when my sister got married. Thank God, I was still in Delhi.' He had been traveling for the past four years. After two years in India with the military, he had then ventured to Kenya where he had spent a year, traveling, and visiting friends, and Edwina loved hearing about all of his adventures. She had begged to go to Africa on their honeymoon, but he thought something a little tamer might be in order. They were planning to spend the autumn in Italy and France, and they wanted to be back in London by Christmas. Edwina secretly hoped that she'd be pregnant by then. She was madly in love with Charles, and she wanted a large family like her own, and a relationship like the happy one she'd always seen between her parents. It wasn't that they didn't fight from time to time, they did, and it almost shook the chandeliers in their San Francisco house when their mother really lost her temper, but along with the anger, there was always love. There was always tenderness and forgiveness and compassion, and you always knew, no matter what, how much Kate and Bertram loved each other, and that was exactly what Edwina wanted when she married Charles. She didn't want anything more or less than that, she didn't need an important man, or a title, or a fancy manor house. She wanted none of the things that had once foolishly drawn her Aunt Liz to Uncle Rupert. She wanted goodness, and a sense of humor, and a fine mind, someone she could laugh with, and talk to, and work hard with. It was true that theirs would be an easy life, and Charles enjoyed sports and going out with friends, and had never been burdened with having to earn a living, but he had the right values and she respected him, and one day he would have his father's seat in the House of Lords.

And just as Edwina did, Charles wanted at least half a dozen children. Her parents had had seven, although one had died at birth, a baby boy who had been between her and Phillip, which had made Phillip feel even more responsible about everything. It was as though he were taking someone else's place by being the eldest son now, and everything he did, or that touched him, seemed to put more responsibility on Phillip's shoulders. All of which made life very simple for George who, at twelve, felt his only mission in life was to amuse everyone, and responsibility was the furthest thing from his mind at any moment. He tortured Alexis and the little ones whenever he could, and felt that it fell to him to lighten his older brother's more austere behavior, and he did that by short-sheeting his bed, or putting harmless snakes in his shoes, a well-placed mouse was useful here and there, and pepper in his morning coffee, just to start his day off right. Phillip clearly felt that George had been visited on him to ruin his existence, and during his rare and extremely cautious pursuits of the opposite sex, George always seemed to appear, ready to lend his expert assistance. George was in no way shy around girls, or around anyone for that matter. On the ship coming over, it seemed as though everywhere Kate and Bertram went, they were greeted by enchanted acquaintances of their second son . . . 'Oh, *you're* George's parents! . . .' as Kate inwardly cringed, wondering what he had done now, and Bertram laughed, amused by the boy's harmless pranks and high spirits. The shyest one was their next born, little Alexis with her halo of white-blond curls and huge blue eyes. The others all had dark hair and blue eyes, like Kate and Bert, except Alexis, who was so fair her hair looked almost white in the sunlight. It was as though the angels had given George all their mischief and courage, and they had given Alexis something very delicate and rare. And everywhere she went, people looked at her and stared and talked about how pretty she was. And within minutes, she would disappear into thin air, only to reappear again, quietly, as though on silent wings, hours later. She was Kate's 'baby girl', and her father's 'special baby', and it was rare that she ever spoke to anyone else. She lived happily within the confines of her family, and was protected by all. She was always there, silent, seeing, yet saying very little. And she would spend hours in the garden sometimes, making garlands for her mother's hair. Her parents meant everything to her, although she also loved Edwina. But Edwina was actually closer to their next born, four-year-old Frances. Fannie, as she was called by everyone; Fannie of the sweet round cheeks, and chubby hands and sturdy little legs. She had a smile that melted everyone's heart, especially her daddy's, and like Edwina, she had blue eyes and shining black hair. She looked exactly like their father, and she had his good nature. She was always happy, and smiling, and content wherever she was, not unlike baby Teddy. He was two, and the apple of his mother's eye. He was talking now, and discovering everything around him, with a headful of curls and a cheerful belly laugh. He loved to run away and make Oona chase him. She was a very sweet Irish girl who had fled Ireland at fourteen, and Kate had been grateful to find her in San Francisco. She was eighteen years old, and a great help to Kate with

18

all of them. Oona would tell Kate reproachfully that she spoiled little Teddy. And she laughingly admitted that she did. She indulged all of them at times because she loved them so dearly.

But what Kate marveled at each year was how different they all were, what totally unique and individual people they were, and how varied their needs. Everything about them was different, their attitudes, their aspirations, their reactions to her, and life, and each other . . . from Alexis's timidity and many fears, to Phillip's staunch sense of responsibility, to George's complete lack of it, to Edwina's strong, quiet self-assurance. She had always been so thoughtful and so kind, thinking of everyone before herself, that it was a relief to Kate to see her now, head over heels in love with Charles, and enjoying it so much. She deserved it. For years, she had been her mother's right hand, and it seemed time to Kate now for Edwina to have her own life.

She only wished that she weren't moving to England. This was the second time in her life that she had lost someone she loved to foreign shores. And she could only hope that her daughter would be happier than her sister Liz had been there, but fortunately Charles was entirely different from Rupert. Charles was charming and intelligent and attractive and kind, and Kate thought he would make a wonderful husband.

They were meeting Charles that morning at the White Star dock in Southampton. He had agreed to go back to the States with them, in part because he couldn't bear the thought of leaving Edwina for the next four months, and also because Bert had insisted that he sail with them as an engagement present. They were sailing on a brand-new ship, on her maiden voyage. And all of them were enormously excited.

They were still sitting in the dining room at Havermoor Manor, and Alexis was starting to laugh out loud, as George said something outrageous in an undertone and then made more vapor with his breath in the frigid air. Bertram was starting to chuckle at his children, when Rupert stood up at last, and they were free to go. Bert came around the table to say good-bye to him, and shook his brother-in-law's hand. And for once, Rupert was actually sorry to see him go. He liked Bert, he had even come to like Kate over the years, although he was still rather tentative about their children.

'It's been wonderful staying with you here, Rupert. Come back to see us in San Francisco,' Bertram said, and almost meant it.

'I'm afraid I'm a bit beyond it.' They had already agreed that Liz would travel to San Francisco for the wedding with Charles's parents. She was just relieved that Rupert would let her go at all, and she could hardly wait. She had already picked her dress in London with Kate and Edwina.

'If you feel up to it, come.' The two men shook hands again. Rupert was glad they had come, and now glad again that they were going.

'Do write and tell us about the ship. She must be quite something.' He looked envious, but only for a moment. And this time Liz was not envious at all. Just thinking about boats of any kind made her desperately seasick. She was already dreading the crossing in July. 'Will you write about it for the paper, Bert?'

Bert smiled. He seldom, if ever, wrote anything for his own paper, except for an occasional editorial, when he couldn't restrain himself. But this time, he had to admit, he had thought about it more than once. 'I might. If I do, I'll send you a copy when we run it.'

Rupert put an arm around Bert's shoulders, and walked him to the door, as Edwina and Kate rounded up the younger children with Oona, the Irish girl, and saw to it that everyone went to the bathroom before they left for Southampton.

It was still shockingly early, the sun was just coming up, and they had a three-hour drive ahead of them to Southampton. Rupert had delegated his chauffeur and two of the stableboys to take them to Southampton in three cars with what little luggage they still had. Most of the trunks had gone down the day before, and would be waiting for them in their staterooms.

And within a few moments, the children had piled into all three cars, Edwina and Phillip with some of the luggage, and George, who insisted on sitting with the stableboy who was at the wheel, Oona with Fannie and little Teddy and the rest of their bags in another car, and Kate and Bertram were going to ride in Rupert's own Silver Ghost with Alexis. Liz had volunteered to come with them, but Kate had insisted that it was too long a journey. They would see each other in four months anyway, and it would be too lonely for her coming back alone in the empty convoy. Instead the two women embraced, and for a long moment, Liz held her fast, not knowing why she felt so emotional this morning.

'Take good care . . . I'll miss you so . . .' It seemed so painful seeing her go this time, as though she just couldn't bear too many more partings. Liz hugged her again, and Kate laughed, straightening the very stylish hat that Bertram had bought her in London.

'It'll be August before you know it, Liz,' Kate whispered gently in her sister's ear, 'and you'll be home again.' She kissed her cheek, and then pulled away to look at her, wishing that Liz didn't look so worn and so dejected. It

21

made her think again of Edwina's moving to England when she married Charles, and Kate could only pray that her daughter's life would turn out to be happier than her sister's. She hated the thought of her being so far away, just as she hated the thought of leaving Liz here now, as Rupert harrumphed, and instructed their drivers, and urged them to leave so they wouldn't miss the ship. She was sailing in just under five hours.

'She's sailing at noon, isn't she?' He pulled out his pocket watch and consulted Bert, as Kate gave Liz a last hug and then climbed into the car, pulling Alexis in beside her.

'Yes, she is. We'll be there in plenty of time.' It was seven-thirty in the morning on the tenth of April.

'Have a marvelous trip! She's a great ship! Good sailing!' He waved as the first car drove away, and Liz stood close to him as the second car followed, and then the last, as Kate waved from the window with a broad smile, with Alexis on her lap, and Bertram sitting next to her with an arm around her shoulders.

'I love you! . . .' Liz called out as they sped away in the roar of the engines. 'I love you . . .' The words faded away as she wiped a tear from her eye, not sure why she felt so worried. It was silly really, she'd be seeing them all again in August. She smiled to herself then as she followed Rupert inside. He locked himself in his library as he frequently did in the morning, and Liz walked back into the dining room to stare at their empty seats, and watch their empty plates being cleared away, and a terrible feeling of loneliness overwhelmed her. Where they had been only moments before, the room that had been so full of life and the people that she loved, was all so empty now, and she was alone again, as the others sped toward Southampton.

2

As they approached the dock at Southampton, the car that Kate and Bertram were in led the convoy of Lord Hickham's automobiles to the place where first-class passengers were embarking. In the second car, George was jumping up and down on his seat, and Edwina finally had to insist that he sit down before he drove her and Phillip utterly crazy.

'Look, look at her, Edwina!' He was pointing to the ship's four impressive smokestacks, as Phillip urged him to calm down. Unlike his more exuberant younger brother, Phillip had done considerable reading about the ship as soon as he knew that they would be sailing on her maiden voyage. She had a nearly identical sister ship, the *Olympic*, which had been in operation since the year before, but this was literally the largest ship in existence. The RMS *Titanic* was marginally bigger than her sister ship, but she was half again as large as any other liner afloat, anywhere in the world, and George was in awe of her when he saw her. His father's newspaper had called her 'The Wonder Ship' when they'd written about her, and on Wall Street she'd been called 'The Millionaires' Special'. It was an extraordinary privilege to be sailing on her maiden voyage. Bert Winfield had reserved five of the twenty-eight special staterooms on B Deck, which were among the many features that set her apart from any other ship in operation. These staterooms had windows instead of portholes and were beautifully decorated with French,

Dutch, and British antiques. The White Star Line had outdone themselves in every way. And the five staterooms of the Winfield party were interconnecting so as to make them seem like one very large suite, rather than several adjoining rooms.

George was going to be rooming with Phillip, Edwina with Alexis, Oona with the two little ones, Fannie and Teddy, and Bertram and Kate were in the largest of the staterooms, in a room just next to the one occupied by their future son-in-law, Charles Fitzgerald. It promised to be a festive crossing, and George could hardly wait to get on the ship, as he dashed out of the car a moment later and headed for the gangplank. But his brother was too quick for him and he grabbed his arm and hauled him back to where Edwina was helping her mother with the others.

'Just where do you think you're going, young man?' Phillip intoned, sounding more like his father than himself as George gave him a look of intense irritation.

'You're beginning to sound like Uncle Rupert.'

'Never mind that. You stay right here until Father tells you that you can board the ship.' He glanced over Edwina's shoulder then and saw Alexis shrinking back against her mother's skirts, and the nurse struggling with the two younger ones, both of whom were crying. 'Go help with Teddy. Oona's trying to help Mother organize the bags.' And their father was in the process of dismissing Lord Hickham's drivers. It was the kind of situation George normally liked, utter chaos, which would allow him to disappear and do exactly what he wanted.

'Do I have to?' He looked horrified at the prospect of having to baby-sit when there was so much to discover. The *Titanic*'s awe-inspiring hulk stood next to them at the pier and all George wanted to do was get on her to discover

24

all her secrets. He had a lot of exploring to do, and he could hardly wait to start. There was not a moment to be wasted.

'Yes, you *have* to help.' Phillip growled again, pushing George in the direction of the younger ones, as he went to assist his father. He noticed out of the corner of his eye then that Edwina was having something of a time with Alexis.

'Don't be silly.' She was kneeling next to her on the pier, in the elegant new blue wool suit that she'd worn when she'd gone to meet Charles's parents. 'What is there to be afraid of? Look.' Edwina gestured toward the huge ship. 'It's just like a floating city, and in a few days we'll be in New York, and then we'll take the train back to San Francisco.' Edwina tried to make light of it, and make it sound like an adventure, but Alexis was clearly terrified of the awesome mass of the ship, and she dived into her mother's skirts and began to cry again as she pulled free of Edwina.

'What's the matter?' Kate glanced over at her oldest daughter and tried to hear what she was saying above the din as the band playing on the bridge launched into ragtime. But aside from that, thus far there had been very little fanfare. The White Star Line had apparently decided that too much fuss would be vulgar. 'What happened?' Kate was trying to calm Alexis.

'She's scared,' Edwina mouthed, and Kate nodded. It was always poor little Alexis who was terrified of new events, new people, new places, and she had been afraid coming over on the *Mauretania*, too, and had asked her mother repeatedly what would happen if she fell in the water.

Kate stroked her silky golden curls with her thinly gloved hand, and stooped to whisper a secret to her. Her words brought a smile to the child's lips, when she reminded her that in five days it would be her birthday. She was going to be six and her mother had promised her a birthday party on the ship, and another when they got back to San Francisco. 'Alright?' she whispered to the frightened child, but Alexis only shook her head as she started to cry all over again and clung to her mother.

'I don't want to go.' And then before she could say more, she felt herself gently scooped up in powerful hands and lifted onto her father's shoulders.

'Sure you do, sugarplum. You wouldn't want to stay here in England without us, would you? Of course not, silly girl. We're all going home now on the most wonderful ship ever built. And you know what I just saw? I saw a little girl just about your age, and I'll bet that before we get to New York you two are best friends. Now, let's go aboard and see what our rooms look like, shall we?' He held her firmly on his shoulders and she had stopped crying by then as he took his wife's arm, and shepherded his family up the gangplank. He set Alexis down when they were safely on board the ship, and she clung tightly to his hand as they walked up the grand staircase to the upper deck and peeked in the gym windows at the much-talked-about electric camel.

People were roaming everywhere, looking at the handsome decor, the beautiful wood paneling and wood carvings, the detailing, the elaborate chandeliers, the draperies, the five grand pianos. Even Alexis was quiet as they walked around the ship, before going to B Deck to their staterooms.

'It's quite something, isn't it?' Bert said to Kate, and she smiled. She loved the idea of being on shipboard with him. It seemed so cozy and safe and romantic, suspended between two worlds, with everyone comfortable and well taken care of. For once, she was planning to let Oona chase after the children more than she usually did, and Kate was going to relax with her husband. He had looked particularly enchanted when he saw the gymnasium, and peeked into the smoking room, but Kate grinned and wagged a finger at him.

'No, you don't! I want to spend some time with you on this trip.' She moved closer to him for a moment and he smiled.

'You mean Charles and Edwina aren't the only young lovers on this ship?' he whispered to his wife, as he continued to hold Alexis's hand.

'I hope not.' Kate smiled meaningfully at him, and gently touched his cheek with the tips of her fingers.

'Alright, everybody, what do you say we go to our staterooms, unpack a little bit, and then do some more exploring?'

'Can't we go now, Dad?' George pleaded. He was about to burst with excitement, but Bert insisted that it would be easier if they let the little ones see their rooms and settle in, and then he would personally escort George on his adventures. But the temptation was too much for George, and before they reached B Deck, two floors below the gym, George had disappeared and Kate was worried about where he had gone to, and she wanted Phillip to go and find him.

'Let him be, Kate. He can't go far. As long as he doesn't get off the ship, he'll be fine, and he's much too excited to be on it to get off for anything in the world. I'll go and look for him myself once we get settled.'

Kate hesitantly agreed, but she was nonetheless worried about what mischief he might get into. But as soon as they saw the lovely staterooms Bertram had reserved for them, they were all far too happy and distracted to think of

27

anything else, and everyone was delighted to see Charles when he arrived a few moments later.

'Is this it?' He stuck his handsome head in the doorway of the main parlor, his dark hair perfectly groomed, his blue eyes dancing as he saw his future bride, and she leapt to her feet as she saw him and ran across the small private sitting room which Kate and Bertram planned to use, if they wanted to get away from the children.

'Charles!' Edwina blushed furiously, as she flew into his arms, her hair the same color as his, her eyes an even deeper blue, and everything about her attesting to their happiness as he swung her right off the floor while Alexis and Fannie giggled.

'What's so funny about that, you two?' He loved to play with the little girls, and he thought Teddy was the sweetest baby he had ever seen. He and Phillip were good friends, and even wild George amused him. It was a wonderful family, and he was deeply grateful to have found Edwina. 'Have you seen the doggies yet?' he asked the girls over their sister's shoulder. Fannie shook her head, but Alexis looked suddenly worried. 'We'll go visit them after your naps this afternoon.' He was almost like a father figure to them, just as Edwina was like another mother.

'Where are they?' Alexis asked worriedly, anxious about the dogs now.

'In cages way, way downstairs, and they can't get out,' Edwina reassured her. Alexis would never leave the stateroom for the rest of the trip, if she thought there might be a danger of running into a dog lurking in the hallways, outside their cabin.

Edwina turned the children over to Oona then, and followed Charles to his stateroom. Her father had reserved him a lovely room, and away from the children's sharply

28

probing eyes, he pulled her closer to him and kissed her gently on the mouth, as Edwina caught her breath, forgetting everything but the powerful presence of her future husband. There were moments, like this one, when she wondered how they would ever wait until August. But there was no question of that, even on this most romantic ship. Edwina would never have betrayed her parents' faith in her, nor would Charles, but it was going to be difficult to restrain themselves until mid-August.

'Would you like to take a walk, Miss Winfield?' Charles smiled at his fiancée as he tendered the invitation.

'I would love to, Mr Fitzgerald.' He laid his heavy coat down on the bed, and prepared to stroll outside on the deck with her. It wasn't particularly cold in port, and he was so happy to see her that he could think of nothing else. They had only been apart for a few days, but every hour seemed too much to them now, and she was glad he was going back to San Francisco with them. It would have been unbearable if he hadn't. 'I missed you terribly,' she whispered as they walked back up the grand staircase to the Promenade Deck just above them.

'So did I, my love. It won't be long now before we never have to be apart again, not even for a moment.'

She nodded happily, as they wandered past the French 'sidewalk café' with its little 'boulevard' in front, and the rapid-fire chatter of the French waiters, as they glanced over at Edwina and smiled in admiration. Many of the first-class passengers seemed to be intrigued by the little 'bistro'. It was a novelty that existed on no other ship, like so many other features of the *Titanic.*

They walked on to the forward half of the Promenade Deck then with its huge glassed-in section that allowed one to look out over the sea, and be sheltered from the weather. 'I have a feeling we're going to find a lot of little cozy corners of our own on this ship, my love.' Charles smiled and pulled her hand more tightly through his arm, and Edwina laughed as he said it.

'So is George. He already got lost on the way to the staterooms. That child is hopeless. I don't know why my mother doesn't throttle him.' Edwina looked exasperated at the mention of her brother.

'She doesn't because he's so charming,' Charles defended him. 'George knows exactly how far to go.' She couldn't really disagree, although at times she would have liked to strangle him herself.

'I suppose so. It's amazing how different he is from Phillip. Phillip would never have done anything like that.'

'Neither would I as a child. Perhaps that's why I admire him now. I wish I had. And George will never have to regret missing anything he "should have done". I'm sure he's done it all.' He laughed and Edwina smiled happily up at him, as Charles put an arm around her shoulders and they watched the huge ship slowly pull away from the dock. She found herself praying that her father had been right, and George hadn't left the ship during his brief excursion. But somehow, like her father, she suspected that he wouldn't, there was too much to see right here, without leaving the ship. And as they looked down, the ship's fiercely resonant whistles gave a blast, rendering all conversation impossible. There was a real feeling of excitement in the air, and Charles pulled her into his arms again and kissed her gently as they listened to the whistles just above them.

Assisted by six tugs, the mammoth ship crept out of the slip and into the channel, headed for Cherbourg, where they were to pick up more passengers before going on to Queenstown and then the high seas and New York. But within moments, there was a brief interlude of excitement that those below were unaware of, but the passengers on deck watched with amazement as the huge ship glided past an American and a British liner, tied up at the quay due to a recent coal strike. The American Line's *New York* had been moored to the White Star's *Oceanic*, and the two small liners stood side by side, rendering the passage for the *Titanic* extremely narrow. There was a sudden sound of what seemed almost like pistol shots, and with no warning the lines tying the *New York* to the *Oceanic* gave way, and the *New York* drifted toward the *Titanic* to within a few feet until it looked as though she would ram the *Titanic* portside. With a series of quick maneuvers, one of the tugs assisting the *Titanic* out of the harbor passed a line to the *New York* and deckhands were able to stop her drift before she collided with the *Titanic*. The *New York* was then towed away, and the *Titanic* was able to steam out of port and head for Cherbourg. But it had been very close, the *Titanic* had almost been rammed. And it was a most impressive series of maneuvers that had spared them. The passengers who had seen it all felt as though they had witnessed an exhibition of remarkable skill. But the *Titanic* seemed invincible, invulnerable to all. The *Titanic* was four city blocks long, or eight hundred and eighty-two feet, as Phillip had precisely informed them earlier, and she was anything but easy to maneuver.

'Was that as close as I thought it was?' Edwina inquired, mesmerized by what she had just seen, and her fiancé nodded.

'I believe so. Shall we have a little glass of champagne at the Café Parisien to celebrate our safe departure?' Edwina nodded happily and they headed back to the 'sidewalk café', where, within minutes, a breathless and slightly rumpled George managed to find them.

'What are you doing here, Sis?' He appeared on the

'boulevard' of the café, with his cap askew, his shirttails out, and one knee of his trousers filthy dirty. But he had never looked happier in his life.

'I might ask you the same question. Mother was looking for you everywhere. What on earth have you been doing?' Edwina scowled at him.

'I had to look around, Edwina.' He looked at her as though she were extremely stupid, and then cast a winning glance at Charles. 'Hello, Charles, how are you?'

'Very well, thank you, George. How's the ship? Sound? Are you pleased with her?'

'She's great! Did you know there are four elevators and they each go nine floors? There's also a squash court, and a swimming pool, and they're carrying a brand-new motorcar to New York, a Renault, and there are some pretty fantastic machines in the kitchen. I couldn't get in to steerage when I tried, but I checked second class and it seems all right, there was a very nice girl there,' he reported, as his future brother-in-law looked vastly amused, and Edwina was horrified at the performance of her younger brother. He had absolutely no self-control, and wasn't even embarrassed by his disheveled appearance.

'I'd say you've had a good look at everything, George. Well done,' Charles congratulated him, and the errant child grinned proudly. 'Have you been to the bridge yet?'

'No.' The boy looked disappointed. 'I haven't really had much time to have a good look at the bridge yet. I was up there, but there were too many people to really see what was going on. I'll have to go back there later. Do you want to go for a swim after lunch?'

'I'd like that very much, if that suits your sister's plans.'

But Edwina was fuming. 'I think you should be put down for a *nap*, with Fannie and Teddy. If you think you

32

can run all over this ship, acting like some wild young hoodlum, you've got another think coming, from me, if not from Mama and Papa.'

'Oh, Edwina,' the boy groaned, 'you don't understand anything. This is really important stuff.'

'So is behaving properly. Wait until Mama sees the way you look.'

'What was that?' Her father's voice spoke from just behind her, and there was a ring of amusement to it. 'Hello, Charles . . . Hello, George, I see you've been busy.' There was even a small smear of grease across his face, and George had never looked more pleased with life or more at ease, as his father looked down at him with open amusement.

'This is just great, Dad.'

'I'm glad to hear it.' But at that exact moment, Kate caught a glimpse of her son as she approached, and scolded him when she reached them.

'Bertram! How can you allow him to look like that! He looks . . . he looks like an urchin!'

'Do you hear that, George?' his father asked calmly. 'I'd say it's time to clean up. May I suggest that you go to your stateroom and change into something a little less . . . uh . . . worn . . . before you overly upset your mother.' But his father looked more amused than annoyed, as the boy grinned up at him with a wide smile that mirrored his own. But Kate was far less amused as she told George to take a bath and change his clothes before reappearing.

'Oh, Mom . . .' George looked imploringly at Kate, but to no avail. She pulled up her sleeve, took his hand in her own, and marched him downstairs, where she left him with Phillip, who was studying the passenger list, hoping to find someone he knew there. The Astors were on board, of course, and Mr and Mrs Isidor Straus, of the family who owned Macy's. There were many, many famous names, and several young people as well, but no one Phillip knew, not yet anyway. But he had seen several young ladies who appealed to him, and he was hoping to meet them during the crossing. He was still studying the passenger list when his mother escorted George into the room and asked her older son to see to it that he clean up and behave himself, and Phillip promised to do his best, but George was already chafing to be off again. He still wanted to visit the boiler room and the bridge, and go back to the kitchen again, there were several machines they hadn't let him use, and there was one elevator he still had to check to see if it went farther up or down than the others.

'It's a shame you don't get seasick,' Phillip said to him mournfully as Kate went back to the others on the Promenade Deck.

She and her husband enjoyed a pleasant lunch with Edwina and Charles, and then met up with Phillip and George and Oona and the younger children after their naps, and Alexis seemed a little less worried about the ship by then. She was fascinated by the people chatting and strolling all around, and by then she had met the little girl that her father had mentioned earlier. Her name was Lorraine, and she was actually closer to Fannie's age. She was three and a half and she had a baby brother named Trevor, and they were from Montreal. She had a doll just like Alexis's. They were grown-up lady dolls, and Alexis called hers Mrs Thomas. She had gotten her from Aunt Liz for Christmas the year before, and Alexis went everywhere with her. Lorraine's had almost the same face, but her hat and coat weren't as fancy as the one Aunt Liz had sent, and Mrs Thomas was wearing a pink silk dress that Edwina had made, under the black velvet coat that she had come with. She had high button shoes, too, and that afternoon Alexis took her for a walk with her as she strolled around the Promenade Deck with her parents.

The ship docked at Cherbourg at Alexis's bedtime that night. The little ones were already asleep, and George had disappeared again. Kate and Edwina were dressing for dinner, while Charles, Phillip, and Bertram waited in the smoking room for the ladies.

They had dinner in the main dining saloon on D Deck that night, the men all in white tie, of course, and the women in exquisite dresses they had bought in London or Paris or New York. Kate wore the incredible pearl and diamond choker that had once been Bertram's mother's. The dining saloon itself was exceptionally beautiful with carved woodwork, shining brass, and crystal chandeliers, and the three hundred first-class passengers dining there looked like visions in a fairy tale in the brightly lit room. Edwina thought she had never seen anything as beautiful as she looked around, and then smiled at her future husband.

After dinner, they sat in the adjoining reception room, where they listened to the ship's band play for hours, and finally Kate yawned and admitted that she was so tired she could barely move. It had been a long day, and she was happy to stroll back to their staterooms with her eldest son and her husband. Edwina and Charles had decided to stay a little longer, and Kate had no objection to it. And when Phillip checked and found George sound asleep in bed they were all relieved to realize that he was no longer on the loose.

At noon the next day, they made their final stop, to pick up steerage passengers in Queenstown, and suddenly as they watched the passengers boarding, from high up

Oona gave a squeal and clutched the railing of the Promenade Deck.

'Oh, my Lord, Mrs Winfield! It's me *cousin*!'

'How on earth can you tell from here?' Kate looked unconvinced. She was a very emotional girl, and not without a vivid imagination. 'I'm sure it can't be.'

'I'd know her anywhere. She's two years older than me, and we was always like sisters. She's got ginger hair, and a little girl, and I see them both . . . Mrs Winfield, I *swear* it! . . . She's been talking about coming to the States for years . . . oh, Mrs Winfield.' There were tears swimming in her eyes. 'How will I find her on the ship?'

'If that's really your cousin, we'll ask the purser. He can check the third-class passenger list, and if it's she, she'll be on it. What's her name?'

'Alice O'Dare. And her daughter is Mary. She'll be five now.' The information wasn't lost on Kate. If she was two years older than Oona, she'd be twenty . . . with a five-year-old daughter . . . she couldn't help but wonder if there was a husband, too, but she didn't want to offend Oona by asking, and she correctly assumed that there probably wasn't.

'Can I play with her little girl?' Alexis asked quietly. She was feeling better today. After a night in a cozy bed, the *Titanic* didn't seem quite so scary. And all the stewards and stewardesses were so nice to her that she was actually beginning to enjoy it. And Fannie thought it was fun too. She had crept into Edwina's bed that morning, and found Alexis already there, and pretty soon Teddy had climbed into bed with them, too, and a little while later, George appeared and sat on the edge of Edwina's bed, tickling all of them, until their squeals and gales of laughter finally woke Oona. She had come running, and then grinned when she saw all of them. Just as she smiled from ear to

36

ear when she found her cousin's name on the passenger list. There it was, plain as day. Alice O'Dare. She went to tell Edwina, while she was dressing for dinner at the A la Carte Restaurant with Charles and her parents.

'Miss Edwina . . . I was right . . . it was my cousin coming on the ship today. I just knew it. I haven't seen her in four years and she hasn't changed a bit!'

'How do you know?' Edwina smiled at her. She was a sweet girl, and she knew that Oona was genuinely fond of the children.

'One of the stewardesses stayed with the little ones for an hour during their naps, while I went down to steerage to see her. She was on the passenger list, the purser said, and I had to see her.' And then, as though to defend herself, 'Mrs Winfield knew. I told her and she said I could go.'

'I'm sure it's alright, Oona.' It was an odd position for Edwina sometimes, neither mistress nor child, and she knew that Oona and others in their house sometimes saw her as a spy, because she might mention something to her mother. 'Your cousin must have been very happy to see you, I'm sure.' She looked kindly at the girl, feeling light-years older. And feeling relieved and happy, Oona smiled.

'She's a beautiful girl, and little Mary is so sweet. She was only a year old the last time I saw her. And she looks just as Alice did as a child! Ginger hair like fire.' She laughed happily, and Edwina smiled, clipping on a pair of her mother's diamond earrings.

'Is she going to New York?'

The young Irish girl nodded, feeling blessed by the fates. 'She was. She has an aunt and some cousins there, but I was after telling her to come to California. And she says she'll try. I'll do anything I can to help her.' Edwina smiled at her. The girl looked so happy, and it was nice for her to have relatives on the ship, and then suddenly she thought of something she knew her mother would have thought about too.

'Did you wash your hands carefully when you came back?'

'I did.' She looked faintly hurt, but she understood. To them, third class was like a disease, a place one never saw and wouldn't want to. But it hadn't been as bad as Oona had expected. It was nothing like her own cabin, of course, and none of the bits and pieces in the cabin were very fancy, but it was decent and clean, and it would get them all to America in one piece, and in the end, that was all that mattered. 'Aren't we lucky, Miss Edwina? To be on the same ship . . . fancy that . . . faith, I never thought I'd have so much good fortune.' She smiled at Edwina again, and went back to her cabin to watch the children, as Edwina walked into the parlor to join her parents and Charles. They were having dinner that night at the elegant A la Carte Restaurant, and Edwina could only agree with Oona as she smiled across the room at her intended. They were all lucky, and blessed, for the lives they led, the people they loved, the places they went to, and this beautiful ship taking them back to the States on its maiden voyage. As she stood holding Charles's hand, in her pale blue satin dress, her hair softly piled high on her head, her engagement ring glistening on her finger, Edwina Winfield knew that in all her life, she had never been as lucky or as happy. And as she drifted into the hall on Charles's arm, as Kate and Bertram chatted cozily, she knew it was going to be a special night, a prelude to a wonderful lifetime.

3

The days on the *Titanic* seemed to glide by with ease and pleasure. There was so much to do, and seemingly so little time in which to do it. It was all too pleasurable, and so easy, suspended between two worlds, on the ship that offered absolutely everything from exquisite meals to squash games and swimming pools and Turkish baths.

Phillip and Charles enjoyed several games of squash and rode the stationary bicycles and the mechanical horses every morning while Edwina tried the novelty of the electric camel. George rode the elevators instead, making friends, and the entire family had lunch together every day. And then, when the little ones went for naps with Oona, Kate and Bertram would go for long walks on the Promenade Deck, talking about things they hadn't had time to discuss for years. But the days went too quickly, and they were over almost before they knew it.

Their evenings were spent dining in either the main dining saloon or the even more elegant A la Carte Restaurant, where the Winfields were introduced to the Astors by Captain Smith on the second day of the trip. Mrs Astor commented to Kate about their lovely family, and from several things she said, Kate deduced that the new Mrs Astor was expecting. She was considerably younger than her husband, and they appeared to be very much in love. Whenever Kate saw them together after that, they were always talking quietly or holding hands, and once she had seen them kissing on their way into their stateroom. The Strauses were a couple Kate had decided she liked too. She had never seen two people so compatible and so obviously in love after so many years, and during her one or two conversations with Mrs Straus she had discovered that she had a wonderful sense of humor.

There were three hundred and twenty-five first-class passengers in all, many of them interesting, some well known, and she had particularly enjoyed meeting a woman named Helen Churchill Candee. She was a writer, and had written several books, and seemed interested in a wide variety of subjects. A wide variety of 'subjects' were interested in her as well. And Kate had noticed repeatedly that the attractive Mrs Candee was seldom surrounded by fewer than half a dozen men, some of them the most attractive on the ship, with the exception of Kate's own husband.

'See what you could have done with your life, if you weren't stuck with me,' Bert teased as they wandered past Mrs Candee's deck chair, where a group of men were waiting breathlessly for every word, and Kate could hear her elegant laughter ring out as they walked away. But she could only laugh herself. It was something Kate Winfield had never even thought of. The very thought of leading a life like Mrs Candee's only made her smile. She loved her own life, with her children, and her husband.

'I'm afraid I'd never do as a femme fatale, my love.'

'Why not?' He looked hurt, as though she were questioning his taste. 'You're a very beautiful woman.'

'Silly thing.' She kissed his neck and then shook her head, with a girlish grin. 'I'd probably always be running around with a handkerchief, blowing someone's nose for them. I think I was just destined to be a mother.'

'What a waste . . . when you could have had all of Europe at your feet, like the illustrious Mrs Candee.' He was teasing, but he was also very much in love with her, as she was with him.

'I'd rather have you, Bertram Winfield. I don't need all that.'

'I suppose I should be grateful.' He smiled down at her, thinking of the years they had shared, the happiness, the joys, the sorrows. They had a good life, and they were not only lovers but good friends.

'I hope Edwina and Charles have what we do one day.' She spoke quietly, and this time Bert knew she meant it.

'So do I.' And despite the chill air that had come on them that afternoon, he stopped and pulled his wife into his arms and kissed her hard. 'I want you to know how much I love you,' he whispered to her, and she smiled. He looked much more serious than usual, and she gently touched his face before kissing him again.

'Are you alright?' He seemed so intense, which was unusual for him.

He nodded. 'Yes, I am . . . but sometimes it doesn't hurt to say the words instead of just think them.' They walked on hand in hand. It was Sunday afternoon, and that morning they had attended Captain Smith's divine service and prayed for 'Those at Sea'. It was a quiet day, and it was growing so cold that almost everyone had gone indoors now. They stopped and looked at the gym, and saw Mrs Candee there, with young Hugh Woolner. Bertram and Kate walked on after that, and finally decided to go inside for tea. It was just too cold to stay outside any longer. And once inside, they noticed John Jacob Astor having tea with his young wife, Madeleine, in a corner of the lounge, and then they saw George, with Alexis in tow, having tea with two elderly ladies across the room.

'Will you look at him?' Bert grinned. 'God only knows

what that boy is going to do when he grows up. I shudder to think sometimes.' He left Kate at their table in the lounge, and went over to introduce himself to the two elderly ladies who were entertaining his children. He thanked them profusely for their kindness, and eventually brought the children back to the table where Kate was waiting for them. 'What on earth are you doing here?' he asked on the way back, and with a look of amusement at Alexis who had seemed quite comfortable with two strangers, which was rare for her, 'And what did you do with Oona?'

George was perfectly happy to answer.

'She went to visit her cousin downstairs, and she left the little ones with a stewardess. I told her I was bringing Alexis to you,' he said, shrugging happily, 'and she believed me.'

'George took me to the gym,' Alexis announced proudly, 'and the swimming pool, and we rode up and down in all the elevators. And then he told me we'd have to find someone to give us little cakes, so we did. They were very nice,' she announced matter-of-factly with her angelic face, satisfied with her big adventure. 'I told them that tomorrow is my birthday.' Which was true. Kate had ordered a birthday cake for her the day before, and Charles Joughin, the head baker, had promised to make it with white icing and pink roses, and it was going to be a surprise for Alexis.

'Well, I'm glad you two had such a lovely time.' Bert was still amused by them, and even Kate laughed as she listened to Alexis's descriptions of what they'd done. 'But perhaps next time you'd better come with us, instead of inviting yourselves to tea with strangers.' George grinned at them both, and Alexis cuddled up to Kate, who gently kissed her cheek, and held her close to her. Alexis loved being near to her mother like that, she loved her warmth and her softness, and the feel of her hair when she turned her head, and the smell of her perfume. There was a special bond between the two. There was no denying it, it just was, and it didn't mean Kate loved the others less. It just meant that at certain times, Alexis was very special. Kate loved all of the others, too, but there was a kind of need Alexis had for her that none of the others seemed to have, which was just as well. It was as though Alexis had never quite pulled away from her, and perhaps she never would, and perhaps, Kate sometimes thought, perhaps she would never have to. At times Kate hoped that she could keep her close to her forever, particularly if Edwina went to live in England.

Edwina and Charles came into the lounge from outdoors a little while later, after their stroll. They waved as they saw Bert and Kate. Edwina was still trying to warm her hands as she approached them.

'It's freezing out there, isn't it, Mama?' Edwina was smiling again. She was always smiling now. Kate thought that she had never seen anyone as happy, except herself maybe when she married Bert. It was almost as though they were made for each other. And Mrs Straus had mentioned it, too, she had noticed the young couple more than once, and commented on them to Kate, about what a lovely young couple they made, and she hoped they would be very happy.

'I wonder why it's so cold,' Edwina said to her father as they ordered tea and buttered toast. 'It's much colder than it was this morning.'

'Our course is quite far north. If we keep an eye out tonight, we might even see a few little growlers,' he said, referring to tiny icebergs.

'Is that dangerous?' Edwina looked concerned, as their

tea and toast arrived, but her father shook his head reassuringly.

'It's not dangerous to a ship like this. You've heard what they say about the *Titanic*. She's unsinkable. It would take a lot more than an iceberg to sink a ship like this, and besides I'm sure that if there is any concern, the captain is proceeding with great caution.' In fact, they had been going close to twenty-three knots all day, which was a good speed for the *Titanic*. And by that afternoon, as they sipped tea and ate toast, the *Titanic* had already received three ice warnings from other ships, the *Caronia*, the *Baltic*, and the *Amerika*, but Captain Smith had not reduced their speed yet. He didn't feel he had to, he was keeping a careful watch on all conditions. He was one of White Star's most experienced captains. And after years with the line, he was retiring after this final prestigious trip.

Bruce Ismay, the head of the White Star Line, was on board too. And he had seen one of the ice warnings earlier as well. He had pocketed it after he and the captain had discussed it.

Kate put the children to bed herself that night, because Oona had gone back to steerage again to visit her cousin, and a stewardess had promised to baby-sit until she returned. But Kate didn't really mind. She liked taking care of the children herself, actually she preferred it. She noticed though that it was even colder than it had been earlier, as she took out extra blankets and tucked the children in more warmly.

When they went to the A la Carte Restaurant that night, and stepped outside for just a second to get some air, it seemed to be absolutely freezing. They were chatting on the way to dinner about Phillip's having found a girl. For several days, he had been staring at her from the deck above. She was in second class, and she was a lovely-looking girl, but there was no way he was ever going to meet her. She had glanced shyly up at him several times, and he dutifully went back to the same spot every day in the hope that he would see her again. And today, Kate feared that he had caught a dreadful cold standing out in the freezing weather. But the girl had apparently been a great deal more sensible, or perhaps her parents were. She hadn't shown up, and Phillip had been depressed all afternoon, and finally decided not to come to dinner at all.

'Poor thing,' Edwina sympathetically said to her mother as they took their seats at the table. Her father was having a word with Mr Guggenheim, and then stopped briefly to say something to W. T. Stead, the well-known journalist and writer. He had written several articles for the Winfield newspaper in San Francisco several years before. And then finally, Bertram joined them.

'Who was that man you were talking to, dear?' Kate was curious. She had recognized Stead, but she didn't know the other man.

'Benjamin Guggenheim. I met him in New York a number of years ago,' he explained, but on this subject he did not appear to be expansive. And Kate knowingly wondered if it was because of the woman he was with, a striking blonde, but something told her she was not his wife, and when she asked, her husband did not look inclined to discuss it with her.

'Is that Mrs Guggenheim?'

'I don't believe so.' The subject was closed, and Bert turned to Charles and asked if he had correctly guessed the day's run. It was five hundred and forty-six miles that day, and Bert had not guessed it correctly yet, but Charles had, and had won a little money doing so, on the first day.

The crossing had actually been a wonderful opportunity for them to get to know each other. And thus far, Bert and Kate liked what they had seen of Charles, and knew that their daughter was going to be very happy once they were married.

'Can I interest anyone in a brisk walk?' Bert suggested when they left the nightly concert in the reception room, but when they set foot outside, it was much too cold. It was absolutely glacial, and the stars were shining brightly.

'My God, it's cold,' Kate shivered despite her furs. 'It's unbelievably cold tonight.' But the night was crystal clear, and what none of them knew was that the radio operator had gotten warnings from two more ships, during dinner, about nearby icebergs. But all concerned were certain they had nothing to fear.

It was ten-thirty when they went downstairs to B Deck, and Bert and Kate chatted softly while they undressed, as Charles and Edwina continued talking over champagne in the parlor they all shared.

It was eleven when Kate and Bertram went to bed, and turned off the light, at approximately the same moment that the nearby *Californian* radioed the *Titanic* about the ice they had just seen. But the *Titanic*'s radio operator, Phillips, was frantically exchanging personal messages from the passengers to the relay station at Cape Race in Newfoundland. Phillips had sharply told the *Californian* not to interrupt him. He had dozens of messages from passengers yet to send, and he had heard about the ice before. But this time he did not think it necessary to warn the captain. The captain had seen the same messages before, too, and had not been impressed by them, so the *Californian* rang off, and did not give this particular iceberg's location. Phillips went on sending his messages to Cape Race, and Kate and Bertram drifted off to sleep, while the children dreamed in their rooms nearby and Edwina and Charles nestled together on the couch in the parlor and talked about their hopes and dreams as the hour approached midnight.

They were still talking when there was a faint shudder of the ship, a kind of jarring, as though they'd hit something, but there was no major jolt, and nothing dramatic occurred. So they both knew that whatever it was, it couldn't have been very important. They continued talking for a few minutes after that, and then suddenly Edwina realized that a certain hum was gone, and with it a familiar impression of vibration. The ship had stopped, and for the first time Charles looked concerned.

'Do you think something's wrong?' Edwina looked worried, as he glanced out the window on the starboard side, but he could see nothing.

'I don't think so. You heard what your father told you today. This ship's unsinkable. They're probably just resting the engines, or changing course, or readjusting something. I'm sure it's nothing.' But he picked up his coat anyway, and kissed her gently on the lips. 'I'll go take a look and let you know what it is in a minute.'

'I'll come too.'

'It's too cold outside, Edwina. You stay here.'

'Don't be silly. It's colder than this at my uncle Rupert's house, inside, over breakfast.' He smiled, and helped her into her mother's fur coat. He was sure that nothing was wrong. And whatever it was, he was sure they were readjusting it, and they'd be on their way again before long.

In the halls, they encountered other curious passengers,

like themselves, people in nightgowns and fur coats, still in white tie and ballgowns, or bathrobes and bare legs. It seemed that a number of people, including John Jacob Astor, sensed something amiss and wanted to know what had happened. But a tour around the deck told them nothing more except what they already knew, that the ship was stopped, and three of the four great funnels were blowing steam into the night sky. But there appeared to be no visible sign of danger. There were no great mysteries to be solved, nothing major seemed to be amiss, and a steward finally explained that they had 'struck a little ice', but there was nothing to worry about. Mr Astor went back to his wife, and Charles and Edwina went back inside to get out of the cold, and were told that they had nothing to fear. In fact, if they wanted to see it, a little bit of the ice could still be seen in the third-class recreation area, and there were people on deck, facing the stern, watching the steerage passengers far below throw snowballs and chunks of ice as they laughed.

But the thrill of that did not appeal to Charles or Edwina and having determined that nothing was seriously amiss, they decided to go back to their staterooms. It was five minutes before midnight by then, and when they got back to their private parlor, they found Bertram waiting for them with a worried frown.

'Is something wrong with the ship?' He was whispering because his wife was still asleep, but he'd been worried since the engines stopped.

'Doesn't appear to be,' Charles answered right away, dropping his heavy coat on a chair, as Edwina peeled off her mother's fur coat. 'Apparently, we've hit some ice, but no one seems particularly concerned. The crew seem to be taking it in stride, and there's nothing to see on deck.' Charles looked relaxed, and Bertram seemed relieved. He felt a little foolish for being worried about it now, but he was a man with a family, and he had wanted to be sure that all was well. He said good night to them then, told Edwina not to stay up too late, and went back to bed, at exactly 12.03, just as far below the decks the stokers fought furiously to put out the huge ship's fires in her boilers, and water gushed across the mail room floor. The *Titanic* had indeed hit an iceberg and her first five so-called watertight compartments were full of water, from the gash the iceberg had caused. On the bridge, Captain Smith, Bruce Ismay, the head of the White Star Line, and Thomas Andrews, the ship's builder, stood in disbelief and tried to determine just how desperate was the situation.

Andrews's conclusions were far from cheering. There was no way around it, with five of her compartments filled with water, the *Titanic* could not stay afloat for long. The unsinkable ship was sinking. They thought they could keep her afloat for a while, but no one could be sure how long, and as Bertram Winfield went back to bed, he thought for just an instant that the floor beneath his feet was listing slightly, but he was certain he was mistaken.

And five minutes after midnight, at Thomas Andrews's urging, Captain Smith looked at the officers on the bridge and told them to uncover the lifeboats. There had been no lifeboat drill until then, no practice, no warnings, no preparation. This was the ship that could not sink, the ship they would never have to worry about, and now all the first-class stewards were knocking on doors, and in an instant Bert was back in the room. He had heard the voices the minute Charles opened the door to the parlor, but he couldn't hear the words. And now he heard them all too clearly. The steward was smiling, and speaking to them gently, as though they were all children and he wanted them to listen to him, but he didn't want them to be startled or frightened. Yet it was obvious, too, that he wanted them to do as they were told, and quickly.

'Everyone up on deck, with life belts on. Right now!' There were no bells, no sirens, no general alarm. In fact, the silence was eerie, but the look in the steward's eyes said that he meant it, and Edwina could feel herself move into another gear, the way she did when one of the children was hurt, and she suddenly knew that she had to move quickly to give her mother a hand with the others.

'Do I have time to change?' Edwina asked the steward before he moved on to the next room, but he only shook his head and tossed the words back over his shoulder.

'I don't think so. Just stay as you are, and put your life belt on. It'll help keep you warm. Just a precaution, but you must go up now.' He was gone then, and for a fraction of a moment she looked at Charles and he squeezed her hand, as her father went to wake her mother and the children. Oona was back by then, but like Kate and the children, she was fast asleep in her cabin.

'I'll help you get the children up,' Charles offered, and went to Phillip and George, got their life belts out for them, and urged them to hurry, while attempting not to frighten them too much, but it was difficult not to. Only George thought it sounded like good fun, but poor Phillip looked terribly worried as he slipped the life belt over his clothes and Charles showed him how to work it.

Edwina woke Alexis up first, with a gentle shake, and a quick kiss, and then she simply lifted Fannie from her bed, and gently shook Oona's arm, but the girl was looking wild-eyed as Edwina tried to explain to her what had happened, without panicking the children.

'Where's Mama?' Alexis looked terrified, and she ran

back to bed as Edwina told Oona to get Teddy, and just then Kate came out of their bedroom, pulling her dressing gown over her nightgown, looking sleepy but composed, and Alexis flew into her arms with a vengeance.

'What's going on?' Kate looked confused as her eyes went from her husband to her daughter, and then to Charles. 'Did I miss something rather crucial while I was asleep?' She felt as though she'd woken in the middle of a drama and she had no idea what it was that had happened.

'I'm not sure.' Bertram was honest with her. 'All I know is that we've hit some ice, they claim it's not serious, or at least that was what they told Charles half an hour ago, but now they want us all up on deck, in life vests, at our lifeboat stations.'

'I see.' Kate was already looking around the room, and glanced at Edwina's feet as she did. She was wearing gossamer-thin silver sandals with delicate heels, and her feet would have been frozen in less than five minutes on deck. 'Edwina, change your shoes. Oona, put your coat on, and put the life vests on Fannie and Teddy at once.' But Charles was already helping her, as Bertram went to put trousers over his pajamas and exchange his slippers for socks and shoes. He put on a sweater that he had brought and not yet worn, and then put on his coat and his life vest, and he brought a warm wool dress to Kate in the room where she was helping Alexis dress, and as he did, he was suddenly aware that the floor beneath his feet was now sloping more acutely, and for the first time since he'd woken up, he was secretly frightened.

'Come on, children, hurry up,' he said, trying to appear confident when he wasn't. Phillip and George were set. Edwina had brogues and her own coat on now, over her blue satin evening dress, and Charles had successfully helped her get clothes and life vests on Fannie and Teddy and Alexis. Only Oona was running around in bare feet and her nightgown. And Kate was pulling the heavy traveling dress Bert had handed her over her dressing gown, as she stepped into walking shoes, and then struggled into her fur coat.

'You have to dress,' Edwina hissed at Oona, not wanting to frighten the children more than they were, but wanting to impress on her the importance of the situation.

'Oh, Alice . . . I must go to my cousin Alice, and little Mary . . .' She was half crying and wringing her hands as she ran around the cabin.

'You'll do no such thing, Oona Ryan. You'll put your clothes on and come with us,' Kate snapped. She was still holding Alexis by the hand, and although the child was terrified, she was no longer protesting. She knew she would be fine, as long as she was with her mother and father. They were all ready, except for Oona, who was suddenly too frightened to join them.

'I can't swim . . . I can't swim . . .' she cried.

'Don't be ridiculous.' Kate grabbed her arm, and motioned to Edwina to start out with the others. 'You don't need to swim, Oona. All you have to do is come with me. We're going upstairs in a moment. But first you are going to put your dress on.' She put a wool dress of her own over the girl's head then, knelt at her feet and helped her slip on shoes, put one of her own coats over the girl's shoulders, grabbed a life vest, and within a matter of minutes they were just behind the others. But now the corridors were crowded with people heading for the decks, in equally peculiar outfits, with life vests and worried faces, although some laughed and said they thought it was all very foolish. It was twelve-fifteen by then, and Wireless Operator Phillips was making his first call for help, as the water level below decks rose rapidly higher, and much faster than Captain Smith had expected. After all, it was only half an hour since they'd hit the berg. But the squash court was filled to the ceiling by then, and Fred Wright, the squash pro, said nothing of it to young Phillip when he saw him on the way to the lifeboats.

'Should I have taken any of my jewelry with me?' Kate suddenly asked Bert worriedly. It was the first time she had even thought of it, and she didn't want to go back now. She had worn only her wedding ring, and it was all she really cared about or wanted.

'Don't worry about it.' He smiled and squeezed her hand. 'I'll buy you some new baubles if you . . . misplace these . . .' He didn't want to say 'lose', for fear of what that implied. He was suddenly terrified of what was going to happen to his wife and their children. They went all the way up to the Boat Deck, and when Bert glanced into the gym, he could see John Jacob Astor and his wife, sitting quietly on the mechanical horses. He wanted her out of the cold, for fear that being frightened and cold might cause her to lose the baby. They were both wearing life vests, and he had a third one across his lap, and as they talked, he was playing with his penknife. The Winfields walked on past the gym then, and they came out on the port side, where the crew were uncovering eight wooden lifeboats as the band started to play. There were another eight being uncovered on the starboard side as well, four toward the bow, four toward the stern, and there were also four canvas collapsible lifeboats. It was not a cheering sight, and as Bert watched them prepare the boats, he could feel his heart pound as he held his wife's hand tightly in his own. She was holding Fannie in one arm, and Alexis was standing as close to her as she could, while Phillip carried little Teddy. They stood closely huddled together in the cold, unable to believe that on this vast, indomitable ship they were actually uncovering the lifeboats and standing there in the middle of the night waiting to load them. There were murmured voices in the crowd, and a moment later, Kate saw Phillip talking to a boy he had befriended at the beginning of the trip. His name was Jack Thayer and he was from Philadelphia. His parents had been to a dinner party that night given by the Wideners, also of Philadelphia, for the captain. But Jack hadn't joined them, and he was talking to Phillip now; the two boys smiled for a moment, and then Jack moved toward another group, still looking for his parents. Kate saw the Allisons of Montreal, as well, with little Lorraine clutching her mother's hand and her beloved dolly. They were hanging back from the others, with Mrs Allison holding tightly to her husband's arm, and the governess holding the little boy in her arms, bundled up in a blanket, to protect him from the icy air of the North Atlantic.

Second Officer Lightoller was in charge of loading the lifeboats on the port side, and everywhere around him there was polite confusion. There had never been a lifeboat drill, nor were there lifeboat assignments for anyone but the crew, and even they weren't quite sure of where they were supposed to be and what they were supposed to be doing. Small groups of men were uncovering each of the lifeboats at random, and tossing in lanterns and tins of biscuits, but the crowds were still holding back as crewmen moved to the davits and began turning the cranks that swung the lifeboats out and then lowered them to where they could be boarded by the extremely hesitant group that stood and watched them. The band was playing ragtime, and Alexis began to cry then, but Kate was holding tightly to her hand and stooped to remind her that at this very moment, it was already her birthday, and later that day there would be presents, and perhaps even a cake.

'And later today, when we're all safely back on the ship, you'll have a very beautiful birthday.' Kate settled Fannie on her hip again, and pulled Alexis closer to her, as she glanced at her husband. He was trying to listen to what was being said in the groups around them, to see if anyone had any information he hadn't yet heard. But no one seemed to know what was going on, except that they were actually going to load the lifeboats, women and children first, and no men whatsoever at this time. Just then, the band began to play even louder and Kate smiled at all of them, belying the terror that was beginning to gnaw at her as she looked at the lifeboats. 'Nothing can be very wrong, or the band wouldn't be playing such pretty music, would they?' She exchanged a long look with Bertram then, and knew that he was frightened too, but there was very little that they could say now with their children all around them. And everything seemed to be happening so quickly.

Edwina was standing close to Charles, and he was chatting with a few young men. She and Charles were holding hands in the chill night air. She had forgotten to bring gloves, and he was trying to warm her icy fingers by holding them in his own. They called out for the women and children then, and everyone seemed to hang back as Second Officer Lightoller told them to step forward quickly. No one could bring themselves to believe that there was really any danger. A number of women seemed to hesitate, and then their husbands took charge. Messrs. Kenyon, Pears, and Wick led their wives forward and assisted them in, as the wives begged them not to make them go without them.

'Don't be foolish, ladies,' someone's husband said for all to hear, 'we'll all be back on the ship in time for breakfast. Whatever the trouble is, they'll have sorted it out by then, and think of the adventure you'll have had.' He sounded so jovial that some laughed, and a few more women timidly stepped forward. Many of them brought their maids with them, but the husbands were clearly told to stand back. They were loading women and children only. Lightoller would tolerate no man's even thinking of getting into a lifeboat. Despite the women's protests that their husbands could help row, Lightoller was having none of it. It was women and children *only*. And as he said the words again, Oona looked at Kate suddenly and started to cry.

'I can't, ma'am . . . I can't . . . I can't swim . . . and Alice . . . and Mary . . .' She began to back away from them, and Kate saw that she was going to start running. She moved away from Alexis briefly then, and tried to comfort Oona as she walked calmly toward her, but suddenly with a great shriek she was gone, running as fast as she could, down into the bowels of the ship, to find the door through which she had previously passed to enter steerage to visit her cousin and her little girl.

'Shall I go after her?' Phillip asked his mother with worried eyes as she walked back to where the children stood, and Kate looked anxiously up at Bertram. Little Fannie was whimpering by then, and Edwina was now holding baby Teddy in her arms. But Bertram didn't want any of them running after Oona. If she was foolish enough to run back, she would have to board a lifeboat on another part of the ship and rejoin them later. He didn't want any of them getting lost, it was imperative that they all stay together.

Kate hesitated, and then turned to him. 'Can't we wait?

I don't want to leave you. Perhaps if we wait, they'll call the whole thing off, and we won't have to put the children through all this for nothing.' But as she spoke, the deck slanted even farther, and Bertram knew that this was no longer an exercise. This was serious, and any delay on their part might be fatal. What he didn't know was that on the bridge, Thomas Andrews had informed Captain Smith that they had little more than an hour or so to stay afloat, and there were lifeboats for less than half the people on board the ship. Frantic efforts were being made to reach the *Californian*, only ten miles away, but she couldn't be roused, despite the radio operator's frantic efforts.

'I want you to go now, Kate.' Bert said the words quietly, and she looked into her husband's eyes and was frightened by what she saw there. She saw that he was worried and afraid, more afraid than she had ever seen him. And with that, she instinctively turned to look for Alexis, who had been next to her only a moment before. For once, she wasn't buried in her mother's skirts, and Kate had let go of her hand when she had hurried after Oona. But now as Kate turned to look, Alexis wasn't there. Kate turned around several times, glanced around in the crowd, and looked over at Edwina to see if she was with her, but Edwina was quietly talking to Charles, while George stood by looking tired and cold and less excited than he had half an hour before. But he cheered up visibly as an explosion of rockets flew up high into the air, lighting the night sky all around them. It was 12.45 by then, barely more than an hour after they'd hit the iceberg that everyone had said couldn't harm them.

'What does that mean, Bert?' Kate whispered, still glancing everywhere distractedly for Alexis. Perhaps she was talking to the Allison child, or comparing dolls, as they'd done before.

57

'It means this is very serious, Kate.' Bert explained the rockets to her. 'You must get off with the children at once.' And this time she knew that he meant it. He held her hand tightly in his own and there were tears in his eyes.

'I don't know where Alexis has gone,' Kate said, with a tone of rising panic in her voice, and Bert looked frantically over the crowd from his height, but still didn't see her. 'I think she must be hiding. I was holding her hand until I ran after Oona . . .' Tears sprang into her eyes. 'Oh, my God, Bert . . . where is she? Where could she have gone?'

'Don't worry, I'll find her. You stay here with the others.' He pressed through the crowd, and he walked through every group, glanced into every corner, running from one cluster of people to another. But Alexis was nowhere. He hurried back to Kate then, and as she stood holding the baby, and trying to keep track of George at the same time, frantic eyes looked up at her husband, asking a question, but he only shook his head in answer. 'Not yet,' was his only answer, 'but she can't have gone far. She never goes very far from you.' But he looked worried and distracted.

'She must have gotten lost.' Kate was on the verge of tears. This was no time for a six-year-old child to disappear in the tense moments as the *Titanic*'s passengers boarded the lifeboats.

'She must be hiding.' Bert frowned unhappily. 'You know how afraid she is of the water.' And how afraid she had been to come on the ship, and how Kate had reassured her that nothing could possibly happen. But it had, and now she had disappeared, as Lightoller called out for more women and children, and the band played on beside them. 'Kate . . .' Bert looked at her, but he already knew that she wouldn't leave without Alexis, if at all.

'I can't . . .' She was looking all around, and overhead the flares were exploding like cannons.

'Send Edwina then.' Perspiration stood out on Bertram's face, this was a nightmare they had never dreamed of. And as the deck continued to tilt beneath their feet, he knew that the unsinkable ship was sinking fast. He moved closer to his wife, and gently took little Teddy from her, unconsciously kissing the curls that fell over his forehead from under the wool cap Oona had put on him when they woke him in the cabin. 'Edwina can take the little ones with her. And you go in the next boat with Alexis.'

'And you?' Kate's face was deathly pale in the eerie white reflection of the rockets, as the band moved from ragtime to waltzes. 'And George and Phillip?' . . . and Charles . . .

'They won't let the men on yet,' Bert answered her question. 'You heard what the man said. Women and children first. Phillip, George, Charles, and I will join you later.' There was, in fact, a large group of men standing beside them now, waving at their wives as the lifeboat filled slowly. It was five minutes after one, and the night air seemed to be getting even colder, as the women continued to beg Second Officer Lightoller to allow their husbands to join them, but he wouldn't have it. And he sternly waved the men back, looking as though he would brook no nonsense.

Kate moved swiftly toward Edwina then, and told her what Bert had just said. 'Papa wants you to get in the lifeboat with Fannie and Teddy. And George,' she added suddenly. She wanted him to at least try to go with the others. He was a child, too, after all. He was only twelve. And Kate was determined to get him into a lifeboat with Edwina.

'What about you?' Edwina was startled, as she looked at her mother, shocked at the prospect of leaving the rest of her family on the ship, and taking only George and the two youngest with her.

'I'll come in the next one with Alexis,' Kate said calmly. 'I'm sure she's hiding right here, she's just frightened to come forward because she doesn't want to get in the lifeboat.' Kate felt slightly less confident than that, but she didn't want to communicate her panic to her eldest daughter. She wanted her to get in the lifeboat with the little ones. And it was no help that Oona had deserted them. Kate wondered how she was faring in steerage with her cousin. 'George can help you until Papa and I come.' But George groaned at the prospect, he wanted to stay till the end with the men, but Kate was firm as she led them all back to Bert, and Charles and Phillip followed. 'Have you found her yet?' Kate asked her husband, referring to Alexis while nervously glancing everywhere, but there was no sign of her anywhere. And Kate was anxious now for the others to get in the lifeboat so she could help Bert in his search for Alexis. But he was thinking of the others now. Lightoller was about to lower lifeboat number eight, the other women that were going were already in, although there were still a number of empty places. There would also have been enough room for the men, but no one would have dared challenge the intense little second officer's commands. There was talk of drawing guns if any of the men tried to board the lifeboat, and no one was anxious to challenge him to do that.

'Four more!' Bert called out to him as Edwina looked frantically at her parents, and beyond them at Charles, watching her in silent anguish.

'But . . .' She didn't even have time to speak as her father pushed her toward number eight with Fannie and George and baby Teddy in her arms.

'Mama . . . can't I wait for you? . . .' Tears sprang into

her eyes, and for an instant she looked as she had as a child, as her mother put her arms around her and looked into her eyes. Teddy started to cry then, and reached his chubby little arms out to his mother again.

'No, baby, go with Edwina . . . Mama loves you . . .' Kate crooned and she touched his face with her own, then kissed his cheek and his little hands, and then, with both hands she touched Edwina's face, looking tenderly at her oldest daughter. There were tears in her eyes, and this time they were not tears of fear, but of sorrow. 'I'll be with you every minute. I love you, sweet girl, with all my heart. Whatever happens, take good care of them.' And then she whispered, 'Be safe, and I'll see you in a little while.' But for an instant, Edwina wondered if her mother really believed that, and suddenly she knew she didn't want to go without her.

'Oh, Mama . . . no . . .' Edwina clutched at her, with little Teddy in her arms, and suddenly they were both crying for their mother, as the men's powerful arms grabbed her and George and Fannie, and Edwina's eyes flew wildly between her mother, her father, and Charles. She hadn't even had a chance to say good-bye to him, and she called out, 'I love you,' as he blew her a kiss and waved and suddenly his gloves came hurtling toward her. She caught them just as she sat down, never taking her eyes from his. He was staring at her strangely, as though he didn't want to let go of her with his eyes. 'Be brave, dear girl. We'll be with you in a minute,' he called out, and at the same instant, the lifeboat was lowered, and Edwina could barely see them. She glanced from her mother to her father to Charles, tears streaming from her eyes, until she couldn't see them anymore. Kate could still hear little Teddy crying as she gave a last wave, fighting back her own tears, as she stood on deck, holding tightly to her husband's hand. Lightoller had balked when they'd put George in the lifeboat, but Bert had been quick to say he was not yet twelve. And he didn't wait for the second officer to comment as he lifted his son into the lifeboat. He had lied by two months, but Bert had feared he might not get George on if he admitted his correct age. George himself had begged to stay with his father and Phillip, but Bert thought Edwina might need his help with the two others.

'I love you, children,' Bert whispered, staring at them till they were gone, as the lifeboat approached the water. Bert had shouted down his last words to them, 'Mama and I will be along soon,' and then turned away so they wouldn't see him crying.

And Kate gave an almost animal groan as they lowered the boat toward the water, and at last she dared to look down. She squeezed Bertram's hand. She could see Edwina holding Teddy, and clinging to Fannie's hand, and George looked up at them as the boat creaked and dropped slowly to the surface of the water. It was a delicate maneuver and Lightoller looked like a surgeon performing a difficult operation, one swift move, one careless gesture and the lifeboat would overturn on the way down, spilling its passengers into the icy water. And the voices below all shouted up at them, a mixture of frantic words, last messages, and I love you's. And then suddenly before they were halfway down, Kate recognized Edwina calling. She saw her waving frantically and nodding her head and pointing. And as Kate looked to the front of the lifeboat, she saw her. The halo of blond curls was turned away, but there was no mistaking Alexis huddled at the front of the lifeboat. And Kate felt a wave of relief pass over her as she shouted down to Edwina, 'I see her! . . . I see her! . . .' She was safe, with the others

62

. . . five children, her five precious babies all in one
lifeboat. Now all she had to do was get off with Phillip
and her husband, and Charles. He was chatting quietly
with some of the other men, who had just put their wives
in the lifeboat, and they were reassuring each other that
everything would be fine, and they would all be off the
ship shortly.

'Oh, thank God, Bert, she found her.' Kate was so
relieved to know where Alexis was that her whole body
visibly relaxed in spite of the continuing tension. 'Why on
earth would she get into the lifeboat without us?'

'Maybe someone grabbed her and put her in when she
walked away from us, and she was too frightened to speak
up. Whatever, she's safe now. Now I want you off next.
Is that clear?' He sounded stern only to mask his own
fears, but she knew him better than that.

'I don't see why I can't wait for you and Phillip and
Charles. The children will be fine with Edwina.' It was an
unnerving feeling, thinking of all of them in the lifeboat
without her, and yet now that she knew that Alexis was
safe in her older sister's care, Kate wanted to stay with
her husband. She shuddered at what it would have been
like to not know that Alexis was safe, and she thanked
God again that Edwina had been able to let her know
Alexis was with her and all right.

The lifeboats below were moving away from the ship,
and as number eight turned on the icy seas below, Edwina
clutched little Teddy to her, and she tried to maneuver
Fannie onto her lap as well, but the seats were too high,
she could barely make it. She wanted to move toward the
front to let Alexis know she was there, but it was
impossible to go anywhere, and George was busy rowing
with the others. It made him feel important, and in truth,
they needed his help. Finally, she asked one of the women

to let Alexis know she was there, and watched pointedly as word was passed along toward the front of the lifeboat, and finally the little girl turned her head, so Edwina could see her, but as she did, Edwina gave a gasp. She was a beautiful child, and she was crying because she'd left her mother on the ship, but she wasn't Alexis. And Edwina knew she had done a terrible thing. She had told her mother that Alexis was there, and they wouldn't look for her now on the ship. A sob broke from her as she stared, and little Fannie started to cry as Edwina clutched her to her.

And at that very moment, Alexis was sitting quietly in her stateroom. She had slipped away when her mother let go of her hand and ran after Oona, and she had gone back as she'd wanted to from the first. She had left her beautiful doll in her bed, and she didn't want to leave the ship without her. And once she had gone back to her room, the doll was there, and it seemed so much quieter here, and so much less scary than on deck. She wouldn't have to get in a lifeboat now, or fall in that ugly, dark water. She could just wait here until it was all over and everyone came back. She would just sit here, with her doll, Mrs Thomas. She could hear the band playing upstairs and the sounds of ragtime came drifting in the open windows, and voices and cries and murmurs. There was no running in the corridor now.

Everyone was on deck, saying good-bye to loved ones and hurrying into lifeboats, as the rockets continued to explode overhead, and the radio operator tried frantically to bring nearby ships to their aid. The *Frankfurt* was the first to reply, at 12.18, then the *Mount Temple*, the *Virginian*, and the *Birma*, but there had been no word at all from the *Californian* since eleven o'clock when she had warned them of the iceberg and Phillips had snapped at her radio operator not to interrupt him. Ever since then, her radio had been silent. In truth, her radio was shut off. But she was the only ship close enough to help them, and there seemed no way to raise her at all. Even the rockets were to no avail. All those who saw them, on the *Californian*, only assumed that they were part of the festivities on the much celebrated maiden voyage. And it never dawned on anyone for a moment that they were sinking. Who would ever have thought it?

At 12.25, the *Carpathia*, only fifty-eight miles away, contacted them and promised to come as quickly as she could. By then, the *Olympic*, the *Titanic*'s sister ship, had chimed in, too, but she was five hundred miles away and too far to help at the moment.

Captain Smith was stepping in and out of the radio shack by then, and after watching Wireless Operator Phillips send the standard distress signal, CQD, he urged them to try the new call signal SOS as well, in the hope that even amateurs might hear it. Any assistance at all would have been welcome and was direly needed now. It was 12.45 a.m. when the first SOS was sent, and at that moment, Alexis was alone in the silent stateroom, playing with her doll and humming softly as she sat quietly, continuing to play. She knew she would be scolded later when they all came back, but maybe they wouldn't be too angry at her for running away, because after all today was her birthday. She was six years old now, and her dolly was much older. She liked to say that Mrs Thomas was twenty-four. She was a grown-up.

On deck, Lightoller was filling another lifeboat, and on the starboard side, several men were climbing into the lifeboats now too. But on the port side, Lightoller was still strictly adhering to women and children only. The second-class lifeboats were being filled as well, and in third class, some of the passengers were breaking through barriers and locked doors, in the hope of boarding in second class or even first, but they had no idea where to go, or how to get there. Members of the crew were threatening to shoot them if they attempted to make their way through the ship, because they were afraid of looting and property damage aboard. The crewmen were telling them to go back the way they had come, as people shrieked and cried and begged to come past the crew members keeping them from the first-class lifeboats. One Irish girl, with another girl her own age, and a little girl, was insisting that she had come from first class in the first place, but the deckhand stolidly kept them from leaving third, he knew better than to believe her.

Kate and Bert walked into the gym for a minute then, to get warm again and escape the agonies of the tears and goodbyes and the visible tension as Lightoller loaded another lifeboat. Phillip stayed outside on deck, with Jack Thayer and Charles, who were helping the women and children into the lifeboats. Dan Martin had just put his bride in the same lifeboat with Edwina, and another man had just sent his wife and baby off with them. And in the gym, Kate and Bert noticed that the Astors were still sitting on the mechanical horses and quietly talking. She seemed in no hurry to get off, and he had their maid and valet on the deck, keeping an eye on the situation.

'Do you suppose the children are alright?' Kate looked worriedly at Bert in the gym, as he nodded, relieved that Edwina had found Alexis, and that at least five of the children had gotten off. He was still worried about getting Phillip and Kate off, and he was hoping that Lightoller would take Phillip in the end. There was less hope for Bert and Charles, and they both knew it.

'I think they'll be alright,' Bert reassured his wife. 'It's

66

certainly an experience none of them will forget. Nor will I,' he added with a serious look at Kate. 'I think she's going to sink, you know.' He had been sure of it for the last half hour, although none of the crew would admit it, and the band played on as if it were all in good fun though a slightly crazy evening. And then, Bert looked at her pointedly and took one of her long, slim hands in his own and kissed the tips of her fingers. 'I want you off in the next lifeboat, Kate. And I'm going to see if I can bribe them to take Phillip with you. He's only sixteen, they ought to be willing to take him. He's barely more than a child.' The problem wasn't convincing her, it was convincing Lightoller.

'I don't see why we don't wait until they start boarding the men too, and I can go with you then. I can't help Edwina now anyway, we'd be in different lifeboats. And she's a very capable girl.' Kate smiled, it was a terrible feeling not to be with them, yet she was sure that they'd be alright. She had to believe that. And Edwina was like another mother to them. All Kate had to worry about now was the safety of her oldest son, and her husband, and Edwina's fiancé, Charles. Once they were in a lifeboat with her, she didn't give a damn what happened to the ship, as long as everyone got off safely, and she saw no reason why they would not. Everything seemed to be moving ahead calmly, and the lifeboats weren't even full as they lowered them, which had to mean that there was plenty of room for everyone, or they wouldn't have lowered them without filling them completely first. And she was sure they had hours before anything serious happened, if anything serious happened at all. There was a false aura of calm that led her to believe they had nothing to fear.

But on the bridge, Captain Smith knew the truth. It

was well after one o'clock by then and the engine room was flooded. There was no doubt that she was going down, the only question was how soon. And he was sure now that it wouldn't be long. Wireless Operator Phillips was sending frantic messages everywhere, and on the *Californian*, their radio still turned off, they watched the rockets high above the *Titanic* without dreaming what they meant. They still thought she was celebrating. At one point, they noticed that she had begun to look very strange, and one of their officers thought she was sitting in the water at an odd angle. But still it never dawned on them that she was sinking. And the *Olympic* radioed and wanted to know if the *Titanic* was coming to meet them. No one understood what was happening, or how fast they were going down. It was inconceivable to all that the 'unsinkable' ship, the biggest ship afloat, was actually sinking. In fact, she was already halfway there.

And this time, when Bert and Kate stepped out of the gym again, the atmosphere was very different. People were no longer calling out to each other quite so gaily, and husbands were begging their wives to be brave and leave the ship in the lifeboats without them. And when the women refused, the husbands forced them into crewmen's arms, and more than one woman was tossed unwillingly into a lifeboat. Lightoller, on the port side, was still following the rule of women and children only, but on the starboard side, for a few men there was hope, particularly if they claimed to know something about boats. They needed all the help they could get to row them. A few people were openly crying now and there were heart-wrenching good-byes everywhere. Most of the children were gone, and Kate was relieved that theirs were, too, with the exception of Phillip, but he would leave with them. And then, out of the corner of her eye, she saw little Lorraine Allison clinging to her mother's hand on the deck, and it reminded her of Alexis, now safely off with her brothers and sisters in lifeboat number eight. Mrs Allison had kept Lorraine with her, and thus far she had refused to leave her husband, but she had put her younger child, Trevor, off with his nurse in one of the early lifeboats. More than once, Kate had seen families separate, and wives and children go on ahead, with the assumption that the husbands would get in the lifeboats that would leave the ship later. It was only toward the very end that it became obvious that almost all of the lifeboats were gone, and there were still almost two thousand people left on board with no way to escape, no way to flee the sinking ship. They were discovering what the captain, the builders, and the head of the White Star Line had known all along, that there weren't enough lifeboats for everyone. If the ship went down, most of them would drown, but who had ever thought the *Titanic* would sink and they would actually need the lifeboats in which to escape her?

The captain was still on the bridge, and Thomas Andrews, the managing director of the firm that had built the enormous ship, was still helping to load people into the lifeboats, as Bruce Ismay, head of the White Star Line, pulled his collar close around his neck and stepped into one of the lifeboats, and no one dared to say a word of challenge. He was lowered to safety with the few chosen lucky ones, leaving close to two thousand souls doomed on the sinking *Titanic*.

'Kate . . .' Bert was looking at her pointedly, as they watched the next lifeboat being swung out on the davits. 'I want you to go in this one.' But she quietly shook her head and looked at him, and this time when her eyes met his, they were quiet and strong. She had always obeyed him, but she knew she wouldn't this time, no matter what he said to sway her.

'I'm not leaving you,' she spoke softly. 'I want Phillip to go now. But I'm staying here with you. We'll leave together when we can.' Her back was very straight, and her eyes firmly locked in his. There was no changing her mind now, and he knew it. She had loved him and lived with him for twenty-two years, and she wasn't leaving him now at the eleventh hour. All but one of her children were safe, and she wouldn't leave her husband.

'And if we can't get off?' Ever since most of their children had gone, his own terror had dimmed a little bit, and he was able to say the words now. All he really wanted now was to get Phillip off with Kate, and Charles if he could. But he was willing to go down himself, as long as the rest of his family survived. It was a sacrifice he was willing to make for her, and for them, but he didn't want her to go too. It just wasn't fair to the children, or to her. The children needed her. And he wanted her to get off while she could. 'I don't want you staying here, Kate.'

'I love you.' The words said everything.

'I love you too.' He held her for a long moment, and silently thought about doing what he had seen others do, force her into the arms of a crewman who would literally throw her into a lifeboat. But he couldn't do that to her. He loved her too much, and they had lived together for too long. He respected what she wanted to do, even though in this case it could cost her her life. But it meant a lot to him that she was willing to die with him. They had always shared that kind of love, mixed with tenderness and passion.

'If you stay, I want to stay too.' She said the words clearly as he held her close to him, willing her to go, yet not willing to force her into doing what she didn't want to. 'If you die, I want to stay with you.'

'You can't do that, Kate. I won't let you. Think of the children.' She already had, and she had made up her mind. She loved them with all her heart, but she loved him too and she belonged with him. He was her husband. And Edwina was old enough to take care of the children, if Kate died. And besides, deep down, she still thought they were all being melodramatic over all this. In the end, they'd all sit in the lifeboats, and they'd be back on the *Titanic* by lunchtime. She tried to say as much to Bert, but this time he shook his head. 'I don't think so. I think this is much worse than we've been told.' And it was, much more so than either of them knew. At 1.40 a.m., the crew on the bridge had just fired the last rocket, and now the last lifeboats were being filled, as in the stateroom, far below, unbeknownst to them, Alexis continued to play with her doll, Mrs Thomas.

'I think you have a responsibility to the children,' Bert went on. 'You *must* leave the ship.' It was his last fervent try. But she refused to hear him.

She squeezed his hands tight in her own and looked into his eyes. 'Bert Winfield, I will *not* leave you. Do you understand me?' Nearby, Mrs Straus had just made the same choice, but she was older than Kate, and had no small children. But Mrs Allison did, and she had decided to stay on with her husband and her little girl, and go down with both of them, if the ship went down, as people now understood it was going to.

'What about Phillip?' Bert decided to stop arguing with her for the moment, but he was still hoping to change her mind.

'Can't you do what you said, and bribe them to take Phillip on?' Kate asked.

They were boarding the last boat on the Boat Deck and there was still one more after that, number four, hanging off the glass partitions of the Promenade Deck, just below. But as Lightoller worked above on the Boat Deck, other crewmen were working to open the windows on the Promenade so that more women could be loaded into the lifeboat through the previously locked windows that, earlier, had gotten in their way. This was going to be the last regular lifeboat to leave the *Titanic*.

Bert approached the officer cautiously, spoke to him as best he could as he continued to work furiously on the now seriously listing ship, and Kate saw Lightoller shake his head vehemently and glance over in Phillip's direction. Phillip was still standing with the Thayer boy, who was conversing quietly with his father.

'He says absolutely not, as long as there are women and children on the ship,' Bert reported to her a moment later. There were some loading now from second class, but all of the first-class children were off, with the exception of little Lorraine Allison, standing next to her mother and holding the doll that looked so much like the one carried everywhere by Alexis. It made Kate smile briefly as she looked at her, and then away. It was as though every scene one saw was too tender, too intimate, too private, to be looked upon by strangers.

And now there was a serious consultation between Phillip, Charles, Bert, and Kate, as to how to get the two younger men off, and if possible, also Bert and Kate, in spite of Lightoller.

'I think we'll just have to wait a little while,' Charles said calmly, a gentleman to the end. Through it all, he had never lost his good manners or his good spirits. 'But I do think that you, Mrs Winfield, should get in one of the boats now. There's no point lingering here with the men.'

He smiled warmly at her, and for some reason realized for the first time how much she really looked like Edwina. 'We'll be fine. But you might as well get off comfortably now, rather than in the last scramble with us. You know how dreadful men are. And if I were you, I'd give a go at taking our young friend here.' But how? The last boy his age who had attempted to get on, in women's dress, had been threatened at gunpoint, although they had finally decided to leave him in the lifeboat because there wasn't time to get him off. But feelings were running a little higher now, and Bert didn't want to tackle Lightoller again, he was clearly brooking no nonsense. None of them knew, of course, that things were slightly different on the starboard side. The ship was just too big for anyone to know that things were different on one side or the other. And as they discussed it, Kate still insisting to Bertram that she wouldn't leave him, Phillip wandered over to talk to Jack Thayer again. Charles sat down in a deck chair and lit a cigarette. He didn't want to intrude on Edwina's parents, even now, and they were clearly engaged in serious discussion, about whether or not Kate was going to get off. And Charles was filled with lonely thoughts of Edwina. He had no hope of getting off now.

Below decks, the cabins were all cleared, the crew had checked them all, and the water in the ship had risen to C Deck. And as she played with her doll in the parlor of the stateroom, Alexis could still hear the band playing pretty music. And every now and then, she would hear footsteps, as crew members dashed past or someone from second class ran by, looking for the way to the first-class Boat Deck. And Alexis was beginning to wonder when they would all come back. She was tired of playing alone, and she hadn't wanted to get in the lifeboat, but she was beginning to seriously miss her mommy and the others.

But she knew that eventually, she'd be in for a scolding. They always scolded her when she ran away, especially Edwina.

She heard heavy footsteps then, and looked up, suddenly wondering if it was her father, or Charles, or even Phillip. But as she glanced up expectantly, a strange face appeared in the doorway. He looked shocked suddenly as he saw her. He was the last steward to leave the deck, and he had known long since that all of the B Deck cabins were empty. But he was checking them one last time before the water came up from C Deck and filled them. He was horrified to see the small child sitting there, playing with her dolly.

'Hey, there . . .' He took a rapid step toward her, as Alexis flew into the next room and started to close the door, but the heavyset steward with the full red beard was quicker than she was. 'Just a minute, young lady, what are you doing here?' He wondered how she had escaped, and why no one had come looking for her. It seemed strange to him, and he wanted to get her up to the lifeboats quickly. 'Come on . . .' She had no hat, and no coat. She had abandoned them in her cabin when she'd come back to the stateroom to play with the doll she called 'Mrs Thomas'.

'But I don't want to go!' She started to cry, as the big burly man swept her up in his arms, grabbing a blanket off one of the beds, and wrapping her in it, with the doll she still clung to. 'I want to wait here! . . . I want my mommy!'

'We'll find your mommy, little one. But there's no time to waste.' He ran up the stairs with his small bundle in his arms, and as he was about to pass the level of the Promenade Deck, one of the crew members called out to him.

74

'The last one's almost gone. No more lifeboats on the Boat Deck. The last one's off the Promenade, and they were about to lower it a minute ago . . . come on, man . . . hurry!'

The heavyset steward ran out onto the Promenade Deck in time to watch Lightoller and another man standing on a windowsill struggling with the davits of number four lifeboat, hanging right outside the open windows. 'Wait, man!' he shouted. 'One more!' But Alexis was screaming and kicking and calling for her mother, who knew none of this, and thought Alexis long since safely stowed in another lifeboat. 'Wait!' Lightoller was already lowering the boat as the crewman ran to the open window with Alexis. 'I've got one more!' The second officer looked over his shoulder, and it was almost too late to stop now. He gestured with his head, as just below him the lifeboat hung in the balance, carrying with it the last women willing to leave the ship, among them young Mrs Astor, and Jack Thayer's mother. John Jacob Astor had asked Lightoller if he might go with them, as his wife was in a 'delicate state', but Lightoller had remained adamant, and Madeleine Astor had boarded with her maid instead of her husband.

The steward glanced down at the lifeboat just below them, and there was no way to bring it back up, and he didn't want to keep Alexis on the ship, so he looked down at her for an instant, and planted a kiss on her forehead as he would on his own child's, and then threw her from the window into the boat, praying that someone would catch her, and if not, she wouldn't fall too badly or break too many bones. There had already been several sprained ankles and broken wrists as people were pushed or thrown into boats, but as Alexis fell, one of the sailors at the oars reached up and broke her fall, as she lay screaming in the

75

blanket, and only one deck above her, her unsuspecting mother stood quietly talking to her husband.

The heavyset steward watched from above as Alexis was safely stowed next to a woman with a baby, and then Lightoller and the others carefully lowered the boat the fifteen-foot drop toward the black icy sea. Alexis sat staring in terror, holding on to her doll, wondering if she would ever see her mother again, and she began to scream again as she looked at the huge ship looming up beside them, as they hit the water. The sailors and the women began to row almost immediately, and feeling as though something terrible were about to happen, Alexis watched the enormous ship as they moved slowly away from it. At 1.55 a.m., they were the last real lifeboat to leave the *Titanic*.

And at 2.00 a.m. Lightoller was still struggling with the four collapsible lifeboats, three of which could not be freed. But collapsible D was finally lowered. And there was no doubt now that this would be the last chance for anyone to leave the ship, if they even made it, which seemed doubtful. A circle of crew members was formed around collapsible D, which was to allow only women and children through. Two unidentified babies were put in, and a number of women and children. And at the last instant, Bert finally induced Lightoller to let Phillip into that lifeboat. He was only sixteen, after all, and then collapsible D was gone too, precariously descending to join the others, as Bert and Kate watched it. And after that, the rescue efforts were over. There was nowhere to go, no way to escape, those who had not made it to the lifeboats would go down with the ship now. And Bert still could not believe that Kate had refused to leave with Phillip. Bert had tried to push her into the boat before it was too late, but she had clung to him. And now he held her close in their final moments.

As the Strauses walked quietly arm in arm, Benjamin Guggenheim stood in full evening dress on the Boat Deck with his valet. And Bert and Kate kissed and held hands and stood talking quietly, about silly things, how they had met . . . their wedding day . . . and the births of their children.

'It's Alexis's birthday today,' Kate said softly, as she looked up at Bert, remembering the day six years before, when Alexis had been born on a sunny Sunday morning in their house in San Francisco. Who would have thought then that this could ever happen? And it was a relief now just to know that their children would survive them, that they would be loved, and cherished, and well cared for by their oldest sister. It was a relief to Kate to know that now, but it made her heart ache to think of never seeing them again, and Bert fought back tears as he held her.

'I wish you had gone with them, Kate. They all need you so much.' He was so sad that it had come to this, an end no one could have dreamed of. If only they had taken another ship home . . . if only the *Titanic* hadn't hit an iceberg . . . if only . . . if only . . . it was endless.

'I couldn't bear to live without you, Bert.' She held him tight, and then reached up to kiss him. They kissed for a long time, and he held her close, as people started to jump from the ship. They watched, and saw Charles leap off. The Boat Deck was only ten feet above the water, and some were reaching the lifeboats safely, but he also knew that Kate couldn't swim, and there was no point trying to jump overboard yet. They would do it when they had to, but not sooner. And they still hoped that perhaps, somehow, when the ship went down, they might reach the lifeboats around them, and survive it.

As they talked, efforts were being made to free two more of the collapsible lifeboats, but even once freed of the ropes that had secured it, it was impossible to get collapsible B off the deck, given the extreme angle at which the ship was now listing. And finally, Jack Thayer jumped overboard as Charles had only moments before, and miraculously reached collapsible D, where he once again met Phillip. They were forced to stand up in the boat, though, because it was taking in so much water.

But just above him his parents were holding each other tight, as the water rushed onto the ship. Kate gave a quick gasp, surprised by the brutal chill of the water. And Bert held her as they went down. He tried to keep her afloat for as long as he could, but the downdraft was too great, and as he held her, the last words she said to him, as the water rose up around them, were 'I love you.' She smiled then, and was gone. She slipped through his hands, and he was struck by the crow's nest moments later just as, very near them, Charles Fitzgerald was relentlessly pulled under.

The radio shack was under water by then, too, and the bridge was gone, as collapsible lifeboat A floated away like a raft on a summer beach, and hundreds dived into the water everywhere, as the huge bow plowed into the ocean. The rag-time sound of the band was long gone by then, and the last anyone had heard from them was what many thought to be the somber strains of the hymn 'Autumn', drifting out toward the lifeboats, to the women and children there, and the men who had been fortunate enough to reach the lifeboats on the starboard side, far from Lightoller's sterner vigil on the port side. The hymn seemed to hang like ice in the frigid night air and it was a sound that would haunt all of them for the rest of their lives.

Now those in the lifeboats sat and watched as the bow

plunged into the ocean so sharply that the stern swung up in midair, pointing at the sky like a giant black mountain. The lights seemed to remain on, strangely, for a long time, blink off finally, come on again, and then disappear for good in the terrifying darkness. But still the stern stood pointing at the sky like a demonic mountain. There was a hideous roar from within as everything possible came loose and shattered, a din mixed with cries of anguish, as the forward funnel broke off and hit the water in a shower of sparks, with a thunderous noise that made Alexis scream as she lay in her blanket beside a total stranger.

And then, as Edwina watched the three giant propellers outlined on the stern against the sky, there was a roar like no other she had ever heard, as though the entire ship were being torn asunder. Many explained it afterward as sounding as though the ship were actually breaking in half, but all were told that this couldn't have happened. And all Edwina knew, as she watched the hideous sight, was that she didn't know where Charles or Phillip or Alexis or her parents were, or if any of them had made it to safety. She clung tightly to George's hand, and for once he had no words for what they had both seen, and she pulled him close to her and hid his eyes as they both cried in lifeboat number eight, watching the tragedy that had befallen the unsinkable *Titanic*.

And as the huge ship finally sank toward the ocean floor, the stern finally disappearing at last, they all gasped in disbelief. It was over. She was gone. On 15 April 1912, at 2.20 a.m. It was exactly two hours and forty minutes after she had struck the iceberg. And Edwina watched, clutching Teddy and Fannie to her, as she sat next to George, praying that the others had survived it.

4

At 1.50 a.m. the *Carpathia* received her last message from the *Titanic*. By then the *Titanic*'s engine room had been full to the boilers. But after that, nothing more was known. They steamed toward the *Titanic*'s location at full speed, fearing that they would find her in serious trouble, but at no time did they suspect that she could have gone down before they reached her.

At 4.00 a.m., they reached the location that she had radioed to them, and Captain Rostron of the *Carpathia* looked around in disbelief. She was gone. The *Titanic* was nowhere to be seen. She had vanished.

They moved cautiously about, anxious to see where she had gone to, but it was another ten minutes before green flares in the distance caught their eye. With luck, it would be the *Titanic*, already on the horizon, but in a moment, Captain Rostron and his men realized what it was. The flares were being fired from lifeboat number two, not on the horizon at all, but quite near them. And as the *Carpathia* edged toward the lifeboat just below, Rostron knew for sure now that the *Titanic* had gone down.

Shortly after four o'clock, Miss Elizabeth Allen was the first to board the *Carpathia*, as passengers from that ship crowded the decks and the corridors and looked on. Through the night, as they felt the *Carpathia* changing course, and caught glimpses of the crew's urgent preparations, the passengers knew that something very serious must have happened. At first, they feared it was trouble on their own ship, and then they heard it from crew members and passed it on . . . the *Titanic* was sinking . . . the unsinkable ship was in trouble . . . an iceberg . . . going down . . . And now, as they looked around them, over an expanse of four miles, they saw the lifeboats all around them. People began to call out, there was waving and shouting from some, and from other boats only silence, as shocked faces looked up. There was no way to tell anyone what had happened, no way to say what they had felt as they looked on, the huge stern sticking straight up into the night sky, toward the stars, and then plunging down, carrying with it their husbands and brothers and friends, gone forever.

As Edwina watched the *Carpathia* move closer to them, she let George hold the baby for a while, and wedged Fannie in between them. George's hands were too cold to row anymore, and still wearing Charles's gloves, she took a turn rowing toward the ship, sitting next to the Countess of Rothes, who had rowed relentlessly for the past two hours. George had done his fair share, too, but Edwina had spent much of the time holding the baby, and trying to comfort Fannie, who had cried for Kate ever since they left the ship, and more than once she had asked for Alexis. Edwina had assured her that they would find them all again as soon as they could.

Edwina assumed somehow that her mother had found Alexis by then, even though Edwina had led her to believe that the child had been put in the lifeboat with them. But it was possible that Alexis would have reappeared, and Edwina also tried to assume that the rest of her family, and Charles, were in another lifeboat nearby. She had to believe that. People were still calling out to other boats as the *Carpathia* neared, hoping to find husbands and friends, asking who was on board, or if they had seen them. Several of the lifeboats had tied up together by then, although number eight and several others were still on their own, moving slowly through the ice-speckled water. And then finally at seven o'clock in the morning, it was their turn, as they hovered near the rope ladder and the rope sling that the *Carpathia* had prepared to bring them up to the deck, where the others were now waiting. There were twenty-four women and children aboard lifeboat number eight, and four crewmen. And Seaman Jones at the oars called up to the men on the ship and explained that there were several very small children. The deck-hands on the *Carpathia* lowered a mail sack then, and with trembling hands, Edwina helped Seaman Jones carefully put Fannie into it as she cried and begged Edwina not to make her do it.

'It's alright, sweetheart. We're going up to the big ship now, and then we're going to find Mama and Papa.' She said it as much for herself as she did for her little sister. And as she watched the tiny dark head at the top of the mail sack, she felt tears sting her eyes, thinking of what they had been through. She felt George squeeze her hand, and she squeezed it back without looking at him. She knew that if she did, she would begin to sob. She couldn't allow herself the luxury of letting go yet. Not until she knew that the others were safe, and in the meantime, she had to take care of Fannie, Teddy, and George, and that was all she could allow herself to think of.

She was still wearing the brogues and the pale blue evening dress under the heavy coat her mother had urged her to put on. Her head was so cold, she felt as though she had nails hammered into it, and her hands felt like marble blocks as she waited for the mail sack to be lowered down again, and then with the help of Steward Hart, she put Teddy into it. The child was so cold that most of his face was blue, and more than once during the night, she feared that he might die of exposure. She had done everything she could to keep him warm, held him, rubbed his arms and legs and cheeks. She had held him between herself and George, but the bitter cold had been hard on him and little Fannie, and now she was afraid for them as she tried to climb the rope ladder, and found she didn't have the strength to take hold. She put George in the swing first, and he looked like a very small child as they raised him to the deck. He was more subdued than she had ever seen him. And then they lowered it down again for her, and Steward Hart gently put her in it. She started to close her eyes on the way up, but as she looked out at the other boats in the soft pink light of the dawn, all she could see was a sea of ice, dotted by tiny icebergs, and here and there, a lifeboat, full of people, anxiously waiting to be rescued. The lifeboats were nowhere near full, and she could only hope that in the other ones, she would find the people she had left only hours before on the *Titanic*'s Boat Deck. She couldn't bear to think of it now and tears filled her eyes as her feet touched the deck beneath her.

'Your name?' A stewardess was waiting on the *Carpathia*'s deck with a gentle smile, and she spoke to Edwina, as a sailor put a blanket over her shoulders. There were coffee and tea and brandy waiting for them just inside, and the ship's surgeon and his assistants were there to check them out. There were stretchers laid out on the deck for those who couldn't walk, and someone had already gone to get George a cup of hot chocolate. But nowhere around her did she see her mother and father . . . Phillip . . . Alexis . . . Charles . . . And suddenly she could barely speak, she was so exhausted.

'Edwina Winfield,' she managed to say as she watched

the other survivors being slowly raised to the deck just as she had been only moments before. And they still had more lifeboats to reach and she was praying the others would be in them.

'And your children, Mrs Winfield?'

'My . . . I . . . oh . . .' She realized suddenly who they meant. 'They're my brothers and sister. George Winfield, Frances, and Theodore.'

'Were you traveling with anyone else?' Someone handed her a mug of steaming tea, and she could feel dozens of eyes on her as her pale blue evening dress fluttered in the wind, and she warmed her hands on the steaming mug as she answered.

'I was . . . I am traveling with my parents. Mr and Mrs Bertram Winfield of San Francisco, my brother Phillip, as well, and my sister Alexis. And my fiancé, Mr Charles Fitzgerald.'

'Do you have any idea where the others are?' the stewardess asked sympathetically as she ushered Edwina into the main dining saloon, which had been turned into a hospital and lounge for the *Titanic*'s survivors.

'I don't know . . .' Edwina looked at her, with tears filling her eyes. 'I think they must have gotten into another lifeboat. My mother was looking for my younger sister when we left . . . and . . . I thought . . . there was a little girl in our boat, and at first I thought . . .' She couldn't go on, and with tears in her own eyes, the stewardess patted her shoulder and waited. There were a number of others in the dining saloon by then, women who were shivering or vomiting, or simply crying, their hands torn to shreds by the rowing and the cold. And the children all seemed to be huddled in one spot, with huge, frightened eyes, many of them crying quietly, as they watched their mothers and mourned their fathers. 'Will you help me

84

look for them, please?' She turned huge blue eyes to the stewardess again, while still glancing at George frequently, but for once, he wasn't a problem. Teddy was being looked at by a nurse, he was still stunned by the cold, but he was beginning to cry now and his face was no longer quite so blue, and little Fannie now clung to Edwina's skirts in silent terror.

'I want Mama . . .' she cried softly as the stewardess left them to speak to some of the others, but she promised to come back as soon as she could, and to tell Edwina if there was news of her parents.

And now, boat after boat was being reached, even the four that had been tied together. The men in collapsible B had been rescued long since by lifeboat number twelve, and it was here that Jack Thayer finally wound up, but when they took him off the overturned canvas boat that was sinking fast, he was too exhausted to notice anyone else in the boat. His own mother was in number four, tied up right next to him, and he didn't even see her, nor she him. Everyone was exhausted and cold and intent on his or her own survival.

Edwina left the two younger children with George, still drinking hot chocolate, and went out on the deck, to watch the rescue operations. There were several other women from the *Titanic* standing there, and among them, Madeleine Astor. She had little hope that her husband had managed to get off after she left, and yet she had to see the survivors boarding from the lifeboats. Just in case . . . she couldn't bear the thought that she had lost him. Just as Edwina prayed that she would see a familiar face coming from the lifeboats now. She stood high up, at the rail, watching as the men climbed the rope ladder, and the women came up in the swing, and the children in the mail sack, although some of the men were too tired to climb, and their hands were all so cold they could hardly hold the rope now. But what Edwina noticed most of all was the eerie silence. No one spoke, no one made a sound. They were all too deeply moved by what they had seen, too cold and too afraid, and too badly shaken. Even the children seldom cried, except for the occasional wail of a hungry baby.

There were several unidentified babies already in the dining saloon, waiting for mothers to claim them. One woman in number twelve spoke of catching a baby that had been thrown to her, but she had no idea by whom, and she thought it might have been by a woman from steerage who had made her way to the Boat Deck and then gave her child to anyone who would take it off the ship. The baby was inside, crying now, along with several others.

The scene in the dining saloon was both touching and chaotic. Women sat together in small clusters, crying softly for their men, being questioned by the stewardesses, the nurses, and the doctors, and a handful of men were there too, but pitifully few, thanks to Second Officer Lightoller, who would not let most of them into the lifeboats. Still, several had survived in spite of it, due to less stringent rules on the starboard side, and ingenuity in some events. Still others had died, in the water, attempting to scramble into lifeboats. But most of those who had jumped from the ship had been left in the water to die by those who were too afraid to pick them up, for fear that they might capsize the lifeboats. They had made a piteous din at first, until at last there was only the terrible silence.

Edwina saw Jack Thayer enter the room then, and a moment later heard his mother scream, as she discovered him too, and she rushed toward him, crying, and then Edwina heard her ask him, 'Where's Daddy?' He saw

Edwina then, and nodded, and finally she walked slowly over to him, afraid of what he might say, yet still hopeful that he might have good news, but he shook his head sadly as he saw her coming.

'Was anyone from my family in your lifeboat?'

'I'm afraid not, Miss Winfield. Your brother was at first, but he slipped out when a wave hit, and I don't know if he was picked up by another lifeboat. Mr Fitzgerald jumped about the same time I did, but I never saw him again. And your parents were still on the deck the last time I saw them.' And he didn't tell her that he had the impression that they were determined to stay together and go down with the ship, if they had to. 'I'm sorry. I don't know what happened to them.' He choked on the words as someone handed him a glass of brandy. 'I'm very sorry.' She nodded, tears spilling down her cheeks. She seemed to cry all the time now.

'Thank you.' She didn't want it to be true. It couldn't be. She wanted him to tell her that they were alive, that they were safe, that they were in the next room. Not that they had drowned, or he didn't know. Not Phillip and Charles and Alexis and her parents. It couldn't be . . . she wouldn't let it. And one of the nurses came to her then. The doctor wanted to see her about little Teddy. And when she went to him, he was lying listless, still wrapped in a blanket, his eyes huge, his hands cold, his little body trembling as he looked at her. She picked him up and held him as the doctor told her that the next several hours would be crucial. 'No!' she said out loud, her hands and body shaking more than the child's. 'No! He's alright . . . he's fine . . .' She couldn't let anything happen to him, not now, not if . . . no! She couldn't bear it. Everything had been so perfect for them. They had all loved each other so much, and now suddenly they were all

87

gone, or most of them, and the doctor had told her that Teddy might not survive the exposure. She held him close to her now, willing her own body heat into him, and trying to make him drink the hot bouillon he refused to swallow. He just shook his head back and forth, and clung to Edwina.

'Will he be okay?' George was staring up at her with huge eyes, as she clung to their little brother, and there were tears running down her cheeks now, and George's, as he began to absorb the implications of all that had happened in the past few hours. 'Will he, Edwina, will he be okay?'

'Oh, please, God . . . I hope so . . .' She looked up at George then and pulled him close to her, and then Fannie, still bundled up in her blanket.

'When will Mama be here?' she wanted to know.

'Soon, my love . . . soon . . .' Edwina found herself choking on the words, as she watched the survivors continue to drift into the Grand Saloon of the *Carpathia*, looking dazed from their ordeal in the lifeboats.

And then, trying not to think of all they had lost, she picked up her baby brother and held him close, crying softly for the others.

5

He came up the ladder with hands so frozen that he could
barely use them, but he refused to come up in the swing
like a girl. He had been picked up by number twelve after
he left collapsible D, and then he had lain on the floor of
the lifeboat almost unconscious with exhaustion. But now,
in some distant part of him he felt the exhilaration of
being saved. Theirs was the last lifeboat in, and it was
eight-thirty in the morning. He came up the ladder just
before the crew, and a moment later he stood on the deck
of the *Carpathia* with tears running down his cheeks,
unable to believe what had happened to all of them. But
he had made it. He had made it alone, without parents or
sisters or brothers, and now he only prayed that they had
made it too. And on shaking, frozen legs, he walked
slowly into the dining saloon, and saw a sea of unfamiliar
faces. Seven hundred and five people had survived, and
more than fifteen hundred had died, but at that precise
moment, the survivors looked like thousands to Phillip.
He didn't know where to begin looking for them, and it
was fully an hour before he even saw Jack Thayer.

'Have you seen any of them, man?' He looked desperate, with his hair still damp, his eyes wild and black-
circled. It was the worst thing that had ever happened to
any of them, and probably ever would. And everywhere
were half-dressed people in blankets and evening clothes
and towels and nightgowns. They couldn't seem to get
away from it even now. They didn't want to go away, or

change, or leave each other, or even speak. They just wanted to find the people they had lost. And now they were all desperately looking through the crowd for familiar faces.

Jack Thayer nodded distractedly, but he was still looking for his own father. 'Your sister is here somewhere. I saw her a while ago.' And then he smiled sadly. 'I'm glad you made it.' The two boys embraced, and held each other for a long time, the tears they had yet to shed choking them now that they were safe on the *Carpathia* and the nightmare had finally ended, or almost.

And then as they parted, Phillip looked frightened again. Looking for the people he loved was frightening; the fear that they might not be there was almost overwhelming. 'Were any of the others with her?'

'I don't know . . .' Jack looked vague. 'I think maybe a baby.' That would be Teddy . . . and the others? Phillip began to wander the crowd, and walked out on the deck, hoping to find her, and then finally, back in the saloon, he suddenly saw the back of her head, the dark hair, the slim shoulders, and George standing next to her with his head bowed. Oh, God, Phillip began to cry, as he pressed through the crowd and hurried toward her. And then without a word, as he reached her, he pulled her around, looking down into her eyes, and pulled her into his arms as she gave a gasp, and a sob, and began to cry.

'Oh, my God . . . Oh, Phillip . . . Oh, Phillip . . .' It was all she could say. She didn't dare ask for any of the others. And everywhere around them, people who had been less fortunate were crying softly too. And it was a long time before he dared to ask the question.

'Who's here with you?' He had seen George, and now he saw Fannie, concealed in her blanket just behind Edwina. And Teddy was lying on the floor, wrapped in blankets, in a makeshift cradle. 'Is he alright?' Her eyes filled with tears again, and as she looked at Phillip, she shook her head. Teddy was still alive, but the child's lips were so blue, they looked almost black now. Phillip took off his own coat then and put it around him, and squeezed Edwina's hand tightly in his own. At least five of them had made it. And by the end of the day, they had found no others.

Teddy was given a bed in the ship's infirmary that night and he was being carefully watched, as was Fannie. They feared frostbite on two of her fingers. And George was sound asleep on a cot in the hallway. And late that night Edwina and Phillip were standing on the deck, staring silently out into the distance. Neither of them could sleep, nor did they want to. She never wanted to sleep again, or think, or dream, or let her mind wander back to those terrible moments. And it was even more impossible to believe now. She felt certain that as the crowd in the dining saloon thinned earlier that day, she would see her mother and father chatting quietly in a corner, with Charles standing right beside them. It was impossible to believe that they hadn't survived, that their parents were gone . . . and Alexis . . . and Charles with them, and there would be no marriage in August. It was impossible to believe, or to understand. The fabric for her wedding gown had gone down and . . . She wondered if her mother had held Alexis's hand . . . if it had been terrible . . . or quick . . . or painful. They were terrible thoughts, and she couldn't even voice them to Phillip, as they stood side by side on the deck, lost in their own thoughts. Edwina had been with Teddy and Fannie all day, and Phillip had kept an eye on George, but through it all, it was as though they were waiting. Waiting for people who would never appear, people who would never come back again, people she had loved so . . . The *Carpathia* had made a last search of the area before steaming toward New York, but there had been no more survivors.

'Phillip?' Her voice was soft and sad in the darkness.

'Hmm?' He turned to look at her with eyes that were suddenly older than his sixteen years. He had aged a lifetime in a matter of hours in the lifeboat.

'What are we going to do now?' What were they going to do without them? It was awful to think about. They had lost so many people they loved, and now she was responsible for those who were left. 'We'll go home, I guess.' She spoke softly in the night. There was nothing else to do, except that Edwina wanted to take Teddy to a doctor in New York . . . if he survived that long. They had told her already that the first night would be decisive. And she knew she couldn't bear another loss. They couldn't let Teddy die. They just couldn't. It was all she could think about now, saving him, her mother's last baby. And as she held him in her arms later that night, listening to his labored breathing, she thought of the babies she would never have . . . Charles's babies . . . all her dreams gone with him, and tears suddenly began streaming down her cheeks as her shoulders shook in silence as she mourned him.

Phillip and George were sleeping on mattresses in the hall and Phillip came back to check on her late that night, looking tired and worried. He had been wondering if his parents had tried to jump free of the ship, and if they had survived for any length of time. Maybe they had tried to swim for the lifeboats, and no one had picked them up, and they had died in the icy water. There had been hundreds of people left to die in the waters around him. No one had wanted to pick them up, and so they called out and swam aimlessly for as long as they could, until finally they went down like the others. It was a horrifying thought, and he had lain awake thinking about it, until he finally gave up the thought of sleep and came to find Edwina. He sat with her in silence for a long time. All over the ship it was like that. The survivors hardly seemed to speak, everywhere there were people standing alone, looking out to sea, or small knots of people, just standing there, but not talking.

'I keep wondering if . . .' It was difficult to find the words in the darkened infirmary. There were several other people there, and in another room, there were a dozen or so unidentified children. 'I keep thinking about the end . . .' His voice cracked and he turned away, as Edwina reached out to touch him.

'Don't think about it . . . it won't change anything.' But all night, she had thought about the same thing . . . her parents, and why her mother had chosen to stay . . . and Charles . . . and Alexis. What had happened to her in the end? Had they found her? Had she gone down with them? Phillip had been horrified to discover that she hadn't been with Edwina. His parents had never realized that she hadn't gotten off the ship with them in lifeboat number eight.

He sighed deeply then, and looked at little Teddy, sound asleep, with his soft baby curls. He looked deathly pale, and every now and then he was racked with coughing. Phillip had caught a terrible cold too, but he didn't even seem to feel it. He insisted that he'd had it the day before, and then she remembered something her mother had said, that he had caught it staring down at the unknown girl in second class. And now she was probably gone too, like so many others.

'How is he?' Phillip asked, looking down at his youngest brother.

'He's no worse . . .' She smiled gently and smoothed his hair, and then bent to kiss him. 'I think he sounds a little better.' As long as he didn't come down with pneumonia.

'I'll stay with him while you get some sleep,' he offered, but she sighed. 'I couldn't sleep anyway.' She kept remembering their careful cruise over the area where the *Titanic* had sunk early that morning. Captain Rostron had wanted to be certain that they didn't leave behind any survivors, but all they saw were deck chairs, and pieces of wood, a few life vests, and a carpet that looked exactly like the one in her room, and a dead seaman floating past them. Just thinking about it now made Edwina shudder. It was all too impossible to believe. The night before, the Wideners had been giving a dinner for Captain Smith, and now only twenty-four hours later, the ship was gone, and with it the captain, Mr Widener, his son Harry, and more than fifteen hundred others. Edwina could only wonder how a thing like that could happen. And again and again, she thought of Charles, and how much she had loved him. He had said he liked the blue satin gown she wore the night before . . . he had said it was exactly the color of her eyes, and he liked the way she'd done her hair. She had worn her sleek black hair swept up on her head, much like the style worn by Mrs Astor. And now, she was still wearing the dress, in tatters. Someone had offered her a black wool dress that afternoon, but she had been too busy with the children to change. And what did it matter now? Charles was gone, and she and the other children were orphans.

They sat side by side for a long time that night, thinking about the past, and trying to sort out the future, and finally Edwina told Phillip to go back to bed, George would be worried if he woke and didn't find him.

'Poor little guy, he's been through it too.' But he had come through it valiantly, and in the past twenty-four hours, he had been both a comfort and a help to Edwina. Had she been a little less tired, she might even have been worried because he was so docile. And little Fannie slept on through the night, just beside her. And once Phillip had gone, Edwina sat quietly, watching both Fannie and Teddy, touching their faces, smoothing back their hair, giving Teddy a drink of water once when he woke up thirsty, and holding Fannie when she cried in her sleep. Edwina sat there and prayed, as she had that morning, at the service conducted by Captain Rostron. Not all of the survivors had attended, but she and Phillip had. But many of the others were just too tired, or too sick, or they thought the service too painful. In one brutal blow, more than thirty-seven women of those who had survived had been widowed. One thousand five hundred and twenty-three men, women, and children had died. There were only seven hundred and five survivors.

Edwina dozed a little finally, and she only awoke when Teddy stirred and looked up at her with eyes so much like their mother's. 'Where's Mama?' he asked, pouting, but he looked more like himself, and when Edwina stooped to kiss him, he smiled, and then cried again for their mother.

'Mama's not here, sweetheart.' She didn't know what to say to him. He was too young to understand, and yet she didn't want to lie to him and promise that she would come later.

'I want Mama too,' Fannie cried, looking woebegone when she heard Teddy wake and ask for their mother.

'Be a good girl,' Edwina urged, with a kiss, and a hug. She got up and washed Teddy's face, and then left him, protesting, with a nurse, while she took Fannie to the bathroom. And when she saw her own face in the mirror, she knew just how bad it had been. In one day she had aged a thousand years, and she felt and looked like an old woman, or so she thought. But a borrowed comb helped, and a little warm water. Still there was nothing lovely about the way she looked, or felt, and when she walked into the dining saloon later to find the boys, she saw that everyone else looked ghastly too. They were still wearing an array of odd, and sometimes barely decent, costumes, now added to with borrowed gear and ill-fitting clothes that only added to their strange appearances and general confusion. People were milling about everywhere, and whenever possible they had been put in crowded cabins together, or on cots in the hall, but there were hundreds sleeping on mattresses in the Grand Saloon, in crew quarters, on couches, or even on the floor. But to them, it no longer mattered. They were alive, although many of them wished they weren't, as they realized how many had been lost.

'How's Teddy?' George asked almost as soon as he saw his older sister, and he was relieved when she smiled. None of them could withstand any more disasters.

'I think he's better. I told him I'd be back in a few minutes.' She had brought Fannie with her, and she wanted to get her something to eat before hurrying back to care for her little brother.

'I'll stay with him if you want,' George volunteered, and then suddenly, the smile froze on his lips, and he stared at something just behind her. He looked as though he had seen a ghost and Edwina stared at him and touched his arm, bending toward him.

'Georgie, what is it?'

He only stared, and then after a minute, he pointed. It was something on the floor, next to a mattress. And then, without a word, he rushed toward it and picked it up and brought it back to her. It was Mrs Thomas, Alexis's doll, she was sure of it, but there was no child in sight, and inquiries of those standing nearby turned up nothing. No one could remember seeing the doll before, or the child who had left it.

'She must be here!' Edwina looked around frantically, and there were several children in sight, but none of them was Alexis. Edwina was holding the doll tightly in her hand, and then her heart sank as she remembered. The Allison child had had a doll like this, too, and she said as much to Phillip, but he shook his head. He would have recognized this one anywhere, and George agreed, and so did Fannie.

'Don't you remember, Edwina? You made her dress with some material from one of yours.' And as he said it, she remembered and tears came to her eyes. How cruel it would be if the doll had survived and Alexis hadn't.

'Where's Alexis?' Fannie looked up at her with enormous eyes, and the look of her father that had always brought him so much pleasure when he was alive. Even he had been able to see their astounding likeness.

'I don't know,' Edwina answered her honestly, and held the doll in a trembling hand, and continued to look around her, but she didn't see her.

'Is she hiding?' Fannie knew her well, but Edwina didn't smile this time.

'I don't know, Fannie. I hope not.'

'Are Mama and Papa hiding too?' She looked so confused and Edwina's eyes filled with tears as she shook her head and continued looking.

But an hour later, they still hadn't found her, and Edwina had to go back to the hospital to Teddy. She still had the doll with her, and she had left Fannie with Phillip and George. And when Teddy saw the doll, he looked suspiciously at his older sister.

'Lexie?' he said. 'Lexie?' He remembered the doll too. In truth, Alexis had seldom been without it. And one of the nurses smiled as she walked past them. He was a beautiful child, and it touched her to see them together. But suddenly Edwina looked up, and then stopped the nurse to ask her a question.

'Is there anyway I can find . . . I was looking for . . .' She didn't quite know how to phrase the question. 'We haven't been able to find my six-year-old sister, and I thought . . . she was with my mother . . .' It was impossible to say the words and yet she had to know, and the nurse understood. She gently touched Edwina's arm and handed her a list.

'We have everyone we picked up listed here, including the children. It's possible that in the confusion yesterday, you might not have found her. What makes you think she's on the ship? Did you see her stowed in a lifeboat before you got off?'

'No.' Edwina shook her head, and then held the doll out. 'It's this . . . she was never without it.' Edwina looked so mournful now, and a quick perusal of the list told her that Alexis wasn't on it.

'Are you sure it's hers?'

'Positive. I made the dress myself.'

'Could another child have taken it?'

'I suppose so.' Edwina hadn't even thought of that. 'But aren't there any lost children who are here without their parents?' She knew there were several unidentified babies in the sick bay, but Alexis was old enough to identify herself, if she wanted to . . . . or wasn't too traumatized . . . Edwina suddenly wondered if she was wandering about, unidentified and lost, and unaware that her brothers and sisters were on the ship with her. She said as much to the nurse, who told her that it was most unlikely.

But it was late that afternoon when she was strolling on the deck, and trying not to think of the hideous outline of the *Titanic* against the night sky just before she went down, her stern rising against the horizon, when she saw Mrs Carter's maid, Miss Serepeca, taking a short walk with the children. Miss Lucille and Master William were looking as frightened as the other children on the ship, and the third child hung back, clutching Miss Serepeca's hand, and seeming almost too terrified to walk on deck, and then suddenly as the child turned, Edwina saw her face, and gasped, and in an instant she was running toward her and had swept her into her arms, off the deck, and she held her with all her love and strength, crying as though her heart would break. She had found her! It was Alexis!

As Edwina held the frightened child in her arms, and smoothed her hair over and over again, Miss Serepeca explained, as best she could, what had happened. When Alexis had been thrown into lifeboat number four, Mrs Carter had rapidly realized that she had no family with her, and once on the *Carpathia*, she had taken responsibility for her until they reached New York. And, Miss Serepeca added in an undertone, ever since the child had seen the ship go down almost two days before, she had not said one word. They didn't know her first name or her last, she absolutely refused to speak to them or say where she was from, and Mrs Carter had been hoping that some member of her family would claim her in New York. And it was going to be a great relief to Mrs Carter, Miss Serepeca said, to find that the little girl's mother was on the ship after all. But as she said the words, Alexis spun her head around, instinctively looking for Kate, and Edwina quietly shook her head, pulling the child closer to her.

'No, baby, she's not here with us.' They were the hardest words she would ever say to her, and Alexis tried to pull away, while bowing her head, not wanting to hear what Edwina was saying. But Edwina wouldn't let her stray far from her. They had almost lost her that way once before. Edwina thanked Miss Serepeca profusely and promised to look for Mrs Carter to thank her for taking care of Alexis. But as Edwina walked back to the shelter of the Grand Saloon, carrying her, Alexis stared at her miserably, and she had still not said a single word to Edwina. 'I love you, sweetheart . . . oh, I love you so much . . . and we've been so worried about you . . .' There were tears streaming down her cheeks as she carried the child. It was a gift finding her again, yet Edwina found herself wishing that she could have found them all, that she could have discovered her parents and Charles hovering in a corner somewhere. They couldn't really be gone. It couldn't have happened like that, except it had . . . and only Alexis was left, like a little ghost from the past. A past that had existed only a short time before, and was gone now, like a dream she would always remember.

When Edwina held her treasured doll out to her, Alexis snatched it from her sister's hand, and held it close to her face, but she wouldn't speak to anyone, and she watched as Phillip cried when he saw her again, but it was George she turned to now, as he stared down at her in amazement.

'I thought you were gone, Lexie,' he said quietly. 'We looked for you everywhere.' She didn't answer him, but her eyes never left his, and she slept next to him that night, holding his hand, and with her other hand clutching her doll, as Phillip kept watch over them both. Edwina was sleeping with Fannie and Teddy in the infirmary again that night, although Fannie was fine, and Teddy was much better. But it was the safest place for her to be with two such delicate children, and Teddy was still coughing pretty badly at night. She had invited Alexis to stay there with her too, but she had shaken her head, and followed George into the Grand Saloon and lay down next to him on his narrow mattress. Her brother lay on his side watching her, before they fell asleep. It was like seeing his mother again, finding her, because the two had always been together so much of the time, and he slept that night, dreaming about their parents. He was still dreaming about them when he woke up in the middle of the night and heard Alexis crying beside him, and he comforted her and held her close to him, but she wouldn't stop crying.

'What is it, Lexie?' he asked finally, wondering if she would finally tell him, or if, like the rest of them, she was just so sad that all she could do was wail. 'Do you hurt? . . . do you feel sick? Do you want Edwina?'

She shook her head, looking down at him as she sat up, clutching her dolly to her. 'I want Mama . . .' She whispered softly, her big blue eyes searching his face, and tears sprang to his own eyes as he heard her and then he hugged her to him.

'So do I, Lexie . . . so do I.' They slept holding hands that night, two of Kate's children, the legacy she had left behind when she had chosen not to leave her husband. They all remembered the great love she had had for them, and the love and tenderness between their parents, but now all that was gone, to another place, another time. And all that was left was the family they had created, six people, six lives, six souls, six of the precious few who had survived the *Titanic*. And for the rest of time, Kate, and Bert, and Charles, and the others were gone. Lost forever.

6

Edwina and Philip stood on the deck on Thursday night, in a sorrowful rain, as the *Carpathia* passed the Statue of Liberty and entered New York. They were home again, or back in the States at least. But it seemed as though there was nothing left for them now. They had lost everything, or so it felt, and Edwina had to silently remind herself that at least they still had each other. But life would never be the same for them again. Their parents were gone, and she had lost her future husband. In only four months, she and Charles would have been married, and now he was gone . . . his gentle spirit, his fine mind, his handsome face, the kindness she had so loved, the tilt of his head when he laughed at her . . . all of it, and with him her bright, happy future, gone forever.

Phillip turned to her then, and saw the tears streaming down her cheeks, as the *Carpathia* steamed slowly into the harbor, assisted by tugs, but there were no sirens, no horns, no fanfare, there was only sorrow and silent mourning.

Captain Rostron had reassured them all the night before that the press would be kept away from them for as long as possible, and he would do everything he could to assure them a quiet arrival in New York. He warned them that the ship's radio room had been besieged by wires from the press since the morning of the fifteenth, but he had answered none of them, and no journalists would be allowed on his ship. The survivors of the *Titanic* had earned the right to mourn in peace, and he felt a responsibility to all of them to bring them home quietly and safely.

But all Edwina could think about now was what they had left behind, somewhere in the bowels of the ocean. Phillip quietly took her hand in his own, as he stood next to her, the tears streaming down his face as well, thinking of how different it all might have been, had the fates been only a little kinder.

'Win?' He hadn't called her that since he was a small child, and she smiled through her tears as he said it.

'Yes?'

'What are we going to do now?' They had talked about it on and off, but she hadn't really had time to think about it, with Teddy so ill, and Alexis so distraught, and the others to worry about too now. George had hardly spoken in the last two days, and she had found herself longing for a little of his naughtiness and mischief. And poor little Fannie cried every time Edwina left her, even if it was only for an instant. It was difficult to think, with all the responsibility she suddenly had. All she knew was that she had to take care of them, and Phillip as well. She was all they had now.

'I don't know, Phillip. We'll go home, I guess, as soon as Teddy is completely well.' He still had a dreadful cough, and the day before he'd been running a fever. And for the moment, none of them were up to the long train ride back to California. 'We'll have to stay in New York for a little while, and then go home.' But the house, and the newspaper? It was more than she cared to think about. All she wanted to do now was look back . . . just a moment . . . a few days . . . to the last night she was dancing with Charles to the happy ragtime music. It was all so simple then, as he whirled her around the floor, and then swept her into the beautiful waltzes she loved best of all. They had danced so much in four days on the ship that she had almost worn her new silver shoes out and now she felt as though she would never dance again, and never want to.

'Win?' He had seen her mind drift away again. She kept doing that. They all did.

'Hmm? . . . I'm sorry . . .' She stared out at New York Harbor, looking at the rain, fighting back tears, and wishing that things were different. And everyone on the *Carpathia* felt the same, as the widows lined the railing, with tears streaming down their cheeks, mourning the men and the lives they'd lost less than four days before. Four days that now seemed like a lifetime.

Many of them were being met by relatives and friends, but the Winfields had no one in New York to meet them. Bert had made reservations for them at the Ritz-Carlton before they left, and they would stay there now until they left for California again. But simple details were now suddenly complicated for all of them. They had no money, no clothes, Alexis had somehow managed to lose her shoes, and Edwina had only her now tattered pale blue evening gown and the black dress someone had given her the day they'd been rescued from the lifeboats. It was a problem for all of them, and Edwina found herself wondering how she would pay for the hotel. She would have to wire her father's office in San Francisco. Suddenly she was having to solve problems that only a week ago she had never even thought of.

They had radioed the White Star Line's London office from the ship and asked them to notify Uncle Rupert and Aunt Liz that all of the Winfield children had survived, but Edwina knew that her aunt would be hard hit by the news of the loss of her only sister. She had also radioed her father's office with the same information. There was suddenly so much to think about, and as she stared out into the New York mist, suddenly a flotilla of tugboats came into view, there was a shrill whistle blast, and then suddenly there were salutes from every boat in the harbor. The spell of the somber silence they had all lived with for four days was about to be broken. It had never occurred to Edwina and Phillip that their tragedy would be big news, and suddenly as they looked at the tugs and yachts and ferries below, crowded with reporters and photographers, they both realized that this was not going to be easy.

But Captain Rostron was as good as his word, and no one except the pilot boarded the *Carpathia* before they reached the pier. And the photographers had to satisfy themselves with whatever photographs they could take from the distance. The lone photographer who had snuck on board had been seized and confined to the bridge by the captain.

They reached Pier 54 at 9.35 p.m., and for a moment all was silent on the ship. Their terrible journey was about to be ended. The lifeboats from the *Titanic* had been taken off first, the davits had been moved into place, and the boats lowered as they had been when they left the sinking ship four days before, only this time the boats were lowered with only a single seaman in each, as the survivors stood at the rail and watched while lightning bolts lit up the night sky, and thunder exploded overhead. The sky seemed to be crying over the empty boats, as the mourners watched them, and even the crowd below stood in silent awe as they were made fast and left there bobbing in the water. And it would be only a matter of hours before looters stripped them.

Alexis and George had joined Edwina and Phillip as the lifeboats were lowered toward the deck, and Alexis started to cry as she clutched Edwina's skirt. She was frightened by the storm, and her eyes were wild with fear as she watched the lifeboats go down and Edwina held her close as Kate had always done. But in the last few days, Edwina had felt like such an inadequate replacement for their mother.

'Are we . . . going in them again?' Terrified, Alexis could barely speak as Edwina tried to reassure her. And Edwina could only shake her head. She was crying too hard to answer . . . those boats . . . those tiny shells . . . and so precious few of them . . . had there been more, the others would have been alive . . .

'Don't cry, Lexie . . . please don't cry . . .' It was all she could say to her as she held her tiny hand. She couldn't even promise her that everything would be alright again. She no longer believed it herself, so how could she make empty promises to the children? She felt as though her heart were filled with sadness.

Edwina saw, as she looked at the pier, that there were hundreds if not thousands of people waiting there. At first, it looked like a sea of faces. And then, as lightning lit up the sky again, she saw that there were more. There were people everywhere. The newspapers said later that there were thirty thousand at the pier, and ten thousand lining the banks of the river. But Edwina was unaware of most of them. And what did they matter now? The people she loved were gone, her parents and Charles. There was no one waiting for them there. There was no one left in the world to care for them. It was all on her shoulders now, and even poor Phillip's. At sixteen, he was no longer a child, he would have to become a man, a burden he had willingly assumed from the moment they were saved, but it seemed so unfair to Edwina as she looked at him, telling George to put his coat on and stand next to Alexis. It made Edwina sad all over again, just looking at them, in their ragged clothes and ravaged faces. They all suddenly looked like what they were. All of the Winfield children were now orphans.

The *Carpathia* passengers disembarked first. There was a long wait then, as the captain gathered all the others in the dining saloon where they had slept for three days, and he said a prayer, for those lost at sea, and for the survivors, for their children and their lives. There was a long moment of silence then, and only the sounds of gentle sobbing. People said goodbye to each other then, a touch on the arm, an embrace, a last look, a shake of the head, a touch of the hand for a moment, and then they shook hands with Captain Rostron. There was little that anyone could say, as the silent group left each other for the last time. They would never be together again, yet they would always remember.

Two of the women reached the gangplank first, hesitated, started to turn back, and then walked down slowly with tears streaming down their faces. They were friends from Philadelphia, and they had both lost their husbands, and they stopped midway as a roar went up from the crowd. It was a roar of sorrow, and of grief, of sympathy, and fascination, but it was a terrifying sound, and poor little Alexis dove into Edwina's skirts again with her hands over her ears and her eyes closed, and Fannie set up a terrible wail as Phillip held her.

'It's alright . . . it's alright, children . . .' Edwina tried to reassure them, but they couldn't hear her above the din. And she was horrified as she watched reporters dash forward and engulf the exhausted survivors. The flash of cameras exploded everywhere, as the heavens rained, and the lightning bolts continued to flash across the sky. It was a terrible night, but no more so than the night that had brought them all to this end only days before. That was the worst night of their lives, and this . . . this was only one more. Nothing more could happen to them now, Edwina felt, as she gently shepherded her brothers and sisters toward the gangplank. She had no hat, and she was soaked to the skin, as she carried Alexis, who clung to her neck with trembling desperation. Phillip carried each of the two youngest ones in his arms, and George walked right beside him looking very subdued and more than a little frightened. The crowd was so huge, it was hard to know exactly what they would do. And Edwina realized as they reached the end of the gangplank that people were shouting names at them.

'Chandler! . . . Harrison! . . . Gates? Gates! . . . Have you seen them? . . .' They were family members and friends, desperately looking for survivors, but with each name, she shook her head, she knew none of them . . . and in the distance, she saw the Thayers being embraced by friends from Philadelphia. There were ambulances and cars everywhere, and again and again, the explosions of light coming from the reporters. There were wails from the crowd, and sobs, as the survivors shook their heads at the names being called out to them. Until then, no complete list of the survivors had been published and there was always hope that the news was wrong, that a loved one may have in fact survived the disaster. The *Carpathia* had refused to communicate with the press, maintaining a barrier of silence around the survivors for their own protection. But now Captain Rostron could no longer do anything to shield them.

'Ma'am . . . ma'am!' A reporter lunged out at her, almost causing Alexis to leap from her arms, as he shouted into Edwina's face. 'Are these all your children? Were you on the *Titanic*?' He was bold and brash and loud, and in the frenzy around them, Edwina couldn't escape him.

'No . . . yes . . . I . . . please . . . please . . .' She started to cry, longing for Charles and her parents, as the dreaded flash went off in her face, as Phillip tried to shield her but he was too encumbered with the younger children to help her very much, and suddenly a sea of reporters surrounded them, pushing George away, as Edwina shouted to him not to lose them. 'Please . . . please . . . stop! . . .' They had done the same to Madeleine Astor when she'd gotten off with her maid, but Vincent Astor, and her own father, Mr Force, had rescued her and taken her away in the ambulance they had brought for her. Edwina and Phillip were not to be as lucky, but they left as quickly as possible, Phillip had gotten them into one of the waiting cars sent by the Ritz-Carlton. They were driven down Seventh Avenue, and walked slowly into the hotel, a ragtag-looking group with no luggage. But there were more reporters waiting there, and a solicitous desk clerk quickly escorted them to their rooms, where Edwina had to fight back a wave of hysterics. It was as though they had never left. The beautiful elegantly appointed rooms were the same as they had been only a month and a half before, and now they were back, and everything had changed completely. They had given them the same rooms as they'd had when they arrived from San Francisco, before they took the *Mauretania* to Europe to meet the Fitzgeralds and celebrate Edwina's engagement.

'Win . . . are you alright?'

She couldn't speak for a moment and then she nodded, looking deathly pale. She was wearing the tattered blue evening dress, her rain-drenched coat, and brogues, the same outfit she had worn when she left the *Titanic*. 'I'm fine,' she whispered unconvincingly, but all she could think about was the last time she had been in these rooms, only weeks before, with Charles and her parents.

'Do you want me to get different rooms?' Phillip looked desperately worried. If she fell apart now, what would they do? Whom would they turn to? She was all they had now, but she shook her head slowly and dried her eyes, and made an effort to reassure the children. For now, she knew only too well that everything rested on her shoulders.

'George, you look for the menus. We need something to eat. And Phillip, you help Fannie and Alexis get into their nightclothes.' She realized again then that they no longer had any. But when they walked through the other rooms, she saw what the owners of the Ritz-Carlton had done. They had provided an assortment of women's and children's clothes, and some things for the boys, too, sweaters and trousers, some warm socks, and some shoes, and laid out on the bed, two little nightgowns for the girls, two new dolls, a nightshirt and a bear for Teddy. The kindness was so great that it made Edwina cry again, and as she entered the main bedroom of the suite, her breath caught. There on the bed were clothes carefully laid out for her parents, and a bottle of champagne, and she knew that in the last bedroom, she would find the same for Charles. Her breath caught on a sob, and with a last look around her, she turned off the light, and closed the door, and went back to the waiting children.

She seemed calmer then, and once the little ones were put to bed, she sat down on the couch with Phillip and George and watched them eat a whole plate of roast chicken, and then some cakes, but even the thought of eating just seemed too exhausting to her. Alexis had that wild-eyed look again just before she went to bed, and all Edwina could do was urge her to hold her old doll, Mrs Thomas, tight, and cuddle her new dolly. Fannie had gone to sleep in the big comfortable bed next to her, and baby Teddy was already sound asleep in a large, handsome cradle in his new nightshirt.

'We'll have to wire Uncle Rupert and Aunt Liz in the morning,' she told the boys. They had wired them and Charles's parents via White Star from the ship, but she owed it to them to let them know they were safely arrived. There was so much to do and to think about. Nothing could be assumed anymore. Nothing could be taken for granted. She had to get clothes for them to get to California, she had to go to a bank, and get the little ones to a doctor. Most of all Edwina wanted to see a specialist to make sure that Teddy was alright and Fannie did not lose her frostbitten fingers. They looked better now, and in spite of the tempestuous arrival, Teddy had not run a fever. In truth, Alexis seemed the worst affected of all of them, the trauma of losing her mother seemed to have left her bereft of any interest in what was happening around her. She was despondent and afraid, and she got hysterical if Edwina tried to leave her even for an instant. But it was hardly surprising after what they'd all been through. The shock of it would stay with them all for a long time, and Edwina could feel her own hands shake whenever she tried to write something down, even her own name, or button the children's buttons. But all she could do was force herself to keep on going. She knew she had to.

She went down to the front desk then and spoke to them about hiring a car and driver for the next day, or at the very least a carriage if all the cars had been hired out, but they assured her that a car and driver would be put at her disposal. She thanked them for the clothes they had left for them, and the thoughtful gifts for the children, and the manager of the hotel somberly shook her hand and extended his sympathy for the loss of her parents. They were old patrons of the hotel, and he had been devastated to learn when she arrived that they had not survived the disaster.

Edwina thanked him quietly and walked slowly back upstairs. She had glimpsed two or three familiar faces from the ship, but everyone was busy now, and exhausted with the business of surviving.

It was almost one o'clock in the morning when she found her two brothers playing cards in the living room of the suite. They were drinking seltzer water and finishing off the last of the cakes, and for an instant, she stood in the doorway and smiled at them. It saddened her to realize that life went on as though nothing had happened, and yet at the same time she realized that it would be their only salvation. They had to go on, they had a whole life ahead of them. They were only children. But Edwina knew that for her, without Charles, it would never be the same. There would never be another man like him, she knew. Her life now would consist of taking care of the children and nothing else.

'Going to bed tonight, gentlemen?' She blinked back tears again as she looked at them. They smiled at her, and then suddenly, looking at her in her now ridiculous outfit, George glanced up at her and grinned. It was the first time she had seen him look like his old self since they'd left the *Titanic*.

'You look awful, Edwina.' He laughed, and even Phillip smiled in spite of himself. She did, and suddenly in the elegantly appointed rooms, her incongruous costume looked less noble and really only foolish.

'Thank you, George.' She smiled. 'I'll do my best to put something decent together tomorrow morning so I don't embarrass you.'

'See that you do,' he intoned haughtily, and went back to his card game.

'See that you two go to bed, please,' she scolded them both, and then went to soak in the luxurious bathtub. And as she took the dress off a few minutes later, she held it for a long moment and stared at it. At first, she thought she would throw it away, she never wanted to see it again, and yet another part of her wanted to save it. It was the dress she had worn the last time she'd seen Charles . . . the last night she'd been with her parents . . . it was a relic of a lost life, of a moment in time when everything had changed, when everything had been lost forever. She folded it carefully then, and put it in a drawer. She didn't know what she'd do with it, but in a way it seemed like all she had left, a shredded evening gown, and it almost seemed as though it had belonged to someone else, a person she had been, and would never be again, and now could scarcely remember.

7

The morning after they arrived, Edwina put on the black dress she'd been given on the rescue ship, and took Fannie and Teddy and Alexis to the doctor the hotel manager had recommended. And when she got there, the doctor was actually surprised at how well the children had survived their ordeal on the *Titanic*. Fannie's two smallest fingers on her left hand would probably never be quite the same, they would be less sensitive and a little stiff, but he doubted very seriously that she would lose them. And he thought Teddy had made a remarkable recovery as well, perhaps even more so. He told Edwina that he considered it quite extraordinary that the child had survived the exposure at all, and in an undertone, he told her he thought the entire experience tragic and amazing. He tried to ask her questions about the night that the *Titanic* went down, but Edwina was reluctant to talk about it, particularly in front of the children.

She asked him to examine Alexis as well, but other than a number of bruises she'd gotten when she was thrown into the lifeboat, she appeared to be surprisingly unaffected and healthy. The problem was that the damage done to Alexis had been to her spirit far more than to her body. Ever since they'd found her again on the *Carpathia*, Edwina felt that she was no longer herself. It was as though she couldn't face the fact that their mother was gone, so she faced nothing at all. She spoke seldom if at all, and always seemed removed and distant.

'She may be that way for quite some time,' he warned Edwina when they were alone for a moment, as the nurse helped the children dress again. 'She may never be the same again. Too great a shock for some.' But Edwina refused to believe that. In time, she knew that Alexis would be herself again, although she had always been a shy child, and in some ways too attached to their mother. But she made a commitment to herself now, not to let the tragedy destroy their lives, not the children's anyway. And as long as she was occupied with them, she had no time to think of herself, which was a blessing. And he told her that within a week, he felt they'd be ready for the journey to San Francisco. They needed a little time to catch their breath before being moved, but then again, so did Edwina.

When they went back to the hotel, they found Phillip and George poring over the story in the papers. Fifteen pages of *The New York Times* were devoted to interviews and accounts of the great disaster. And George wanted to read everything to Edwina, who didn't want to hear it. She had already had three messages from *The New York Times* herself, from reporters wanting to speak to her, but she had thrown the messages away, and had no intention of spending any time with reporters. She knew her own father's paper would carry the story of his death, and the circumstances of the giant ship going down, and if they wanted to speak to her when she got home, she knew she would have to. But she wanted nothing to do with the sensationalism of what was happening in the papers in New York. And she growled at a photograph of herself leaving the ship with her brothers and sisters.

She had also gotten another message that morning when she got back to the hotel. A Senate subcommittee was to begin meeting the next day, at the Waldorf-Astoria Hotel, and they were inviting her to come and speak to them within the next few days, about the *Titanic*. They wanted the details of what had occurred, from all the survivors who were willing to speak to them. It was important that the committee understand what had happened, who, if anyone, was to blame, and how a similar disaster could be avoided in the future. She had told Phillip about that, and that she was nervous about appearing but felt she should, and he tried to reassure her.

They had lunch in their rooms at the hotel, and then Edwina announced that she had work to do. They couldn't live forever in borrowed clothes, and she had to do some shopping.

'Do we have to go?' George looked appalled, and Phillip buried himself again in the papers, as Edwina smiled at them. For a minute, George had sounded just like their father.

'No, you don't, as long as you stay here and help Phillip take care of the others.' It reminded her of the fact that she would need to hire someone to help her once she got home. But even that thought reminded her of poor Oona. Whatever she thought of just now always took her back to painful memories of the sinking.

She went first to the bank, then to Altman's, on the corner of Fifth Avenue and Thirty-fourth Street, and bought as much as she could for all of them. And then she went to Oppenheim Collins and bought the rest of what she needed. Her father's office had wired her a fairly large sum, and she had more than enough money for herself and the children.

It was after four o'clock when she got back to the hotel in a somber black mourning dress she had bought at Altman's. And she was startled to see George playing cards again with Phillip.

'Where are the others?' she asked as she deposited her bundles on the floor of the sitting room, as the driver staggered in with the rest. She realized suddenly that it took a great many things to properly outfit five children. And she had bought five serious black dresses for herself. She knew she would be wearing them for a long time, and when she'd put the somber-looking gowns on in the store, she realized with a sad pang how much they made her look like her mother.

But now as she looked around the suite, she couldn't see any of the younger children. Only her two brothers playing one of their passionate card games. 'Where are they?'

Phillip grinned, and pointed toward the bedroom. Edwina quickly crossed the room, and gasped when she saw them. The two little girls and their two-year-old brother were playing with one of the maids and what must have been at least two dozen new dolls, and a rocking horse, and a train just for Teddy.

'My word!' Edwina looked stunned as she looked around the room. There were still unwrapped boxes halfway to the ceiling. 'Where did all that come from?'

George only shrugged, and threw a card down that infuriated his brother, and then Phillip glanced over at Edwina, still gazing around in awe. 'I'm not sure. There were cards on everything. I think most of it is stuff from people here at the hotel . . . there's something from *The New York Times* . . . the White Star Line sent some things too. I don't know, they're just gifts, I guess.' And the children were having a wonderful time tearing through them. Even Alexis looked up happily and grinned at her sister. It was the birthday party she had been cheated of on the day they sank, and more. It looked like ten birthdays and a Christmas.

Edwina walked around it all in amazement, as Teddy sat happily on his new horse and waved at his big sister. 'What are we going to do with all this?'

'We'll just have to take it home, of course,' George answered matter-of-factly.

'Did you get everything you needed?' Phillip asked as she attempted to make some order in the room, and divide up her purchases according to whom they were for. He looked up at her then and frowned. 'I don't much like the dress, it's kind of old-looking, isn't it?'

'I suppose,' she said quietly, but it had seemed appropriate to her. She didn't feel young anymore, and wondered if she ever would again. 'They didn't have much in black at the two stores I went to.' She was so tall and slim that it wasn't always easy to find exactly what she wanted. Her mother had had that problem too, and they had shared dresses sometimes. But no longer. They would never share anything again . . . not their friendship, their warmth, their laughter. Like Edwina's childhood, it was all over.

Phillip looked up at her again then, and realized why she was wearing black. He hadn't thought of that at first, and he wondered if he and George would have to wear black ties and black armbands. They did when their grandparents had died. Mama had said it was a gesture of respect, but Papa had said that he thought it was silly. Which reminded Phillip of something he had forgotten to tell her.

'We got a Marconigram today from Uncle Rupert and Aunt Liz.'

'Oh, dear.' Edwina frowned. 'I meant to send them a wire this morning and I forgot, with all the excitement of going to the doctor. Where is it?' He pointed to the desk and she picked it up and then sat down with a sigh. It was

not exactly news that she wanted, although she appreci-
ated their good intentions. Uncle Rupert was putting Aunt
Liz on the *Olympic* in two days, and they were to wait for
her in New York, and she would then bring them back
with her to England. Edwina felt her heart skip a beat as
she read it, and she felt sorry for her aunt's having to
come over, knowing how desperately seasick she got.
Besides which, the very thought of an ocean crossing now
made Edwina feel ill. She knew she would never get on a
ship again for as long as she lived. She would never forget
the sight of the *Titanic*'s stern sticking straight up out of
the water and outlined against the night sky as they sat
watching her from the lifeboats.

She wired an answer back to them later that evening,
urging Aunt Liz not to come, and telling them that they
were going back to San Francisco. But another response
came back to them the next morning.

'No discussion. You will return to England with your
aunt Elizabeth. Stop. Regret circumstances for all of you.
Must make the best of it here. See you shortly. Rupert
Hickham.' The very prospect of going back to Havermoor
Manor to live almost made her shudder.

'Do we have to, Edwina?' George looked up at her with
ill-concealed horror, and Fannie started to cry and said
she was always cold there and the food was awful.

'So was I cold, now stop crying, you silly goose. The
only place we're going is home. Is that clear?' Five heads
nodded and five serious faces hoped that she meant it. But
it was going to be a little more difficult convincing their
uncle Rupert. Edwina fired off an answer to him at once.
And a two-day battle ensued, culminating in their aunt
Liz's coming down with a ferocious case of influenza,
which forced her to postpone the crossing. And in the
interim, Edwina made herself more than clear to her

uncle. 'No need to come to New York. We are going home to San Francisco. Much to settle, many things to work out. We will be fine there. Please come and visit. We will be home by May 1st. All love to you and Aunt Liz. Edwina.' The last thing any of them wanted now was to go and live in England with Aunt Liz and Uncle Rupert. Edwina wouldn't consider it for a moment.

'Are you sure they won't come to San Francisco and just take us?' George's eyes were huge in his face, and Edwina smiled at the obvious concern there.

'Of course not. They're not kidnappers, they're our aunt and uncle, and they mean well. It's just that I think we can manage on our own in San Francisco.' It was a brave statement for her to make, and one she had yet to prove, but she had decided that she was determined to do it. The paper was run by a fine staff well chosen by her father, and well directed by him over the years. There was no reason why anything had to change now, even without Bert Winfield at the helm of the paper. He had often said that if anything ever happened to him, no one would ever know it. And they were about to be put to the test, because Edwina had no intention of selling the paper. They needed the income, and even though it wasn't vastly profitable like *The New York Times*, or any of the truly great papers, it was still a very comfortable little venture, and she and the others would need the money, if they were to survive and stay together in their home in San Francisco. And she had no intention of letting Rupert, or Liz, or anyone else force her to sell the paper, or the house, or anything else that had belonged to their parents. She was anxious to get home now to see that everything was sorted out, and no one made any decisions that affected her and that she didn't approve of. She had decided they were going home. But what she didn't know was that Rupert had already made plans to have her close up the house and put the paper up for sale. As far as he was concerned the Winfield children would not be returning to San Francisco, and if so, not for long. But he had not fully reckoned with Edwina, and her determination to keep her family where they belonged. Together, at home, in San Francisco.

The Winfield children spent the next week in New York, went for long walks in the park, saw the doctor again, and were pleased with the reports about Teddy's health and Fannie's two fingers. They had lunch at the Plaza, and went shopping again, because George informed Edwina that he wouldn't be caught dead wearing the jacket she had bought him. It was a time to relax and to rest, and to be slowly restored, but at night they were all still strangely quiet, haunted by their own thoughts and fears, and the ship that had caused them. Alexis still had nightmares, and she slept in Edwina's bed now, with Fannie in another bed just beside her, and Teddy in a crib close beside them.

They had dinner in their rooms at the hotel on the last night, and they spent a quiet evening, playing cards, and talking, and George made them laugh with embarrassingly accurate impersonations of Uncle Rupert.

'That's not fair,' Edwina tried to scold him, but she was laughing too. 'The poor thing has gout, and he means well.' But he was funny anyway, and easy prey for George's wicked sense of humor. And only Alexis didn't laugh with them, she hadn't smiled in days, and if anything, she was growing more withdrawn, as she silently mourned their parents.

'I don't want to go home,' she whispered to Edwina late that night, as they lay cuddled close to each other in bed, and Edwina listened to the gently purring breath of the others.

'Why not?' she whispered, but Alexis only shook her head, and her eyes filled with tears as she buried her face in Edwina's shoulder. 'What are you afraid of, sweetheart? There's nothing to hurt you there . . .' Nothing could hurt them as much as the loss they had sustained on the *Titanic*. And there were times when even Edwina wished that her own life had been lost, there were times when she didn't want to go on without Charles or her parents. She had so little time alone to think about him, to mourn him, to just let her thoughts drift back to their happy moments. And yet, thinking about Charles at all was so painful, she could hardly bear it. But with the little ones counting on her, she knew she had to pull herself together. She could only allow herself to think of them and no one else. 'You'll be safe in your own room again,' she crooned to Alexis, 'and you can go to school with your friends . . .' But Alexis shook her head vehemently, and then looked up miserably at her older sister.

'Mama won't be there when we get home.' It was a sad fact they all knew, and Edwina also knew that a part of her was somehow childishly hoping that they would be there, and Charles with them, and it would all be a cruel joke, and none of it would have happened. But Alexis knew better, and she wisely didn't want to have to face it when they went home to San Francisco.

'No, she won't be there. But she'll be there in our hearts, she always will be. They all will – Mama, and Papa, and Charles. And once we go home, maybe we'll even feel closer to Mama there.' The house on California Street was so much a part of her, she had done so many things to make it lovely for them, and the garden was entirely magic of her mother's making. 'Don't you want to see the rosebushes in Mama's secret garden?' Alexis only shook her head, and her arms went around Edwina's

neck in quiet desperation. 'Don't be afraid, sweetheart
. . . don't be afraid . . . I'm here . . . and I always will
be . . .' And as she held the little girl close to her, she
knew she would never leave them. She thought of the
things her mother had said in the past about how much
she loved her children. Edwina thought about it, as she
drifted off to sleep holding her little sister . . . it was true,
she remembered how much her mother had loved her
. . . and there was no greater love than she would have to
have now for her brothers and sisters. And as she drifted
off to sleep, and thought of Charles and her father, she
remembered her mother's face and felt the tears sliding
into her pillow, as she held Alexis near her.

8

The Winfields left New York on 26 April, on a stormy Friday morning eleven days after the *Titanic* had gone down. The car from the Ritz-Carlton Hotel took them to the station, and the driver helped Edwina check in their bags. There were precious few of them now, and they carried with them only the things she had bought for them in New York. The toys and gifts from well-wishers had been packed and sent on ahead by train. And now there was nothing left for them to do but go home, and begin to live their life without their parents. For the little ones nothing much had changed, but Phillip felt an enormous responsibility to them all now, and for a boy of not quite seventeen, it was an awesome burden. And George felt the difference too. With Edwina, he didn't dare be quite as wild, because she was stricter with him than his parents had been, but he felt sorry for her too. She had so much to do now to take care of the younger children. She always seemed to have one of them in her arms. Fannie was always crying, Teddy always needed to be changed, or had to be carried, and Alexis was either clinging to her skirts, or hiding from people in a remote corner or behind the curtains. It seemed as though Edwina needed to be an octopus now, and although George still liked keeping amused, he no longer dared to do it at the expense of his older sister.

In fact, both boys seemed absolutely angelic to her as they helped her board the train and settle the younger children. They had two adjoining compartments on the train, and after sleeping on mattresses on the floor of the *Carpathia* for three days, she knew no one would ever complain again about the accommodations. They were grateful to be safe and warm, and to be going home, and as the train pulled slowly out of the station, Edwina felt a wave of relief sweep over her. They were going home again, to a familiar place where they would be safe, and nothing terrible would ever happen to them again, at least she hoped not. It was odd for Edwina now. At times she was so preoccupied with taking care of all of them that she didn't have time to think, or to remember, and at other times, like at night, in bed with Alexis or Fannie, all she could think of was Charles, and his last kisses, the touch of his hand . . . their last dance . . . and his good spirits when she had last seen him on the *Titanic*. He had been an elegant, kindhearted young man, and she knew he would have made her a wonderful husband. Not that it mattered now. And yet she tortured herself thinking about it, and she did again on the train, hearing his name repeated over and over and over again as she listened to the sound of the wheels speeding along the train tracks . . . Charles . . . Charles . . . Charles . . . I love you . . . I love you . . . I love you . . . she wanted to scream as she imagined the words and she could hear his voice calling her. And finally she closed her eyes just to shut out the face that still seemed so real to her in the darkness. She knew she would never forget him. And she envied her parents staying together till the end. Sometimes she wished she had gone down on the ship with Charles, and then she had to force her thoughts back to the children.

Edwina and the children read the newspapers as they crossed the States, and news of the *Titanic* was everywhere. The Senate subcommittee hearings were still continuing. Edwina had appeared before them briefly in New York. And it had been emotional and painful, but she had felt it her duty to oblige them. And their conclusion thus far was that a three-hundred-foot-long gash on the starboard side had caused the *Titanic* to founder. It no longer seemed to matter now, but people appeared to have a need to find a reason, a cause, as though that would make it all seem right, but Edwina knew only too well that it wouldn't. More importantly, people were outraged at the loss of life, and the fact that there had been lifeboats for less than half of those aboard. The committee had asked her how the officers had conducted themselves and what her impression was of how people had behaved in the lifeboats. There was a general outcry over the fact that there had been no lifeboat drill, and not even the crew knew which were their stations. The most appalling fact of all was that the lifeboats had been sent off the ship half empty, and had then refused to pick people up out of the water after the ship sank, for fear of overturning. The whole episode was one that would go down in history as a heart-wrenching tragedy of monumental proportions. Testifying had left her feeling spent and desolate, as though going there somehow might have changed it, but it didn't. The people they had loved were gone, and nothing was ever going to bring them back. Somehow, talking about it now only made it more painful. It was even more so to read in the newspaper on the train that three hundred and twenty-eight bodies had been recovered, but Edwina already knew before she left New York that none of them had been her parents or Charles.

She had gotten a touching telegram from the Fitzgeralds in London, offering their condolences to her, and assuring her that in their hearts she would always be their daughter. And for some odd reason, it made her think of the beautiful wedding veil that was being made, and Lady Fitzgerald was to have brought over in August. What would happen to it now? Who would wear it? And why did she care? She had no right to mourn the little things, she told herself, or to care about things like that now. Her wedding veil was no longer important. And at night, on the train, she lay awake, trying not to think about all of it, and staring out the window. Charles's gloves, which he had thrown to her to keep her own hands warm as she left the ship, were still in her valise. But she couldn't bear to look at them now. Even seeing them was painful. But just knowing that she still had them was a comfort.

She was awake when the Rockies appeared high in the morning sky, with the first pink streaks of dawn splashed across them, on their last day on the train, and for the first time in exactly two weeks, she felt a little better. Most of the time, she didn't have time to think about how she felt, which was just as well, and that morning she woke all of them and told them to look outside at the beautiful mountains.

'Are we home yet?' Fannie asked with big eyes. She couldn't wait to get home again, and she had already told Edwina several times that she was never going to leave home again, and the first thing she was going to do when she got back was make a chocolate cake just like Mama's. It had been one of Kate's frequent treats for them, and Edwina had promised that she'd help her do it. George had already said that he was not going back to school, he tried to convince Edwina that the trauma had been too much for him, and it would be better for him to rest at home for a while before resuming his school-work. Fortunately, his sister knew better than to believe him. And poor Phillip was worrying about school. He had only one more year before going east to Harvard, like his father. At least that was what the plan had been, but now it was difficult to plan anything. Perhaps, Phillip thought to himself, as they rode home on the train, he might not even be able to go to college. But he felt guilty for his thoughts in the face of their far greater losses.

'Weenie,' Fannie asked, using the name that always made Edwina laugh.

'Yes, Frances?' Edwina pretended to look very prim and proper.

'Don't call me that, please.' Fannie looked at her reproachfully and then went on. 'Are you going to sleep in Mama's room now?' She looked at her oldest sister matter-of-factly, and Edwina felt as though she had been punched in the stomach.

'No, I don't think so.' She couldn't have slept in that room. It wasn't hers. It was theirs, and she didn't belong there. 'I'll still sleep in my own room.'

'But aren't you our mama now?' Fannie looked puzzled, and Edwina saw tears in Phillip's eyes as he turned away to look out the window.

'No, I'm not.' She shook her head sadly. 'I'm still just Weenie, your big sister.' She smiled.

'But then who'll be our mama now?'

What to say? How to explain it? Even George looked away, the question was too painful for them all. 'Mama is still our mama. She always will be.' It was all she could think of to say to them. And she knew the others understood, if not Fannie.

'But she's not here now. And you said you'd take care of us.' Fannie looked like she was about to cry as Edwina tried to reassure her.

'I will take care of you.' She pulled the child onto her lap, and glanced at Alexis sitting huddled in the corner of the seat, with her eyes on the floor, willing herself not to hear what they were saying. 'I'll do all the things that Mama did, as best I can. But she's still our mama, no matter what. I couldn't be Mama, no matter how hard I tried.' And she wouldn't have wanted to try to replace her.

'Oh.' Fannie nodded her head, satisfied finally, and then she had a last thought to clear up before they got home. 'Then can you sleep in my bed every night?' But Edwina just smiled at her.

'Your bed might collapse, you know. Don't you think I'm a little too big for it?' She had a beautiful little bed that their father had had made for Edwina years before. 'I'll tell you what. You can visit me in my bed sometimes. How does that sound?' She saw that Alexis was watching her mournfully then, and she didn't like hearing about their mother's being gone. 'And you too, Alexis. You can sleep in my bed with me sometimes.'

'What about me?' George teased, and then he tweaked Fannie's nose, and snuck a little piece of candy to Alexis. Edwina had noticed repeatedly how much he had changed in the past two weeks, and how much more subdued he was now. The prospect of going home again was beginning to worry all of them. Seeing their home, knowing that their parents would never come back to it, was going to be very painful.

They were all thinking about it on the last night on the train, and no one spoke as they lay awake long into the night. Edwina slept less than two hours, when she finally got up at six o'clock and washed her face and dressed in one of her finest black dresses. They were due to arrive shortly after 8.00 a.m., and as worried as she'd been about going home, looking out at the familiar countryside was somehow a comfort. She woke the younger children up, and knocked on the door to the adjoining compartment where Phillip and George had slept. And they were all in the dining car at seven o'clock having breakfast. The boys ate a hearty meal, and Alexis played with a scrambled egg, as Edwina cut Teddy's and Fannie's waffles up, and by the time they had finished, and gone back to their compartments, and she had washed the little ones' faces, and straightened their clothes, the train was rolling slowly into the station. She had seen to it that they were all properly dressed in their new clothes, their hair shining and clean and well combed, and she had carefully tied Fannie's and Alexis's ribbons. She didn't know who would come to meet them at the station, but she knew they would be scrutinized, and perhaps even photographed by reporters from their father's paper. And she wanted the children to do him proud. She felt she owed that to her parents. She felt the wheels come to a jagged stop, and Edwina looked up with a sharp intake of breath and then glanced at the others. Not a word was said, but they all felt the sharp, bittersweet pang of coming home. They were back, so different than when they left, so totally changed, so alone, and yet so close to each other.

9

The flowers and the trees were all in bloom as Edwina and the children stepped off the train in the early May sunshine. Somehow she expected it to look the same as it had when she left. But it didn't. Like her own life, suddenly everything was different. She had left home a happy, carefree girl, with her brothers and her sisters and her parents. Charles had been with them and they had talked endlessly all the way across the States, about what they wanted and what they believed and what they liked to read and do and think, and even how many children they thought that they wanted. But now nothing was the same, least of all Edwina herself. She had come home a mourner and an orphan. And she was wearing a black dress that made her look taller and thinner and so much older. She was wearing a serious black hat with a veil that she had bought in New York, and as she stepped down from the train and looked around her, she saw reporters waiting for them, just as she had suspected they would be. They were from her father's paper, and rival newspapers too. And for a moment it looked as though half the town had come to see them. As she looked at them, a reporter stepped forward and with an explosion of light, snapped her picture. Once again, it was on the front page the next day, but she turned away from him, and tried to ignore the staring crowds and the photographers. She helped the children off the train. Phillip carried Alexis and Fannie, and Edwina lifted Teddy into her arms as

George went to find a porter. They were home now. In spite of the curious crowds, they felt safe here and yet they were all afraid to go home, knowing what they wouldn't find there.

As Edwina struggled with their few bags, a man hurried forward and she turned and recognized Ben Jones, her father's attorney. He had been her father's friend for years, they were the same age, and twenty-five years before, they had been roommates at Harvard. Ben was a tall, attractive man, with a gentle smile and gray hair that had once been sandy, and he had known Edwina since she was a little girl. But he saw no child in her now, only a very sad young woman, struggling to bring her sisters and brothers home safely. He parted the crowd as he came toward her, and people moved aside without a murmur.

'Hello, Edwina.' His eyes were filled with grief, but hers were more so. 'I'm so sorry.' He had to say it quickly so he wouldn't cry himself. Bert Winfield had been his best friend, and he had been horrified when he had first heard about the *Titanic*. He had checked with the paper at once, to see if they knew anything, and by then they had heard from Edwina, steaming toward New York on the *Carpathia* with her brothers and sisters, but no fiancé, and no parents. And Ben had cried at the loss of his good friend and his wife, and for the terrible sorrow of the children.

The children were happy to see him there and George was grinning as he hadn't in weeks. Even Phillip looked relieved. He was the first friend they had seen since they had survived the disaster. But none of them were anxious to talk about it, as Ben tried to keep the reporters at a distance. By way of conversation, George made an announcement to him. 'I learned two new card tricks on the way home.' But the child looked tired and sad and pale, Ben noticed, seeing that George wasn't his old self, but he was trying valiantly to be entertaining.

'You'll have to show me your new tricks when we get to the house. Do you still cheat at cards?' Ben asked and George let out a great guffaw in answer, and as he looked around, Ben noticed that Alexis's face was completely without expression. He also noticed how pale and tired the younger children looked, and how terribly thin Edwina had become in the short time since she had left California. In truth, she had only gotten thin since escaping the *Titanic*.

'Mama's dead,' Fannie announced as they stood in the sunlight waiting for their bags, and Edwina felt the words hit her in the stomach like bricks as Fannie spoke them.

'I know,' Ben said quietly as they all held their breath, wondering what she would say next. 'I was very sorry to hear it.' He glanced at Edwina and she was pale beneath the veil. In truth, they all were. They had been through a nightmare and it showed, and it tore at his heartstrings to see it. 'But I'm glad that you're alright, Fannie. We were all very worried about you.'

She nodded, pleased to hear it, and then told him of her perils as well. 'Mr Frost bit my fingers.' She held out the two fingers she had almost lost, and he nodded soberly, grateful that they were all alive. 'And Teddy got a cough, but he's fine now.'

Edwina smiled at the report, and they all got into the car he had brought from her father's paper. It was a car they sometimes used to go on trips, and he had brought the carriage for their bags, not that they had very many with them. He hadn't known how much they would have, or if they might even come home empty-handed.

'It was nice of you to pick us up,' she said, as they drove toward the house.

He knew only too well how painful it would be, having lost his wife and son in the earthquake of '06. It had almost broken his heart, and he had never remarried. The boy would have been George's age by then. And because of that George had always had a special place in his heart.

Ben chatted with him on the way to the house, and the rest of them lapsed into pensive silence. They were all thinking the same thing. How empty the house was going to be now without their parents. And it was even worse than Edwina had expected. The flowers their mother had planted before she left were in full bloom now, and they stood out in brilliant colors, offering them a bittersweet welcome.

'Come on, everyone, let's go in.' Edwina spoke softly as they hesitated for a long time in the garden. They all seemed to drag their feet, and Ben tried to chat and make it easier for them, but no one seemed to want to talk. They just walked inside and stood looking around as though it were not their home anymore, but a stranger's. And Edwina herself knew that she was listening for sounds that were no more . . . the rustle of her mother's skirts . . . the sound of her bracelets. The sound of her father's voice as he came up the stairs . . . But there was only silence. And Alexis looked as though she were hearing voices. She strained as though she could hear something, but she only wanted to, and they all knew that she couldn't. There was nothing to hear. And the tension was unbearable as they looked around, and Edwina felt as though they were waiting, as Teddy pulled at her sleeve with a curious expression.

'Mama?' he asked, as though sure that there was some reasonable explanation. Even though he had last seen her on the ship, in his two-year-old mind, he knew that she belonged here.

'She's not here, Teddy.' Edwina knelt down next to him to explain it.

'Bye bye?'

'That's right.' She nodded as she took her hat off and tossed it onto the hall table. Without it, she looked younger again, and she stood up, unable to explain it any further. She just held his hand in her own and looked sadly at the others.

'It's hard being back here, isn't it?' Her voice was hoarse, and the two boys nodded, and Alexis walked slowly up the staircase. Edwina knew where she was going and she wished that she wouldn't. She was going to their mother's room, and maybe it was just as well. Maybe here she would be able to face it. Phillip looked at Edwina questioningly, but she only shook her head. 'Let her go . . . she's alright . . .' They were all sad, but at least they were safe here.

The driver from the paper brought their pitifully few bags in, and Mrs Barnes, their elderly housekeeper, appeared, wiping her hands on her starched white apron. She was a cozy woman, and she had adored Kate. And now she burst into tears as she hugged Edwina and the children. It was not going to be easy, Edwina realized then. There would be countless people offering condolences and wanting painful descriptions and explanations. Just thinking about it was exhausting.

Half an hour later, Ben finally left them. She walked him to the door, and he asked her to let him know when she was ready to talk business with him.

'How soon do I have to do it?' she asked with a worried look.

'As soon as you're ready.' He spoke quietly, not wanting to frighten her or the children, but the others were already out of earshot. George was already upstairs, destroying his

135

room, and Phillip was checking his mail and sorting through his books, and little Fannie had gone to the kitchen with Mrs Barnes for some cookies, with Teddy in hot pursuit, but still looking over his shoulder, as though at any moment he expected to see Mama and Papa.

'You have a lot of decisions to make,' Ben went on, standing in the hallway with Edwina.

'About what?' She needed to know. She'd been worried about it for a week. What if they didn't have enough money to survive? She had always thought they did, but what if they didn't?

'You have to decide what you want to do about the paper, this house, some investments your father has. I suppose I should tell you, too, that your uncle thinks you should sell everything and move to England, but we can talk about that later.' He hadn't wanted to upset her, but her face was suddenly flushed and her eyes grew bright and angry as she listened.

'What does my uncle have to do with all this? Is he my guardian?' She looked horrified, she hadn't even thought about that as a possibility, but Ben was shaking his head to reassure her.

'No, your aunt is, according to your mother's will. But only until you're twenty-one.'

'Thank God.' Edwina smiled. 'That's in three weeks. I can wait that long.' Ben smiled in answer. She was a bright girl, and she would do well, it was just a shame that she had to face this. 'Will I have to sell the newspaper?' She looked worried again, and Ben shook his head.

'One day you might want to, but right now there are good people running it, and it will provide the income you need. But if Phillip hasn't put a hand to it in a few years, you'll probably have to sell it. Unless you want to give it a try, Edwina?' They both smiled at that. That was the last thing she wanted.

'We can talk about this next week, but I'll tell you right now, Ben, I'm not going anywhere. And I'm not selling anything. I'm going to keep everything just as it is now . . . for the children.'

'That's quite a responsibility to put on your shoulders.'

'Maybe so.' She looked sober as she walked to the door. 'But that's where it belongs now. I'm going to do everything I can to keep things just as they were when my parents were alive,' and he knew without a doubt that she meant it.

He admired her for trying, but a part of him wondered if she would be able to do it. Raising five children was no small task for a girl of twenty. But he also knew that she had her father's brains and her mother's warm heart and courage and she had every intention of making it work, no matter what it took. And maybe she was right. Maybe she could do it.

When he was gone, Edwina closed the door behind him with a sigh and looked around her. The house had the look of a place where people have been away for a long time. There were no flowers in the vases, no pretty, fresh smells, there were no happy sounds, no signs that people cared, and Edwina realized that she was going to have a lot to do there. But first, she needed to check on the children. She could hear the two youngest ones playing in the kitchen with Mrs Barnes, and on the second floor, Phillip and George were having a heated argument over whose tennis racket George had apparently broken, and in Alexis's room, she found no one. It was easy to guess why, and passing her own room on the way, she walked slowly upstairs to what had been her parents' sunny quarters.

It was painful just walking up the stairs now, knowing that they wouldn't be there. And it was hot and airless up there, as though it had been months since anyone had opened the windows. But it was sunny, and they had a beautiful view of the East Bay.

'Alexis?' She called softly. She knew she was there. She could feel her. 'Darling . . . Where are you? . . . Come back downstairs . . . we all miss you.' But she missed her mother more, and Edwina knew it. She knew she would find Alexis there, and it broke her heart as she walked into her mother's pretty pink satin dressing room, with the perfumes all lined up, and the hats neatly put on the shelf, and the shoes all perfectly arranged . . . the shoes she would never wear again. Edwina tried not to look at them, as her own eyes filled with tears. She hadn't wanted to come up here yet, but she had to now, if only to find Alexis. 'Lexie? . . . Come on, baby . . . come on back downstairs . . .' But all around her there was silence, and only the relentlessly happy sunshine, and the smell of her mother's perfume. 'Alex . . .' Her voice died on the word as she saw her, holding her beloved doll, and crying silently as she sat in her mother's closet. She was holding on to her skirts, smelling their perfume and just sitting there, alone in the May sunshine. Edwina walked slowly toward her, and then knelt down on the floor and held the child's face in her hands, kissing her cheeks, her own tears mingling with her sister's.

'I love you, sweetheart . . . I love you so much . . . maybe not exactly the way she did . . . but I'm here for you, Alexis . . . trust me.' She could barely speak, as the sweet fragrance of her mother's clothes tore at her memories and her heart. It was almost unbearable being here now that Kate was gone. And across the hall, she could see her father's suits hanging in his dressing room. And for the first time in her life, she felt as though neither she nor Alexis belonged here.

'I want Mama,' the little girl cried as she sank against Edwina.

'So do I,' Edwina cried with her and then kissed her again as they knelt there, 'but she's gone, baby . . . she's gone . . . and I'm here . . . and I promise I'll never leave you . . .'

'But she did . . . she's gone . . .'

'She didn't mean to leave us . . . she couldn't help it. It just happened.' But it hadn't, and Edwina had been fighting back the thought of that for days, ever since they'd left the *Titanic* without her. Why hadn't she come in the lifeboat with Edwina and the children? Or later, after she thought she saw Alexis in the lifeboat? There had been other boats . . . later ones, she could have gotten in one. But instead she had chosen to stay on the ship with her husband. Phillip had told her about their mother's decision to stay with him. How could she do that to all of them? . . . to Alexis . . . to Teddy . . . Fanny . . . the boys . . . and somewhere, deep within her, Edwina knew that she was angry at her for it. But she couldn't admit that now to Alexis. 'I don't know why it happened, Lexie, but it did. And now we have to take care of each other. We all miss her, but we have to go on . . . that's what she would have wanted.' Alexis hesitated for a long time, and then let Edwina stand her up, but she still looked unconvinced as she stood in her mother's closet.

'I don't want to come downstairs . . .' She balked as Edwina tried to lead her out of the room, and she looked around her as though in a panic, as though she were afraid she might never see this room again, or touch her mother's clothes, or smell her delicate perfume.

'We can't stay up here anymore, Lexie . . . it'll just make us sad. I know she's here, so do you, she's everywhere . . . we take her with us in our hearts. I always feel her with me now, and so will you, if you think about her.' Alexis seemed to hesitate, and very gently Edwina picked her up and carried her downstairs to her own room, but the child didn't look as frightened now, or as desolate. She had finally come home, the thing they had all wanted and feared most, and they had found that it was true. Their mother and father were gone. But the memories lived on, like the flowers in her garden. And without saying anything, Edwina left a little bottle of her mother's perfume on Alexis's dresser that night. And from then on, she always smelled it on Alexis's doll, Mrs Thomas. It was a faint whiff of what their mother had been, a dim memory of the woman they had loved, and who had chosen to die with her husband.

10

'I don't give a damn.' Edwina was looking ferociously at Ben Jones. 'I will *not* sell the paper.'

'Your uncle thinks you should. I had a long letter from him only yesterday, Edwina. At least think about what he's saying. He thinks that it can only run down slowly as long as there is no family member left to run it. And he strongly feels that you, and all the children, belong in England.' Ben looked apologetic but firm, as he repeated her uncle's opinions.

'That's nonsense. And there will be someone to run the paper, in time. In five years, there will be Phillip.'

Ben sighed. He knew what she wanted, and she could be right, but so could her uncle. 'A twenty-one-year-old boy cannot run a paper.' It was how old Phillip would be five years later. And in the meantime he wasn't sure either that a twenty-one-year-old girl should be responsible for five younger children. It was an unfair burden on her, and perhaps moving to England with them would be simpler.

'There are perfectly good people running the paper now. You said so yourself,' Edwina insisted. 'And one day Phillip will run the business.'

'And if he doesn't? What then?' To her, it seemed an absurd question at the moment.

'I'll face that when it happens. But meanwhile, I have other things to do. I have the children to think about, and there is absolutely no reason to worry about the business.' She looked tired, and her temper was short, and there

to learn now. Her father had some
her mother had had a few too. And
e of real estate in southern Califor-
o sell that. And to keep the house.
the paper. It was all so damn
children were still upset. And
ll at school, and suddenly the boys
seemed to fight all the time, and Phillip was afraid of
failing his exams, so she was studying with him at night,
and then there were the cries . . . and the tears at midnight
. . . and the constant nightmares. She felt as though she
were living on a merry-go-round and she could never get
off. She just had to keep going around and around and
around, taking care of other people's needs, learning new
things, and making decisions. There was no room anywhere for her and what her needs were . . . nowhere for
the constant aching memories of Charles . . . There was
no one to take care of her now, and she felt as though
there never would be.

'Edwina, wouldn't it be easier for you to go to England
and stay with the Hickhams for a while? Let them help
you.'

She looked insulted at the idea. 'I don't need help. We
are fine.'

'I know you are,' he apologized, 'but it's unfair for all
the responsibility to fall on you, and they want to help you.'

But she didn't see it that way. 'They don't want to help
me. They want to take everything away.' Tears filled her
eyes as she spoke. 'Our house, our friends, the children's
schools, our way of life. Don't you understand?' She looked
up at him mournfully. 'This is all we have left now.'

'No.' He shook his head quietly, wishing he could reach
out to her. 'You have each other.'

He didn't mention the Hickhams again, and she went

over the paperwork with Ben, definite about what she wanted to do, no matter what anyone thought of it. She was going to hang on to the paper for her brothers, and to the house for all of them.

'Can I afford to keep it all, Ben?' Everything seemed to boil down to that now. And she had to ask questions she had never even thought about before, and fortunately, he was always honest.

'Yes, you can. For now nothing has to change. Eventually, it might become counterproductive. But for right now, the paper will actually bring you a very decent income, and the house is no problem.'

'Then I'll keep both. What else?' She was amazingly matter-of-fact at times, and so capable it shocked him. Maybe she was right to keep everything as it was. For the moment, it was certainly the greatest gift she could give the children.

And eventually she explained it for the ten thousandth time to their uncle Rupert. And this time he understood it. In truth, he was relieved. It was Liz who had begged him to let them come, and he had wanted to do his duty. Edwina told him how grateful they all were to him but that the children were still far too upset by everything that had happened, and so was she. What they needed now was to stay home, and catch their breath, and have a quiet, happy life in surroundings that were familiar. And that although they loved him and Aunt Liz, they just couldn't leave California at the moment. He responded that they were always welcome to change their minds, and a flurry of letters began to arrive from Aunt Liz, promising to come and visit them the moment she was able to leave Uncle Rupert. But somehow, Edwina always found the letters extremely depressing, although she did not share that viewpoint with the younger children.

'We're not going,' she finally told Ben. 'In fact,' she said, looking at him seriously across his desk at the law firm where he was a partner, 'I doubt very much if I will ever get on a ship again. I don't think I could do it. You don't know what it was like,' she said softly. She still had nightmares about the stern of the giant ship rising into the night sky with the propellers dripping, and she knew the others did too. She wouldn't have put them through it for anything in the world, no matter what Rupert Hickham thought was best for them, or what he felt he owed them.

'I understand,' Ben said quietly. And he thought she was extremely brave to try to cope alone. But she seemed to be doing very well, much to his amazement.

There were times when he wondered how she was going to do it all. But she was so determined to carry on where her parents left off, and he admired her greatly for it. Any other girl her age would have been crying in her room over the fiancé she had lost, but not Edwina, she was carrying on as best she could, without a word of complaint, and only a look of sorrow in her eyes, which never failed to touch him.

'I'm sorry to bring this up, by the way,' he mentioned one day. 'But I've had another letter from White Star. They want to know if you're going to file a claim for your parents' death, and I want to know what to tell them. In some ways, I think you should, because you'll have to bear the expenses for everything in your father's absence, yet it won't bring them back. I don't even like mentioning it, but I have to know what you want to do. I'll do anything you want, Edwina . . .' His voice drifted off as he met her eyes. She was a beautiful girl, and he was growing fonder of her every day. She had grown up hard and fast, and she wasn't a child anymore. She was a very lovely young woman.

'Let it go,' she said softly, and turned away to walk slowly to the window. She was thinking of what it had been like, and how anyone could pay you for that, and how they had almost lost Alexis when she ran away . . . and little Teddy from the brutal exposure to the freezing temperatures, and Fannie with her two little stiff fingers . . . and their parents . . . and Charles . . . and all the nightmares and terrors and sorrows . . . the wedding veil she would never wear . . . the gloves that had been his that she kept locked in a little leather box in her chest. She herself could hardly bear to look at the bay anymore, and she felt ill just glancing at a ship . . . how did they pay you for that? How much for a lost mother? . . . a lost father? . . . a lost husband? . . . a damaged life? . . . What price did people put on all that? 'There is nothing they could pay us that would make up for what we lost.'

Ben was nodding sadly from where he sat. 'Apparently, the others have thought pretty much the same thing. The Astors, the Wideners, the Strauses, no one else is suing either. I think some people are suing for their lost luggage. I can do that if you want me to. All we really have to do is file a claim.' But she only shook her head again, and walked slowly toward him, wondering if they would ever forget, if it would ever go away, if life would ever be even remotely as it once had been before the *Titanic*.

'When does it stop, Ben?' she asked sadly. 'When do we stop thinking about it night and day and pretending that we aren't? When will Alexis stop sneaking upstairs so she can feel Mama's fur coats, and the satin of her nightgowns . . . when will Phillip stop looking as though he's carrying the weight of the world . . . and little Teddy stop looking for Mama? . . .' There were tears sliding down her cheeks, as he came around the desk and put an arm around her shoulders. She looked up at him then as if he were the father she had lost and buried her face in his shoulder. 'When will I stop seeing them every time I close my eyes? When will I stop thinking Charles will come back from England? . . . oh, God . . .' He held her for a long time while she cried, and wished he had the answers, and eventually she pulled away and went to blow her nose, but even the handkerchief she carried had once been her mother's, and nothing he could say would change what they had been through or what they had lost, and how they felt about it.

'Give it time, Edwina. It hasn't been two months yet.'

She sighed and then nodded.

'I'm sorry.' She smiled sadly and stood up again, kissed him on the cheek and absentmindedly straightened her hat. It was a lovely one her mother had bought in Paris. He walked her out of his office again and saw her downstairs to her carriage. And as she turned back to wave at him as they drove away, he couldn't help thinking what a remarkable girl she was. And then he silently corrected himself. She wasn't a girl anymore. She was a woman. A very remarkable young woman.

11

The summer passed leisurely for all of them, doing simple things and just being together. And in July, just as they always had when her parents were alive, Edwina took them to the lake to a camp they had always borrowed from friends of her father's. They had always spent part of their summers at Lake Tahoe, and as much as possible Edwina wanted their lives to remain the same now. The boys fished and hiked, and they stayed in a cluster of rugged, pretty cabins. She cooked their dinners at night and went swimming with Teddy and the girls while Phillip and George went hiking. It was a simple, easy life, and here, finally, she felt that they were all beginning to recover. It was exactly what they needed, and finally, even she no longer had the same anguished, troubled dreams of that terrible night in April. She lay in her bed at night, thinking of what they'd done all day, and now and then she would let herself think of being there with Charles the previous summer. No matter what she did, her mind always drifted back to him, and the memories were always tender and painful.

Everything had been different before. Her father had organized adventures with the boys, and she had taken long walks with her mother, picking wildflowers around the lake. They had talked about life, and men, having children, and being married, and it was there that she had first admitted to her how much she was in love with Charles. It had been no secret to anyone by then, and

George had been merciless with his teasing, but Edwina didn't care. She was ready to admit it to all the world. And she had been ecstatic when Charles had come up to stay with them from San Francisco. He brought little treats for the girls, a new unicycle for George, and a series of beautifully bound books for Phillip. His gifts delighted everyone, and he and Edwina had gone for long walks in the woods. She thought about it now sometimes, and it was hard not to cry as she forced her mind back to the present. It was a challenging summer for her mostly, though, trying to take her mother's place, and sometimes feeling so small in her shadow. She helped Alexis learn to float, and watched Fannie play at the edge of the lake with her dolls. Little Teddy went everywhere with her now, and Phillip talked to her for long hours about getting into Harvard. She had to be everything to them now, mother, father, friend, mentor, teacher, and adviser.

They'd been there for a week when Ben came up from town, to surprise them. And as he had in years before, he brought presents for everyone, and some new books for Edwina. He was interesting and fun, and to the children, he was like a favorite uncle, and they were happy to see him.

Even Alexis had laughed happily as she ran toward him. Her blond curls were flying loose, and she had just come up from the lake with Edwina, and their feet and legs were bare. She looked like a little colt, and in his big sister's arms, Teddy looked like a little bear, and it almost brought tears to Ben's eyes as he watched them. He thought of how much his lost friend had loved them all, how much Bert's family had meant to him, and he felt his loss again the moment he saw them.

'You all look very well.' He grinned, happy to see them, as she set Teddy down, and he chortled as he ran after Alexis.

Edwina smiled happily as she pushed away a lock of her dark, shining hair. 'The children have been having fun.'

'It seems as though it's done you good too.' He was pleased to see her looking healthy and relaxed and brown, and a moment later, before he could say more, the children swarmed him.

They played together for hours, and that night she and Ben sat quietly in the twilight.

'It's been wonderful being here again.' She didn't say that it reminded her of her parents, but they both knew it. But still she knew she could say things to Ben she couldn't say to anyone else because he had been so close to her parents. And it was odd coming back to the places she'd always gone to with them. It was as though she expected to find them there, but one by one, as she went back to their favorite haunts, she came to understand, as the children did, that they were gone forever. It was the same with Charles. It was hard to believe he was never coming back from England . . . that he hadn't gone there for a while, and would be coming home soon. None of them would be back again. All of them had moved on. But she and the children had to live with their memories, and for the first time in a long time, they were having fun and relaxing. And as she sat in the mountain twilight, she found herself talking about her parents to Ben. And even laughing about some of their past summer adventures. And he was laughing too, remembering the time Bert had pretended to be a bear and scared Kate and Ben and Edwina half to death wandering into the cabin beneath a huge bear rug.

They talked about fishing expeditions in some of the hidden streams, and entire days on the lake in the little boat they'd rented. They talked of silly things, moments they'd all shared, and memories they both cherished. And for the first time in months, it wasn't so much painful as a source of comfort. With Ben, she was able to laugh at memories of them, they became human again, and no longer godlike. And she realized as they chuckled into the night that this was something she wanted to share with the other children.

'You're doing a beautiful job with them,' Ben said, and she was touched. Sometimes she wasn't sure she was.

'I'm trying,' she sighed, but Alexis was still afraid, and Phillip so subdued, and the two little ones still had nightmares on occasion. 'It isn't always easy.'

'It's never easy raising children. But it's a wonderful thing to do.' And then finally he dared say something to her he'd thought for months but hadn't wanted to mention. 'You ought to get out more, though. Your parents did. They did more than just raise all of you. They traveled, they saw friends, your mother was involved in a lot of things, and your father was busy with the paper.'

'Are you suggesting I get a job?' She grinned, teasing him, and he shook his head as he watched her. He was a good-looking man, but she had never thought of him as anything but her father's friend and her adopted uncle.

'No, I meant that you should go out, see friends.' She had gone out almost constantly with Charles during their engagement. Ben had loved seeing her in beautiful gowns with dancing eyes, as she left the house on Charles's arm, whenever he dined with her parents. She was meant for all that, not for living the life of a recluse, or a widowed mother. Her whole life still lay ahead, altered perhaps, but certainly not over. 'What happened to all those parties you . . . used to go to?' He was suddenly afraid to mention Charles, for fear it would be too painful, and Edwina lowered her eyes as she answered.

'It's not the time for that now.' It was too soon, and it

would only have reminded her of Charles and made his absence infinitely more difficult to bear. She never wanted to go out again, or so she thought at the moment. And in any case, she reminded Ben, she was still in full mourning for her parents. She still wore only black, and she had no desire to go anywhere, except with the children.

'Edwina,' Ben sounded firm, 'you need to get out more.'

'I will one day.' But her eyes weren't convincing, and he hoped it would be soon. She was twenty-one years old and she was leading the life of an old woman. Her birthday had gone almost unnoticed that year, except for the fact that she was now legally of age and could sign all her own papers.

Ben slept in the same cabin with the boys that night and they enjoyed his company. He took them fishing at 5.00 a.m., and when they returned, victorious, and very smelly, Edwina was already cooking breakfast. She had brought Sheilagh, the new Irish girl, with her, and she was pleasant, but no one seemed to have adjusted to her yet. They all still missed Oona. But Sheilagh endeared herself to the fishermen by cleaning their fish, and Edwina grudgingly cooked them for breakfast. But everyone else was extremely impressed that they had actually caught some fish this time, instead of just explaining why they didn't.

It was a happy few days with Ben, and they were all sorry when he had to go. They had just finished lunch and he said good-bye, and Edwina realized she hadn't seen the boys since just before lunchtime. They had said that they were going for a walk, and after that they were going swimming, and then suddenly as she and Ben talked, Phillip exploded into the clearing.

'Do you know what that little rat did?' Phillip shouted at her, barely coherent. He was angry and out of breath and obviously very frightened, as Edwina could feel her heart pound, fearing what might have happened. 'He left while I was asleep, next to the fishing hole, way in back, at the creek . . . I woke up and found his shoes and his hat and his shirt floating in it . . . I've been digging everywhere with sticks . . . I dove all the way to the bottom of it . . .' And as he spoke, Edwina saw that his arms were badly scratched, his clothes wet and torn, and his hands were covered with mud, his fingernails broken. 'I thought he had *drowned!*' he shouted at her, choking on tears of fear and fury. 'I thought . . .' He turned away so they wouldn't see him cry, and his whole body shook as he made a lunge at George as he entered the clearing. Phillip cuffed him hard on the ear, grabbed his shoulders, and then shook him again. 'Don't you ever do that again . . . the next time you leave, you tell me about it!' He was shouting at him, and they could all see that George was fighting back tears, too, as he punched him.

'I would have told you if you weren't sleeping. You're always asleep or reading . . . you don't even know how to fish!' He shouted back the only thing that came to mind, and Phillip just kept shaking him.

'You know what Papa said last year! *No one* goes anywhere without telling someone else where he's gone. Do you understand that?' But it was more than that now. It was all compounded by the agony of losing their parents, and the fact that all they had was each other. But George wouldn't back down as he glared at his brother.

'I don't have to tell you *anything*! You're *not* my father!'

'You answer to *me* now!' Phillip grew more heated by the moment, but George was furious now too. He swung at him again and missed his mark as Phillip ducked.

'I don't answer to *anyone*!' George screamed with tears

running down his face. 'You're not Papa and you never will be, and I hate you!' They were both in tears, as Ben finally decided to step in and stop it. He reached out quietly and separated them as tears rolled down Edwina's cheeks. It broke her heart to see her brothers fighting.

'All right, boys, enough!' He took George gently by the arms, and led him away, still sputtering, while Phillip calmed down. He looked at Edwina ferociously, walked to his cabin, and slammed the door. And once inside, he lay on his bed and sobbed because he thought George had drowned, and he desperately missed their father.

It was an incident that illustrated how shaken they still were, and how great a strain it was on the boys to no longer have a father. The boys calmed down eventually, and Ben said good-bye to them, and once again took leave of Edwina. The episode between the two boys only reminded him of what he had thought in the beginning. The family was too great a burden for Edwina alone, and he wondered for a moment if he should have tried to force her to go to England to her aunt and uncle. But one look into her eyes told him that she would have hated it. She wanted this, her family, in the familiar places they had always lived, even if sometimes it wasn't easy.

'They're alright, you know,' she reassured Ben. 'It's good for Phillip to let off steam, and it's good for George to learn that he can't play his tricks all the time. He'll think twice next time.'

'And what about you?' Ben asked. How could she manage them all alone? Two lively boys who were nearly men, and three other very young children. And the truth was there was no one to help her. But he had to admit, she didn't seem to mind it.

'I love this, you know.' She said it calmly, and it was easy to believe that she meant it. 'I love them.'

'So do I. But I worry about you anyway. If you need anything, Edwina, just whistle, and I'll come running.' She kissed him gratefully on the cheek, and he watched her for a long time, as she waved, and he drove slowly back toward the station.

12

They were all sad to leave the lake. But she had things to do back in San Francisco. She attended a monthly meeting at the newspaper now, with Ben, to show everyone that she was interested in what was going on, and she had to approve certain policy decisions, which was interesting. But she still felt uncomfortable in her father's place, and there was so much to learn even for her meager involvement. She had no desire to run the paper herself, but she wanted to preserve it over the next few years, for Phillip. And she was always grateful for Ben's advice at the meetings.

But the day after their August meeting was a hard one for her. She was working in the garden, pulling weeds, when the mailman came with what looked like an enormous parcel, from England. She imagined that it was something from Aunt Liz, and couldn't imagine what she had sent. She asked Mrs Barnes to leave it in the front hall for her, and when she came in later with dirt all over her hands, and bits of grass and leaves on her black dress, she glanced at it, and felt her heart give a lurch. The sender's name on the parcel was not Hickham, but Fitzgerald. And it was written out in the careful, elaborate hand that Edwina had long since come to recognize as Charles's mother's.

She went into the kitchen to wash her hands, and came back to carefully take the parcel to her bedroom. And as she touched it her hands were shaking. She couldn't imagine what Lady Fitzgerald would be sending her, and yet she somehow feared that it might be something of Charles's, and she was more than a little afraid to see it.

The house was quiet as she walked upstairs, the boys were out with friends, and Sheilagh had taken the three younger children to Golden Gate Park to see the new carousel, and they had left the house in high spirits. There was no one to interrupt her now, and Edwina carefully unwrapped the package that Lady Fitzgerald had sent her. It had come by mail steamer, and then by train, and it had taken well over a month to arrive from England. Edwina noticed that the parcel was very light. It almost felt as though there was nothing in it.

The last bits of paper fell away, and there was a smooth white box with a letter attached on blue stationery with the Fitzgerald crest engraved in the upper left-hand corner. But she didn't read the letter, she was too curious to see what was in the box, and as she untied the ribbon and lifted the lid, her breath caught as she saw it. There were yards and yards of white tulle, and a delicately made white satin crown, embroidered in elaborate patterns with the tiniest white seed pearls. It was her wedding veil, the one Lady Fitzgerald was to have brought over when she came, and with a rapid calculation, Edwina realized that the next day was to have been her wedding day. She had tried to force it from her mind, and she had all but succeeded. And now all that was left was the veil, held in her trembling hands, as the miles of tulle floated across her room like a distant dream. Her whole body ached as she put it on, and the tears slid solemnly down her cheeks, as she looked in the mirror. It looked just as she thought it would, and she wondered what the dress would have been like. Surely, just as beautiful, but no one would ever know. The fabric they were bringing back to the States had gone down on the *Titanic*. She had hardly let herself think of that until now, it seemed so pointless. But now suddenly, here was her veil, and all it had stood for was gone forever.

She sat down on her bed, crying softly, still wearing the veil, and opened Lady Fitzgerald's letter. For the first time in months, she felt hopeless and alone, as she sat in her black mourning dress, with her wedding veil floating around her.

'My very dearest Edwina,' she began, and it was like hearing her voice again as Edwina cried as she read it. She and Charles had looked so much alike, tall and aristocratic, and very English. 'We think of you a great deal, and speak of you much of the time. It seems difficult to believe that you left London only four months ago . . . difficult to believe all that has happened in the meantime.

'I am sending you this now, with trepidation and regret. I very much fear that it will upset you terribly when you receive the veil, but it has been finished for some time, and after thinking about it a great deal, Charles's father and I feel that you should have it. It is a symbol of a very beautiful time, and the love that Charles had for you until he died. You were the dearest thing in his life, and I know that the two of you would have been very happy. Put it away, dearest child, do not think of it too much . . . and perhaps only look at it once in a while, and remember our beloved Charles, who so greatly loved you.

'We hope to see you again here one day. And in the meantime, to you and your brothers and sisters, we send our dearest love, and most especially to you, Edwina dear . . . our every thought, now and forever.' She had signed it 'Margaret Fitzgerald,' but Edwina was blinded by tears by the end of the letter and could barely read it. And she sat on her bed, in her wedding veil, until she heard the front door slam heavily downstairs and the children's voices in the stairway, looking for her. They had been to the carousel, and come home, and all afternoon, she had sat there, in her wedding veil, thinking of Charles, and the wedding day that was to have been tomorrow.

She took the veil off carefully, and set it back in the box, and she had just tied the lid when Fannie burst into the room with a broad, happy smile, and hurled herself into her big sister's arms. She didn't see the tears, or the ravaged look in her eyes. She was too young to understand what had happened. Edwina put the box away on a shelf, and listened as Fannie rattled away about the carousel in the park. There were horses and brass rings and gold stars, and lots of music, and there were even painted sleds if you didn't want to ride a horse, but the horses were really *much* better.

'And there were boats too!' she went on, but then she frowned. 'But we don't like boats, Teddy, do we?' He shook his head, having just come into the room, and Alexis was just behind him. She looked at Edwina strangely then, as though she knew something was amiss, but she didn't know what it was. And only Phillip saw it later, after the children had gone to bed, and he asked Edwina cautiously as they walked upstairs together.

'Is something wrong?' He was always worried about her, always concerned, always anxious to play the fatherly role with the others. 'Are you alright, Win?'

She nodded slowly, almost tempted to tell him about the veil, but she just couldn't say the words. And she wondered if he remembered what the date was. 'I'm alright.' And then, 'I had a letter from Lady Fitzgerald today, Charles's mother.'

'Oh.' Unlike George, who was still too young and wouldn't have understood the implications, Phillip knew immediately what she was feeling. 'How is she?'

'Alright, I guess.' She looked sadly at Phillip then. She had to share it with someone, even if it was only her seventeen-year-old brother, and her voice was low and gruff as she said it. 'Tomorrow was . . . would have been . . .' It was almost impossible to say the words, and she turned away as they reached the second-floor landing. But Phillip gently touched her arm and she turned to him with tears streaming from her eyes. 'Never mind . . . I'm sorry . . .'

'Oh, Winnie.' There were tears in his eyes too, as he pulled her close to him and she held him.

'Why did it happen?' she whispered to him. 'Why? . . . why couldn't there have been enough lifeboats?' It would have been such a small thing . . . lifeboats for everyone on the ship . . . and it would have made all the difference. But there were other whys too . . . like why the *Californian* had turned her radio off and never heard their frantic CQDs, their distress signals going out to ships all over the Atlantic. They had only been a few miles away, and they could have saved everyone, had they only heard . . . there were so many whys and if onlys, but none of them mattered anymore, as Edwina cried in her brother's arms, the night before what should have been her wedding.

13

Predictably, Christmas was difficult for them that year. Or for the older ones, at least. Edwina kept the little ones so busy baking and making things that they scarcely had time to think about things being different. Ben came to visit and took the boys to an exhibition of new motorcars, and he took all of them to see the lighting of the Christmas tree at the Fairmont Hotel to help them through the holidays. And other friends of their parents invited them too. But sometimes the invitations were too painful, and made them feel more like orphans.

Alexis was still the most withdrawn of all of them, but Edwina was tireless in her efforts to help her recover. Edwina still found her upstairs in her mother's bedroom from time to time, and she didn't make a big fuss about it when she did. She just talked to her for a little while, sitting on the little pink settee in her mother's dressing room, or on the bed, and eventually, the little girl would come back to the others.

It always made Edwina feel strange being up there, it was as though it was a sacred place now, and to all of the children, it was a kind of shrine to their parents. Bert's and Kate's clothes still hung in the closets, and Edwina didn't have the heart to remove them. Her mother's hairbrushes and solid gold dresser set lay where she had last set them down. Mrs Barnes dusted up there carefully, but even she didn't like going up there anymore. She said it always made her want to cry. And Sheilagh flatly refused to go up there at all, even to retrieve Alexis.

And Edwina never mentioned it, but she went up there now and then too. It was a way of staying close to them, of remembering what they'd been like. It was difficult to believe that it was only eight months since they'd died. In some ways, it seemed like only moments, in others it seemed aeons. And on Christmas night, once the younger children were in bed, Edwina said as much to Phillip.

They had survived the holidays, their first alone, and for Edwina it had been exhausting. But she had handled it gently and well, and the little ones had hung their stockings as they always did, and sang carols, and baked cookies, and gone to church. Just as their mother had always done, Edwina had spent days before wrapping presents. And Phillip had thanked her from all of them that night, just as Bert used to thank Kate, with a sleepy yawn, and it touched Edwina as she remembered.

Ben came to visit them on Christmas Day, and everyone was happy to see him. He brought presents for everyone, a wonderful hobbyhorse for Teddy, and dolls for the girls, an enormously elaborate magic set for George, which he adored, and a beautiful pocket watch for Phillip, and for Edwina an exquisite cashmere shawl. It was a delicate blue, and she longed to wear it when she abandoned her mourning in April. He had thought of buying it for her in black so she could wear it now, but the thought of doing that depressed him.

'I can't wait to see you in colors again,' he said warmly as she opened the gift and thanked him. The children had all made him gifts. Even George had mastered a small oil painting of Ben's dog, and Phillip had carved him a very handsome pen stand. And Edwina had carefully selected a pair of her father's very favorite sapphire cuff links. She knew they would mean a lot to him, and she had asked George's and Phillip's permission before she gave them to him. She didn't want to give away anything that either of them seriously wanted, but both boys had liked the idea of Ben having their father's cuff links. He was their best friend, and he had been incredibly kind to them ever since their parents' death and long before that.

It was a loving day for all of them. And Christmas was always difficult for Ben too. It always brought back painful memories of the family he had had six years earlier, before the earthquake. But together, they all brought each other cheer, and they ended with laughter and smiles, and many tender moments. In the end, Teddy fell asleep on Ben's lap. And Ben carried him upstairs and put him to bed while Edwina watched him. In truth, he was wonderful with all of them, and the girls loved him just as much as the boys did. Fannie begged him to put her to bed too. And before he left, he even tucked in a smiling Alexis.

He had one last glass of port with the older ones before he left, and he went home feeling warm and contented. For a potentially difficult Christmas, it had actually been filled with blessings.

Unlike New Year's, which seemed to be filled only with tears and anguish. Their aunt Liz arrived on New Year's Day, and she cried incessantly from the moment she arrived, without seeming to stop for a single moment. The black gown she wore was so severe and so grim that when Edwina first saw her, she suddenly wondered if their uncle had died and she didn't know it. But Liz was quick to reassure her that Rupert was in the very worst of his poor health, and in an exceptionally appalling humor. He had been suffering abysmally with gout since the fall, and Liz said he was half out of his mind with pain and temper.

'He sends his love, of course,' she was quick to add, dabbing at her eyes, and crying at each remembered object and photograph as she toured the house on Edwina's arm.

And she cried even harder each time she saw the children, which completely unnerved them. But she couldn't bear the thought of her beloved sister being gone, and her children being reduced to orphans. But it was difficult for Edwina to listen to her, because in the past eight months they had struggled so hard not just to survive, but to thrive, but their aunt Liz absolutely refused to see it. She said the children looked terrible and pale, and she inquired immediately of Edwina who the cook was, or if they even had one.

'The same one we've always had, Aunt Liz. You remember Mrs Barnes.' But Liz only cried more, and said how awful it was, how *dangerous* even, for Phillip and George to be brought up only by their sister, although she did not specify the exact nature of the peril. But in the past eight months she herself seemed to have sunk into a terrible depression. She almost fainted when she entered her sister's dressing room and saw all her belongings still hanging there, and she literally screamed when she saw the bedroom.

'I can't bear it . . . I can't bear it . . . oh, Edwina, how *could* you! How could you do such a thing?' Edwina was not sure what she'd done, but her aunt was quick to tell her. 'How could you leave everything there, as though they left only just this morning,' Liz sobbed hysterically as she shook her head and looked accusingly at Edwina. But in some ways it was comforting for them to have everything still there, her father's suits, her mother's clothes, the familiar gold and pink enamel hairbrush. 'You must pack everything up at *once*!' she wailed, and Edwina only shook her head. This was not going to be easy.

'We haven't been ready to do that yet,' Edwina said quietly, handing her the glass of water that Phillip had discreetly brought her. 'And Aunt Liz, you must try not to be so upset. It is very difficult for the children.'

'Oh, how could you say such a thing, you insensitive child!' She broke into sobs again, which seemed to reverberate everywhere, as Edwina sent the children out for a walk with Sheilagh. 'If you knew how I've mourned her all these months . . . what her death meant to me . . . my only sister.' But she had been Edwina and the other children's only mother. Not to mention Bert . . . and Charles . . . and even poor Oona . . . and all the others . . . But Liz seemed bent on celebrating only her own grief and ignoring everyone else's. 'You should have come to England when Rupert told you to,' she said plaintively to her oldest niece. 'I could have cared for all of you.' And instead, selfishly, Edwina had robbed her of her last chance to mother children. She had refused to come and insisted they stay in San Francisco. And now Rupert said that the attorney wrote that they were doing extremely well, and Rupert said he was no longer well enough to have them. She had ruined everything by being so stubborn. She was clearly just like her father. 'It was wicked of you not to come when you were told to,' she said, and Phillip suddenly began to look angry.

'There is nothing "wicked" about my sister, ma'am,' he said through clenched teeth, and Edwina urged him to go back downstairs and see what George was up to.

She stayed for twenty-six days, and at times Edwina thought that she would go crazy if her aunt stayed a moment longer. She made the children nervous all the time, and she cried during her entire stay. And in the end, she actually forced Edwina to pack up at least part of her parents' bedroom. They put most of the clothes away, although Edwina refused to give them away. She kept it all, and Liz packed a few of Kate's things to take back to England, mostly mementos of their youth, which meant little to Edwina or the younger children.

And at last, after almost four weeks, they escorted her to the ferry to go to the train station, in Oakland. And it seemed to Edwina that she had never stopped crying. And she stayed angry at Edwina until the end. She was mad at everyone and the Fates for the hand that had been dealt her. She was angry that her sister had been lost, angry that Edwina and the children had refused to come to her afterward, angry that her own life seemed to be over. And angry, finally, at Rupert for the unhappy life she had led with him in England. It was as though, in the past nine months, she had given up, and there were times when Edwina wasn't sure if Liz was mourning her sister's death or her own disappointments. Even Ben had finally avoided her, and coming home from the ferry building with the children the morning Liz left, Edwina sank back against her seat, exhausted. The children were quiet too. They hadn't known what to make of her, but this time, one thing was sure, they hadn't liked her. She picked on Edwina all the time, or so it seemed, and she complained about everything, and the rest of the time she was crying.

'I hate her!' Alexis said on the way home, as Edwina gently chided her.

'No, you don't.'

'Yes I do.' And her eyes said she meant it. 'She made you put away Mama's clothes and she had no right to do that.'

'They're not put away,' Edwina said quietly. And maybe her aunt had been right after all. Maybe it was time. But it hadn't been easy. 'It doesn't matter anyway,' Edwina reassured the child. 'We can't put Mama away. You know she's always with us.' There was silence the rest of the way home, as they all thought about what Edwina had said, and how close their mother still was to them, and how different she was from her sister.

14

The anniversary of their parents' death was a difficult day for them. And yet the service Edwina had said at their church was tender and gentle and human. It reminded everyone of how kind her parents had been, how interested in everyone, how full their lives, how involved in the community, and how rich in the blessings of their children. The Winfield children sat together in the first pew, listening, and occasionally dabbing at their eyes, but they were a proud legacy to the memory of Kate and Bertram Winfield.

Edwina had invited several of her parents' friends to lunch in their garden afterward, and it was the first time they had entertained since the fateful voyage on the *Titanic*. It was a beautiful April afternoon, and they also celebrated Alexis's seventh birthday. There was a beautiful cake made by Mrs Barnes, and the day turned out to be a warm, festive occasion. And people Edwina had barely seen all year were happy to see all of them again, and were offering all kinds of invitations now that their year of mourning was over. Several people noticed that she still wore her engagement ring on her left hand, and the minister had mentioned Charles as well, but Edwina was a beautiful girl and she was almost twenty-two years old, and there was no denying that she was going to be a handsome catch for someone. Ben noticed several of the younger men watching her after lunch, and he was surprised to find himself feeling protective.

'It was a lovely afternoon,' he said quietly as he found her sitting on a swing in the garden with the children near her.

'It was, wasn't it?' She looked pleased. It had been a fitting tribute to her parents. And then she smiled up at him. 'They would have liked it.'

He smiled and nodded too. 'Yes, they would. They'd be proud of all of you.' Especially their eldest daughter. What an amazing woman she'd turned out to be. Not a child, not a girl, but a woman. 'You've done an incredible job in the last year.'

She smiled, flattered, but she knew there was always more to do. Each of the children needed help in different ways, and Phillip was especially anxious about getting into Harvard. 'Sometimes I wish I could do more for each of them,' she confessed to Ben. Especially for Alexis.

'I don't see how you could do more,' he commented, as people came and went and stopped to thank her. There were anecdotes about her parents, stories about her father particularly, and when the last guest but one finally left, she was exhausted. The children were eating leftovers in the kitchen by then, with Sheilagh and Mrs Barnes in attendance. And Edwina was in the library with Ben, still chatting about the party.

'You seemed to be getting a lot of invitations.' He was pleased for her, and yet, much to his own surprise, he was jealous. It was as though he had actually liked it when she was in deep mourning and saw only him. But she only smiled at him in answer.

'I was. People are being very kind to me. But nothing's going to change much now that the year is over. I already have my hands full. Most people don't understand that.'

Relief? Was he relieved, he asked himself, unable to believe what he was feeling. She was a child, wasn't she?

His best friend's child . . . barely more than a baby. And yet, he knew that none of that was true, and he looked deeply worried as she laughed and offered him a glass of sherry.

'Don't look so upset.' She knew him well, or so they both thought.

'I'm not,' he lied.

'Oh, yes, you are. You remind me of Aunt Liz. What are you afraid of? That I'll disgrace myself or the Winfield name?' she teased.

'Hardly.' He took a sip of sherry and set it down, as he looked at her intently. 'Edwina, what do you think about doing with your life now?' He glanced at the ring on her left hand and wondered if she was going to think he was crazy. He was beginning to think so himself. 'I'm serious,' he pressed for an answer, which surprised her. 'Now that this year is over . . . what do you want to do?' She stopped and thought about it, but the answer had been clear to her since the previous April.

'Nothing different than I'm doing now. I want to take care of the children.' It seemed so clear to her. There were no choices anymore, only duty and love for them, and the promise she had made to her parents as she stepped into the lifeboat. 'I don't need more than that, Ben.' But at not yet twenty-two, that seemed crazy to him.

'Edwina, one day you'll regret that. You're too young to give up your whole life for your brothers and sisters.'

'Is that what I'm doing?' She smiled at him, touched by his obvious concern for her. 'Is it really so wrong?'

'Not wrong,' he said softly, his eyes never leaving hers, 'but it's a terrible waste, Edwina. You need more than that in your life. Your parents had much more than that. They had each other.' They both thought of the things the minister had said about Kate and Bert only that morning. And Edwina thought to herself that she had almost had a life with Charles, and then she had lost that. And she wanted no one else . . . only Charles . . . but Ben was looking at her so intensely. 'You don't know what I'm talking about, do you, Edwina?' He smiled gently at her and she looked confused for a moment.

'Yes, I do,' she said quietly, 'you want me to be happy, and I am. I'm happy in my life here with the children.'

'And that's all you want, Edwina . . .' He hesitated, but only for a moment. 'I want to offer you more than that.' Her eyes opened wide and she looked extremely startled.

'You do? Ben . . .' She had never even thought of that, never suspected for a moment that he loved her. Nor had he at first, but he had come to understand it in recent months, and he had been able to think of nothing else but Edwina ever since Christmas. He had promised himself he'd wait to say anything to her until at least April . . . until they'd been gone a year, but now he was suddenly afraid that he should have waited longer. Perhaps in the end, that might have made a difference. 'I never thought . . .' She was blushing and looking away from him, as though the very thought of his wanting her was embarrassing and almost painful.

'I'm sorry.' He moved forward quickly and took her hands in his own. 'Should I not have said anything, Edwina? I love you . . . I have for a long time . . . but more than anything, I don't want to lose our friendship. You mean everything to me . . . and the children too . . . please, Edwina . . . I don't ever want to lose you.'

'You won't,' she whispered, forcing herself to look at him then. She owed him that much. And she loved him, too, but as her father's dearest friend, and nothing more. She just couldn't. She couldn't have worn the wedding veil for him . . . she still loved Charles. In her heart, she was still his bride, and she knew that she always would be. 'I can't, Ben . . . I love you . . . but I can't.' She didn't want to hurt him, but she had to be truthful with him.

'Is it too soon?' he asked hopefully, and she shook her head.

'Is it the children?' He loved the children, too, but she was shaking her head again as he watched her, aching over the fear of losing her. What if she never spoke to him again? He had been a fool to tell her that he loved her.

'No, it's not the children, Ben, and it's not you . . .' She smiled as tears sprang to her eyes, and she promised herself she'd be honest with him. 'I think it's Charles . . . I would feel so unfaithful to him if . . .' She couldn't say the words, as the tears slipped slowly down her cheeks, and he reproached himself again for trying to force the issue too early. Perhaps in time . . . but now he knew. He had risked everything, and he had lost, to the fiancé she had lost on the *Titanic*.

'Even widows remarry eventually. You have a right to happiness, Edwina.'

'Maybe,' she said, but she didn't sound convinced. 'Maybe it is too soon.' But in her heart she knew she would never marry. 'But to be honest with you, I don't think I'll ever marry.'

'But that's absurd.'

'Maybe it is.' She smiled up at him. 'But it seems easier this way, because of the children. I couldn't give any man what he'd deserve, Ben, I'd be too busy with them, and sooner or later any decent man would resent it.'

'Do you think I would?' He looked hurt, and she smiled.

'You might. You deserve someone's full attention. Mine won't be available for another fifteen years at least, until little Teddy goes off to college. That's a long wait.' She smiled gently at him, touched by his intentions.

He shook his head and grinned. He was beaten and he knew it. She was a stubborn girl, and if she said it, he knew she meant it. He knew that well by now, and it was also part of why he loved her. He loved the things she stood for, and her courage, and indomitable strength and wonderful ability to laugh . . . he loved her hair and her eyes, and her delicious sense of humor. And in a way, he knew that she loved him, too, but not the way he wanted. 'Fifteen years might be a little long for me, Edwina. I'll be sixty-one years old by then, and you might not want me.'

'You'll probably be a lot livelier than I will. The kids will have worn me out by then.' Her eyes sobered as she held a hand out to him. 'That's all part of it, Ben. My life is theirs now.' She had made a promise to her mother to take care of them, no matter what. And she couldn't think of herself anymore. She had to think of the children first. And no matter how fond she was of Ben, she knew she didn't want him, or anyone else, as a husband. But he was clearly worried now, as he frowned. He was desperately afraid he would lose her.

'Can we still be friends?'

Tears filled her eyes and she smiled as she nodded. 'Of course we can.' She got up and put her arms around him. He was her best friend, her dearest friend, not just her father's friend now. 'I couldn't manage without you.'

'You seem to be doing just fine,' he said wryly, but at the same time he pulled her close, and held her fast for a moment. He didn't try to kiss her, or argue with her anymore. He was grateful not to have lost her affection and her friendship, and maybe it was just as well he had spoken up after all. Maybe it was better to know where he stood, and how she felt. But he still had a heavy heart when he left her that night, and he turned to look back at her as he got in his car, and he waved, and drove away, wishing that things could have been different.

The telegram came from Aunt Liz the next day. Uncle Rupert had died on the anniversary of Kate and Bert's death. And Edwina was subdued when she told the children at dinner. She was quiet all day, thinking of what Ben had said the night before. And she was still touched, but she was sure she had made the right decision.

The children weren't overly distraught at Edwina's news from Aunt Liz, and Phillip helped compose a telegram to her shortly after dinner. They assured her of their prayers and warmest thoughts, but Edwina made a point of not saying that they hoped their aunt would visit soon. She decided that she really couldn't bear it. Her visit three months before had left them all far too shaken.

Edwina contemplated going into mourning again, and then decided it didn't make sense for an uncle they barely knew and had never been very fond of. She wore gray for a week, and then went back to wearing the colors she had found again only days before, the colors she hadn't worn since the previous April. She even wore Ben's beautiful blue cashmere shawl, and she saw him almost as often as before, although not quite. He seemed a little bit more careful of her now, and faintly embarrassed, although she always acted as though nothing had happened between them. And the children weren't aware of it at all, although once or twice, she thought she saw Phillip staring at them, but there was nothing he could detect except an old, well-worn friendship.

In May, Edwina went out for the first time. She accepted an invitation to a dinner party from old friends of her parents', and she felt awkward when she went, but she was surprised to discover that she had a very pleasant evening. The only thing she didn't like was that she somehow suspected that she had been invited to entertain their son, and the second time they invited her she was certain. He was a handsome young man of twenty-four, with a large fortune and a small mind, and a wonderful estate near Santa Barbara. But he was of no interest to her, nor were the other young men she suddenly found herself paired off with whenever she accepted invitations from her parents' friends. Her own friends all seemed to be married now, and most of them were busy having babies, and spending too much time with them only reminded her of Charles, and the life they would never share, and it never failed to depress her. It was easier being with her parents' friends. In some ways, she had more in common with them since she was bringing up children of the same ages as theirs, and she found it easier to be viewed without the added tension of sexual interest. She had no interest whatsoever in young men, and she made it clear to all of them when, eventually, they pressed her. She continued to wear her engagement ring and to think of herself as still belonging to Charles. She didn't want anything more than her memories of him, and her busy life with her brothers and sisters. And in the end, it was a relief when they left the city and went to Lake Tahoe in August. It was a special summer for them. Phillip had been accepted at Harvard months before, and he would be leaving them for Cambridge in early September. It was hard to believe he'd be gone, and Edwina knew that they would all feel his absence, but she was happy for him that he was going. He had offered to stay home with her, to help her manage the little ones and the exuberant George, and Edwina had refused to even discuss it. He was going, and that was that, she announced. And then she packed the entire family up, and they boarded the train for Lake Tahoe.

And once they were there, on a moonlit night, Phillip finally dared to ask her the question. He had been wondering for a while, and more than once, he had gotten seriously worried about it.

'Were you ever in love with Ben?' he finally whispered on a moonlit night.

She was startled not only by what he asked, but by the way he looked when he asked it. It was a look that said Edwina belonged to him, and the others, and she suddenly wasn't quite sure what to answer.

'No.'

'Was he in love with you?'

'I don't think that's very important.' Edwina spoke softly. The poor boy really looked worried.

But he had nothing to fear and she smiled as she reassured him. She took a deep breath, thinking of the wedding veil hidden in her closet. 'I'm still in love with Charles . . .' And then a whisper in the dark, '. . . Perhaps I always will be . . .'

'I'm glad,' and then he flushed guiltily. 'I mean . . . I didn't mean . . .'

But Edwina smiled at him. 'Yes, you did.' She belonged to them . . . they owned her now . . . they didn't want her marrying anyone. She was theirs. For better or worse, until the day she died, or her services were no longer needed. She accepted that, and in a way she loved them for it.

It was odd, she thought to herself, her parents had a right to have each other, but the children felt that she should love only them. She owed the children everything, even in the eyes of Phillip. He had the right to go away to school, as long as she stayed there, waiting for him, and caring for the others.

'Would it make a difference if I did love him? It wouldn't mean I love you less,' she tried to explain, but he looked hurt, as though she had betrayed him.

'But do you?'

She smiled again, and shook her head, reaching up to kiss him. He was still a boy, she realized, whether or not he was going to Harvard. 'Don't worry so much. I'll always be here.' It was what she had said to all of them, ever since her mother died. 'I love you . . . don't worry . . . I will always be here . . .'

'Good night, Phillip,' she whispered, as they walked back to their cabins, and with an easy smile he looked at her, relieved by what she'd said. He loved her more than anything. They all did. She was theirs now, just as their parents had been. And she had them . . . and she had a wedding veil she would never use, hidden on a shelf . . . and Charles's engagement ring, still sparkling on her finger.

'Good night, Edwina,' he whispered, and she smiled and closed her door, trying to remember if life had ever been different.

15

The train stood in the station with all of the Winfields standing in Phillip's compartment. Ben had come too, and Mrs Barnes, and a handful of Phillip's friends, and two of his favorite teachers. It was a big day for him. He was leaving for Harvard.

'You'll write, won't you?' Edwina felt like a mother hen, and then asked him in an undertone if he had all his money hidden in the money belt she'd given him. He grinned and ruffled her elegant hairdo. 'Stop that!' she scolded, as he went to talk to two of his friends, and she chatted with Ben, and tried to keep George from climbing out the window. She couldn't see Alexis then, and a faint wave of panic rose in her, remembering another time when Alexis had disappeared, but a moment later she saw her with Mrs Barnes, staring sadly at the brother who was about to leave them. Fannie had cried copiously the night before, and at three and a half even Teddy knew he was being deserted.

'Can I come too?' he asked hopefully, but Phillip only shook his head and gave him a ride on his shoulders. He could touch the ceiling in the compartment then, and he chortled happily as Edwina pulled Fannie closer to her. They were all sad to realize that the group at home was shrinking. To Edwina, it felt like the beginning of the end, but that morning, she had reminded Phillip of how proud their father would have been. It was an important moment in his life, and one he should always be proud of.

'You'll never be quite the same,' she had tried to explain to him, but he didn't yet understand what she meant. 'The world will grow, and you'll see us differently when you come home. We'll seem very small to you, and very provincial.' She was wise for her years, and the long talks she'd had with her father for years had given her a perspective that was rare for a woman. It was something Charles had loved about her from the first, and something Ben admired greatly. 'I'll miss you terribly,' she said to Phillip again, but she had promised herself not to cry and make it harder for him. More than once, he'd offered not to go at all, and to stay and help her with the children. And she wanted him to have this opportunity. He needed it, he had a right to it, just as their father had, and his father before him.

'Good luck, son.' Ben shook his hand as the conductor began calling, 'All aboard.' And Edwina felt her heart fill with tears, as he called good-bye to his friends, shook hands with his teachers, and then turned to kiss the children.

'Be good,' he said soberly to little Fannie, 'be a good girl, and listen to Edwina.'

'I will,' she said seriously, two big tears rolling down her cheeks. For over a year, he had been like a father to her, not just an older brother. 'Please come back soon . . .' At five and a half, she had lost two teeth, and she had the biggest eyes Edwina had ever seen. She was a sweet child and all she wanted in life was to stay close to home, and her brothers and sisters. She talked about wanting to be a mama one day, and nothing more. She wanted to cook and sew, and have 'fourteen children.' But what she really wanted was to be safe, and cozy and secure forever.

'I'll come back soon, Fannie . . . I promise . . .' He

kissed her again, and then turned to Alexis. There were no words between those two. There didn't need to be. He knew only too well how much she loved him. She was the little ghost who slipped in and out of his room, who brought him cookies and milk on silent feet when he was studying late, who divided everything she had with him, just because she loved him. 'Take care, Lexie . . . I love you . . . I'll be back, I promise . . .' But they all knew that to Alexis, those promises meant nothing. She still stood in her parents' room sometimes, as though she still expected to see them. She was seven now, and for her the pain of losing them was as great as it had been a year before. And now losing Phillip was a blow Edwina feared would truly shake her far more than it would the others.

'And you, Teddy Bear, be a good boy, don't eat too many chocolates.' He had eaten a whole box of them the week before, and gotten a terrible stomachache, and he laughed guiltily now, as Phillip carefully lifted him off his shoulders.

'Get out of here, you rotten kid,' he said with a grin to George, as the conductor called, 'Alllllllll aboooarrrrddd' for the last time, and waved them off the train. Edwina scarcely had time to hold him close and look at him for a last time.

'I love you, sweet boy. Come home soon . . . and love every minute of it. We'll all be here forever, but this is your time . . .'

'Thank you, Winnie . . . thank you for letting me go . . . I'll come home if you need me.' There were tears in her eyes and she nodded then, barely able to answer.

'I know . . .' She clutched him one more time, and it reminded her too much of the good-byes they'd never had time to say on the ship, the good-byes they should have said and didn't. 'I love you . . .' She was crying as Ben helped her off, and he had an arm around her shoulders, to comfort her, as the train pulled out of the station. They saw Phillip waving his handkerchief for a long, long time, and Fannie and Alexis cried all the way home, the one in loud, gulping sobs of grief, the other in silent furrows of tears that rolled down her cheeks and tore through her heart and Edwina's when she watched her. None of them were good at grief, none were impervious to pain, and none were happy at the thought of Phillip leaving.

The house was like a tomb once he was gone. Ben left them at their front gate, and Edwina walked them all inside with a look of sorrow. It was hard to imagine life without him.

Fannie helped her set the table that night, while Alexis sat quietly, staring out the window. She said not a word to anyone. She only sat there, thinking of Phillip. And George took Teddy out to the garden to play, until Edwina called them in. It was a quiet group that night, as she served them their favorite roasted chicken. And it was odd now, she never thought of taking her mother's place. It no longer occurred to her. After a year and a half, it seemed as though this was what she had always done. At twenty-two, she was a woman with five children. But the void Phillip had left reminded her now of a ne'er-to-be-forgotten pain, and they were all quiet as she said grace, and asked George to carve the chicken.

'You're the man of the house now,' she said, hoping to impress him, as he pierced the roasted bird straight through and lopped the wing off as though using a dagger. At thirteen, he had neither matured nor lost his passion for mischief and what he considered humor. 'Thank you, George, if you're going to do that, I'll do it myself.'

'Come on, Edwina . . .' He lopped off another wing, and both legs, like a mercenary carving up the spoils, as chicken gravy splashed everywhere and the children laughed, and suddenly in spite of herself, Edwina was laughing too, until tears came to her eyes and rolled down her cheeks. She tried to force herself to be serious and reproach him, but she found that she couldn't.

'George, stop it!' He whacked the carcass in half and handled the knife like a spear. 'Stop it! . . . you're awful . . .' she scolded, and he bowed low then, handed her her plate, and sat down with a happy grin.

It was certainly going to be different having him underfoot as the oldest child, instead of the far more dignified, responsible Phillip. But George was George, an entirely different character than his brother.

'After dinner, let's write a letter to Phillip,' Fannie suggested in a serious voice, and Teddy agreed. And Edwina turned to say something to George just in time to see him flinging peas at Alexis. And before Edwina could say anything, two of the peas hit Alexis on the nose and she exploded into laughter.

'Stop that!' Edwina intoned, wondering why, suddenly feeling like a child herself . . . stop making us laugh! . . . stop making me feel better! . . . stop keeping us from crying! . . . She thought about it for a moment, and without a sound, Edwina put three peas on her own fork and silently hurled them across the table at George, as he retaliated in glee, and she threw three more peas back at him, while the younger children squealed with excitement. And far, far away . . . Phillip rolled relentlessly toward Harvard.

16

The first few days after Phillip left, they all felt the pain, and for them, the pain of loss was far too familiar. It was a leaden feeling, and within a week, Edwina saw signs of the strain telling on Alexis. She began to stutter, which she had done before, for a brief time after they first lost their parents. The stutter had disappeared fairly quickly then, but this time it seemed to be more persistent. She was having nightmares again, too, and Edwina was worried about her.

She had just mentioned it to Ben that day, during a board meeting at the newspaper, and when she came home, faithful Mrs Barnes told Edwina that Alexis had spent all afternoon in the garden. She had gone out there as soon as she had come home from school, and she hadn't come in since. But it was a lovely warm day, and Edwina suspected that she was hiding in the little maze that their mother had always called her 'secret garden'.

Edwina left her alone for a little while, and then shortly before dinner, when she hadn't come back in, Edwina went back outside to find her. She called her, but as often was the case with the child, there was no answer.

'Come on, silly, don't hide. Come on out and tell me what you did today. We have a letter from Phillip.' It had been waiting for her in the front hall, along with one from Aunt Liz that mentioned her not being very well, and having sprained her ankle when she went to London to see the doctor. She was one of those people that unhappy things happened to. And she had just asked Edwina again if she'd finally emptied her mother's room, and the question had annoyed her. In fact, she hadn't yet, but she still didn't feel ready to face it, or to do it to Alexis. 'Come on, sweetheart, where are you?' she called, glancing at the rosebushes at the far end, sure she was hiding there, but when she walked the length of the garden, and peeked into all the familiar places, she still couldn't find her. 'Alexis? Are you there?' She looked some more, and even climbed up to George's old, abandoned tree house, and she tore her skirt as she jumped down, but Alexis was nowhere.

Edwina went back into the house and asked Mrs Barnes if she was sure she'd been out there, but the old woman assured her that she had seen Alexis sit for hours in the garden. But Edwina knew only too well that Mrs Barnes paid very little attention to the children. Sheilagh was supposed to do that, but she had left shortly after Easter, and Edwina took care of them herself now.

'Did she go upstairs?' Edwina asked pointedly, and Mrs Barnes said she didn't remember. She'd been tinning tomatoes all afternoon, and she hadn't been paying close attention to Alexis.

Edwina checked Alexis's room, her own, and then finally walked slowly upstairs, remembering Liz's words in her letter only that day. '. . . it's high time that you faced it, and cleared those rooms out. I've done it with all Rupert's things . . .' But it was different for her, Edwina knew, and all she wanted now was to find where Alexis was hiding, and solve whatever problem had driven her to it.

'Lexie? . . .' She pulled back curtains, rustled her mother's skirts, and noticed that there was a musty smell in the room now. They had been gone for a long time, almost eighteen months. She even looked under the bed, but Alexis was nowhere.

Edwina went downstairs and asked George to help her look around, and finally, an hour later, she was beginning to panic.

'Did something happen today at school?' But neither Fannie nor George knew anything about it, and Teddy had been with Edwina when she went to the paper. The secretaries there were always happy to baby-sit for him, while she went to her meetings. And at three and a half, he was a little charmer. 'Where do you suppose she is?' she asked George. Nothing special had gone wrong, and no one seemed to have any idea where she'd gone. The dinner hour came and went, and Edwina and George conducted another search in the garden, and they finally came to the conclusion that she was nowhere in the house or on the grounds. Edwina went into the kitchen then, and after some hesitation, decided to call Ben. She didn't know what else to do, and he promised to come over at once to help her find Alexis. And he was frantically ringing the doorbell ten minutes later.

'What happened?' he asked, and for an odd moment, Edwina thought he looked like her father. But she didn't have time to think of it now, as she brushed her stray hair off her face. Her upswept hairdo had been torn apart while she searched for Alexis in the garden.

'I don't know what happened, Ben. I can't imagine. The children said nothing happened in school today, and Mrs Barnes thought she was in the garden all afternoon, but she wasn't, at least not by the time I got there. We've looked everywhere, inside the house and out, and she's just not here. I don't know where she could have gone to.' She had few friends at school, and she never wanted to play at their houses. And everyone in the family knew that she had always been the sensitive one, and she had never totally recovered from their mother's death. She was just as likely to disappear as she was not to speak for days on end. It was just the way she was, and they all accepted her that way. But if she'd run away, God only knew where she was or what it meant, and what would happen to her when she got there. She was a beautiful child, and in the wrong hands, anything might have happened.

'Have you called the police yet?' Ben tried to appear calm, but he was as worried as she was. And he was glad that Edwina had called him.

'Not yet. I called you first.'

'And you have no idea where she's gone?' Edwina shook her head again, and a moment later Ben walked into the kitchen and called the police for her. Mrs Barnes had already helped put Fannie and Teddy to bed, and she'd told them it was very, very naughty to run away, and Fannie had cried and asked if they would ever find her.

George was standing with Edwina as Ben called the police, and half an hour later they rang the front doorbell and Edwina went to answer. She explained that she had no idea where her sister had gone, and the sergeant who had come asked in some confusion who the child's parents were. Edwina explained that she was Alexis's guardian, and he promised to search the neighborhood and report back to her in an hour.

'Should we come?' she asked worriedly, glancing at Ben.

'No, ma'am. We'll find her. You and your husband wait here with the boy.' He smiled at them comfortingly and George glared at Ben. He liked him as a friend, but he didn't like him being referred to as Edwina's 'husband'. Just like Phillip, he was possessive about his older sister.

'Why didn't you tell him?' George growled at her, when the policeman had left.

'Tell him what?' Her mind was totally on Alexis.

'That Ben isn't your husband.'

'Oh, for heaven's sake . . . will you please concentrate on finding your sister and not this nonsense?' But Ben had heard it too. After a year and a half of her full attention, night and day, they all felt as though they owned her. It wasn't a healthy thing for any of them, he thought, he also knew that it was none of his business. Edwina wanted to run her family as she chose, and unfortunately he had no reason to interfere with them. He looked up at her worriedly again, and they went over the possibilities, of where Alexis might have gone, and with whom, and he volunteered to drive her in his car to the child's various friends' houses, and Edwina jumped to her feet with a hopeful look and told George to wait for the policeman.

But a tour of three neighboring houses turned up nothing at all. They said that Alexis hadn't been to visit in weeks, and more and more Edwina found herself thinking of how upset Alexis had been ever since Phillip left for Cambridge.

'You don't suppose she'd do something crazy like try to hop a train, do you, Ben?' It was her idea, but Ben thought it more than unlikely.

'She's afraid of her own shadow, she can't be far from here,' he said as they walked up the front steps again. But when Edwina mentioned it to George, he narrowed his eyes and started thinking.

'She asked me how long it takes to get to Boston last week,' George confessed with an unhappy frown, 'but I didn't think anything of it. God, Win, what if she does try to catch a train? She won't even know where she's going.' And she could get hurt . . . she could trip on the tracks, fall trying to get into a freight car . . . the possibilities were horrifying as Edwina began to look frantic. It was ten o'clock at night by then and it was painfully obvious that something terrible had happened.

'I'll take you down to the station, if you like, but I'm sure she wouldn't do anything like that,' Ben said quietly, trying to reassure them both, but George only snapped at him. He was still amazed at the policeman's assumption that Ben was Edwina's husband.

'You wouldn't know anything about it.' From close family friend, he had suddenly become a threat to George. Phillip's jealousy of him before he left for school had not been entirely lost on him either. And although Edwina normally kept a firm grip on them, this time she was far too worried about their younger sister to pay much attention to what George was saying.

'Let's go.' She picked a shawl up off the hall table, and ran out the front door, just as the policeman returned, but the man at the wheel only shook his head.

'No sight of her anywhere.'

Ben drove her down to the station in his Hupmobile with George in the backseat, and all along the way, Edwina glanced nervously out the window, but there was no sign of Alexis anywhere. And at ten-thirty at night the station was almost deserted. There were the trains to San Jose, and it was a roundabout way of going east instead of taking the ferry to Oakland station.

'This is a crazy idea,' Ben started to say, but as he did, George disappeared, running through the station, and to the tracks behind it.

'Lexie! . . .' he called. 'Lexie! . . .' He cupped his hands and shouted, and the words echoed in silence. There was the occasional grinding of an engineer shifting wheels as they sidetracked a locomotive or a car here and there, but on the whole there was nothing and no one, and no Alexis.

Edwina had followed him by then, and she didn't know why, but she trusted George's instincts. In some ways he knew Alexis better than anyone, better even than Edwina or Phillip.

'Lexie . . .' he shouted for her endlessly, and Ben tried to get them to turn back, just as they heard a train wailing in the distance. It was the last Southern Pacific freight train that came in every night shortly before midnight. There was a long beam of light in the distance, and as it approached, Edwina and Ben stood safely behind a gate, and then with a sudden flash there was a quick movement, a tiny white blur, a something, an almost nothing, and George took off like a shot across the tracks before Edwina could stop him. And then she realized what he'd seen. It was Alexis, huddled between two cars, frightened and alone, she was carrying something in her hand, and even from the distance Edwina could see that it was the doll she had rescued from the *Titanic*.

'Oh, my God . . .' She grabbed Ben's arm, and then started under the gate to go after them, but he pulled her back.

'No . . . Edwina . . . you can't . . .' George was headed in a straight line across the tracks in front of the oncoming train, toward the child who lay huddled next to the tracks. If she didn't move, she would be hit, and George had seen it all too clearly. 'George! No! . . .' she screamed, tearing herself from Ben, and heading across the tracks after her little brother. But her words were lost in the scream from the oncoming train as she headed after him. Ben looked around frantically, wanting to pull a switch, an alarm, to stop everything, but he couldn't, and he felt tears sting his cheeks as he waved frantically at the engineer, who didn't see him.

And through it all, George was hurtling toward Alexis

like a bullet, and Edwina was stumbling toward him, falling over the tracks, her skirt held in her hands, and screaming soundlessly for him, and then with the rush of, a hurricane, the train sped past her, and it seemed an interminable wait for it to go by. But when it was gone, sobbing uncontrollably, she ran ahead looking for them, sure that she would find them both dead now. But instead, what she saw was Alexis, covered with dirt, her blond hair caked with dust, as she lay under a train, her brother's arms around her, lying in the place where he had pushed her. He had reached her, just in time, and the force of his body hitting her much smaller one, as he dove for her, had pushed them both to safety. She was wailing in the sudden stillness of the night, as the train shrieked away into the distance, and Edwina fell to her knees looking at them both, and holding them, as Ben ran to where they lay, and looked down at them with tears pouring down his own cheeks. There was nothing he could say, to either of them, or even to Edwina. In a moment, Ben helped her up, and George pulled Alexis out from under the train. Ben swept her up into his arms, and carried her to the car, as George put an arm around Edwina. She stopped before they reached the car, and looked down at him. At thirteen, he had become a man, as surely as their father had been. Not a boy, or a clown, or a child anymore, but a man, as she cried and held him to her.

'I love you . . . oh, God . . . I love you . . . I thought you were . . .' She started to sob again, and she couldn't finish her sentence. Her knees were still shaking as they walked slowly to the car, and on the way home Alexis told them what George had instinctively known, she had been going to find Phillip.

'Don't *ever* do that again!' Edwina told her as she bathed her at the house, and put her between the clean sheets of her own bed. 'Never! Something terrible could have happened to you.' There, and on the *Titanic*, twice now she had almost lost her life from running away, and the next time, Edwina knew she might not be as lucky. If George hadn't pushed her out of the way of the train . . . she couldn't bear to think about it, and Alexis promised her she would never do it again, it was just that she missed Phillip. 'He'll come home again,' Edwina told her thoughtfully, she missed him too, but he had a right to what he was doing.

'Mama and Papa never came back,' Alexis said quietly.

'That was different. Phillip will. He'll be home in the spring. Now go to sleep.' She turned off the light and went back downstairs to Ben. George was in the kitchen having something to eat, and as she looked at herself, she realized that she was covered with the dirt from the train tracks, her skirt was torn, her blouse was filthy, and her hair looked even worse than Alexis's.

'How is she?' Ben asked.

'She's alright.' As alright as she ever would be. For the rest of her life, she would never really trust anyone . . . she would never believe that anyone was coming back, and in a part of her she would always be lost without their mother.

'You know what I think, don't you?' He looked unhappy tonight after all they'd been through, unhappy and almost angry. He had called the police for her while she put Alexis to bed, and he had felt George's eyes questioning him as they came back from the station. 'I think this has gone far enough. I don't think you can manage them alone, Edwina. It's too much. It would be for anyone. At least your parents had each other.'

'We're fine,' she said quietly. George's hostility toward Ben that night had not been lost on her either.

'Are you telling me you're going to carry on like this till they grow up?' His own fears for the child had now exploded into irritation with Edwina, but she was too drained and shaken to argue.

'What do you suggest I do?' she snapped. 'Give them up?'

'You can get married.' She had called him to help her that night. That was all. But he looked suddenly hopeful.

'That's not a reason to marry anyone. I don't want to marry someone because I can't manage the children. I can manage them, most of the time. And if I can't, I'll hire someone to help me do it. But I want to marry someone because I love him, the way I loved Charles. I don't want anything less than that. I won't get married because I "can't manage".' She was thinking of what her parents had had, and what she'd felt for Charles, and she didn't feel that for Ben, and she knew that she never would, no matter how angry it made him tonight, or how much she cherished his friendship. 'Besides, I don't think the children are ready for me to marry anyone.' She didn't know it, but George had just come out of the kitchen and was listening to them. It had been a rough night and their voices were sharp now.

'If that's what you're waiting for, Edwina, you're dead wrong. They'll never be ready for you to have someone in your life. They want you to themselves, all of them . . . they're selfish and all they think of is themselves . . . Phillip . . . George . . . Alexis . . . the little ones . . . they don't want you to have a life. They want you there every minute of the day as their nursemaid. And when they grow up, when they're all through with you, you'll be alone, and I'll be too old to help you . . .' He started toward the door, and she said not a word, and then he turned slowly to face her. 'You're giving your life up for them, Edwina, you know that, don't you?'

She looked at him and nodded slowly. 'Yes, Ben, I know that. It's what I want to do . . . what I have to do . . . it's what they would have wanted.'

'No, it isn't.' He looked sad for her. 'They wanted you to be happy. They wanted you to have what they did.' But I can't, she wanted to cry . . . I can't have it . . . they took it with them . . .

'I'm sorry . . .' She stood very quietly, as George watched her, relieved somehow that she wasn't marrying Ben. He didn't want her to. And he instinctively knew that Phillip didn't either.

'I'm sorry too, Edwina,' he said softly, and closed the door behind him. And as he did, she turned and saw George watching her, and she was suddenly embarrassed. She wasn't sure if he'd been listening all along, but she suspected that he had been.

'Are you okay, Sis?' He walked slowly toward her, covered with grime, and his eyes were worried.

'Yes.' She smiled at him. 'I am.'

'Are you sad you're not going to marry Ben?' He wanted to know what she felt, and he knew that most of the time she was honest with him.

'No, not really. If I really loved him, I'd have married him the first time he asked me.' George looked more than a little startled and she grinned.

'Do you think you'll ever get married?' He wore a worried look and she laughed suddenly. She knew now that she never would. If nothing else, she wouldn't have time to. Between running after children under trains, getting them through school, and making cookies with Fannie, it was unlikely there would ever be a man in her life again, and she knew that in her heart of hearts, she didn't want one.

'I doubt it.'

'Why not?' He was curious as they walked upstairs.

'Oh . . . for a lot of reasons . . . maybe just because I love all of you too much.' She took a breath and felt a pull somewhere near her heart again. 'And maybe because I loved Charles.' And maybe because loving someone that much meant that part of you died . . . that you gave everything up and went down with them, the way her mother had done, by choice, with her husband. Edwina had given her all to Charles, and to the children, and there was nothing left for anyone else now.

She kept George company while he washed the dirt of the train yard off in her bathroom, and then she put him to bed as she would have little Teddy. She turned off the light, and tucked George in after kissing him good night, and she checked on Fannie and Teddy sound asleep in their own rooms, and she walked past Phillip's empty room as she went back to her own, where Alexis purred softly beneath the sheets, her little golden head on the pillow. She sat down on her bed then, and looked at her, and for the first time in a long time, she reached high up into her closet. She knew it was still there in the box that had come from England, carefully tied with blue satin ribbons. And she pulled it down and set it carefully on the floor, and opened it, as the crown of tiny pearls and white satin shimmered in the moonlight. And as she held her wedding veil, with its sea of tulle floating around her like faded dreams, she knew she had told George the truth that night . . . she would never wear a veil like this, there would never be another man in her life again . . . there would be Phillip and George and Alexis and the others . . . but for Edwina there would be nothing more than that. It was too dangerous and too dear and too painful . . . for Edwina, there would be no husband.

She set the bridal veil back in its box carefully, and she didn't even feel the tears that fell as she tied the ribbons. It was over for her, all that . . . over on a long-distant night at sea, with the man she had loved, the man who was no more . . . she had been desperately in love with Charles, and she knew with absolute certainty, there would never be another.

17

The train pulled into the station on the fourteenth of June, 1914, and Edwina stood behind George, waving as hard as she could, while Phillip hung out of his compartment window grinning at them. It felt like a thousand years since he'd been home, instead of the nine months he had just spent completing his freshman year at Harvard.

He was on the platform before anyone else, his arms around them all, and Edwina felt tears roll down her cheeks, as George let out a wild whoop of glee, and the little ones jumped up and down shouting in the excitement. Alexis just stood there and grinned, staring at him in disbelief, as though she'd been sure he would never come back again, in spite of everything Edwina had said, and her promises that he would be back home again in time for summer.

'Hi there, little love.' He turned quietly toward Alexis, and hugged her to him, as she just closed her eyes and beamed. He was home again, and all was right with the world for all of them. It was like a dream come true, and George punched him in the chest and pulled his hair at least a dozen times as Phillip grinned at him and put up with it. He was just so happy to be home, he could hardly stand it.

And as he climbed back on the train and passed his things to George through the compartment window, Edwina realized how much bigger and broader he had grown in the year that he'd been gone. He looked sophisticated and poised and very grown up. He was clearly a man now. He was nearly nineteen, and suddenly he looked even older.

'What are you looking at, Sis?' He glanced over George's head and she smiled and saluted him.

'Looks like you did some growing up while you were away. You look alright.' Their eyes were the same blue, and she knew that they both looked a great deal like their mother.

'You look pretty good too,' he admitted grudgingly, and he didn't tell her that he had dreamed of coming home, almost every night. But he liked Harvard too. Ben Jones had been right, it was wonderful just being there, but there were times when it seemed like it was on a different planet than California. And it was so far away. Four days by train. It seemed to take an eternity to get here. He had spent Christmas with his room-mate's family in New York that year, and he had been desperately homesick for Edwina and the children, though not quite as lonely as they were for him. And there were times when Edwina wondered if Alexis would survive it.

Phillip noticed that Ben wasn't there, and raised an eyebrow as they walked to the car parked just outside the station. 'Where's Ben?'

'He's away. In L.A.' She smiled. 'But he said to send his love. He'd probably love to have lunch with you sometime, to talk about Harvard.' And she wanted to hear about it too. His letters had been fascinating, about the people he met, the courses he took, the professors he was studying with. It made her envious at times. She would have loved to go to a place like Harvard. She had never even thought about things like that before Charles and her parents died. All she had wanted to do was get married

195

and have babies then. But now she had so many responsibilities, she had to be so well informed when she went to meetings at the paper, and she felt as though she should be teaching the children something more than just baking cakes and how to plant daisies in the garden.

'Who drove you here?' Phillip was trying to keep George from spilling all the books he had brought home in a large box, while still holding Alexis's hand and keeping an eye on Fannie and Teddy. It was the usual juggling act, and Edwina laughed as she answered.

'I did.' She looked very proud of herself, and Phillip laughed, thinking she was joking.

'No, seriously.'

'I am serious. Why, don't you think I can drive?' She was grinning happily at him, standing next to the Packard she had bought for all of them, as a gift to them and herself on her twenty-third birthday.

'Edwina, you don't mean it?'

'Sure I do. Come on, dump all your stuff in here, and I'll drive you home, Master Phillip.' They stowed everything in the trunk, and lashed the rest to the top of the handsome dark blue car she had bought, and Phillip was wildly impressed as she drove them home without a problem. The children were all chattering, and George was so excited he could hardly keep his questions straight. There was so much going on all at once that by the time they got home, Phillip jokingly said he had a headache.

'Well, I see nothing's changed here.' And then he looked at her carefully. She looked well, and even prettier than he had remembered her. She was a beautiful girl, and it was odd to realize that this beautiful young woman who took such good care of them was not his mother but his sister, and that she had opted for this strange, lonely life, taking care of them, but it seemed to be what she wanted. 'You're alright?' he asked her quietly as they walked into the house behind the others.

'I'm fine, Phillip.' She stopped and looked up at him then. He had grown much taller in the months he'd been gone, and now he towered over her, and she suspected that he was even a trifle taller than their father. 'Do you like it there? Really, I mean . . .' He nodded at her, and he looked as though he meant it.

'It's a long way from home. But I'm learning wonderful things, and meeting people I like. I just wish it were a little closer.'

'It won't be long,' she said optimistically, 'three more years and you'll be back here running the paper.'

'I can hardly wait.' He grinned.

'Neither can I. I'm getting awfully tired of those meetings.' And sometimes it was a strain having to do business with Ben. He had been so disappointed the last time she'd turned down his proposal, the night Alexis was almost hit by the train. But they were still friends. They just kept a little more distance than they used to.

'When do we go to Tahoe, Win?' Phillip was looking around the house as though he'd been gone for a dozen years, drinking it all in, touching things. She couldn't begin to imagine how much he had missed it.

'Not for a few weeks. I thought we'd go in July as we always do. I wasn't sure what you wanted to do in August.' And in September, he'd be going back to Cambridge again but he had two and a half months to enjoy with them before that.

They did all the things that he wanted to do for the first week. They had dinner at all his favorite restaurants, and he went to see all his friends, and Edwina noticed that by early July, there was even a certain young lady in his life. She was a very pretty young girl, she was very delicate and fair and she seemed to hang on Phillip's every word when she came to dinner. She was just eighteen, and she made Edwina feel as though she were a thousand years older. She treated her with the deference with which one would have treated a woman twice her age, and Edwina wondered how old the girl thought she was. But when she mentioned it to Phillip the next day, he just laughed and told her she just wanted to impress her. Her name was Becky Hancock, and conveniently, her parents had a house at Lake Tahoe, near where Edwina and the children stayed.

They saw a lot of her in July, too, and on several occasions she invited Phillip, George, and Edwina over to play tennis. Edwina played a good game of it, and when Phillip and Becky left the courts, she and George enjoyed a few slam dunk games, and she was extremely pleased when she beat him.

'You're not bad for an old girl,' George teased, and she playfully threw a ball at him.

'See if I let you learn to drive in my car.'

'Okay, okay, I apologize.' Phillip drove the car to chauffeur Becky, but whenever it was free, Edwina was teaching George how to drive. At fourteen, he was remarkably good at it, and he was a little less mischievous these days, and she noticed that he was starting to keep an eye on the ladies. 'Phillip is dumb to get stuck with that girl,' he announced one day as they were driving along with George at the wheel, while Phillip was back at their familiar camp, keeping an eye on the younger children.

'What makes you say that?' She wasn't sure she disagreed, but she was curious as to why he thought so.

'She likes him for all the wrong reasons.' It was an interesting observation.

'Such as?'

He looked pensive as he took a turn expertly, and Edwina complimented him on his driving. 'Thanks, Sis.' And then his thoughts returned to Becky again. 'Sometimes I think she just likes him because of Papa's paper.' Her father owned a restaurant and two hotels, and they were hardly destitute, but the Winfield paper turned a far bigger profit and had much more prestige. Phillip would be an important man one day, just as their father had been. She was a smart girl, if she was looking for a husband. But Phillip was still awfully young to be thinking of marriage, and Edwina didn't think he was, at least she hoped not, not for a long time.

'You could be right. But on the other hand, your brother is an awfully handsome guy.' She smiled at George and he shrugged disdainfully, and then glanced at her thoughtfully as they drove back toward the house.

'Edwina, would you think I was terrible if, when I grow up, I didn't work at the paper?'

She was startled by his words, but she shook her head slowly. 'Not terrible, but why wouldn't you?'

'I don't know . . . I just think it would be boring. It's more for Phillip than me.' He seemed so serious that Edwina smiled at him. He was still so young, and only months before he had been totally wild. But recently he seemed so much more grown up to her, and now he had decided that he didn't want a career at the paper.

'What is "your" kind of thing then?'

'I don't know . . .' He looked hesitant, and then glanced at her, prepared to confess as she listened. 'One day, I think I'd like to make movies.' She looked at him in astonishment, and then realized that he meant it. The idea was so farfetched that she laughed at him, but he went on to explain just how exciting it was, and then he went on to tell her all about a film he had seen recently with Mary Pickford.

'And when did you see that?' She didn't recall letting him go to the movies recently, but he grinned broadly at her.

'When I cut school last month.' She looked horrified and then they both started to laugh.

'You're a hopeless beast.'

'Yeah,' he said happily, 'but admit it . . . you love me.'

'Never mind.' She made him turn the wheel over to her again, and they drove home easily, chatting about life, and their family, the movies he was so crazy about, and the family paper. And as they reached the camp and she stopped the car, she turned to look at him with surprise. 'You're serious, George, aren't you?' But how could he think seriously about anything? To her, they were the dreams of a baby.

'Yes, I am serious. I'm going to do that one day.' He smiled happily at her. She was his best friend as well as his sister. 'I'll do it, while Phillip runs the paper. You'll see.'

'I hope one of you runs the paper anyway. I'd hate to hang on to it for nothing.'

'You can always sell it and make a bundle,' he announced optimistically, but she knew only too well that it wasn't as easy as all that. The paper had been having some labor problems recently, and some profit troubles as well. It wasn't the same as when the owner was actually running the paper. And she had to keep it alive for three more years, until Phillip finished Harvard. And right now, three years seemed like a long time to Edwina.

'Did you have a nice drive, you two?' Phillip smiled at them as they returned. Teddy was asleep in the hammock under a tree, and Phillip had been having a long, serious talk with Fannie and Alexis.

'What were you all talking about?' Edwina smiled

happily as she sat down next to them, and George went to change into fishing gear. He had a date to go trout fishing with one of their neighbors.

'We were talking about how pretty Mama was,' he said quietly, and Alexis looked happier than she had in a long time. She loved hearing about her, and sometimes at night, when she slept in Edwina's bed, she would make Edwina talk for hours about their mother. It was painful at times for the older ones, but it kept her alive for the little ones, and Teddy loved to hear stories about their father.

'Why did they die?' he'd asked Edwina one day, and she had answered the only thing she could think of.

'Because God loved them so much he wanted to be closer to them.' Teddy had nodded, and then looked at her with a worried frown.

'Does he love you too, Edwina?'

'Not that much, sweetheart.'

'Good.' He had been satisfied and they'd gone on to talk about something else. And it saddened Edwina to realize that Teddy had been so young when they died, that he would never know them. But Alexis still had memories of them, and Fannie did, a little. It had been more than two years since they'd died, and for all of them the pain had dimmed a little. Even for Edwina.

'Did you pick up a newspaper today?' Phillip asked casually, but Edwina said that she hadn't had time, and he told her he would buy one when he went to visit Becky.

He had been intrigued weeks before by the assassination of the heir to the Austrian throne, and had insisted several times to Edwina that the event had much broader implications than people suspected. He had gotten very involved in politics in the last year, and was talking about majoring in political science when he went back to Harvard.

When he found a newspaper that afternoon, he was stunned to discover that he'd been right. It was a copy of the Winfield paper, the *Telegraph Sun*, and it ran a banner headline. EUROPE AT WAR, the paper said, as people gathered around and stared. The assassination of the Archduke Franz Ferdinand and his wife at Sarajevo had given the Austrians just the excuse they wanted to declare war on Serbia, and then for Germany to declare war on Russia, and within two days, Germany had declared war on France and invaded neutral Belgium as well, and the day after that the English declared war on the Germans in return. It seemed like utter madness, but in the space of a week almost all of Europe was at war with each other.

'What does this mean for us?' Edwina asked as they drove back to San Francisco a few days later. 'Do you suppose we'll get into it as well?' She looked at Phillip with concern, but he smiled and was quick to reassure her.

'There's no reason why we should.' But Phillip was fascinated with all of it, and he devoured everything he could find to read about it. Once back in San Francisco, he went straight to his father's paper. And when Ben turned up there too, they spent hours dissecting and discussing the news in Europe.

For the rest of the month, the war news seemed to be the center of every conversation, with Japan getting into the war against Germany, and the German air strikes on Paris. Within a month it had become a full-scale war, as the world stood by and watched in amazement.

He was still fascinated with it when he left for Harvard in early September, and at each stop along the way, he bought the newspapers and talked to people on the train about what he'd read. He had a youthful zeal about it all, but his interest in the war made Edwina more aware of it too. She read up on everything so she would know what they were talking about when she went to the paper for her monthly meetings. But she had her own problems, too, with unions causing trouble at the paper. There were times when she wondered if she could hang on to the paper for the next two and a half years. Waiting for Phillip to finish his education now seemed endless. Her decisions at the monthly meetings were cautious as a result. She didn't want to take any chances and jeopardize anything, and no matter how criticized she was for her conservative decisions, she knew there was nothing else she could do for the moment.

In 1915, as Phillip struggled through his sophomore year at Harvard, the Great War grew more intense, and the German U-boat blockade of Great Britain began. She was still able to get mail from Aunt Liz from time to time, but it was becoming increasingly difficult. Her letters always had a sad, plaintive tone. She seemed so far away now to the children and Edwina. She was someone they had seen a long time ago, and whom they felt they didn't really know. She was still nagging at Edwina to put the rest of her parents' clothes away, which she had finally done long since, and sell the newspaper and the house and come to live at Havermoor with her, which Edwina would never do, and didn't even bother to mention in her letters.

The Panama-Pacific Exposition opened in San Francisco in February, in spite of the war, and Edwina took all the children to it. They had a marvelous time and after that they insisted that they wanted to go every week. But the most exciting thing of all was that in January long-distance telephone service had been established between New York and San Francisco, and when Phillip went to New York to visit friends, he asked permission to make a call to San Francisco, promising to reimburse them.

The children were all at dinner one night when the phone rang, and Edwina thought nothing of it as she picked up the receiver. The operator connected it, told her to hang on, and then suddenly she was speaking to Phillip. The connection wasn't great, and there was lots of static on the line, but she could hear him, and she waved to all the children so they could hear him too. Five heads clustered as one and each shouted a message into the phone, as he listened and then he sent them all his love and said he had to get off. It was an exciting change for them, and it made him seem a little less remote as they waited for him to come home from Harvard.

At Harvard, Phillip was invited to a ceremony that was difficult for him and brought back some of the painful memories that had been beginning to fade. Mrs Widener invited him to the dedication of the Harry Elkins Widener Memorial Library founded in her son's name. They had last met on the *Titanic*, and Phillip remembered him well. He had gone down with his father, and he had also been a friend of Jack Thayer's. It was a sad reunion when they all met for the dedication, and Jack and Phillip chatted for a while, and then drifted away. It was strange to think that they had once been in the same lifeboat, and for a day or two the local papers wanted to interview Phillip as one of the survivors, but eventually, much to his relief, they forgot him. They had all lost too much, and too much time had passed now to want to talk about it anymore. He wrote to Edwina about seeing Jack Thayer again, but she didn't mention it when she wrote back. He knew that with her as well it was a difficult subject. She seldom spoke of it anymore, and although he knew she still thought of him, she almost never talked of Charles. It was still agonizing for her, and he suspected that it always would be. Her life as a young girl had ended that night forever.

But the real blow came in May. Phillip was on his way across the campus when he heard it, and for a moment he stopped, thinking of an icy night almost exactly three years before.

The *Lusitania* had been sunk, torpedoed by the Germans, and the world was stunned. To all appearances, an innocent passenger ship had been attacked, and she had gone down in eighteen minutes, carrying with her 1,201 people. It was a brutal blow, and one that Phillip understood all too well. All morning, as he thought of it, he thought of his sister, and how hard the news of it would hit her. It was too close to home for all of them. And he was right. When Edwina heard, she closed her eyes, and walked all the way home to California Street from her father's paper. Ben offered her a ride when he saw her go, but she only shook her head. She couldn't speak and it was almost as though she didn't see him.

She walked slowly home, thinking, as Phillip had, of that terrible night three years before and all that it had changed for them. She had wanted the memories to fade, and they had, but the loss of the *Lusitania* brought them all back with a vengeance. The memories were all too vivid again, and all she could think of were her parents and Charles as she walked into the house. It was as though she could see their faces again through a mist of tears, as she said a prayer for the souls on the *Lusitania*.

And as she remembered back to three years before, she could almost hear the band on the *Titanic* playing the mournful hymn just before the ship went down. She remembered the icy wind on her face, hearing the terrible ripping, roaring, tearing sounds . . . and never again seeing people she had loved so much and lost so quickly.

'Edwina?' Alexis looked frightened when she saw her sister's face as she walked through the front door, and carefully lifted her veil and took her hat off. 'Is something wrong?' Alexis was nine years old by then, but Edwina didn't want to remind her of their own loss, and touching the child's face gently with her hand, she only shook her head, but her eyes told their own story.

'It's nothing, sweetheart.' The child went back outside to play, and Edwina stood watching her for a long time, thinking of the people they had lost, and now those that had died on the *Lusitania*.

Edwina was quiet all day, and Phillip called her that night, knowing how she would have felt when she heard the news. 'It's an ugly war, isn't it, Win?'

'How could they do a thing like that? . . . a passenger ship . . .' The very thought of it made her wince with remembered pain.

'Don't think about it.' But it was impossible not to think about it. Thoughts of the *Titanic* kept drifting into her head . . . the night of the ship going down . . . the screech of the lifeboats being lowered . . . the wails of the people in the water as they drowned. How did one forget memories like that? When did it ever go away? She had begun to think it never would, as she lay in bed that night, thinking of her parents, and Charles, and the lives she had led with them, in sharp contrast to the life she led now, alone with the children.

18

Shortly after the *Lusitania* went down, Italy annulled its allegiance to Germany, and declared war on Austria as well. And by September of that year, Russia had lost all of Poland, Lithuania, and Courland, as well as a million men. The Great War was taking a shocking toll, and America was still watching from the sidelines.

The following year, in 1916, the Germans and the French lost almost 700,000 men between them at Verdun alone, and well over a million men died at the Somme. The Germans continued extensive attacks with their U-boats, sinking merchant vessels and passenger ships as well as warships. It caused a tremendous hue and cry, and by then Portugal had been drawn into the war as well, and the airship raids on London continued. And in November, Wilson had been reelected, mainly for keeping the States out of the war. But all eyes were turned toward Europe as the slaughter continued.

On 31 January 1916, Berlin notified Washington that unrestricted submarine warfare had been resumed, and within two months, they announced that submarines would sink any ship bringing supplies to the Allied countries. Wilson finally took a stand within days, and although earlier he had said that there was such a thing as a nation 'being too proud to fight' about the United States, he now announced that he would defend the kind of freedom Americans had always enjoyed and quite simply expected.

Edwina continued to hear from her aunt Liz, although letters were few and far between, and they were coming out of Europe by circuitous routes, but she seemed to be alright in spite of dreadful weather and terrible shortages of fuel and food. But she urged Edwina to take care, and said that she longed to see all the children. She hoped that when the war was over they would all come over and visit her, but even the thought of it made Edwina tremble. She was no longer able to take even the ferryboat to Oakland.

She went to the newspaper frequently, though, and it was always interesting to listen to the men there discussing the war news. She had made her own peace with Ben by then, and they were still close. He realized that she didn't want to marry anyone, and she was content with her life with the children. She enjoyed his friendship and his male views, and they would talk endlessly about the war, and about the problems they were having with the paper. Phillip was in his last year at Harvard by then, and Edwina was glad of it, she knew the paper desperately needed a family member to run it. The competition was stiff, and the other papers were all run by people and families who understood the business, particularly the de Youngs, who were the most powerful newspaper family in San Francisco. And the healthy empire her father had been building for years had been powerfully affected by his absence. Five years was a long time, and it was time for Phillip to take over. And she also knew that it would be a year or two before Phillip had a good grasp on everything, but she hoped that he would be able to bring the paper back to what it once had been. Even their income had been diminished somewhat over the past two years, but they still had enough coming in for their way of life not to be affected. She was just grateful that Phillip would be coming home soon. And in the fall, George would be beginning his four-year stint at Harvard.

But on 6 April, the United States finally entered the war, and Edwina came home from her monthly meeting at the newspaper, looking sober. She was worried about the boys, she had talked to Ben for a long time about what it would mean for them, and their conclusion had been that for all intents and purposes Phillip and George wouldn't be affected. Phillip was in college. George was too young, and she was glad for that. All she could remember were the terrible stories she had read at her father's paper, about the staggering casualties in the course of the battles.

When she got home, Alexis told her that Phillip had called and he would call her later that night, but he never did, and Edwina forgot about it after that. Sometimes he liked to call her just to discuss world events, and although she discouraged that kind of extravagance, she was always flattered that he wanted to talk to her. She was so used to spending her days picking up dolls, and tying ribbons on braids, and scolding Teddy for leaving his soldiers everywhere that it was refreshing discussing more important topics with her older brothers. George was interested in the war too, but he was far more interested in the movies that were being made on the subject. He went to see them whenever he could, and took any one of his innumerable girfriends with him. It always made Edwina smile, just watching him, it reminded her a little bit of her own youth, when the most important thing in her life had been going to parties and balls and cotillions. She still went from time to time, but it was all different without Charles, and no one else had ever mattered to her. Nearly twenty-six, she was content with the life she led, and she had no interest in finding a husband.

George scolded her sometimes about going out. He

thought she should go out more. He still remembered how it had been 'before,' with their parents dressed up and going out, and Edwina wearing beautiful gowns when she went out with Charles in the evening. But when he talked about it, it only made Edwina sad, and her younger sisters would clamor and beg to see the gowns she'd worn, but the prettiest ones were long since put away, if not entirely forgotten. Lately she wore more serious things, and sometimes she even wore some of her mother's gowns. They made her look more like a young matron.

George asked her, 'Why don't you go out more?' but she insisted that she went out quite enough. She'd been to a concert only the week before, with Ben and his new lady.

'You know what I mean.' George looked annoyed, he meant with men, but that was a subject she didn't choose to discuss with her brother. They had mixed feelings about it anyway. In some ways they thought she should have more fun, and in others, they were possessive about her. But Edwina didn't want a man in her life anyway. She still dreamed of Charles, although, after five years, the memories were a little dim now. But in her heart, she still felt as though she belonged to him, and she hated the whispers, and the things people said when she overheard them . . . tragic . . . terrible . . . poor thing . . . very pretty girl . . . fiancé went down on the *Titanic*, you know . . . parents too . . . left to bring up the children. She was too proud to let them know she cared, and too sensible to care if anyone called her a spinster. But she was, she knew. At twenty-five, she didn't let herself care, and she insisted that it didn't matter. That door was closed for her now, that part of her life definitely over. She hadn't even looked at her bridal veil in years. She couldn't bear the pain of it anymore. She doubted if she would ever look at it again, but it was there . . . and it had almost been . . . that was enough . . . and perhaps one day it would be worn by Alexis or Fannie on her wedding day . . . in memory of a love that had never died, and a life that had never been. But there was no point thinking about it now. She had too many other things to do. She wondered then if Phillip would call again, to discuss the fact that the United States had entered the war, but in spite of his promise to Alexis when he'd called earlier that day, he didn't.

George came home full of talk about it, though, and several times expressed regret that he wasn't old enough to go, much to Edwina's chagrin, and she told him as much, which he felt was extremely unpatriotic.

'They're looking for volunteers, Win!' He frowned at her, noticing in spite of himself as he always did, that she was even more beautiful than their mother had been. She was tall and graceful and thin, with long shining black hair that she wore straight down her back sometimes when she wasn't going anywhere. It made her look like a very young girl, unlike the more serious hairdos she wore when she was going downtown, or to meetings at their father's paper, or to a dinner party in the evening.

'I don't care if they are looking for volunteers.' She glared pointedly at him. 'Don't get any ideas into your head. You're too young. And Phillip has a paper to run. Let someone else go to the war, it will be over soon anyway.' But there was no sign of it, as millions continued to fall in the trenches in Europe.

Five days after Congress had declared war, Edwina was walking in from the garden with an armful of her mother's roses, when she suddenly looked up and her face went deathly pale. Standing in the kitchen doorway looking handsome and tall, and with a painfully serious face, was her brother Phillip. She stopped where she was and walked slowly toward him, afraid to ask why he was there, why he had come all the way from Boston. She only dropped the roses on the grass next to her, and hurried into his open arms and he held her for a long time. It was odd to realize how grown up he was now. He was twenty-one years old, and unlike Edwina, he looked much older. The responsibilities he'd shouldered in the past five years had left their mark on him, as they had on Edwina, too, but although she felt them, she didn't show them.

'What is it?' she asked slowly, as she pulled away from him, but a terrible pain in her heart told her what she didn't want to know, but already suspected.

'I came home to talk to you.' He wouldn't have done anything that important without consulting her. He respected and loved her too much not to ask her opinion, if not her permission.

'How did you manage to leave school? It's not your holiday yet, is it?' But she already knew, she just didn't want it to be what she feared. She wanted him to tell her it was something else, anything, even that he had been thrown out of Harvard.

'They gave me a leave of absence.'

'Oh.' She sat down slowly at the kitchen table and for an instant, neither of them moved. 'For how long?'

He didn't dare tell her. Not so soon. There was so much he wanted to say to her first. 'Edwina, I have to talk to you . . . can we go in the other room?' They were still in the kitchen, and Mrs Barnes was rustling somewhere in the larder behind them. She hadn't seen Phillip since he'd come in, and he knew that once she did, there would be a big fuss and he wouldn't be able to talk to Edwina.

Edwina said not a word and walked solemnly into the front parlor. It was a room where they seldom sat, except when they had guests, which wasn't often. 'You should have called before you came home,' she reproached him. Then she could have told him not to come home at all. She didn't want him to be here, didn't want him to look so grown up and as though he had something terrible to tell her.

'I did call, but you were out. Didn't Alexis tell you?'

'Yes, but you never called again.' She felt tears sting her eyes as she looked at him. He was still so sweet and so young, despite his serious airs and his almost grown-up ways, and the polish he'd acquired at Harvard.

'I took the train that night, Edwina.' He took a quick breath. He couldn't avoid it any longer. 'I've enlisted. I leave for Europe in ten days. I wanted to see you first, to explain . . .' But as he said the words, she stood up, and walked nervously around the room, wringing her hands, and turning to glare at him.

'Phillip, how *could* you? What right did you have to do that, after all we've all been through? The children need you so much . . . and so do I . . . and George will be gone in September . . .' There were a thousand good reasons she could think of why he shouldn't go, but the simplest one was that she didn't want to lose him. What if he got hurt, or died? The very thought of it made her feel faint. 'You can't do that! We all depend on you . . . We . . . I . . .' Her voice trailed off and tears filled her eyes as she looked at him and then turned away. 'Phillip, please don't . . .' she said in muffled tones, and he walked toward her and gently touched her shoulder, wanting to explain it to her, but not entirely sure that he could.

'Edwina, I have to. I can't sit over here, reading about battles in the newspapers, and still feel like a man. I have an obligation to do my duty now that this country is at war.'

'Nonsense!' She spun around to face him, and her eyes flashed just as their mother's would have years before. 'You have an obligation to two brothers and three sisters. We've all been waiting for you to grow up, and you can't run out on us now.'

'I'm not running out on you, Win. I'll be back. And I promise, I'll make it up to you then. I swear!' She had made him feel guilty for deserting them, and yet he felt that he owed his country something more. And in his heart, he knew that their father would have approved of his going. It was something he had to do, no matter how angry it made Edwina. Even his professors had understood it at Harvard. To them, it was merely part of being a man. But to Edwina, it was a kind of betrayal, and she was still crying and looking angrily at him, as George rushed through the front door a little while later.

He was about to dash past the front parlor, as he always did, and then he caught a glimpse of his sister, head bowed, her long dark hair cascading down her back, as it had been in the garden when she dropped the roses, and he couldn't see his brother from where he stood near the door.

'Hey, Win . . . what's up? . . . something wrong?' He looked startled and she turned slowly to face him. He had a stack of books in his arms, and his dark hair was ruffled, he looked healthy and young, and his cheeks were warm from the spring air. But as he looked at her with concern, his brother took several steps toward him. George saw him then, and looked even more worried by what he saw in his eyes. 'Hey . . . what's wrong? . . .'

'Your brother has enlisted in the army.' She said it as though he had just murdered someone, and George stared at him, not sure what to say. And then his eyes lit up, and for a moment he forgot Edwina, as he took a step toward his older brother and clapped him on the shoulder.

'Good for you, old man. Give 'em hell!' And then he rapidly remembered Edwina. She took an angry step toward them both and tossed back her long hair with a vengeance.

'And what if they give him hell, George? What if they do it to him? What if they kill him? What then? Will it be so exciting then? Will you be as pleased? And what will you do then, go over there and "give 'em hell" too? Think of it, both of you. Think of what you're doing. Think of this family before you do anything, and what you'll be doing to all of us when you do it.' She swept past them then, and turned with a last anguished look at Phillip, and she spoke in an iron voice. 'I won't let you go, Phillip. You'll have to tell them it was a mistake. But I will not let you.' And with that she slammed the door and hurried upstairs to her own room.

19

'Why did Phillip come home?' Alexis asked with curiosity as she combed her doll's hair. 'Did he flunk out of school?' She was interested, as were Fannie and Teddy, but Edwina refused to discuss it with them as she served breakfast the next morning.

The two boys had gone out to dinner the night before, to their father's club, and she knew they had met Ben, but she had not spoken to Phillip since the previous afternoon.

'Phillip decided he missed us, that's all.' She spoke very seriously, and offered nothing further. And as they watched the look on her face, even Teddy knew that something was wrong that she wasn't saying.

She kissed them all before they left for school after breakfast, and she walked out to the garden then, and picked up the roses she had dropped the day before on the lawn when she first saw Phillip. She had forgotten all about them, and they were more than a little wilted, but they seemed so unimportant now. Everything did, in light of what Phillip had told her. She didn't know what she could do, but she knew she was going to do everything she could to stop him. He had no right to go away and leave them like that, and more importantly, risk his life. She took the roses into the house, and she was thinking about calling Ben to discuss it with him, when George walked into the room. He was late for school, as he always was, and she looked up and was about to scold him, but the look in his eyes told her it was too late for that. Like Phillip, he was almost a man now.

'Are you really going to try and stop him, Win?' The words were spoken quietly, with a sad look. It was as though he knew she had already lost, but he understood it all better, because he was a man and she wasn't.

'Yes, I'm going to try and stop him.' She put the roses in a vase with a certain vehemence and then looked up at him with grief and anger. 'He had no right to do that without asking me first.' And she wanted to be sure that George also got that message. She wasn't going to tolerate either of them doing that, and George was just impulsive enough to try and follow his older brother into the war in Europe.

'You shouldn't do it, Win. Papa wouldn't approve of your stopping him. He believed in standing up for what you believe in.'

Her eyes pierced into his like darts and she didn't mince words. 'Papa isn't here anymore,' she said harshly, and George realized that she had never been that blunt about it before. 'Papa wouldn't want him leaving us alone either. Things are different now.'

'You have me,' he said gently, but she only shook her head.

'You're going to Harvard next year.' He had already been accepted and he was following the family tradition, and it wasn't that she was trying to hang on to them, but she didn't want them to get killed. 'Don't get involved in this, George,' she warned, 'this is between me and Phillip.'

'No, it's not,' he said, 'it's between him, and him. It's up to Phillip to stand up for what he believes in. You wouldn't want him to be less than that, Win. He's got to

217

do what he thinks is right, even if it hurts us. I understand that, and you have to too.'

'I don't have to understand anything.' She spun around so he wouldn't see the tears in her eyes, and spoke to him over her shoulder. 'Go on, now, you'll be late for school.'

He left reluctantly, just as his brother came downstairs and whispered to George across the main hallway. 'How is she?' They had talked about it long into the night, and there was no doubt in Phillip's mind. He had to go.

'I think she's crying.' George whispered back, and smiled as he saluted his brother and flew out the front door. He would be late for school, as usual, but it didn't matter anymore. School was almost over. He was going to graduate from Drew School in six weeks, and he was off to Harvard in September. And to him, school was a place where you made friends, and chased girls, and had a good time before you went home to your family and ate dinner. He had always liked school, but he had never been the serious student that Phillip was. He was sad, too, that his brother was going to war, but he was certain that Phillip was doing the right thing, and equally so that Edwina was wrong. Their father would have told her so, had he been alive, but unfortunately he wasn't. And Phillip was no longer a little boy.

He tried to tell her that himself a little while later in the garden, but she was furiously pulling weeds, and pretending not to hear him, and then finally she turned to him with tears running down her cheeks, and with the back of her hands, pushed the hair back from her face.

'If you're not a child anymore, then act like a man and stand by us. I've held on to that damn paper for you for five years, and what do you expect me to do now? Close the doors?' The paper had nothing to do with it and they both knew it. All she really wanted to tell him was that she was scared. So scared that she couldn't bear the thought of him leaving, and she would have done anything in her power to stop him from going to the war in Europe.

'The paper will wait while I'm gone. That's not the point and you know it.'

'The point is . . .' She started to justify herself again, but this time the words failed her. She couldn't go on, as she turned and saw the look on his face. He looked so strong and so young, and so damn hopeful. He believed in what he'd done and he wanted her to believe in it too, for him, but she just couldn't do it. 'The point is . . .' she whispered as she reached out to him and he went to her, '. . . the point is I love you so much,' she sobbed, '. . . oh, please, Phillip . . . don't go . . .'

'Edwina, I have to.'

'You can't . . .' She was thinking of herself, and Fannie and Teddy, and Alexis. They all needed him so much. And if he left, they would have only George. Silly George of the endless mischief, the tin cans tied behind horses, the cranks 'borrowed' from motorcars, the mice let loose in classrooms . . . the sweet face that kissed her at night, the arms that always hugged Fannie . . . the boys they had been, and no longer were . . . and in the fall, George would be gone too. Suddenly, everything was changing as it had once before, except that the children were all she had left now and she didn't want to lose them. 'Phillip, please . . .'

Her eyes begged and he looked at her unhappily. He had come all the way to California to tell her, and he had half expected this, but it was so painful for all of them. 'I won't go without your blessing. I don't know how I'd get out of it, but if you really mean what you say, if you can't manage without me, then I'll have to tell them I can't go.' He looked heartbroken as he said it, and the look in his eyes told her there was no choice. She had to let him do it.

'And if you don't go?'

'I don't know . . .' He looked sadly around his mother's garden, remembering her, and the father they had loved, as he looked back into his sister's eyes. 'I think I'd always feel that somehow I had failed them. I have no right to let someone else fight this war for us. Edwina, I want to be there.' He looked so sure, and so calm, it broke her heart just to see him. And she didn't understand the lure of war for men, but she knew that he had to go with it.

'Why? Why do you have to be the one?'

'Because even though to you I'm still a child, I'm a man now. Edwina . . . that's where I belong.'

She nodded silently and stood up, shaking out her skirt and dusting her hands off, and it was a long moment before she looked up at him again. 'You have it then.' She sounded solemn and her voice was shaking, but she had made up her mind, and she was glad he had come home to tell her. If he hadn't, she would never have understood it. And she wasn't sure she did now, but she had to respect him. And he was right. He was no longer a boy anymore. He was a man. And he had a right to his own principles and opinions.

'What do I have?' He looked confused, and suddenly surprisingly boyish as she smiled at him.

'You have my blessing, silly boy. I wish you wouldn't go, but you have a right to make up your own mind.' And then her eyes grew sad again. 'Just be sure you come home.'

'I promise you . . . I will . . .' He threw his arms around her and hugged her close, and they stood that way for a long time, as little Teddy watched them from an upstairs window.

20

The two oldest boys had talked for hours the night before, as Phillip packed some of his things, and told George he could take anything of his he wanted to Harvard, and it had been long after midnight when they went downstairs and decided to have something to eat in the kitchen.

George talked animatedly, waving a chicken leg, and wished him Godspeed, and then teased him about the girls he would meet in France, but that was the last thing on Phillip's mind.

'Be easy on Edwina,' he urged, and then reminded George not to go wild when he got to Harvard.

'Don't be silly.' George grinned as he poured a beer for himself and his older brother. All of Phillip's bags were packed, and they had nothing left to do until morning. They could talk all night if they wanted to, and George knew that Edwina wouldn't have minded if they stayed up all night, or even got drunk. As George saw it, they had a right to.

'I mean it,' Phillip said again. 'It's been hard on her having to take care of all of us for all these years.' It had been exactly five years since their parents had died.

'We haven't been so bad.' George smiled as he sipped the beer, and wondered how his brother would look in a uniform. When he thought about it, he envied him and wished he were going with him.

'If it weren't for all of us, she might be married to someone,' Phillip said pensively. 'Or maybe not. I don't think she's ever gotten over Charles, maybe she never will.'

'I don't think she wants to get over him,' George said. He knew his older sister well, and Phillip nodded.

'Just be good to her.' He looked lovingly at his younger brother as he set his own glass down, and then as he tousled George's hair, he smiled. 'I'll miss you, kid. Have a good time next year.'

'You too.' George smiled, thinking of his brother's adventures in France. 'Maybe I'll see you over there sometime.'

But at that Phillip only shook his head. 'Don't you dare. They need you here.' And his eyes said he meant it, as George nodded at him with a sigh of envy.

'I know.' And then, looking unusually sober for him, 'Just be sure you come back.' It was what Edwina had said too, and silently Phillip nodded.

The two brothers walked upstairs arm in arm, shortly after 2.00 a.m., and the next morning, everyone was ready and waiting when they came down to breakfast. Edwina had made their breakfast herself, and she looked up and smiled at the two boys, looking tired from the night before, and their long hours of talking in the kitchen.

'Did you get to bed late last night?' she asked, pouring coffee for both as Fannie stared at Phillip. She couldn't believe he was leaving them again, and this time she knew that Edwina wasn't happy about it.

They were all going to the station to see him off, and there was an aura of false gaiety as Edwina drove them through town in the Packard.

There were other boys like him waiting at the station for the train. Many had enlisted in the past few days. It was only nine days since the United States had entered the war. And for Alexis it was a sad and special day, it was her eleventh birthday. But it was a doubly sad day for her, because Phillip was leaving.

'Take care of yourself,' Edwina said softly as they waited for the train, and George cracked an endless series of old jokes. They kept the younger children distracted anyway, and Edwina suddenly felt an arrow pierce her heart, as in the distance, they heard the train begin to wail as it approached them.

It swept into the station then, and George helped him carry his things, as the younger children waited with sad eyes and unhappy faces.

'When will you come back again?' Teddy asked unhappily as a tear trembled in the corner of his eye, and then slid down his cheek.

'Soon . . . be good . . . don't forget to write . . .' His words were interrupted by the whistle of the train as it prepared to pull out. Everything was happening too rapidly as he kissed each of them, and then squeezed Edwina close to him. 'Take care . . . I'll be alright . . . I'll be back soon, Win . . . oh, God . . . I'll miss you so . . .' His voice broke on the words.

'Stay safe,' she whispered, 'come home soon . . . I love you . . .' And then, they hurried to the platform as the conductor shouted, 'All aboard.' She held Teddy close to her, and George stood holding Alexis's and Fannie's hands, as slowly, relentlessly, the train moved out of the station.

Edwina felt a terrible pull at her heart, and prayed that he would come home safely. And then they all waved and he was gone, and as the train sped away, they couldn't see the tears rolling down Phillip's cheeks. He was doing what he knew he had to do . . . but God . . . he was going to miss them . . .

21

It seemed like an endless wait for him. He wrote to Edwina and the children occasionally, and by winter, Phillip was in France, at the battle of Cambrai. His unit was fighting with the British there and for a while, they were doing well, better than the nearly half million who had died at the battle of Passchendaele. But ten days after the battle of Cambrai began, the Germans counter-attacked, and the British and Americans lost ground and had to fall back, almost to where they had started.

The loss of men was staggering and as Edwina read accounts of the battles there, her heart would sink, thinking of her brother. He wrote of mud and snow and discomfort everywhere, but he never told them how afraid he was, or how disheartened, watching men die by the thousands day after day, as he prayed that he'd survive it.

In the States, there were the recruitment posters everywhere, showing a stern invitation from Uncle Sam. And in Russia the Czar had fallen that year, and the imperial family was in exile.

'Is George going to be a hero too?' Fannie asked one day just before Thanksgiving, as Edwina trembled at the thought of George following in Phillip's footsteps.

'No, he's not,' she answered somberly. It was hard enough worrying about Phillip night and day, and fortunately George had been at Harvard since the fall. He called infrequently, and his rare letters showed that he was happy there, although he talked of none of the things Phillip had when he'd been there. He talked of the people he met, the men he liked, the parties he went to in New York, and the girls he dated constantly. But he also surprised Edwina by saying that he missed California. And he wrote a funny letter raving about the latest movies he'd seen, a new Charlie Chaplin called *The Cure*, and something with Gloria Swanson called *Teddy at the Throttle*. His fascination with films lived on, and he had written a long, technical letter about both films, telling how they could have been better. It made her wonder if he really was serious about going to Hollywood one day and making movies. But the world of Hollywood seemed a long, long way from Harvard.

Phillip was still in France with frostbitten fingers and men dying all around him.

Fortunately, Edwina was unaware of it, as they said grace and prayed for him at their Thanksgiving table.

'. . . and God bless George, too.' Teddy added solemnly, 'Who isn't going to be a hero, because my sister Edwina won't let him,' he offered by way of explanation, as she smiled at him. At seven, he was still a pudgy, cuddly little elf with a special attachment to her. Edwina was the only mother he remembered.

They spent a quiet day, and sat in the garden after their Thanksgiving meal. It was a warm, pretty day, and Alexis and Fannie sat on the swing, as Teddy kicked a ball from one to the other. It was odd now, with both of the big boys gone, and having only the younger children at home. Edwina suggested that they write to Phillip that night. And she hoped that George would call. He was spending Thanksgiving with friends in Boston.

Everyone was still full when they went to bed, and Edwina was still awake late that night, when she heard the doorbell. She sat up, startled by the noise, and then hurried downstairs before the persistent bell could wake the children.

She was still struggling into her dressing gown as she reached the front door, in bare feet with her hair in braids, and she opened the door cautiously, expecting to see one of George's friends, drunk and looking for him, having forgotten that he'd gone to Harvard.

'Yes?' she said, looking very young in the darkened hall, her face shining in the moonlight.

There was a man she didn't recognize outside, with a telegram in his hand, and she stared at him in surprise. 'Is your mother home?' he asked, adding to her confusion.

'I . . . no . . . I think you mean me.' She frowned. 'Who is that for?' But a finger of fear was tracing its way around her heart and she found herself short of breath as he read her name loudly and clearly. He handed the telegram to her, and scurried down the stairs like a rat in a bad dream, as she closed the front door and leaned against it for an instant. There could be nothing good in it. Good things did not come in telegrams shortly after midnight.

She walked into the front parlor then, turned on a lamp, and sat down slowly to read it. The envelope tore open easily in her hands, and her eyes raced over it as her breath caught and she felt her heart writhe within her. It couldn't be . . . it wasn't possible . . . five years before, he had survived the sinking of the *Titanic* . . . and now he was gone . . . 'regret to inform you that your brother, Private Phillip Bertram Winfield, died with honor on the battlefield today in Cambrai on 28 November 1917. We at the Department of the Army extend our condolences to your entire family . . .' and it was signed with a name she had never heard of. A sob tore at her throat as she read it a dozen times, and then stood up silently and turned the light off.

With tears streaming down her cheeks, she walked upstairs, and stood in the hall where he had lived, and they had grown, and knew that he would never come home again . . . like the others . . . five borrowed years he had lived after them, long enough to grow to be a man, and be killed by German soldiers.

And then, as she stood there, crying silently, holding the hated telegram, she saw a little face peering at her in the dark. It was Alexis. She stood there, staring at her for a long time, knowing something terrible was wrong, but not daring to approach Edwina. And then at last, Edwina saw her there and held out her arms, and instinctively Alexis knew that he was gone, and they stood there in the hall for a long, long time, until at last Edwina dried her eyes, and took Alexis to bed with her, where they lay clinging to each other like two lost children until morning.

22

'Hello? . . . Hello!' Edwina shouted across three thousand miles. The connection was terrible, but she had to reach George. She had already waited two days for him to get back to Harvard after the Thanksgiving weekend. And finally, at his end, someone answered. 'Mr Winfield, please,' she shouted into the phone, and then there was endless staccato again, while someone went to find him. And at last, George was on the line, and for an instant he heard only silence.

'Hello!' he shouted back at her, '. . . hello! . . . who is this?' He was sure that they had lost the connection, but at last she took a breath and spoke, not sure how to begin. It was hard enough telling him, without having to shout it over the long-distance wires, and yet she hadn't wanted to give him the shock of a telegram, or spend days waiting for a letter to reach him. He had a right to know, just as the others did. The children had cried for days. They were familiar tears to them, tears they had already shed once before, even if they didn't remember.

'George, can you hear me?' Her voice barely reached him.

'Yes! . . . are you alright?'

The answer was a hard one, and tears filled her eyes before she spoke, as suddenly it seemed a mistake to have called him. 'Phillip . . .' she began, and before she said another word, he knew, as he felt his blood run cold, and listened to her from Boston. 'We got a telegram two days ago,' she began to sob, which George knew was unlike her. 'He was killed in France . . . he . . .' suddenly it seemed important to tell him all the details, '. . . he died honorably . . .' And then she couldn't go on. She couldn't say another word, as the children stood on the stairs and watched her.

'I'm coming home,' was all he said, as tears rolled down his cheeks. 'I'm coming home, Win . . .' They were both crying then, and Alexis walked slowly upstairs, all the way to the top floor where she hadn't been in so long. But she needed to go there now, to be alone with her thoughts of her oldest brother.

'George,' Edwina tried to go on, 'you don't have to do that . . . we're . . . alright . . .' But this time, she was far from convincing.

'I love you . . .' He was still crying openly, thinking of Phillip and her, of all of them, and how unfair it was. Edwina had been right. She should never have let him go. He knew that now. Too late. For Phillip. 'I'll be home in four days.'

'George, don't . . .' She feared that they would take a dim view of it at Harvard.

'Good-bye . . . wait . . . are the little ones alright?' They were, more or less, except Alexis, who seemed very badly shaken. The others were clinging to Edwina for fear that it could mean she might die and leave them.

'They'll do.' She took a breath, and tried not to let herself think of Phillip and how he must have died, alone, in the freezing mud. Poor baby . . . if only she could have held him . . . 'See you in four days, then.'

She was about to tell him not to come, but he was gone by then, and she slowly set the phone down, and turned to see Fannie and Teddy sitting on the stairs crying softly, just above her. They came to cuddle with her then, and she took them back upstairs to their own rooms, but that night they slept with her, and eventually Alexis came back downstairs and joined them. Edwina had left her alone, knowing where she'd gone, and that she needed to be alone with her memories of Phillip. In some ways, they all did.

They talked about him until late that night, and all the things they loved about him. How tall and distinguished he had been, how kind, how serious about things, how responsible, how loving, and how gentle. There was a long list of attributes that came to mind, and as she thought about him, Edwina realized with a gash of pain again, how terribly she would miss him.

And as they huddled together late into the night, she realized that it was once again like being in the lifeboat, afraid, alone, clinging to each other in stormy waters, wondering if they would all find each other again. Only this time, she knew they wouldn't.

It was a long four days of quiet thoughts, and tears, and silent anger, waiting for George to come home, but when he did, the house came alive again, as he hurried up or down stairs, slammed doors, or rushed into the kitchen. It made Edwina smile just seeing him again, and when he walked through the front door when he arrived, he hurried out to find her in the garden. He strode toward her, pulling her close to him, and they stood together for a long time and cried for their lost brother.

'I'm glad you came,' she admitted later on, when the little ones were all tucked into bed upstairs. And then she looked sadly at George. 'It's so lonely here without him. It's different suddenly, knowing that he's . . . gone . . . that he's not coming back. I hate going into his room now.' George understood. He had gone in and just sat down and cried that afternoon when he'd gotten home. A part of him had expected Phillip to be there.

'It's so strange, isn't it?' he said. 'It's as though he's still alive somewhere out there, and I know that he'll be back someday . . . except he won't, Edwina . . . will he?'

She shook her head, thinking of him again, and how serious he had been, about everything, how responsible, and how he had always helped her with the children. Unlike George, who was always busy putting frogs into people's beds, except that now, she was grateful to see him.

'I used to feel that way about Mama . . . and Papa . . . and Charles . . .' Edwina admitted. 'That they would come back one day, but they didn't.'

'I guess I was too young to understand that then,' he said quietly, getting to know her better now. 'It must have been terrible for you, Win . . . with Charles and everything.' And then, 'You've never cared about anyone else, have you? I mean . . . after him . . .' He knew about Ben liking her, but he also knew that Edwina had never been in love with him. And he didn't think there had been any serious suitors since then.

She smiled and shook her head. 'I don't suppose I will love any other man again. Maybe that was enough in one lifetime. Just Charles . . .' Her voice drifted off as she thought of him.

'That doesn't seem fair . . . you deserve more than that.' And then, 'Don't you want children of your own someday?'

But at that, she laughed, and wiped the tears off her face that she had shed for her brother, 'I think I've had quite enough, thank you very much. Wouldn't you say five is sufficient?'

'That's not the same, though.' He was still looking serious and she laughed again.

'I'd say it's close enough. I promised Mama I'd take care of all of you, and I have. But I'm not sure I need more than that. And besides, I'm too old now anyway.' But she didn't look as though she regretted it. All she regretted was losing so many people she had loved so much. It made those who were left now even more precious. 'When do you have to go back?'

He looked at her for a serious moment before he answered. 'I want to talk to you about that . . . but not tonight . . . maybe tomorrow . . .' He knew she'd be upset, but he had made his mind up even before he'd left to come home to California.

'Is something wrong? Are you in trouble, George?' It wouldn't have been a total shock, in George's case, but now she smiled lovingly. He was still such a boy, and so full of life, no matter how serious he appeared. But he was shaking his head, looking faintly insulted.

'No, I'm not in trouble, Win. But I'm not going back either.'

'What?' She looked shocked. All the men in her family had graduated from Harvard. For three generations. And after George did, one day Teddy would go, and one day, their children.

'I'm not going back.' He had made his mind up, just as Phillip had when he went to war, and Edwina sensed it.

'Why?'

'Because I belong here now. And to be honest with you, I never did belong there. I had a good time, but it's not what I want, Win. I want something very different. I want the real world . . . something new and exciting and alive . . . I don't want Greek essays and mythological trans-lations. That was fine for Phillip . . . but it just isn't for me. It never was. I want something else. I'd rather go to work out here.' The suggestion shocked his sister, but she

232

already knew it would be pointless to try and dissuade him. Perhaps if she let him be, one day he'd go back of his own choice and finish. She hated to think of him not getting his diploma. Even Phillip had planned to go back and finish.

They talked about it for several days, and eventually she discussed it with Ben, and two weeks later, George began an apprenticeship at their father's paper. She had to admit that maybe for him, it made more sense, and with Phillip gone, now there would be no one else to run the paper. George was a long way from being there, but perhaps after a year or two, he would have learned enough to try his hand at it. God knew, there was no one else to.

And she smiled to herself as she watched him leave for the paper every morning. He looked like a child, pretending to be his father. First, he would fall out of bed, invariably late, and with his coat and tie askew, he would eventually appear at the breakfast table, just in time to tease and distract the children. Then, after spilling three glasses of milk, and feeding his oatmeal to the cat, he would grab two pieces of fruit, and fly out the door, telling her that he'd call her at lunchtime. He called her religiously every day, but usually to tell her a joke, and ask if she minded if he went out to dinner, which, of course, she didn't.

George's romances were legendary all over town, and as soon as people knew he was back, invitations poured in for him almost daily. The Crockers, the de Youngs, the Spreckleses, everyone wanted him, just as they had always wanted Edwina, but a lot of the time, she preferred to stay home now. She went out occasionally with him, and he made a very handsome escort, but Edwina no longer thrived on going to parties. But George enjoyed it all thoroughly, much more than he enjoyed his apprentice-ship at the paper.

She forced him to go to monthly meetings with her for several months, but then she discovered that he was out every afternoon, and careful investigation told her that he was sneaking out to go to the movies.

'For God's sake, George, be serious. This business is going to be yours one day,' she scolded in June, and he apologized, but the following month it was the same thing, and she had to threaten to cancel his salary if he didn't stick around and earn it.

'Edwina, I can't help it. It's not me. And everybody bows and scrapes, and calls me Mr Winfield, and I don't know anything about all this. I keep looking over my shoulder, thinking they must mean Papa.'

'So, learn it, dammit. I would, in your shoes!' She was furious with him, but he was tired of being pushed, and he said so.

'Why the hell don't you run the paper yourself, then? You run everything else, the house, the children, you'd run me if you could, just the way you used to run Phillip!' She had slapped him then, and he was aghast at what he'd said. He had apologized profusely but he had cut her to the quick and he knew it. 'Edwina, I'm sorry . . . I didn't know what I was saying . . .'

'Is that what you think of me, George? You think I run everything? Is that what it looks like to you?' There had been tears running down her face by then. 'Well, just exactly what did you think I should do when Mama and Papa died? Give up? Let all of you run wild? Who did you think was going to keep it all together for us? Aunt Liz? Uncle Rupert? You, maybe while you were busy putting frogs in everyone's bed? Who else was there, for heaven's sake? Papa was gone, he had no choice.' She was sobbing by then and something she had held back for years was about to escape her. 'And Mama chose to go with him . . . they wouldn't let him or Phillip in the boats because they were men . . . you were the last little boy to get in a lifeboat that night because the officer in charge wouldn't let boys or men on . . . so Papa had to stay . . . but Mama *wanted* to stay with him. Phillip said she wouldn't get in the last lifeboat that left. She *wanted* to die with Papa.' It was something that had torn at her for five years. Why had Kate wanted to die with their father? 'So who was left, George? Who was there? There was me . . . and you, and you were only twelve years old . . . and Phillip, and he was only sixteen . . . that left me. And if you don't like the way I've done it, then I'm sorry.' She turned away from him then, with tears running down her cheeks in the room that had once been her father's office.

'I'm sorry, Win . . .' He was horrified at what he'd done. 'I love you . . . and you've been wonderful . . . I was just upset because this isn't me . . . I can't help it. I'm sorry . . . I'm not Papa . . . or Phillip . . . or you . . . I'm me . . . and this isn't.' There were tears in his eyes now too, because he felt he'd failed her. 'I just can't be like them. Harvard doesn't mean anything to me, Win. And I don't understand anything about this paper. I'm not sure I ever will . . .' He started to cry, and turned back to look at her. 'I'm so sorry.'

'What do you want then?' she asked gently. She loved him as he was, and she had to respect him for what he was, and what he wasn't.

'I want what I've always wanted, Win. I want to go to Hollywood and make movies.' He was not yet nineteen and the thought of his going to Hollywood to make films seemed ridiculous to Edwina.

'How would you do that?'

His eyes lit up and danced at the question. 'I have a friend from school whose uncle runs a studio, and he said that if I ever wanted to, I should call him.'

'George,' she said with a sigh, 'those are pipe dreams.'

'How do you know? How do you know I wouldn't turn out to be a brilliant producer?' They both laughed through their tears and a part of her wanted to indulge him, but a more serious side of her told her she was crazy. 'Edwina.' He looked at her pleadingly. 'Will you let me try?'

'And if I say no?' She looked at him soberly, but the disappointment on his face touched her deeply.

'Then I'll stay here and behave. But I promise, if you let me go, I'll come home and check on you every weekend.'

She laughed at the thought. 'What would I do with the women you'd drag along behind you?'

'We'll leave them in the garden.' He grinned. 'Well, will you let me try it?'

'I might,' she said slowly, and then looked at him sadly. 'And then what do I do with Papa's paper?'

'I don't know.' He looked at her honestly. 'I don't think I could ever run it.' It had been a headache to her for a long time, and one day soon, with no one strong enough to run it, it was either going to die quietly, or start costing them a great deal of money.

'I suppose I should sell it. Phillip was the one who really wanted to try his hand at this.' And God only knew what Teddy would do one day, he was only eight years old, and she couldn't hold on to it forever.

George looked at her with regret. 'I'm not Phillip, Win.'

'I know.' She smiled. 'But I love you just as you are.'

'Does that mean . . .' He didn't dare ask, but she laughed as she nodded and put her arms around his neck and hugged him.

'Yes, you wretch, go . . . desert me.' She was teasing him. He had come home to her when she needed him, seven months before when Phillip died, but she knew he would never be happy languishing at their father's paper. And who knew? Maybe one day he'd be good at making movies. 'Who is this man, by the way, your friend's uncle? Is he any good? Is he respectable?'

'The best.' He told her a name she'd never heard of, and they walked out of her father's office hand in hand. She still had a lot to think about, a lot to decide, but George's fate was sealed. He was off to Hollywood. And it sounded more than a little mad to Edwina.

23

George left for Hollywood in July, right after their annual trip to Lake Tahoe. They still went to the same camp they had gone to for years, borrowed from old friends of their parents', and Edwina and the children still loved it. It was a place to relax, and go for long walks, and swim, and George was still the master at catching crayfish. And this year, it was especially nice for them to be together, before he left on his Hollywood adventure.

They talked about Phillip a lot when they were there, and Edwina spent a lot of time trying to decide what she was going to do with the paper. She had already made her mind up to sell it, but the question was when.

And when they went back to San Francisco, she asked Ben to offer it to the de Youngs, two days after George had left for Los Angeles. The house still seemed to be in an uproar after he left, and his friends were still calling night and day. It was difficult to think of him having a serious career anywhere, but maybe Hollywood was the place for him if the stories one read were true, which Edwina doubted. There were always tales of mad movie stars draped in white fox, driving fabulous cars, and going to wild parties. He still seemed a little young for all that, but she trusted him, and she had decided that it was better for him to get it out of his system, and either make a success of it or forget it forever.

'Do you suppose I should wait before I sell the paper, Ben? What if he changes his mind and the paper's gone by then?' She was worried about it, but the truth was that the paper had been sliding downhill badly recently, along with its profits. It just couldn't survive anymore without her father, and George was far too young and too uninterested to take over.

'It won't last long enough for him to grow into it.' Ben was always honest with her, although he was sad to see her sell it. But there was just no point in keeping it anymore. Her father was gone, as was her brother Phillip, who might actually have done good things with it, and George had already demonstrated his lack of interest.

The de Youngs turned them down summarily, but in a matter of a month, they got an offer from a publishing group in Sacramento. They had been looking for a San Francisco paper to buy for quite some time, and the *Telegraph Sun* fit the bill perfectly. They made Edwina a decent offer, and Ben suggested that she take it.

'Let me think about it.' She hesitated, and he told her not to drag her feet, or the people in Sacramento might change their minds. The money they offered her was not fabulous, but it would allow her to live on it for the next fifteen or twenty years, and educate her remaining brother and sisters. 'And then?' she asked Ben quietly. 'What happens after that?' In twenty years, she was going to be forty-seven years old, with no husband, no skills, and no family to take care of her, unless George or one of the others decided to support her. It was hardly an idea that appealed to her, and she had to think about that now. But on the other hand, keeping the paper wasn't a solution either.

It made Ben feel sorry for her, but he would never have said as much to her. 'You have time over the next several years to make some investments, to save money. There are a lot of things you could do, with time to think about it.' And things that she could have done too, like marry him or anyone else. But at twenty-seven, marriage no longer seemed likely. She was far past the marrying age by then. Women just didn't suddenly get married at twenty-seven. And she no longer thought about it at all. She had done what she had to do, and that was that. She had no regrets. And it was only for the merest moment when George left that she looked into his face and saw the sheer excitement there, and felt as though life had somehow passed her by. But it was crazy to feel that, she knew. And she had gone home from the station with Fannie and Alexis and Teddy, and gotten busy with them on a project they were making in the garden.

She wouldn't have known what to do in Hollywood anyway, with all the movie stars and people he wrote to them about now. He made them roar with laughter with tales of women trailing rhinestones and furs, with wolfhounds running behind them, one of whom had lifted his leg on a starlet's pet snake, causing a near riot on the first set he'd been invited on. He was already having a good time, and he was knee-deep in the movie world within days of his arrival. His friend's uncle had actually come through, as promised, and had given him a job as an assistant cameraman, learning the trade from the ground up. And in two weeks he was going to be working on his first movie.

'Will he be a movie star one day?' Fannie had wanted to know shortly after he left. She was ten years old, and it all seemed fascinating to her. But it was even more so to Alexis, who, at twelve, was already a beauty. She had grown up to be even more beautiful than she'd been as a child, and her wistful reticence made her look almost sultry. It frightened Edwina sometimes to see how remarkable the child was, and how people stared when she took her out, and it still seemed to frighten Alexis. She had never really fully recovered from her parents' death. And the blow of Phillip's being killed as well had made her seem even more remote. And yet, with Edwina, she was always outspoken and intelligent and assured, but the moment there were strangers around her, she still panicked. And she had had an almost eerie attachment to George before he left. She followed him everywhere, and she sat on the stairs sometimes for hours at night, waiting for him to come back from parties. Ever since Phillip had died, she had clung to George, as in the distant past, she had clung to her parents.

She was anxious to know if they would go to Hollywood to visit him, and Edwina promised her they would, although he had promised to come up and visit them for Thanksgiving.

It was shortly before that when the paper finally sold, to the Sacramento people who'd wanted it. And dragging her feet had succeeded in bringing Edwina more money. It was a decent sum, but it was not a fabulous amount, and she knew that now she'd have to be even more careful. There would be no new clothes, new cars, no expensive trips anywhere, none of it things she would miss in any case. All she needed was enough to bring up the children. But it was emotional for her anyway, when the newspaper sold. And she went down on the last day before the sale, to sign the papers in her father's old office. It was occupied now by the managing editor he had left in his place. But in everyone's mind it was still Bert Winfield's office. And there was a picture of her on the wall as a child, standing next to her mother. She took it down, and looked at it. The rest of his things had been packed long since, and now she put this last photograph away, wrapped up carefully, and she sat down and signed the final papers.

'I guess that's it.' She looked up at Ben. He had come in specially to watch her sign them, and complete the transaction, as her attorney.

'I'm sorry it had to be this way, Edwina.' He looked at her and smiled sadly. He would have liked to see Phillip running it, but then again, so would Edwina.

And then as he walked out, 'How's George?'

She laughed before she answered, remembering the absurdities of his last letter. 'I don't think he's ever been happier. It all sounds a little mad to me. But he loves it.'

'I'm glad. This wasn't for him.' He didn't say it, but in his opinion George would have destroyed the paper.

They stood outside the paper for a long time, and she knew she would see him about other matters she consulted him on, but he walked her slowly to her car and helped her in with a feeling of nostalgia. 'Thank you for everything.' She said it softly. He nodded, and she started the car, and drove slowly home, feeling sad. She had just given up the paper her father had so deeply loved. But with him gone . . . and Phillip gone . . . it was finally the end of an era.

24

George came home for Thanksgiving as promised, full of wild tales and crazy stories of even crazier people. He had met the Warner brothers by then, and seen Norma and Constance Talmadge at a party, and he regaled the children with tales of Tom Mix and Charlie Chaplin. It was not that he knew any of them well, but Hollywood was so open, so alive, so exciting, and the film industry so new, it was open to everyone, he claimed, and he loved it. It was exactly what he had wanted.

His friend's uncle, Sam Horowitz, sounded like a character as well, and according to George, he was a shrewd businessman and knew everyone in town. He had started the most important studio in Hollywood four years before, and he was going to own the whole town one day, because he was so smart about what he did, and everybody seemed to like him. George described him as a big man, in stature as well as importance, and the fact that he had a very pretty daughter wasn't entirely lost on Edwina. According to George, she was an only child, who'd lost her mother as a little girl in a train disaster in the East, and she had grown up alone with her adoring father. He seemed to know a lot about the girl, but Edwina refrained from making comment as he told them one amusing story after another.

'Can we come and see you sometime?' Teddy asked with adoring eyes. His brother was a big man to him, more important even than a movie star! And George reveled in their excitement over what he was doing. It wasn't that he was that fascinated with the technical end of it, and being an assistant cameraman was only temporary, he assured them all, but one day he wanted to produce the films and run the studio, the way Sam Horowitz did, and he was sure he could do it. Sam had even promised him an office job within a year if he behaved himself and was serious about the business.

'I hope you work harder than you did at the newspaper,' Edwina reminded him, and he grinned.

'I promise, Sis. Harder than at Harvard too!' He was penitent about his sins, and he had found something he really loved. She was only sorry Phillip hadn't lived to see what his brother had undertaken. But then again, if Phillip were alive, George would probably still have been cutting classes at Harvard.

The war had ended a few weeks earlier, and Edwina and he talked about it during his few days in San Francisco. It seemed cruel that their brother had died only a year before. All of it seemed so senseless. Ten million dead among all the Allied countries, and twenty million maimed. It was a staggering toll that was difficult to even conceive of. And talking about the war in Europe reminded her that she hadn't heard from Aunt Liz in a long time, and she wanted to write to her, to tell her about George's new life in Hollywood, and give her news of the other children. She had been desolate when Edwina wrote to tell her of Phillip's death the year before, but she had hardly written to them since. Edwina imagined that it was because it had been so difficult to get letters out of England.

She wrote to her after George went back to Los Angeles, and it was after Christmas before she got an answer. By then, George had come home again, to celebrate the holidays with them, and tell them more stories about the stars he'd seen. Edwina noticed several more mentions of Helen Horowitz during his brief stay with them, and she suspected that George was very taken with her. She wondered if she should go down and visit him there or let him enjoy his independence without intruding. In a way, he was half boy, half man. At nineteen, he considered himself the consummate sophisticate, and yet she knew that in his heart of hearts, he was still a child, and perhaps he always would be. It was what she loved about him the most. When he was home he played endlessly with the children. He brought the girls beautiful new dolls, and a new dress for each, and a handsome bicycle and a pair of stilts for Teddy. And for Edwina, he had brought a fabulous silver fox jacket. She couldn't imagine wearing it, and yet she remembered her mother having one years before, and she felt glamorous and beautiful when she tried it on. And he had insisted that she wear it to the breakfast table on Christmas morning. He was always generous and kind, and endlessly silly, as he walked around the house on Teddy's stilts, and went out to greet their neighbors on them from the garden.

And he had already left again when Edwina finally heard from her aunt's solicitor in London. He had written her a very formal letter, and regretted to inform her that Lady Hickham had passed away in late October, but due to the 'inconveniences' of the last days of the Great War, he had been unable to advise her sooner. But he had been meaning to write to her anyway, as soon as things were sorted out, he said. As she undoubtedly knew, Lord Rupert had left his lands, and his estate, to the nephew who was the heir to his title. However, he had, quite understandably, left his personal fortune to his wife, and according to Lady Hickham's last will and testament, she had left all of it to Edwina and her brothers and sisters. He quoted a sum that, as closely as he could figure it, was an approximation of what she had left them. And Edwina sat staring at the letter in amazement. It wasn't an amount which would leave them rolling in tiaras and Rolls-Royces, but it was a very handsome sum, which would leave each of them secure, if they were careful with it, for most of their lifetime. For her, it was the answer to a prayer, because all of them were young enough to have jobs and careers one day, or for the girls to find husbands who would care for them at least, but Edwina knew she wouldn't. For her it would mean being independent until the day she died, and never having to be dependent on her siblings. And she read the letter again with silent gratitude to the aunt she had scarcely known and barely liked in the course of her last visit. As a final gift to them, she had saved them. It was a far greater amount than what Edwina had derived from the sale of the newspaper and carefully split into five accounts, one for each of them, but once divided it wasn't an enormous fortune. This was a great deal more.

'Good Lord,' she whispered to herself as she sat back in her chair in the dining room and folded the letter. It was a Saturday afternoon and Alexis had just wandered in and watched her read the letter from England.

'Is something wrong?' She was too used to tragedy and bad news, which too often came in telegrams or letters, but Edwina smiled as she looked up at her and shook her head.

'No . . . and yes . . . Aunt Liz has died,' she said solemnly, 'but she's left us all a very generous gift, which you'll be very happy to have one day, Lexie.' She was going to speak to her banker about the safest ways to invest it, for herself, and the children . . .

Alexis seemed unimpressed by the bequest as she looked seriously at Edwina. 'What did she die of?'

'I don't know.' Edwina opened the letter again, feeling guilty that she wasn't more upset by the loss of her mother's only sister. But she had always been so nervous and unhappy, and her last visit to them hadn't been all that pleasant. 'It doesn't say here.'

But it might have been the Spanish influenza. It had already killed so many that year, in Europe, and the States. It was a dreadful epidemic. She tried to figure out how old Liz had been then, calculating rapidly that she would have been fifty-one, as their mother would have been forty-eight that year. It was odd, too, that she had survived Rupert by so little. 'It was nice of her to think of us, Alexis, wasn't it?' Edwina smiled as Alexis nodded.

'Are we rich now?' Alexis looked intrigued as she sat down next to her, and Edwina smiled as she shook her head, but she herself certainly felt greatly relieved by the money Liz had left them. 'Can we move to Hollywood with George now?'

Edwina smiled nervously at the idea. 'I'm not sure he'd be too thrilled by that. But we can certainly paint the house.' . . . and hire a cook and a gardener . . . Mrs Barnes had retired the summer before, and except for cleaning help, Edwina had been doing it all herself to spare their funds now that they'd sold the paper.

But the idea of moving to Hollywood was not one that appealed to Edwina. She was happy where she was, and at almost thirteen Alexis was hard enough to keep track of in sleepy San Francisco. Men followed her everywhere, and she was beginning to respond flirtatiously to their advances. It was already a source of great concern to Edwina.

'I'd rather go to Hollywood,' Alexis announced matter-of-factly, with her wild blond mane framing her face and cascading over her shoulders. She still had the kind of looks that stopped people on the street, and wherever they went people stared at her, whereas Fannie had Edwina's quieter but perfectly etched features. It was odd to think about sometimes. Both of her parents had been handsome, but neither of them had had the shocking beauty of Alexis. And Phillip had been a good-looking boy. Teddy had some of that star-blessed quality to him, and George had rugged good looks like their father.

But the thought of taking Alexis to Hollywood filled Edwina with dread. It was exactly where she would most not have wanted to take her. All she needed were matinee idols trailing after her, thinking that she was twenty.

But when George called a few days later and she gave him the news about Liz, he suggested they come down to celebrate, and then he sounded suddenly apologetic.

'I'm sorry, Win . . . is that tactless of me? Should I be feeling sad or something?' He was so ingenuous that she laughed at him, she always loved the openness he had about his feelings. When he was happy, he laughed, and made others laugh with him, and when he was sad, he cried. It was as simple as that. And the truth was that none of them had ever been close to Aunt Liz and Uncle Rupert.

'I feel the same way,' Edwina confessed. 'I know I should be sad, and I guess in a little part of me, I am because she used to be close to Mama. But I'm excited about the money. It sure makes a difference knowing I won't have to be sitting on a corner with a tin cup in my old age.' She grinned and looked like a kid again as the children pretended not to listen.

'I'd never let you do that anyway.' He laughed. 'Not unless you cut me in on a share of it. Hell, who taught you everything you know?'

'Not you, you brat! Cut you in on a share, my eye!' But they were both laughing and happy. He invited them to come down again, and as a lark, she agreed to come down during the children's Easter vacation.

And when she hung up the phone, Teddy looked at her, much impressed, and asked if she was really going to sit on a corner with a tin cup, and she laughed out loud.

'No, I'm not, you little eavesdropper! I was just teasing George.'

But Alexis had picked up something much more interesting in the conversation, and she was beaming at her older sister. 'Are we going to Hollywood to visit George?' She stood there looking like a vision in a dream, and Edwina wondered again if she was making a mistake taking her there, but they were all so excited, and after all, they were only children. It didn't matter that Alexis looked twice her age, and men chased after her constantly. Edwina would be there to protect her.

'Maybe. If you behave yourselves. I told George we might go for Easter.' In unison, they let out a scream and jumped up and down, while Edwina laughed with them. They were good children, and she had no regrets about her life. Everything really seemed very simple.

She heard from her aunt's solicitor two more times, and he inquired if there was any possibility she'd like to come to Havermoor herself to settle things and see it for a last time before it passed into Lord Rupert's nephew's hands, but Edwina wrote back to tell him there was absolutely no possibility of her coming to England. She did not explain why. But Edwina had absolutely no intention of ever getting on a ship again. Nothing on this earth could have induced her to go over. She sent a polite letter to him explaining that due to her obligations to her family, she was unable to go to England at this time, which he in turn assured her presented no problem whatsoever. The very thought of going over there made her shudder.

They marked the anniversary of their parents' death, as they always did, with a quiet church service, and their own private memories of them. But George didn't come home for it that year. It had been seven years since they'd died, and he couldn't get the time off from the movie he was currently making. He sent Alexis a birthday gift, a new dress with a matching coat. They always celebrated her birthday on the first of April now, because celebrating it on the day the *Titanic* had gone down was just too painful.

She turned thirteen that year, and Edwina bought her a new grown-up dress for their trip to Hollywood, and Alexis was justifiably proud of it. They had bought it at I. Magnin, and it was sky-blue taffeta with a delicate collar and a matching jacket, and when Edwina saw her in it she almost cried at the sheer beauty of her. Alexis stood there, smiling at her, with her silky blond hair piled up on her head, and she looked just like an angel.

They were all beside themselves as they boarded the train to Los Angeles a few days after that. 'Hollywood, here we come!' Teddy shouted excitedly as they pulled slowly out of the San Francisco station.

25

Their visit to George in Hollywood was beyond even Alexis's wildest expectations. He picked them up at the station in a borrowed Cadillac, and drove them to the seven-year-old Beverly Hills Hotel, a palace of luxury perched on a hilltop. He assured them that all the movie people stayed there, and that at any moment they might run into Mary Pickford, Douglas Fairbanks, or even Gloria Swanson. They even saw Charlie Chaplin arrive, being driven by his Japanese chauffeur. Fannie and Alexis were staring everywhere, and Teddy was so excited about the cars people drove that he almost got run over several times, and Edwina was constantly grabbing him and telling him to pay attention.

'But look, Edwina! It's a Stutz Bearcat!' On the first day, they saw two of those, four Rolls-Royces, a Mercer Raceabout, a Kissel, and a Pierce-Arrow. It was almost more than Teddy could stand, but the clothes were what fascinated the girls, and even Edwina. She had bought herself a few new clothes when she'd gone shopping with Alexis, and she had brought the silver fox jacket that had been a Christmas gift from George, but she felt like her own grandmother now in the clothes she had brought from San Francisco. Everyone was wearing long, tight slinky dresses, and showing quite a bit more leg than Edwina was used to exposing. But there was something wonderfully exciting about being here. She let George talk her into buying several hats, and when they went to dinner one night at the Sunset Inn in Santa Monica, she insisted that her brother teach her the fox-trot.

'Come on . . . that's it . . . good God, my foot . . .' he teased, and he guided and they laughed, and she hadn't had so much fun in such a long time that she couldn't even remember when, and for just a fraction of a moment, she felt a chord of memory rip through her.

In some ways, George was so much like their father, and she remembered his teaching her to dance when she was a little girl, and George was only a baby. But she wouldn't let herself think about it now. They were having too much fun, and now she understood why George was so happy here. This was a world of excited, young happy people, bringing pleasure to the entire world with their wonderful movies. And the people who were involved in making them were young and alive and fun, and it seemed as though everybody down here was involved in making movies. She heard people talking about Louis B. Mayer, D. W. Griffith, Samuel Goldwyn, and Jesse Lasky. They were all making the kind of pictures that George was learning about with Samuel Horowitz. And Edwina was fascinated by all of it. But the children were even more excited when George took them to the latest Mack Sennett comedy and Charlie Chaplin movie. They thought they had never had so much fun. He took them to Nat Goodwin's Café for lunch in Ocean Park, and with Edwina's permission he even took them to the forbidden Three O'Clock Ballroom in Venice, and Danceland in Culver City. And when they drove back to town, he took them all to the Alexandria Hotel at Spring and Eighth to see the stars dining there. And they were lucky that night, Gloria Swanson and Lillian Gish were there, and Douglas Fairbanks with Mary Pickford. It was rumored that their romance was serious, and Edwina just beamed as she watched them. It was even better than going to the movies.

He took them to the Horowitz studios as well, and the children watched for a whole afternoon as he worked on a film with Wallace Beery. Everything seemed to move unbelievably quickly, and George explained to her that they could complete a movie in less than three weeks. He had already worked on three since he'd been there. He wanted to introduce her to Sam Horowitz, too, but he was out that day, and George promised to introduce Edwina to him later.

That night, he took them all to the Hollywood Hotel, where they had dinner, and the children looked around them in awe at the elegance of the decor, but they were even more impressed by what Teddy referred to as 'George's lady.' Helen Horowitz met them at the hotel in a shimmering white gown, her blond hair swept off her face, and her skin like cream that had just been poured as the white dress molded her amazing body. She was almost as tall as George, but she was reed-thin, and very shy. She was eighteen years old, and the dress had been made for her by Poiret in Paris, she explained innocently, as though everyone had their dresses made there. She was polite and shy, and in a funny innocent yet sophisticated way, she reminded Edwina of Alexis. She had the same ethereal beauty and the same gentle ways, and she seemed to be totally unaware of her own effect on those around her. She had grown up in Los Angeles, but her father apparently didn't like her spending a lot of time with people 'in the business,' and she much preferred riding horses anyway. She invited them all to ride at their ranch in the San Fernando Valley. But Edwina had gently explained that Alexis was afraid of horses. Teddy would have been happy to have gone, but he was content enough staring at the cars they saw everywhere. Edwina was beginning to wonder how she would ever get him to settle down again in San Francisco.

'Have you known George long?' Edwina asked, watching her. She was so beautiful, and in a funny way, also very simple. She had no conceited airs, she was just a very lovely girl, in a very expensive dress, and she looked as though she was very taken with Edwina's brother. It was heady stuff, and he was very gentle with her. And Edwina watched them as they danced. There was something very sweet about the pair, something wonderfully striking and healthy and young and innocent. They were two people totally unaware of their own beauty. And as Edwina watched, she realized how much George had grown up since he left home. He was truly a man now.

'It's a shame my father's out of town,' Helen said. 'He's in Palm Springs this week, we're building a house there,' she announced, as though everyone did. 'But I know he would have liked to meet you.'

'Next time,' Edwina said, watching George again. He had just met some friends, and he brought them all over to meet Edwina. They were all a racy crowd, and yet they didn't look like bad people. They just looked like they were having fun. They were in a business which almost required it, and which brought fun to thousands of other people. And whatever it was that they did, or didn't do, it was easy to see how much George loved it.

The children hated to leave, and after agreeing to extend their stay by a few days, they went back to the studio to watch him work again, and on that particular day one of the directors asked Edwina if she would allow Alexis to appear in a movie. She hesitated, but much to her surprise, George shook his head, and when he declined, Alexis was in dark despair almost until they left. But when

Edwina and George talked about it later, he told her that he thought it would have been the wrong thing for her.

'Why let them exploit her? She doesn't even know what she looks like. It's fun down here. But it's for grown-ups, not children. If you let her do this now, she's going to want to come down here and go wild. I've seen it happen, and I don't want that for her. Neither would you, if you could see it.' She didn't disagree with him, but she was surprised at his conservative position *vis-à-vis* his sister. For a boy of nineteen years, nearly twenty, he reminded her more than once, he was surprisingly mature, and he seemed to fit in extremely well in the sophisticated life of Hollywood. She was proud of him, and she was suddenly doubly glad that she had sold the paper. If this was what he wanted, then he would never have been happy there. She had done the right thing. And so had he, when he had come to live here.

The children were despondent when they checked out of the Beverly Hills Hotel, and they made her promise that they would come back often.

'How do you know George will want us to?' she teased, but he looked over their heads at her and made her promise that she would come down and bring them.

'I should have my own place by then, and you can even stay with me.' He was planning to buy a small house with the money he had inherited from Aunt Liz. But for the moment he was still sharing an apartment with a friend in Beverly Hills, just outside the city. There were a lot of things he still wanted to do, and he knew he had a lot to learn, but he was excited about all of it, and for the first time in his life, he wanted to be a diligent student. Sam Horowitz had given him the chance, and he was going to do everything he could to live up to his expectations.

He took them all to the train station then, and the

children all waved as they left. It was like a whirlwind that had come and gone for them, an exciting dream, a flash of tinsel that was suddenly gone, as they sat staring at each other on the train, wondering if it had ever happened.

'I want to go back there again one day,' Alexis said quietly as they rolled toward San Francisco.

'We will.' Edwina smiled. She had had the best time she'd had in years, and she felt eighteen herself again, instead of nearly twenty-eight. Her birthday was in another week, but she had just had enough celebration to last her for the year. She smiled to herself as Alexis looked at her intently.

'I mean I'm going back there to live one day.' She said it as though making a plan that nothing in this world could interfere with.

'Like George?' Edwina tried to make light of it, but there was something in Alexis's eyes that told her she meant it. And then, halfway home, Alexis looked at her again with a puzzled frown.

'Why didn't you let me be in the movie that man asked me to be in?'

Edwina tried to make light of it, but Alexis had that same intent look in her eyes that she had had for days. It was a look of intensity and purpose that Edwina had never seen there. 'George didn't think it was a good idea.'

'Why not?' she persisted, as Edwina busied herself rolling up Fannie's sleeves and then glanced out the window before she looked back at Alexis.

'Probably because that's a world for grown-ups, Alexis, people who belong there, not amateurs who get hurt doing things they don't understand.' It was an honest answer after giving it some thought, and Alexis seemed to accept it for the moment.

'I'm going to be an actress one day, and nothing you do will ever stop me.' It was an odd thing to say, and Edwina frowned at the vehemence of the child's words.

'What makes you think I'd try to stop you?'

'You just did . . . but next time . . . next time will be different.' She sat looking out the window then, as Edwina stared at her in amazement. And who knew? Maybe she was right. Maybe she'd go back one day and work with George. She had a feeling that he was going to make it. She found herself wondering about Helen, too, about what she was really like, and how much she cared about George and if it might be serious one day. There was a lot for all of them to think about on the way home. And eventually, Edwina fell asleep listening to the wheels as they carried them home, and on either side of her, the younger children slept, leaning their heads against her shoulders. But across from them, Alexis sat staring out the window most of the way home, with a purposeful look that only she understood, and the others could only guess at.

26

The next four years in Hollywood were exciting years for George and the people who had become his friends. The films made included *The Copperhead*, *The Sheik*, De Mille's *Fool's Paradise*, his comedy *Why Change Your Wife?*, and the budding movie industry rapidly turned to gold for everyone involved. With Sam Horowitz teaching and protecting him, George had an opportunity to work on dozens of important movies, and from cameraman he went to third assistant director, and eventually, he began producing, which had always been his dream. The promise he had made Edwina four years before when he first left for Hollywood in 1919, was a reality for him by 1923.

Early on, Horowitz had even loaned him out to Paramount and Universal, and George knew everyone now, but most of all he knew his business. And like the Warner brothers that year, Sam Horowitz had just taken out incorporation papers, and hired several writers and directors. And Sam was the first to go to Wall Street and interest serious investors by convincing them that in Hollywood there was real money to be made. Mary Pickford and Douglas Fairbanks had joined D. W. Griffith and Charlie Chaplin to form United Artists, and there were similar groups forming too. It was an exciting era to be involved down there, and Edwina loved hearing about it. It still amazed her that her little brother's wild dreams had come true. And he'd been right, it was certainly a far cry from running their father's paper, and this was much more his style than staying in sleepy San Francisco would have been.

Edwina and the children went down to visit him two or three times a year, and stayed in his house on North Crescent Drive. He had a butler, a cook, and an upstairs and a downstairs maid. He was quite the man about town, and Fannie insisted that he was more handsome than Rudolph Valentino, which only made him laugh. But Edwina had long since noticed that the girls around Hollywood seemed to think so too. He took out dozens of actresses and starlets, but the only girl he seemed to really care about was Helen Horowitz, his mentor's daughter. She was twenty-two years old by then, and even more beautiful than Edwina had thought her when they first met. She had a startling sophistication about her now, and the last time Edwina had seen her with George, she had worn a skin-tight silver lamé dress that took people's breath away as she sauntered casually into the Cocoanut Grove on George's arm. She seemed oblivious to the stares and the cameras, and Edwina asked him later why Helen was never in her father's movies.

'He doesn't want her having any part of all that. It's all right as long as she's on the sidelines. I suggested the same thing to him years ago, but he wouldn't have it. I guess he's right. Helen's untouched by all this. She likes hearing about it, but she just thinks it's funny.' And something about the way he talked about her always suggested to Edwina that something might come of their friendship one day, but thus far nothing more than a longtime romance ever had, and Edwina didn't want to press it.

Edwina had just taken the children to see *Hollywood* at home in San Francisco, and was arguing with Alexis about why she could *not* go to see *Loves of Pharaoh*, when the telephone rang, and it was George calling from Los

Angeles. He wanted Edwina to come down and go to the premiere of his biggest movie with him. They had borrowed Douglas Fairbanks for it, and he said that the opening parties would be terrific.

'It'll do you good to get away from the little monsters for a while.' Once in a while, he liked to bring Edwina down alone. But the outcry was too great this time to allow it, and finally two weeks later, Edwina left for Hollywood with all of them in tow. Alexis was seventeen by then and just as lovely as Sam Horowitz's daughter, except that her hair wasn't bobbed, and she had never worn silver lamé. But she was still a strikingly beautiful girl, now even more so. And people still stared wherever she went. Alexis was a beauty. And it was all Edwina could do to keep her suitors from knocking down their door. She had no fewer than five or six admirers at any given time, but she was still a relatively shy child, with a fondness for Edwina's much older friends because she felt safer with them. Fannie was fifteen, and surprisingly domestic. She was happy in the garden and baking cakes, and she was happiest when Edwina was too busy doing other things to run the house. Edwina had made several wise real estate investments, and now and then she had to go somewhere to check on them with Ben. He had long since forgotten his romantic dreams about Edwina, and now they were only good friends. He had married two years before, and Edwina was pleased that he seemed very happy.

And at thirteen, Teddy was already talking about going to Harvard. He liked Hollywood, but what really appealed to him at this point was running a bank. It seemed an odd choice for a thirteen-year-old child, but he had the solidity of their oldest brother, and he reminded her of Phillip much of the time. George was the only one thus far with a wild flair for the unexpected, but for him the quixotic world of Hollywood was exactly what he needed.

They stayed at the Beverly Hills Hotel this time, because George had other houseguests, but the children, as Edwina still called them, much to Alexis's disgust, thought it more exciting at the hotel. Pola Negri was staying there, Leatrice Joy, Noah Beery, and Charlie Chaplin. And Teddy went crazy when he saw Will Rogers and Tom Mix in the lobby.

And Edwina was very flattered when her brother invited her to the opening gala at Pickfair. She bought an incredible gold lamé Chanel dress, and in spite of her age, she felt like a young girl. She was thirty-one years old, soon to be thirty-two, but she hadn't really changed in years. Her face was smooth and unlined, her figure even better than it had been years before. She had had her shining black hair cut in a shingled bob that year, at her brother's insistence, and she felt very chic in the gold dress, as they walked into the house Douglas Fairbanks had built for Mary Pickford as a wedding gift three years before. They seemed very happy there, and it was one of those rare marriages that worked in spite of the glamorous world they lived in. Few relationships seemed to last from one of Edwina's visits to the next, except this one.

'Where's Helen?' she asked George as they stood in the garden at Pickfair, drinking and watching the others dance. He hadn't mentioned her this time, which for George was very rare. He seemed to go everywhere with her, everywhere that mattered to him, although they still saw other people, but it was Helen who made him smile, Helen he cared about when she had the smallest problem or the merest cold, Helen who had his heart. But he seemed in no particular rush to get married, and Edwina had always hesitated to ask him about it.

'Helen's in Palm Springs with her father,' he said quietly, and then he glanced at Edwina. 'Sam thinks we shouldn't see each other anymore.' It explained the sudden invitation to the premiere, and her absence now. Edwina had been thinking for several hours that this was a party he should have gone to with Helen.

'Why not?' Edwina was touched by the look in his eyes. Beneath the jovial exterior, he looked crushed, which was unlike him.

'He thinks that after four years of seeing each other, we should either be married or forget it.' He sighed and accepted a refill of champagne from a passing butler. He had drunk a little too much champagne, but ever since the onset of Prohibition three years before, everyone had. It was a favorite sport going to speakeasies and hidden bars, and at private parties, the bootleg liquor flowed like water. The Volstead Act had seemed to have turned a lot of innocent people into alcoholics. But fortunately, George didn't have that problem, it was just that tonight he was so damn lonely for Helen, and Edwina could see that he looked unhappy.

'Why don't you marry her, then?' She dared to say something she never had to him before, she had never wanted to press him, but maybe now was the time, and she had had a bit of champagne as well. 'You love her, don't you?'

He nodded, and smiled down at her sadly. 'Yes. But I can't marry her.'

Edwina looked startled. 'Why not?'

'Think of what everyone would say. That I married her to get in tighter with Sam . . . to tie things up with her father. That I married her for the money . . . for a job.' He looked unhappily at his sister then. 'The truth is that Sam offered me a partnership six months ago, but as I see it, it's the girl or the job. If I marry her, I almost have to leave Hollywood, so people don't think I married her for the wrong reasons. We could go back to San Francisco, I guess.' He looked at Edwina miserably. 'But what would I do there? I left four years ago, and I don't know anything about any other kind of business. Except for what I do here, I don't think I could get a job. And I spent the money from Aunt Liz, so how would I support her?' He had a good income there, probably even a great one, but away from Hollywood he had nothing. And he had spent the money he'd inherited from their aunt on a beautiful estate, fast cars, and a stable full of expensive horses. 'So if I marry her, we starve. And if I take the partnership with Sam, no Helen . . . I can't marry her, and become partners with Sam, it just looks too awful. It looks like nepotism of the worst kind.' He set down his glass again, and this time when the butler came by again, he covered the glass with his hand. He didn't even want to get drunk tonight. He just wanted to cry on his sister's shoulder, and he was sorry for not showing her a better time after inviting her down for the premiere.

'That's ridiculous,' she insisted, looking at the anguish in his eyes. 'You know the score with Sam. You know why he wants you to be his partner. Look at the compliment that is, at your age, that's unbelievable. You'd be one of the biggest success stories in Hollywood.'

'And the loneliest.' He laughed. 'Edwina, I just can't do it. And what if she thought I married her to get ahead? That would be even worse. I just can't do it.'

'Haven't you talked to her about any of this?'

'No. I only talked to Sam. And he said he'd understand whatever I decided, but he thinks the romance has gone on long enough. She's twenty-two years old, and if she doesn't marry me, he thinks she ought to marry someone else.' And he was not yet twenty-four and he had almost everything he wanted, except a partnership with the most powerful man in Hollywood, and the woman whom he loved as his wife. He could have had both, but somehow he kept insisting that he couldn't, and Edwina understood his fears about it, but she thought it could be worked out, and she spent most of the evening trying to change his mind. But George was adamant as they drove her back to the hotel finally in his Lincoln Phaeton. 'I can't do it, Win. Helen is not a bonus I get along with the business.'

'Well, dammit.' Edwina was getting exasperated with him. 'Do you love her?'

'Yes.'

'Then marry her. Don't waste your life going out with other girls you don't care about. Marry her while you can. You never know what's going to happen in life. When you have the chance for what you want, grab it.' There were tears in her eyes when she spoke to him, and they both knew she was still thinking of Charles. He was the only man she had ever loved, the only man she had ever thought of, and he was long gone, and with him, he had taken an important part of her life. 'Do you want the job?' she went on, determined to solve the problem that night, in spite of his reservations. 'Do you want the partnership with Sam?' she asked again, and he hesitated this time, but only for an instant.

'Yes.'

'Then take it, George.' Her voice softened and she put her hand on his arm. 'Life only gives you so many chances. And it's given you everything you ever dreamed of and more. Take it, love it, hold it, keep it, be grateful for everything you have. Do what you *want* to do . . . don't waste your life giving things up for ridiculous reasons. Sam is offering you a fabulous opportunity, and

Helen is the woman you love. If you ask me, I think you'd be crazy to give either of them up. You know that you're not marrying her to get closer to Sam. You don't have to. He's already asked you to be his partner. What more do you want? Go after it, and to hell with what people think. You know what, even if someone does think something about it, or even dares to say it, by next week they'll have forgotten. But you never will, if you give it up. You don't belong in San Francisco, you belong here, in this crazy business you're so good at, and one day Sam's studio will be yours, or you'll have your own. You're twenty-three years old, kid, and you'll be at the top of all this one day. You already are. And now you've got a girl that you love too . . . Hell,' she said, smiling at him as the tears spilled from her eyes, 'grab the gold ring, George . . . you've got it, it's yours : . . you deserve it.' He did, and she loved him. She wanted him to have everything that she had never had. She had no regrets about her life, but she had given up her own life, in a sense, for these children, and now she wanted each of them to have everything, all their dreams, and everything life had to offer.

'Do you really mean it, Sis?'

'What do you think? I think you deserve it *all*. I love you, you silly boy.' She rumpled the carefully slicked-down hair, and he returned the favor. He liked her hair in a bob, and she looked so pretty. It was a shame that she had never married, that there had been no one since Charles. And then, because of the champagne and the closeness of the moment, he dared to ask her something he'd wondered about for a long time.

'Are you sorry you never had more than this, Win? Do you hate your life now?' But he thought he knew the answer anyway, it was in her eyes.

'Hate it?' She laughed, and she looked surprisingly

content for a girl who had spent eleven years bringing up her mother's children. 'How could I hate it when I love you all so much? I never thought about it years ago, it was just what I had to do, but the funny thing is you've all made me so happy. I would have loved to be married to Charles, of course, but this hasn't been a bad life.' She talked about it now as though it were almost over. And in some ways, for her, it was. In five more years, Teddy would go to Harvard. Fannie and Alexis would probably be married by then, or on their way. And George's life was certainly on the right track, except for torturing himself just then, but five years from then it would be long solved. And she would be alone then, the children she had raised would be grown. It was a time she didn't like to think about now. 'I have no regrets,' she said to George as she leaned over and kissed his cheek. 'But I'd hate to see you miss out on spending the rest of your life with someone you love. Go to Palm Springs and get Helen, and tell Sam you'll be his partner, and forget about what people will think. I think it's great, and you can tell Helen I said so.'

'You're amazing, Win.' And later when he walked her into the hotel, he thought of what a great girl she was, and how lucky any man would have been to have married her. And there were times when he still felt guilty about her not getting married. He still felt that he and the children had taken so much from her. He was about to say something about it, when they both saw the same thing at the same time, and stopped. Alexis was walking across the lobby in a gray satin evening gown that was Edwina's, her hair piled high on her head, held back by a spangled headband with a white feather that she had concocted from somewhere, and she was on the arm of a tall handsome man whom George recognized, and

Edwina didn't. They were obviously coming home from somewhere, and Alexis had not yet spotted George and Edwina.

'My God,' Edwina whispered, thunderstruck, she had thought that Alexis was at home in bed, while they were at the party. 'Who is that?' He looked to be about fifty years old, and he was undeniably good-looking, but he was three times her sister's age, and he looked more than a little drunk, and very taken with Alexis.

George's face was set as he advanced across the lobby, speaking in an undertone to Edwina. 'His name is Malcolm Stone, and he's the biggest son of a bitch I know. He goes after young girls all the time, and I'll tell you one thing, I'll kill the bastard before he gets Alexis.' It was unlike him to use language like that or lose his temper around his sister, and Edwina was momentarily stunned. George looked as though he was going to murder him. 'He's a big new star down here, or at least that's what he thinks. He's only been in a couple of pictures so far, but he has big ideas. And when he's not working, he keeps busy with the ladies, mostly other people's wives or daughters. Very young ones seem to be his specialty.' And the way he was looking at Alexis said that George wasn't wrong. He had also had an eye on Helen, which had seriously irritated George several weeks before, and he wanted her for all the reasons George didn't. Because she was beautiful and rich, and because he wanted a conduit to Sam, her father.

'Stone!' George's voice boomed out across the lobby, and the pair stopped and Alexis turned, with a look of terror as she saw George. She had wanted to get home before they did, but she had had such a good time dancing at the Hollywood Hotel that they'd forgotten the time. She had met Malcolm several times in the lobby, and when they'd introduced themselves eventually, the third time they met, he had recognized her name. He had asked her if she was related to George Winfield of Horowitz Pictures, and when she said she was, he had taken her to lunch at the hotel. Edwina had been at the La Brea tar pits with the children that day, but Alexis had stayed at the pool to enjoy the sunshine.

'Just exactly what are you doing with my sister?' George spat the words at him as he strode across the room and stood in front of Malcolm Stone.

'Absolutely nothing, dear boy, except having a lovely time. It has all been very aboveboard, hasn't it, my dear?' He had a phony English accent and Edwina could see from where she stood that Alexis was smitten by him. For a shy child, she had a strange affinity for older men. 'Your sister and I have been dancing at the Hollywood Hotel, haven't we, my dear?' Malcolm smiled down at her, but only Alexis didn't see that the look in his eyes was anything but benign.

'Are you aware that she is not quite seventeen years old?' George was absolutely steaming, and Edwina was equally upset. It was very wicked of Alexis to have snuck out while they were gone.

'Aha.' Stone smiled down at the girl. 'I believe there's been a little misunderstanding.' He gently took her hand from his arm, and offered it to George. 'I believe we said that we were about to have our twenty-first birthday.' Alexis flushed beet red with embarrassment, but in truth Malcolm Stone didn't look as though he cared. It was only embarrassing to have her age pointed out to him by her older brother. He had been aware all night long that she was far younger than she had claimed to him, but she was a beautiful child, a pretty girl, and being seen with her couldn't do any harm. 'Sorry, George.' He looked far more amused than penitent. 'Don't be too hard on her, she's a very charming young girl.'

George didn't mince words with him as they stood there. 'Stay away from her.'

'Of course, as you say.' He bowed low to the three of them, and walked quickly away.

George stood staring at her then, and grabbed her arm as they hurried toward Edwina's cottage, and Alexis had begun to cry as her older sister frowned. 'What ever possessed you to go out with him, for heaven's sake?' George was furious with her, which was rare for him. He was always his younger siblings' benefactor, intervening for them when he thought Edwina was being too severe. But not this time. This time he would have liked to give Alexis a good spanking, except that she was far too old for that, and, of course, Edwina wouldn't have let him. But he wanted to strangle her for falling prey to a man like Malcolm Stone. 'Do you know what he is? He's a phony and a four-flusher! He's crawling his way around Hollywood to get ahead, and he'll use anyone he can!' George was well acquainted with the world he lived in, and men like Malcolm Stone were all over town, a dime a dozen.

But Alexis was sobbing openly by then as she wrenched away her arm. 'He is *not* what you say he is! He's sweet and kind, and he thinks I should be in movies with him. You've never said that to me, George!' she said accusingly as the tears poured down her face, and in his estimation Malcolm Stone was anything but 'sweet and kind'. He was a snake of the very worst species.

'You're damn right I've never said that to you! Do you think I want you hanging around people like him? Don't be ridiculous! And look at you, you're a baby! You don't belong down here, or in pictures, at your age!'

'That's the meanest thing you've ever said to me!' she wailed, as George almost dragged her into the living room of their suite and she collapsed sobbing into a chair as Edwina watched them.

'May I interrupt to ask why you didn't ask my permission to go out with him, or even introduce us?' That had occurred to her from the first, and it worried her now. Ever since she was a child, Alexis had been going off on her own, and eleven years before it had almost cost her her life on the *Titanic*.

'Because . . .' Alexis sobbed even more vehemently, clutching her handkerchief, and drenching Edwina's dress, which she had 'borrowed' for her tryst. 'I knew you wouldn't let me.'

'That's sensible of you, Alexis. May I ask how old the gentleman is?' Edwina was clearly disapproving.

'He's thirty-five,' Alexis answered primly, and her brother shouted in derision.

'My eye! He's fifty if he's a day! My God, where have you been all your life!' George interrupted, but Edwina knew that wasn't fair, she was a child from a sleepy town compared to this hotbed of glamor and illicit behavior in the South Land. She couldn't be expected to identify roués and cads at a mere glance like her older brother who worked and lived here. 'Do you have any idea what someone like that will do with you?' Alexis shook her head, crying harder, and he turned to Edwina in exasperation. 'I'll let you explain that to her.' And then he turned back to his younger sister. 'And you'll be damn lucky if I don't send you home before your birthday.'

They had agreed to celebrate it in Los Angeles over her Easter holiday, but the rest of the week proved to be more than a little strained. Alexis was in obvious disgrace and Edwina had had several serious talks with her. The trouble was that she was a beautiful girl and she was far too visible to the men in Hollywood. Even here, everywhere they went, people stared at her, particularly men. She overshadowed everyone around her, even her sisters. And to complicate matters further, two days after her evening with Malcolm Stone, a scout approached her in the hotel lobby and asked if she would like to make a movie for Fox Productions. Edwina gently declined for her, and Alexis flew to their room in fresh gales of tears, accusing Edwina of trying to ruin her life forever. She took to her bed and that night George asked Edwina what was wrong with her, she had never been this way before, but he also hadn't lived at home for the past four years. And Alexis had never been the easiest child, and she wasn't now either. Although she was shy, and somewhat unaware of her dazzling looks, she was dying for a career in the movies.

'It's a difficult age,' Edwina said to George calmly when they were alone. 'And she's a beautiful girl. That's confusing sometimes. People offer her all kinds of treats, and we say she can't have them. Men run after her, and we say she can't go. In her eyes, it's not much fun, and we're all the villains. Or at least, I am.'

'Thank God.' He had never realized how hard it had been for Edwina. Bringing up children was not as easy as he had sometimes thought. 'What are we going to do with her now?' He acted as though she had committed a crime in Los Angeles, and Edwina laughed.

'I'm going to take her home, and hope that she settles down. And pray that she finds a husband before she's much older, and then he can worry about how pretty she is.' She laughed, and he shook his head in bewildered amusement.

'I hope I never have daughters.'

'I hope you have twelve,' she laughed. 'Speaking of which,' she said, looking at him pointedly, feeling like a much older sister again, 'what have you done about Helen? Why aren't you in Palm Springs?'

'I called and now they're visiting friends in San Diego. I left a message at the hotel, but I'm going to wait till they get back. I'm sorry you didn't get to see Sam, by the way.' Edwina had met him once, three years before, and she had liked him. He was an impressive man, with intelligent eyes and the face of a wise man, and everything about him, from his great height, to his powerful hand-shake, exuded power.

'I'll see him next time. But listen, you,' she said, looking at him severely, 'don't mess up your life. You remember what I said, and do the right stuff. You got that?' She grinned at him then, but they both knew she meant it.

'Yes, ma'am. You'd better tell your sister that too.' But after a day of crying about her blighted movie career, Alexis calmed down enough to enjoy her birthday. They had one day in Los Angeles left, and Edwina wanted to take the two youngest children on the set of George's latest movie. He was busy in the production office, but the children were able to meet Lillian Gish, which was the high point of their visit. And seeing him in his working environment allowed Edwina to ask him a question she'd been wondering about since the scout from Fox Productions approached Alexis.

'Would you ever let her do a picture for you?'

He thought about it for a minute and sat back in his chair with a long sigh. 'I don't know. I never thought about it before. Why? Are you her agent?'

Edwina laughed as he teased her. 'No, I just wondered. She seems to have the same fascination with all this that you did.' It was true, and she was certainly pretty enough to be a star. She was just a little young, but maybe one day . . . it would have cheered Alexis to know that.

'I don't know, Edwina. Maybe. But I see so much go on here. Would you really want her in the midst of all this?' He didn't. He wouldn't even have wanted it for his own children, if he had any. Just as Sam didn't want it for Helen. And as a result, George thought, she was a nicer person.

'Helen seems to have survived it,' she pointed out, and he nodded.

'That's true. But she's different. And she's not in the front lines. Her father would lock her up before he'd let her appear in a movie.' Edwina had often wondered why she wasn't, but that explained it.

'It was just a thought. Never mind.'

'Where is Alexis?'

'Resting at the hotel. She didn't feel well.'

'Are you sure?' He was suspicious of everything now, and all the men he saw looked like rapists, hell-bent on attacking his sister. Edwina teased him about it as she went back to the set to pick up the others.

George took them all out to lunch afterward, and he dropped them off at the hotel and went back to his office. But when they went back to the rooms, Alexis wasn't there, and Edwina sent Teddy to the pool to find her.

'She's not there. Maybe she went for a walk some-where.' He went back outside to see if he could see Tom Mix in the lobby again, and Fannie started to pack, to help Edwina. But by dinnertime, Alexis still hadn't reappeared, and Edwina was beginning to panic. She wondered suddenly if George had been right to be sus-picious, even though she hated to think that way about her younger sister. But Alexis had always been different

from the rest of them . . . shy . . . distant . . . removed
. . . afraid of everything as a small child, although she
was better now. But she had always clung to the adults in
her life, and she did now. She was desperately attached
to Edwina, and to George, and in some ways Edwina had
always felt that she had never recovered from Phillip's
death, even more than that of their parents. She seemed
to have an almost unnatural need to attach herself to her
friends' fathers and uncles and older brothers, not in a
sexual way, at least not in her mind, but it was as though
she were eternally searching for a big brother like Phillip,
or a daddy.

Edwina called George finally, at eight o'clock. He had
had plans for that night, and he was going to take them
to the station in the morning. And with fear in her voice,
she explained to George that Alexis was missing. She was
glad that he had not yet gone out, and he arrived at the
hotel in evening clothes to discuss the situation with
Edwina.

'Have you seen her with anyone?' Edwina said she
hadn't. 'Could she be with Malcolm Stone again? Do you
think she could be that stupid?'

'Not stupid,' Edwina explained, fighting back tears,
'young.'

'Don't tell me about young. I was young too.' He still
was, Edwina thought, smiling, although at nearly twenty-
four he didn't think so. 'I didn't disappear every two
minutes and chase around with fifty-year-old deadbeats.'

'Never mind that, what are we going to do, George?
What if something's happened?' But somehow, he didn't
think she'd been kidnapped or hurt, unlike Edwina, who
was convinced of it and wanted him to call the police.
But he hesitated to do that.

'If she's not hurt, and she's with Stone again, or

someone like him, the press is going to get hold of it, and make a big stink, and you don't want that either.' Instead he walked around the hotel, handing out big tips and asking questions, and in twenty minutes he had their answer. And he was fuming. She had gone to Rosarita Beach, with Malcolm Stone. He had borrowed a car, and left with a beautiful, very young blond girl, and taken her to the famous hotel where everyone went to drink and gamble and have illicit affairs, just across the Mexican border.

'Oh, my God . . .' Edwina burst into tears, and ordered the children into the other room. She didn't want them to hear it. 'George, what are we going to do?'

'What are we going to do?' he blazed. It was eight-thirty by then, and it would take him two and a half hours to get there, driving as fast as he could. It would be eleven o'clock by then, and with luck it wouldn't be too late . . . maybe. 'We are going to drive to Mexico, that's what we're going to do. We are going to get her. And then I'm going to kill him.' But fortunately she knew her brother better than that. At his orders, she grabbed a coat, and ran out the door after him a moment later, calling over her shoulder to Fannie and Teddy *not* to leave the room, no matter what, and they would be back very late.

Edwina flew through the lobby behind George, and he wasted no time flooring the car and heading south. And it was twenty to eleven when they got there. The hotel was a rambling affair on the beach, and there were expensive American cars parked all around it. People came down from Los Angeles all the time to get drunk and wild and more than a little crazy.

They walked into the hotel and George fully expected to have to pull every bedroom door off its hinges to find her, but they were still sitting at the bar, which was lucky. Malcolm Stone was gambling and very drunk, and Alexis was a little drunk and very nervous. And she almost fainted when she saw George and Edwina. George crossed the bar to where they were, in two strides, grabbed her by the arm, and literally yanked her off the barstool.

'Oh . . . I . . .' She couldn't even speak, it happened so fast, and Malcolm Stone looked up with bland amusement.

'We meet again,' he said coolly with a Hollywood smile, but George wasn't smiling at him.

'Apparently you didn't understand me the first time. Alexis is seventeen years old, and if you come near her again I'm going to have you run out of town and then put in jail. You can kiss your movie career goodbye right now if you come near her again. Now, are we clear this time? Do you understand me?'

'Perfectly. My apologies. I must have misunderstood the last time.'

'Fine,' George said, dropping his tailcoat on a chair, and aiming one punch at Stone's midriff, and the next at his chin before stepping back again. 'See that you don't misunderstand me this time.' And as Malcolm Stone knelt dazed on the floor as people stared at him in amazement, George picked up his coat, grabbed Alexis by the arm, and walked back out of the bar with Edwina behind him.

27

The drive back to Los Angeles was painful for all, but particularly so for Alexis. She cried copiously all the way, not because she was afraid of the punishment they would mete out, but mostly because she'd been frightened and embarrassed. But the humiliation they had caused was not quite as unnerving as the realization had been that Malcolm wasn't planning to take her home that night. She had just figured that out when George appeared in the bar, like a knight in shining armor. It had come a little close for her this time, and even though she liked Malcolm, and he treated her like a little girl, 'his little baby' he kept calling her, and it made her feel all warm and happy inside, it was a relief to be going home to the safety of her life with Edwina.

'You are never coming down here again,' George told her in no uncertain terms when they got back to the hotel, in addition to a barrage of reproaches he had pelted her with on the drive north from the Mexican border. 'You are unmanageable and you can't be trusted. And if I were Edwina, I would lock you up in a convent. You're just lucky you don't live with me. That's all I have to say!' But he was still spluttering when she went to bed, and he poured himself a drink with Edwina. 'Christ, doesn't she realize what that guy would have done? That's all we'd need, his little brat running around nine months from now.' He took a sip of the drink and collapsed on the couch as Edwina stared at him in disapproval.

'George!'

'Well, what do you think would have happened to her? Can't she figure that out?'

'I think she has now.' Alexis had explained it to her while she undressed and Edwina tucked her into bed like a sad, naughty child. It was difficult for Alexis, she was a woman, and yet still a baby. And Edwina suspected she always would be. The shocks in her life had taken their toll, and she needed more than anyone had to give. What she really needed was what she could never have. She needed a mommy and a daddy, and since she was six years old, she had never had them. And there had been the terrible night when she had thought she'd lost everyone, when they'd thrown her into the lifeboat with her doll, just moments before the ship sank.

'He told her he was going to bring her home tonight,' Edwina explained to George as he sipped his whiskey. It had been a long drive and a long night and his hand hurt from where he had hit Malcolm Stone. Edwina did not mention how impressed she had been by her brother's stellar performance. 'And she'd only just figured out that he'd lied to her when we turned up, like heroes in a movie.'

'She's damn lucky. Most of the time there are no heroes when you're dealing with people like Malcolm Stone. I swear, I'll kill him if he ever comes near her.'

'He won't. We'll be back in San Francisco by tomorrow, and by the time we come back again, he'll be gone, or he'll have forgotten all about her. This is quite a town you live in.' She grinned, and he laughed. It had all ended well at least, there was no harm done, and he was happy they had found her. 'Actually,' Edwina grinned mischievously, 'old as I am, I rather like it.'

'Stick around, Win.' He laughed at the look in her eyes.

If anything, she looked prettier in the excitement. Her eyes were shining and her bobbed hair framed her face, and he was reminded again, as he often was, of how lovely she was, and what a waste it was that she had never gotten married. 'Hell, if you stick around, maybe we'll find you a husband.'

'Terrific,' she laughed at him, it was not a high priority on her list of concerns. She was only interested in finding husbands for Fannie and Alexis, and at the moment, marrying him off to Helen. 'You mean like Malcolm Stone? What an incentive.'

'I'm sure there must be someone else around.'

'Great. Let me know if you find him. Meanwhile, my love . . .' She stood up and stretched. It had been a long night and they were both tired. 'I'm going home to San Francisco where the only excitement is a dinner party at the Templeton Crockers, and the only scandal is who bought a new car, and who winked at someone's wife at the opening night of the opera.'

'Christ,' he groaned, 'no wonder I moved down here.'

'But at least up there,' she said, walking him to the door with a grin and a yawn, 'no one has ever abducted your sister.'

'There's a point in its favor. Good night, Win.'

'Good night, love . . . thanks for saving the day.'

'Anytime.' He kissed her on the cheek then, and walked back to his car. His beloved Lincoln was covered with dust from their wild ride, and he drove slowly home, thinking about how much he missed Helen, and how fond he was of his older sister.

28

It was two months later when George came to San Francisco to visit them, and Edwina wondered why he had come. He hadn't called her in a while, and she had just assumed that he was busy. But he had come, it turned out, to tell her that he had proposed to Helen and she had accepted. He beamed when he told her, and she cried when she heard the news. She was happy for them, and he looked as though he had the world on a string.

'And the partnership with Sam?' She looked suddenly worried and he grinned boyishly. She knew how much his association with Sam Horowitz meant to him too, and she wanted him to have both. He deserved it.

'Helen said the same thing you did, and so did Sam. I talked it out with both of them, and Sam said I was crazy. He knew I was marrying Helen because I loved her, and he still wants me to be his partner.' He beamed and Edwina shouted with glee.

'Hurray! When are you two getting married?' It was June then, and Helen had insisted that she needed time to plan the wedding.

'September. Helen says she couldn't put it together any sooner than that. It's being directed by Cecil B. De Mille,' he laughed, 'we're hiring four thousand extras.' It was going to be a grand wedding in true Hollywood style, but he had never looked as happy. 'And the truth is, I came up here to talk to you about something else. I think I'm probably crazy to even consider it, but I want your advice.' She was flattered, and excited about his news.

'What is it?'

'We have a movie we've been saving for two years. We wanted just the right person to do it, and no one has turned up. And then Sam had a crazy idea. I don't know, Edwina.' He looked deeply worried and she frowned, not understanding what he was getting to as she watched him.

'What do you think about Alexis trying out for our movie?' She was stunned for a moment as he looked at her, they had laughed at the idea of the Fox Productions scout wanting her, and now he wanted the same thing. But at least with her brother in control, Edwina knew that no harm could come to Alexis.

'I know I'm crazy to even consider it. But she's so perfect for the part, and she's been driving me crazy, sending me letters, telling me she wants to be in the movies. And what do I know? Maybe she's right. Maybe she does have talent.' He felt torn, but also extremely tempted. And he knew she was perfect for his movie.

'I don't know.' Edwina hesitated, thinking about it. 'I've been wondering too. She's so desperate to be an actress. But when we were in Los Angeles two months ago, I asked what you thought about Alexis making movies one day and you didn't seem to like the idea then. What's different?' She wanted to be cautious, but she also trusted George.

'I know,' he said thoughtfully. 'I didn't want her exploited, and I still don't. But maybe if she signs an exclusive with us, we can control it. If,' he added, looking ominously at his oldest sister, 'we can control her. Do you think she'll behave herself down there?' He was still smarting from the experience of rescuing her from the clutches of Malcolm Stone, and he had no desire to do it again. The drive to Mexico with Edwina was one he would always remember.

'She would if we kept an eye on her. She needs to feel that someone's taking care of her and then she's fine.'

He laughed at his sister's words. 'She sounds like every other star I've ever met. She'll be perfect.'

'When would you want her to start?'

'In a few weeks, by the end of June. And she'd be through by the end of the summer.' It was perfect for the children's schedules, Edwina knew, because Alexis had just graduated and the others had already started their summer vacation. And Alexis had no desire to go on to college, few girls did, and she knew Fannie wouldn't either. But if Alexis was finished by the end of August, she could come home in time to get the others back into school in September. Teddy would be starting eighth grade and Fannie still had two more years of high school to finish at Miss Sarah Dix Hamlin's. 'It would screw up your plans for Tahoe this year, but you could all go to the Del Coronado for a few days and get some sea air, or Catalina. And you'll have to come down for the wedding anyway.' She smiled at the thought. 'What do you think? The real question, of course, is not where to spend the summer with the kids, it's whether or not we should expose Alexis to the demands and pressures of making a movie.'

Edwina was nodding, thinking about it, as she slowly circled the room and then looked out the window, into the garden. Her mother's rosebushes were still blossoming there, along with all the newer things she herself had planted. And then, slowly, she turned to face her brother.

'I think we ought to let her do it.'

'Why?' He wasn't sure himself, which was why he had come to San Francisco to discuss it with Edwina.

'Because she'll never forgive us if we don't.'

'She doesn't have to know. We don't have to tell her.'

'No,' Edwina agreed as she sat down again. 'But I think she'd be good at it, and I think she deserves more than San Francisco has to give her. Look how beautiful she is.' She smiled proudly at George and he grinned. Edwina sounded like a proud mother hen, but he felt the same way about all of them. 'I don't know, George, maybe we'll be sorry one day, but I think we should give her a chance. If she misbehaves, we'll bring her back and lock her up forever.' They both laughed at the thought, but then Edwina looked seriously at him. 'I think everyone deserves their chance. You did.' She smiled.

'And you?' He looked gently at her and she smiled again.

'I've been happy with my life . . . let's give her a chance.' George watched her and nodded slowly.

And just before dinnertime, they called her in. Alexis had just come in from a trip downtown, shopping with a friend from Miss Hamlin's. Neither she nor her younger sister was an avid student. Edwina, Phillip, and Teddy were the family 'brains,' according to their father years before, and George had certainly done well in Los Angeles, there was no denying that. With his quick mind and his easy ways, he had fallen into just the right thing, and not for a moment had he ever regretted leaving Harvard.

'Is something wrong?' Alexis looked at them nervously, when they called her in, and all George could think of was how beautiful she was and how perfect she was going to be for their picture.

'Noooo.' Edwina smiled gently at her. 'George has something to tell you, and I think you're going to like it.'

That made it more interesting, and a little less ominous to be called into the front parlor by her older siblings.

'You're getting married?' She had guessed, and he nodded and grinned happily at her.

'But that's not what this is all about. Helen and I are getting married in September. But Edwina and I have some plans for you before then.' For a moment her face fell, she was sure they were going to send her to some kind of finishing school, and she couldn't think of anything less amusing. 'How would you like to come to Los Angeles,' he began, and she looked a little more hopeful '. . . and be in a movie?' She stared at him for a long moment and then she sprang off the couch and ran to put her arms around him.

'Do you mean it? . . . do you mean it? . . .' She turned quickly to Edwina then. '. . . Can I? . . . can I really? . . . Oh, will you let me?' She was wild with joy, and George and Edwina were laughing, as she almost strangled him when she hugged and kissed him.

'Alright, alright . . .' He pulled himself free of her embrace and then wagged a finger at her. 'But I want to tell you something. If it weren't for Edwina, you wouldn't be doing this. I'm not entirely sure I would have let you after your little performance two months ago.' Her eyes dropped, as he reminded her of her near disgrace with Malcolm Stone, she was still embarrassed about it, although she defended it to Edwina. 'If you pull anything like that again,' he went on, 'I will lock you up and throw away the key, so you'd better behave yourself this time.'

She threw her arms around his neck and attempted to strangle him with gratitude again as he laughed at her. 'I promise, George . . . I promise I'll be good. And after the movie, will we live in Hollywood?' It was something they hadn't even thought of.

'I think your sister will want to come back here to put Fannie and Teddy back in school.'

'Why can't they go to school there?' Alexis asked matter-of-factly, but none of them was prepared to think about all of that yet, and then Alexis had an even better idea, much to George's chagrin. 'Why can't I live with you and Helen?'

He groaned at the thought, as Edwina laughed at him. 'Because I'd wind up divorced or in jail by Christmas. I don't know how Edwina puts up with all of you. No, you may not live with me and Helen.' She looked crestfallen for an instant, and then came up with an even better suggestion.

'If I'm a big star, can I have my own house? Like Pola Negri? . . . I could have lots of maids, and a butler . . . and my own car, just like yours . . . and two Irish wolf-hounds . . .' She had the entire scene set in her mind, and she drifted out of the parlor again as though in a dream, as George smiled and looked ruefully at Edwina.

'We may come to regret this, you know. I told Sam I'd sue him if this picture ruined my sister.'

'And what did he say?' Edwina grinned. She didn't know him well, but she liked everything she had heard about George's partner.

'He said that he'd already given to God and country, and now my sister and his daughter were my problem.' But George didn't look as though he minded.

'He sounds like a sensible man.' She stood up and got ready to go into dinner.

'He is. He wants to take us all out to dinner when you come to L.A. to celebrate our engagement.'

'Now that,' she said, kissing him on the cheek as she took his arm, 'I approve of.'

The children were heartily pleased when she told them at dinner that George and Helen were getting married. And they were all excited at the prospect of another trip to Los Angeles, and they were fascinated at the thought of Alexis's making a movie. Edwina had wondered briefly if Fannie would be jealous in any way, but her sunny little face lit up with delight and she ran around to hug Alexis and ask if she could watch, and then she looked at Edwina worriedly.

'We are coming back here, aren't we? I mean home, to San Francisco.' It was all she wanted, all that she loved, the home she had lived in all her life, and her comfortable pursuits there.

'I certainly plan to, Fannie,' Edwina said honestly. She thought it a far better plan than Alexis's idea of moving to Hollywood and acquiring Irish wolfhounds.

'Good.' She settled down happily in her seat again with a happy smile, as Edwina wondered how children born of the same parents could all be so different.

29

They went to Los Angeles two weeks after George had visited them, and this time they stayed with him. He didn't want Alexis going wild in the hotel again, and he thought that being in his large, rambling house would be easier for Edwina. He rented a car for her use while she was there, and Teddy immediately busied himself riding George's horses. Edwina was watching him ride the next afternoon, when a limousine drove up, and stopped very near her. It was a long black British Rolls, and for a moment, Edwina couldn't tell who was in it. She assumed it was one of George's friends, perhaps even a lady. But as the liveried chauffeur opened the door and stood back, she saw quickly that it was a huge man. He was tall, with broad shoulders, she saw that he was powerfully built as he stood to his full height in the summer sunshine. He had a mane of white hair, and he had an expectant look as he turned and studied Edwina. Her dark hair was cut short, and she stood looking very slim and tall in a navy blue silk dress that was elegant and discreetly set off her figure. She had been smoking a cigarette while she watched, and now suddenly she felt silly. The man appeared to be studying everything about her, and then suddenly she smiled, realizing who he was. She dropped the cigarette and held out her hand with an apologetic look.

'I'm sorry. I didn't mean to stare. I didn't realize who you were at first. It's Mr Horowitz, isn't it?' He smiled slowly, watching her. She had poise and charm, and she was a beautiful woman. And he had long since admired her, although he'd only met her once a few years before. But he liked the things George said, and what he believed in and stood for, and he knew that much of that was her doing.

'I'm sorry too . . .' He looked almost sheepish. 'For a moment, I was wondering what a beautiful young woman was doing here, visiting my future son-in-law.' But he recognized her now, and he couldn't help but admire her again. She was really lovely, and despite the simple dress, the lack of flashy clothes and jewels, she had a definite air of sophistication. She had made a point of buying some new clothes before she came back to Hollywood, so she wouldn't embarrass her brother. And he'd been impressed with what he'd seen. She had wonderful taste, just as their mother had, and now, thanks to Aunt Liz, Edwina had the money to indulge it.

'I wanted to welcome you to Los Angeles myself. I know how happy George is to have you here, before the wedding, and to watch them do the film. And Helen and I are very pleased that you're going to be here.' Although everything about him exuded power and strength, from his size to the way his chauffeur reacted to him as he watched his every movement, still there was a gentleness to the man, a kindness, a simplicity, which Edwina had already admired in Helen. There was no pretentiousness, nothing pompous, or rude. He was very quiet, very friendly, and in an interesting way very subtle. He came to stand next to her, and for a moment they watched Teddy ride. He rode very well, and he was a handsome boy. He waved happily at them, and Sam waved back. He had never met the younger children, but he knew they all meant a great deal to George, and Sam liked that about him. He also knew that Edwina had brought them up herself, and he admired her for that as well. And as he glanced at her cautiously, standing at her side, it was obvious that she was quite a woman.

'Would you like to come in for a cup of tea?' she asked him pleasantly, and he nodded, relieved not to be offered champagne at eleven o'clock in the morning. People in Hollywood drank too much, as far as Sam was concerned, and he had never liked it.

He followed her inside, and forced himself not to admire her legs as her new navy dress swayed, and her hips with it.

She asked the butler for tea for both of them, and then escorted Sam through the library, and into the south garden. There were pretty chairs and a table set up there, and it all looked very English.

'Do you like Los Angeles?' he asked easily, as they waited for the tea tray, which came very quickly.

'Very much. We always have a wonderful time when we come down here. And I'm afraid this time the children are even more excited, over this movie of Alexis's. That's quite an event for us. She's a very lucky girl.'

'She's luckier to have all of you.' He smiled. 'Helen would have given anything to have a family like yours while she was growing up, instead of being an only child, alone with her father.'

Edwina looked wistful for a moment, and in spite of the fact that she looked away, he was touched when he saw it. 'Both of our families have had their absences and their losses.' She knew that Helen had lost her mother when she was only a baby. 'But we manage.' Edwina smiled victoriously at Sam, over their tea, and he found himself admiring her again. She was an unusual girl, not just because she was pretty and well dressed, but there was a quiet strength to the girl that struck you the moment you met her. He had noticed it before, when he met her a few years ago, but now that he saw her again, she seemed even more impressive.

'What are you planning to do while you're here? Some sightseeing? A few plays? Visit with friends?' He was curious about her, and it was abvious that he liked her. He reminded her of his daughter in some ways, and yet she was obviously extremely independent, and she was laughing now at the naiveté of his question. He obviously knew nothing about Alexis.

'I am going to be keeping an eye on your star, Mr Horowitz.' She smiled and he grinned in answer. He knew what that was like, although Helen had always been a very docile girl, but nonetheless from time to time, even she had required a little closer supervision. 'She's with George today, which is why I'm here with the two younger ones. But from tomorrow morning on, I have my work cut out for me, as dresser, bodyguard, and mentor.'

'It sounds like hard work.' He smiled, setting down his cup and stretching his long legs out before him. And she was watching him too. She knew he was somewhere in his fifties, but he didn't look it, and she had to admit it he was extremely handsome. And part of his charm was that he didn't seem to know it. He was completely natural and totally at ease, and he looked up with added interest as Teddy left his horse and joined them in the garden. Edwina introduced him to Sam, and the boy was enthusiastic and polite when he shook the older man's hand, and then exploded with delight about the horses.

'They're fantastic, Win. I've ridden two of them, and they're just gorgeous.' The first one had been Arabian, and the stableboy had suggested Teddy try something a little tamer. 'Where do you suppose George got them?'

'I have absolutely no idea.' Edwina smiled happily and Sam grinned.

'He got one of them from me. In fact, the one you were just riding. He's a fine piece of horseflesh, isn't he? Sometimes I really miss him.' Sam was warm and friendly with the boy, just as he had been with Edwina.

'Why did you give him up?' Teddy was curious about everything, and absolutely crazy about horses.

'I thought George and Helen might enjoy him more. They ride together quite a bit, and I really don't have time. And besides,' he smiled ruefully at the child who looked so much like his sister, 'I'm getting too old to ride all the time.' He pretended to growl, and Edwina dismissed the thought with a wave of the hand.

'Don't be absurd, Mr Horowitz.'

'Sam, if you please, or you'll make me feel even older. I'm practically a grandfather!' he announced, and they all laughed and Edwina raised an eyebrow after a burst of laughter.

'Oh? Is there anything in particular I should know about this wedding?' But they were only teasing and he was quick to shake his head and reassure her. But he was looking forward to grandchildren, and hoped that George and Helen would oblige him soon. And he had always hoped that his future son-in-law wanted a large family like his own. Sam loved the idea of lots of children running around. He had always wanted more himself until . . . Helen's mother had died. And he had never remarried. 'I wonder what it'll be like to be an aunt,' she said pensively as she poured them both more tea. It seemed very strange to her. She was so used to having the children as her own, it was going to be very odd when they were someone else's.

Sam invited them to dinner at his home then. He had

come to tender the invitation himself, and assured her that she and all of the children were welcome.

'That would be a terrible imposition, Mr . . . sorry, Sam.' She blushed and he smiled graciously.

'Not at all. It would be an honor. Please be sure you bring Teddy, and Fannie, and Alexis, and, of course, George. Do I have all the names right?' he asked as he stood up to his full height and she looked up at him in amazement. He was very tall indeed, and very handsome. But it was absurd to keep thinking that about her future sister-in-law's father. 'I'll send the car for you at seven. I know how unreliable my partner can be about things like that, and he may want to come directly from the office.' Sam smiled at her and she nodded.

'Thank you very much.' She walked him back to his car as Teddy bounded beside them like an exuberant Irish setter.

'We'll see you tonight, then.' He seemed to hesitate for a long moment before shaking her hand and sliding back into the Rolls. And then a moment later, the chauffeur started the car, Sam waved, and he was gone, just as Fannie came out to see them.

'Who was that?' she asked, but with no particular interest.

'Helen's father,' Edwina said matter-of-factly, as Teddy continued to rhapsodize about the horses, and then stopped long enough to say how much he liked Sam, before going on to say that he wanted to try the Arabian again, but Edwina didn't think he should, and she warned him to be careful.

'I am.' He looked offended by her remark and she looked pointedly at her youngest brother.

'Not always.'

'Alright . . .' he conceded, 'but I will be.'

'I hope so.'

'Do we have to go out to dinner?' Fannie asked. She always preferred staying home, not unlike Edwina. But she was far too young to keep herself cooped up all the time and Edwina insisted that she join them.

'It'll be fun.' Edwina was sure of it. They were good people, and he had been incredibly nice to come to the house himself to ask them. 'And we're all invited.'

But Alexis was far more enthusiastic when she got home and all she wanted to know was what she should wear, preferably something of Edwina's. She was all excited about her day on the set. She had had fittings for all her clothes and she and George had signed the contract.

'How late can we stay?' she asked repeatedly while they dressed, and she almost fainted when she saw the elegant car that Sam sent to bring them.

George decided to drive his own, in case he and Helen decided to go out afterward, which sounded sensible to Edwina.

The Horowitzes had a beautiful home, and even Edwina was more than a little in awe when she saw it. It made even Pickfair look like a hovel. The rooms were enormous, the ceilings vast, the furniture was all antiques he had brought back from England and France, and there were wood-paneled rooms and marble floors and exquisite Aubusson carpets, and Impressionist paintings. And in the midst of it all, Sam Horowitz greeted them with total ease, and he kissed Edwina on the cheek, as he would a child he had known for her entire lifetime. He made the younger children feel completely at home. And even Helen shone here, although she was sometimes shy. She showed Fannie her old dolls, and her bedroom, although Alexis was far more impressed with her sunken pink marble bathtub. And while they were touring Helen's rooms, Sam took Edwina and Teddy out to the stables to see his horses. They were a remarkable lot, all Arabian, all champions from Kentucky. And suddenly Edwina could see why George had been afraid to propose to Helen for so long, this was a great deal to live up to. And yet, in spite of all of it, Helen was a surprisingly simple girl, and Edwina had to admit that she looked ecstatic with her brother. And she didn't seem to be demanding or spoiled. She wasn't fabulously bright, but she was very loving. And in an odd way, she reminded Edwina of an older, far more sophisticated Fannie. All she wanted to do was cook, and stay home and have babies. And listening to them, as they dined, Alexis made a face and said they were all crazy.

'And what would you rather do, young lady?' Sam asked, with a look of amusement.

She didn't hesitate for a beat as she answered. 'Go out, have fun . . . go dancing every night . . . never get married . . . make movies.'

'Well, you've got part of your wish, haven't you?' he said kindly. 'But I hope all your wishes don't come true. It would be a shame if you never got married.' And then suddenly he realized what he'd said, and he looked at Edwina with a mortified expression. But she only laughed, and teased him a little bit, and put him at ease again quickly.

'Don't worry about me. I *like* being a spinster.' She was laughing but Sam wasn't.

'Don't be ridiculous,' he growled. 'That's an absurd thing to call yourself.' But he was aware of the fact that she wasn't young either.

'I'm thirty-two years old,' she said proudly, 'and quite happy being single.' Sam stared at her for a long moment. She was an odd girl in some ways, and yet he liked her.

'I'm sure you wouldn't be single if your parents were alive,' he said quietly, and she nodded . . . no . . . and, of course, if Charles were, they would have been married for eleven years by then. By now, it was almost impossible to imagine.

'Things work out the way they're meant to.' She looked perfectly at ease, and Helen smoothly changed the subject, and only much later in the evening, chided her father.

'I'm sorry . . . I didn't think . . .' he said apologetically as she reminded him of Edwina's lost fiancé, drowned on the *Titanic*, and he felt even worse. And as though to make it up to them, a little while later he suggested they go dancing. He thought they should take the 'children' home, and he invited Helen and George and Edwina to join him at the Cocoanut Grove, and everyone thought it a wonderful idea, except Alexis, who was furious not to be invited. Edwina reminded her in an undertone that she was too young, and she was not to make a fuss, there would be other opportunities for her to go out, if she behaved herself, and did not give in to tantrums. She pouted all the way home in the limousine, but Edwina saw her safely inside with the others, and then went back out to Sam. Helen was riding with George in his car, just behind them. And Edwina was smiling and happy when she returned to the waiting Rolls to find Sam pouring two glasses of champagne from the bottle that had been chilling for several hours.

'This could be dangerously addictive.' Edwina smiled at him, touched by all the little attentions, and amused by the constant extravagances of Hollywood.

'Could it?' He looked her squarely in the eye, he already knew her better, and she saw his blue eyes sparkle in the moonlight. 'I'm not sure I believe you. You seem more sensible than that.'

'I suppose I am. And a little bit less demanding.'

'Quite a bit, I suspect, or you couldn't have given up your own life to raise five children.' He toasted her silently and she raised her glass and toasted George and his bride, and Helen's father smiled at her. It had already been a very pleasant evening.

And once they got to the Cocoanut Grove, it was even more so. The four of them danced for hours, exchanged partners, chatted, and laughed at funny stories. They were like four good friends, and more than once Edwina saw Helen squeeze her father's hand or touch his arm, and he always looked at her with adoration. But she and George were close too, and they danced almost professionally for six straight tangos.

'You two are quite a team!' Sam said admiringly as George took Helen off to the floor without even pausing for breath after dancing with his sister.

'So are you.' Edwina grinned. 'I saw you two out there.'

'Did you? Then perhaps you and I ought to try it again, just to make sure we don't step on each other's feet at the wedding.'

Edwina was sure they had danced all night, and she had a fabulous time getting to know him. She already knew how much she liked Helen.

And Edwina was surprised at how easy it was to glide around the room in Sam's arms. He reminded her of someone, and she wasn't sure who, and then she realized later on, that he reminded her of her father when she had danced with him when she was a little girl. Sam Horowitz was so much taller and stronger than she was that it made her feel like a child again, and in a funny way, she realized that she liked it. She liked him, and his constant thoughtfulness and kind eyes, which seemed to take everything in and understand it. He had brought his daughter up alone too, after his wife died when Helen was only a baby. 'It wasn't easy sometimes, and she always thought I was too strict.' But it was easy to see she didn't think so now, and that he adored her. She was truly a beautiful girl, and she obviously doted on Edwina's brother. Edwina was happy for both of them. It made her feel both happy and sad. It was a bittersweet time, and more than once they reminded her of her last days with Charles, when they had gone to England to announce their engagement. She had put her engagement ring from him away finally, a few years before, and she looked at it now and then, when she went to get something else out of her jewel box.

Sam asked her to dance one last time, and from his arms, she watched her handsome brother glide his fiancée smoothly across the floor in a final tango, but she and Sam didn't do badly either.

All in all, the two couples had a wonderful time and they went home at three in the morning.

And when Sam dropped her off, Helen got into the car with him outside George's house. And Helen and Sam waved good night to the Winfields. Edwina thanked him again for a wonderful evening, and George kissed Helen again, as Sam and Edwina pretended not to notice.

'We'll have to do this again, soon,' Sam said softly, and for an instant, Edwina felt a pang of regret that their lives hadn't been different.

And the next day, Alexis started work on the picture. It was far more arduous than she had thought it would be, and there were days when it was grueling, but no matter how hard it was, or how demanding the director was with her, it was obvious how much she loved it. Edwina was with her on the set almost every day, but after a while she felt superfluous. Alexis was doing a beautiful job, she felt totally at ease, and it was obvious that everyone on the set, from the star to the last extra, loved her. And just as George had known from the moment he came to Hollywood that he had found his home, so did Alexis. It was a fairyland of make-believe where she would always be a child and people would always take care of her, which was exactly what she wanted. And it warmed Edwina's heart to see her so happy and so involved in what she was doing.

'She's like a different person,' Edwina said to George late one night, when she was dining with him and Helen, at the Cocoanut Grove, which was Helen's favorite nightspot. Edwina had been enjoying watching Rudolph Valentino dance with Constance Talmadge, and she found herself suddenly missing Sam. They had become good friends, and she enjoyed going out with him with George and Helen, but he was in Kentucky, buying two new horses.

'I have to admit,' George said, as he poured more champagne for his sister and his future wife, 'Alexis is very good in the picture. Much better than I thought she would be. In fact,' he said, looking pointedly at Edwina, 'it's going to pose something of a problem.'

'What kind of problem?' She looked surprised. Thus far, everything had gone so smoothly.

'Pretty soon it may all be out of my hands. If she's good in this, she's going to be getting more offers to make other pictures. And then what are you going to do?'

Edwina had been thinking of that for the past week and she hadn't yet solved it. 'I'll think of something. I really don't want to stay down here with the other two.' And George had his own life now, and in spite of what Alexis thought, she wasn't old enough to live alone in Los Angeles. 'Don't worry about it. I'll think of something.'

But fortunately, when the picture ended, there was a

lull, and they all went back to San Francisco to put Fannie and Teddy back in school. Edwina found that she hated leaving Hollywood, but she felt that she had to go home, and she had promised the younger children. But she was sad to leave George and Helen and even Sam, and she missed their elegant evenings of dining and dancing. But they were going back to Los Angeles at the end of September anyway, for George and Helen's wedding. By then, there was talk of another picture for Alexis, and Alexis was begging Edwina to let her get her own apartment, which Edwina said would only work if she could find a suitable chaperone. In fact, it was becoming a rather complicated situation. And she was still trying to sort it out when they went back down on the train for the much-heralded wedding.

George picked them up himself, and Edwina laughed at how nervous he was when he took them to the hotel. She had been determined not to get in his way, and she had booked them into the Beverly Hills Hotel again, which the children enjoyed and she had always liked too. And George was just beside himself with nerves as he told the bellboy where to put their luggage.

His bachelor party was scheduled for that night, and the rehearsal dinner was the following night at the Alexandria Hotel, and the night before they had been given a huge party at Pickfair.

'I may not live through the week,' George groaned, and fell onto the couch in the suite's living room and looked up at Edwina. 'I had no idea it was so exhausting, getting married.'

'Oh, shut up,' she teased, 'you're loving every minute of it, and so you should. How is Helen?'

'A tower of strength, thank God. If it weren't for her I couldn't get through this. She remembers absolutely everything we're supposed to do, she knows who gave what gifts, who's coming and who isn't, and where we're supposed to be when. All I have to do is get dressed, try not to forget the ring, and pay for the honeymoon, and I'm not even sure I could do that much without her.' Edwina was impressed, as she had been months before when Helen asked her to be her maid of honor. There were going to be eleven other bridesmaids, eleven ushers, a best man, four flower girls, and a ring bearer. And George hadn't been kidding when he said it should have been directed by Cecil B. De Mille. It sounded like one of his epics.

The wedding itself was going to take place in the Horowitzes' garden, under a gazebo covered in roses and gardenias that had been specially grown just for Helen and George, and the reception was going to be in the house, and two huge tents that had been put on the grounds, with two bands, and every name in Hollywood who would be there to see Helen marry George. It brought tears to Edwina's eyes each time she thought about it, but when they'd come down in June she had brought with her a very special gift for Helen.

'Have a good time tonight.' She kissed her brother as he left to get ready for his bachelor party that night. And as she went to take a bath, Alexis, Fannie, and Teddy took off like a band of roving urchins to check out the lobby. 'Behave yourselves, please,' she urged, but she assumed that as long as they were together they couldn't get into too much trouble. After all, this was where Alexis had met Malcolm Stone, but that had been months before, and Alexis was reformed now.

30

The Horowitzes' Duesenberg appeared for them at the hotel at exactly eleven-thirty, and Edwina and the three children got in and they were driven to the Horowitz estate, where everything was orchestrated to perfection.

The tents were in place, both bands had already set up their stands and their music. Paul Whiteman and his orchestra and Joe 'King' Oliver's Creole Jazz Band were going to be playing from six o'clock until the wee hours of the morning. The caterers were in full swing. The Horowitz staff had everything in control. And an exquisite luncheon was being served to everyone but the bride in the dining room at precisely twelve o'clock. And when Sam Horowitz appeared to greet them, he looked calm and collected. He was wearing a business suit, and he thought Edwina looked very pretty in a white silk dress and a long rope of pearls that had been her mother's. It was a big day for all of them, and all of the Winfield children were very excited. George had asked Teddy to be his best man, which had flattered him and touched Edwina deeply. She was going to be Helen's maid of honor, Alexis was a bridesmaid, and Fannie a flower girl, so they each had a role. At two o'clock, the girls went to the room where the bridesmaids were being combed and coiffed and made up and perfumed, Teddy joined the men, and Edwina went to find Helen.

'See you later,' Sam said quietly, and touched her arm just before she left. 'It's a big day for both of us, isn't it?'

She was more like the mother of the groom than the maid of honor and they both knew it, and he had to stand in, as he had for all of Helen's life, as both father and mother.

'She's going to look beautiful.' Edwina smiled at him, knowing what a wrench it had to be for him. She was feeling it, too, and George hadn't lived at home in more than four years, and still, for all of them, it was an important moment.

And much to her surprise, she found Helen sitting calmly in her bedroom, looking beautiful and composed, her hair already done, her manicure perfect, her wedding dress all laid out. She had nothing more to do except relax and wait for five o'clock when she would walk down the aisle on her father's arm and become Mrs George Winfield.

Edwina had never realized when they met how organized she was, how capable, and how much she was like her father. She just quietly went about what she did, smiling, being pretty and pleasant, and taking care of everyone and seeing to their comfort. It made Edwina happy seeing that, and she knew without a moment's doubt that she and George were going to be very happy. And yet, for a moment, just then, she felt almost sorry for her. It was a time when she should have had a mother and not simply a friend, to fuss over her, and send her on her way with a warm hug and a tear as she walked down the aisle, but they were two young women alone, the one who had never known her mother at all, the other who had had to take her mother's place and bring up five children.

As Edwina looked around the room, she saw the miles and miles of Chantilly lace, hundreds of tiny buttons, rivers of tiny pearls, and a twenty-foot train, but there was no veil, and then as she walked into Helen's dressing room, she saw it. It had been pressed, and it was propped up on a hat stand high up on a chest of drawers, as it drifted across the room, fully as long as Helen's train, and as Edwina saw it, tears filled her eyes. It looked just as it was meant to, a whisper to cover a virgin's face, and make her groom long for her as she drifted toward him. It looked as it would have eleven years before, if she'd married Charles. She had given it to Helen and now she was deeply touched that she was going to wear it. And she turned at a sound, as Helen came into the room behind her, and gently touched her shoulder. They were sisters now, and not just friends. Sisters who had only each other, and as Edwina turned to embrace her, there were tears running down her face, as she remembered Charles as though she had seen him only moments before. With all the years since he'd been gone, he was still fresh in her mind and her heart, and if she closed her eyes, she could see him as she did her parents.

'Thank you for wearing it,' she whispered as they hugged, and Helen was crying too. She could only guess at how much the gift meant to Edwina.

'Thank you for letting me . . . I wish you had worn it too . . .' But what she really meant was that she wished Edwina had had the joy that Helen had now.

'I did, in my heart.' She pulled away and smiled at her new younger sister. 'He was a wonderful man, and I loved him very much.' She had never talked about him to Helen before. 'And George is a wonderful man too . . . may you always be happy.' Edwina kissed her again, and a little while later, she helped her dress, and it took her breath away when she saw her. She looked more beautiful than any bride she had ever seen, in real life or any movie. Her blond hair seemed to frame her face, and it was swept around her head like a halo, artfully woven with little sprigs of baby's breath and lily of the valley, and the crown of Edwina's wedding veil fit carefully above the silken hair, with its shimmering pearls, and its miles of white tulle. It took six of her bridesmaids to help her down the stairs, and Edwina cried again as she watched her.

Her own dress was pale blue lace, and it had a matching coat that trailed far behind her, and a beautiful hat made in Paris by Poiret that dipped low and almost concealed one eye, and made her look at the same time both demure and sexy. The dress was cut low to reveal her creamy bosom, but the coat covered her for the ceremony and the pale sky blue made her shining black hair look like raven's wings. She didn't know it, but her brother thought she had never looked more beautiful.

Sam was startled by her, too, and then, a moment later, there was a hush and there was Helen. The extraordinary dress and the magical wedding veil transformed her into everyone's dream, and reminded Sam that she was no longer a little girl and he was about to lose her. A tear crept slowly from Sam's eye, and a moment later he held his daughter tight and everyone sobbed, watching them. She looked so beautiful, and he looked so loving and so strong, and Edwina knew everything Helen meant to him, and also what she meant to her brother. Helen was a lucky girl. She was precious to both men, and she knew how much they both loved her.

The music started up and the bridesmaids and flower girls moved down the aisle, and then at the very end, Edwina moved out just ahead of Helen and Sam, in measured steps, holding her bouquet of white orchids. The bridesmaids all looked like little girls to her, and she could see Alexis and Fannie giggling far ahead, but as she looked toward him she could see George, waiting expectantly with his young, shining face, for his life to begin with Helen. And seeing him there made Edwina wish again that her parents were alive to see him now, as she moved to the side, and Helen appeared like a miracle suddenly in everyone's field of vision. There were sighs throughout the crowd, and people straining to see, and as Edwina took her place, Sam Horowitz stood solemnly and looked down at his only child with a small, sad smile, and gave her delicate white-kid-gloved hand to her husband.

Edwina could feel a rustle in the crowd, and as Helen and George took their places under the canopy that was a tradition in Helen's faith, she watched and cried silently, tears of joy for them, and as she thought of the love she had lost so long ago, there were tears of sorrow and longing.

The wedding was beautiful, and the ceremony just what it should have been, as George broke a glass beneath his foot. They weren't Orthodox, but Helen had wanted a wedding in her own faith, and after that it didn't bother her that she and George were of different religions.

It took hours to get through the reception line, and Edwina stood beside Sam, drained at first, from all the emotions she felt, and then laughing at Sam's jokes, as he shook hands, introduced all their friends, and spoke in a series of whispers whenever he could to Edwina. He was a great source of strength and warmth throughout the wedding. And Edwina introduced him to their friends who had come down from San Francisco, mostly their parents' old friends, and Ben, of course, with his wife, who was expecting a baby. And after Helen danced with Sam, and George with Edwina, then Edwina danced with Sam, and with Teddy, and with movie stars and friends, and people she didn't know and would probably never see again, and they all had a wonderful time. And at last at midnight, the bride and groom left, in the Duesenberg

Sam had given George as a wedding gift. And in the morning, they would leave for New York by train, and to Canada from there. They had talked about going to Europe, but George had balked at the thought of going on a ship, and Helen hadn't pressed it. She knew they would someday, and she didn't want to rush him. She was happy going anywhere with him. And she had looked blissful as they drove off, and Edwina turned to Sam with a sigh, wondering where Alexis and Teddy and Fannie were. She had seen them on and off all night, and they were having a ball, particularly Alexis.

'It was beautiful.' Edwina smiled at him.

'Your brother's a fine boy,' he said admiringly.

'Thank you, sir.' She curtsied, smiling up at him in her blue gown. 'And you have a lovely daughter.'

He shared the last dance with her, and as Edwina looked around the floor, she was startled to see Malcolm Stone there. She suspected he had come with someone, because she knew that otherwise, he would never have been invited. And a little while later, she rounded up her family, thanked Sam again, and went home, exhausted but happy. And it was only later that night, as they undressed, and she chatted with Alexis, that she thought to ask her if she'd seen Malcolm.

Alexis didn't answer for a moment, and then nodded her head. She had. She had danced with him. But she didn't want to admit that to Edwina, and she wasn't sure if her sister had seen them. She had been surprised to see him there too, and he had laughed when he told her he'd crashed and pretended to have forgotten his invitation.

'Yes, I saw him there,' she said noncommittally as she took off the pearls she had borrowed from Edwina.

'Did he talk to you?' Edwina frowned, as she sat down, looking faintly worried.

'Not really,' which was a lie.

'I'm surprised he had the courage to turn up.' But this time, Alexis didn't answer her, and she didn't say that they had made a lunch date for the next day, to talk about her next picture. He said he had auditioned for a part in it, which surprised Alexis because so far nothing was set, and Alexis hadn't even been formally signed yet. 'It was a beautiful wedding, wasn't it?' Edwina decided to change the subject. There was no point talking about Malcolm Stone anymore. All of that was in the past now.

And they all decided that Helen had looked absolutely gorgeous, and as she went to bed that night, Edwina smiled to herself, tired, happy, sad, and glad that she'd given her the veil. But Alexis was not thinking of the bride, as she drifted off to sleep. She was dreaming of Malcolm, and their date tomorrow.

31

Alexis and Malcolm Stone met the next day at the Ambassador Hotel for lunch, and when she arrived she was very nervous. Edwina had gone to George's house to do some things for him, and Alexis had told Fannie she was going out to meet a friend. Fannie had been reading a book in the room, and Teddy was at the pool when Alexis asked the doorman to get her a cab at the hotel, and she had just gone, without telling anyone where she was going.

'My sister will be furious if she hears about this,' Alexis admitted to him. She looked lovelier than ever in a cream-colored suit and a matching hat with a veil that all but obscured her eyes, as she looked up at him like a trusting child.

'Well, then, we'll see that she doesn't hear about it, won't we?' He was handsomer than ever, and a little frightening as he reached for Alexis's hand. There was something very sexual about him, and yet at the same time he always made her feel like a little girl, and he was going to take care of her, and it was that side of him that she liked, not the other. 'At least your charming brother's not in town.' He laughed, as though amused by him. 'Where did he go for his honeymoon?'

'To New York and Canada.'

'Not to Europe?' He looked amazed. 'How surprising.' But Alexis did not explain why. 'How long will they be gone?'

'Six weeks,' she told him openly, as he kissed the inside of her palms with interest.

'Poor baby . . . what will you do without him? He's going to be all wrapped up with his little wifey, and that leaves you all alone in the world now, doesn't it?' It didn't, of course, it left her with very capable Edwina, but as he said it, she began to feel as though she had no one left in the world. 'Poor little love, Malcolm will just have to take care of you, won't he, love?' he said, and she nodded, the memory of Rosarita Beach fading from her mind as he murmured.

He asked about the timing of her next picture, and she admitted that Edwina and George wanted her to wait to sign anything until he got back.

'Then you're free for the next two months?' He looked enchanted.

'Well . . . yes . . . except that I have to go back to San Francisco, because my sister and brother are still in school.' And suddenly, beneath the veil, even to him, she still looked like a child. She had the face and the body of an angel, and with the right direction, she could almost pretend to be a vamp. But left to her own devices, she was still deliciously childish. It was part of her charm, but in the face of Malcolm's advances, she felt awkward, and she was suddenly anxious to get back to the hotel. 'I really ought to go,' she said finally, as he lingered, kissing her again and again and playing with her hair. He had had a lot to drink over lunch, and he seemed to be in no hurry. And he tried to tempt her to drink some wine with him, and finally she did, hoping that after that, he would finally take her back to the hotel. But when she did, she found that she liked it, it tasted better even than the champagne they'd had the night before. And by the end of the afternoon, they were still sitting there, drinking wine and giggling and kissing, and by then she had forgotten that she had to go anywhere at all. She laughed as they drove back to his apartment. Everything seemed terribly funny now, especially Edwina waiting for her, God only knew where. Alexis couldn't remember.

He gave her more wine when they got to his place, and he kissed her until she was breathless, and suddenly she knew that there was more she wanted to do with him, but she couldn't quite remember what. She remembered they had gone somewhere together once, and for a minute she thought that they were married, but then a moment later, that thought was a blur as well. She was unconscious when he put her back in his car with a suitcase. He had thought about this all night, and decided that it was a great idea, and would solve all his problems. He left the money he owed for the rent on the table, and he was planning to leave the car with a note at the station. It wasn't his anyway, he had borrowed it from someone on his last picture.

The train was still in the station when they got there, and Alexis was half conscious again by then, and she sat up and looked around her.

'Where are we going?' She looked around at him, but the compartment seemed to be swaying around her, and she couldn't figure out where she was, or where she was going.

'We're going to see George in New York,' he told her, and in the condition she was in it sounded fine to her.

'We are? Why?'

'Don't worry about it, little love,' he said again, and kissed her. He had the perfect plan. Alexis was going to be his ticket to stardom. And once he had compromised her sufficiently, George would have no choice. Particularly now that he was married to Sam Horowitz's daughter, he would be far from anxious to have his younger sister labeled as a whore all over the business.

The train pulled out as Alexis snored loudly on the seat next to Malcolm, and as he looked down at her and smiled, he had to admit to himself that he could have done worse, she was a very pretty girl. In fact, she was a beauty.

32

'What do you mean you don't know where she went?' At
the exact moment the train pulled out carrying Alexis,
Edwina was questioning Fannie, who was close to tears.

'I don't know . . . she said she was going to see a friend
or something . . . I think someone from her movie . . . I
don't remember . . .' Fannie was getting panicked, and
Teddy hadn't even been there.

'Did you see anyone?' Fannie shook her head again,
terrified that something awful had happened to Alexis.

'She was all dressed up, and she looked very pretty,'
Fannie added, and as she said the words, a chill ran
through Edwina, and she instantly suspected Malcolm
Stone. She suddenly had the feeling that the night before,
Alexis had been lying. She had thought so then but she
hadn't wanted to press her.

The doorman told her that her sister had left in a cab.
And when she hadn't come back by nine o'clock that
night, she finally called Sam. She apologized for disturb-
ing him, and told him about her problem. She wanted to
track Malcolm down to see if Alexis was with him.

It was two hours later before he called her back, and
the other children were asleep then. All he had was an
address another actor had given him, and it was in a rotten
part of town.

'I don't want you going there. Do you want me to go
there now or in the morning?' He was more than willing
to help, but Edwina insisted that she could handle it

herself. They argued about it for a little while, and finally Edwina agreed to let him go there with her. It was midnight by the time they arrived and it was obvious that no one was at the apartment.

She decided to call the police by then, no matter how much scandal it caused. And Sam reluctantly left her with them at the hotel at one in the morning. Edwina said she was alright with them, and she didn't seem to want Sam to stay with her. She tried to tell the police what she could. But all she knew, in truth, was what Fannie had told her. Alexis had gone to meet a friend, and had never come back. But by the next morning, Edwina was truly panicked. There was no sign of the girl. And the police had no leads at all. No body had been found, no one had seen anything. And no one of her description had turned up at any of the hospitals in town. She had to be somewhere, but Edwina had no idea where, or with whom, or why. Her only thought was Malcolm Stone, but she realized she could be wrong about that. Their last run-in with him had been months before, and surely he had learned his lesson.

It was noon when Sam Horowitz called, and Edwina was frantic by then. And what he had to say told her that she had been right. With a little careful checking, Sam had learned that Malcolm Stone had left his room paid for and deserted. Sam had discovered when he went back that morning, and by sheer luck he'd been able to find out, through an actor he knew, that he'd left the car he used at the station, with a note, and one could assume that he'd left town. But the question was, did he have Alexis with him? That was what she needed to know, and she had no idea how to do it.

'You could tell the police he kidnapped her,' Sam suggested, but Edwina was loath to do a thing like that.

What if he didn't? If Alexis said she'd gone willingly with him, which Edwina assumed she had, then it would be all over the papers, and her reputation would be ruined forever. As Edwina thought about it, she found herself missing George. 'Is there anything I can do to help?' Sam offered again, but she told him that she would try to find a solution, and let him know what was happening, as soon as she knew herself. But she didn't want to impose on him. He had done enough, and this wasn't his problem. It was also embarrassing to admit to him that she was unable to control her own sister. And suddenly, Edwina was afraid to disgrace George, and Sam, and Helen.

And there was certainly no way to stop Malcolm and Alexis now, or even to catch them if they had left town, and all she could think of to do now was to go back to San Francisco, and wait for Alexis to call her. She called Sam later that afternoon and told him her plan, and the next morning she took Fannie and Teddy home to San Francisco. They were a quiet threesome on the long train ride home. Edwina's thoughts were filled with worry for her little sister, and Fannie felt guilty that she hadn't questioned her more, or told her not to go wherever she was going.

'That's silly,' Edwina tried unsuccessfully to reassure her. 'It's not your fault, sweetheart.' What Alexis had done was her own fault.

'But what if she never comes back again?' Fannie started to cry, and Edwina smiled sadly. She would come back again . . . but God only knew when, or how, or in what condition. But it was actually more comforting to think of her with Malcolm Stone than to fear that some unknown fate had befallen her. Edwina wasn't sure which fate was worse, as she and the younger ones rolled into San Francisco.

It was three days before they heard from her, and by then Edwina thought she would go crazy. The call came to San Francisco at ten o'clock at night.

'My God, do you realize how worried we've been? Where *are* you?'

Alexis's voice trembled. She had been almost too embarrassed to call, but even Malcolm thought she should. It had been the worst week of her life. First she had been so sick on the train, she thought she would die, and then he had told her she had slept right through their wedding night. He told her they'd gotten married just before getting on the train, and to prove it, he'd made love to her all during the second night. It had been awful and not at all what she had expected, and now she couldn't imagine why she'd married him in the first place. He wasn't anything like he'd been in Los Angeles, and all he talked about were the pictures they would star in, and no matter how handsome he was, in broad daylight, to Alexis, he looked ancient.

'I'm alright,' she said faintly, but even over the long-distance wires, she wasn't convincing. 'I'm with Malcolm.'

'I figured out that much,' Edwina said, tears of relief choking her. 'But why? Why on earth would you do something like this, Alexis?' It made Edwina want to ask herself where she had gone wrong. 'Why did you lie to me?'

'I didn't. Not really. I hardly talked to him at the wedding. I just danced with him once and agreed to meet him for lunch.'

'So where are you?' It had certainly been the longest lunch in her life, and by now Edwina had no illusions about what had happened. After five days, even Edwina knew what must have transpired.

'I'm in New York,' Alexis answered nervously, as Edwina gasped, and then shook her head, wondering if she could contact George, but she hated to bother him now on his honeymoon, and there was very little that could be done. More than anything, Edwina wanted to hush it up. She was planning to tell Sam that she had found her, and maybe even swear the other children to secrecy, and never tell George at all. The fewer people who knew about this, the better it would be for Alexis, and that was all she could think of now.

'Where are you in New York? What hotel?' Her mind was racing.

'At the Illinois Hotel,' Alexis answered, and she gave Edwina an address far up on the West Side. This was certainly not the Plaza or the Ritz-Carlton, but Malcolm Stone was not that kind of man. 'And Edwina . . .' Her voice broke, she knew it would break Edwina's heart, but she wanted to tell her. 'I'm married.'

'*What?*' Edwina almost leapt into the phone. 'You are?'

'Yes, we got married before we got on the train.' She didn't tell her that she had been drunk and had no recollection of it, it seemed enough just to say she was.

'Are you coming back now?' Edwina had every intention of getting it annulled, and seeing to it that Alexis came to her senses, but first she had to get her home before she could do that.

'I don't know . . .' She sounded tearful. 'Malcolm says he wants to try out for a play in New York.'

'Oh, for God's sake. Look . . .' She closed her eyes for a moment and made some rapid calculations. 'Stay where you are, I'm coming to get you.'

'Are you going to tell George?' At least she had the grace to sound embarrassed, Edwina was relieved to hear.

'No, I'm not. I'm not going to tell anyone, and neither

316

are you, and neither is Malcolm. The fewer people who *ever* know about this, the better. I'm bringing you home with me, and that will be the end of this nonsense. We'll have the marriage annulled, and that will be the end of it.' And she just prayed that, as George had put it several months earlier, there would be no 'brat' as a gift from Malcolm. 'I'll be in New York in five days to get you.'

But suddenly, after they'd hung up, Alexis was sorry she had called her. Malcolm was suddenly nice to her again, and this time when he made love to her, she liked it, and she didn't want to go back to California, she wanted to stay in New York, with him. The hotel where they were staying was dark and dingy, and there were things about being with him that she didn't like. And she didn't like the way he'd tricked her into leaving California, but now that she was here with him, there were moments when she thought she was in love. And he was very good-looking, of course, although he drank too much and when he did, his hands were rough, but he was sweet to her too, and he treated her like a baby, and it made her feel very grown up when he introduced her as his wife. By the next day, she was absolutely sure of it, she was sorry she had told Edwina to come, or even where she was. But when she called and tried to tell her not to come, Fannie told her that Edwina had already left for New York.

'Why did you do it, Lexie?' Fannie wailed into the phone, as Alexis felt Malcolm's hand slide up her thigh and she trembled.

'We're going to be in movies together,' Alexis explained, as though that changed everything. 'And I wanted to be Malcolm's wife.' Fannie gasped with horror. Edwina hadn't told her that Alexis had married Malcolm. All she knew was that Lexie was in New York.

'What? You got married?' Fannie almost jumped

through the phone as Teddy listened with interest. Edwina hadn't told them that, and then suddenly Alexis remembered that she wasn't supposed to tell.

'Well, sort of.' But if she did tell, then Edwina couldn't annul it, or could she? It was all very confusing now, and Alexis was sorry she had called at all. And when she hung up, she told Malcolm that she was sorry she had called Edwina, and he was in a bad mood anyway, because there seemed to be no work for him in New York at any of the theaters.

'I have an idea,' he announced, pulling her down on the bed next to him, and slipping her blouse off. He had bought her some cheap clothes outside the station in Chicago, but to Alexis it was all exciting now. It was like playing a part in a picture.

They made love again, and afterward he left her at the hotel for a long time, and that night he came back with two tickets. And he was very drunk. Alexis had been frantic without him, but he promised her that the next day everything would be alright. They were going to London, he explained, and he was going to act in a play there, on the stage, and then after that, they would go back to California. And by then, it would be too late for her sister to do anything. With luck, as he saw it, by then Alexis might be pregnant. And even if she wasn't, the scandal would have gone on long enough that they wouldn't dare do anything, and he would spend the rest of his life in style, living off George Winfield.

33

Before Edwina left California, she had called and reassured Sam that everything was fine. It had all been a big misunderstanding, she said, and Alexis had been upset about something Edwina had said, and she had gone back to San Francisco on the train alone. Supposedly, according to Edwina, they had found her there, penitent about all the trouble she'd caused, and perfectly fine. It was all a lot of excitement about nothing.

'And Malcolm Stone?' he asked suspiciously. He wasn't sure he believed her.

'Nowhere in sight,' Edwina said convincingly, and thanked him for all his kindness. And then she had made arrangements to leave Fannie and Teddy with the housekeeper while she was gone, and the next morning she had left for New York to bring back Alexis.

She had sworn everyone to secrecy, in case George should call, and she told them she would be back as soon as she could. But whatever they did, under no circumstances were they to say anything to George if he called them.

She took the train to New York, filled with dread and painful memories. The last time she had traveled in that direction had been more than eleven years before, with her parents and brothers and sisters and Charles on the way to board the *Mauretania* in New York. She had too much time to think as they traveled east, and by the time she reached the Illinois Hotel, she was overwrought. She had gone straight there from the station, expecting to find a distraught Alexis, and she was going to threaten Malcolm Stone with the law. Instead, she found a letter from them, in Alexis's childish hand, explaining that Malcolm wanted to be on the London stage, and Alexis had gone with him as a dutiful wife. She read between the lines to see that Alexis was completely besotted, so much so that she was willing to get on a ship with him, which Edwina knew was no small task. She wondered if he had any idea what he had gotten himself into. And if Alexis had said anything about having been on the ill-fated *Titanic* eleven years before.

When Edwina left the Illinois she was in tears, wondering what to do next, whether to pursue them to London to bring her back, or if there was any point pursuing her at all. Maybe she really did want to be married to him, and maybe it was much too late now. What if they really were married, as Alexis said, or if she had gotten pregnant? Then what could Edwina do? She couldn't very well have the marriage annulled if Alexis was carrying his baby.

She was crying softly in the backseat of the cab when they reached the Ritz-Carlton, and she checked in and walked into a room that reminded her too much of the ones where she stayed the last time they were in New York. And she wished suddenly that there was someone to help her. But there was no one . . . her parents and Phillip were gone . . . George was married . . . she scarcely knew Sam . . . she didn't want to tell Ben how she'd failed . . . there was no one to turn to, and she knew, as she lay in bed that night, that she had to make the decision herself. There was no choice really. She knew she couldn't get on a ship again, not after what had happened on the *Titanic*, yet she couldn't let Alexis go on with him, without at least trying to bring her back. Alexis had called, after all, and she had told Edwina where she was. It had to mean that she wanted Edwina to save her.

Edwina thought about it all night and again all morning. She knew what ship they were on. And she could have wired, but in Alexis's besotted state, that wouldn't have brought her back. Edwina knew she had to do something, and soon, if anything was to be done at all. And then, as though it was the only answer, she could see her mother's face in front of her, and knew what she would have done. She would have gone after Alexis. And that afternoon, Edwina booked her passage on the *Paris*. Alexis had left three days earlier on the *Bremen*.

34

When Alexis boarded the *Bremen* in second class she was quiet and pale, and Malcolm tried to bolster her spirits. He told her how much fun they would have, and assumed she had never been on a ship before. He ordered champagne, and kissed her frequently, and all he could think of was the life that they would lead one day, on more luxurious ships, traveling in first class. 'Just think of it,' he teased her, slipping a hand into her dress, but this time Alexis wasn't smiling.

She didn't say a word to him as they sailed, and when they went to their cabin and he stood close to her, he could feel her tremble.

'You don't get seasick, do you?' he asked, in high spirits with her. He could think of worse fates than having a young wife who was the sister of a major studio head, even if he had just spent the last of his money on their passage. It was a dreary ship, but the Germans liked to laugh and drink, and if nothing else he could gamble a little bit, play cards with the men, and show off his 'wife.' But she was clinging to their bed as they slipped into the harbor, and by dinnertime that night she couldn't catch her breath. She lay there gasping and wild-eyed, and he ran for the steward in terror, and asked him to call a doctor at once. Alexis looked as though she were dying.

'*Mein Herr?*' the steward inquired, glancing into the room behind him. He had noticed the American's pretty bride. They were a handsome pair, but the husband looked old enough to be her father.

'My wife . . . she isn't well . . . we need a doctor, and fast!'

'Certainly.' The steward smiled. 'But may I bring her a cup of bouillon and some biscuits? It is the perfect answer for seasick, sir. She has never sailed before?' But as he spoke, she let out a terrible groan, as though of pain, and when Malcolm turned to look at her, he saw that she had fainted.

'The doctor, man, quick!' She looked as though she had died, and suddenly Malcolm was terrified. What if she did die? George Winfield would kill him, and he could forget Hollywood and Duesenbergs and anything else he'd had in mind with sweet little Alexis beside him.

The doctor came at once, and bluntly asked Malcolm if she was pregnant, and if there were signs of a miscarriage. He hadn't even thought of that and it seemed too soon, as she had been a virgin when they left California. He said he didn't know, before the doctor asked him to step outside, and he paced the halls, smoking, and wondering what had happened to make her faint, and look so ill before that.

It was a long time before the doctor came out, and frowned at him. He beckoned him to walk down the corridor, as Malcolm followed hesitantly. 'Is she alright?'

'Yes. She will sleep for a long time. I have given her an injection.' He ushered him to a small sitting area and sat down and looked at Malcolm. 'It was important that you go to Europe?' The doctor seemed to be almost angry at him, and he didn't understand why.

'Yes, I . . . I'm an actor . . . I'm going to perform on the London stage.' And like everything else in his life, it was a lie. He had no idea if he would find work there. But

323

the handsome, fading blond lit another cigarette and smiled nervously at the German doctor.

'She has not told you, has she?' He stared at him, wondering suddenly if they were truly married. She was too young, too frightened, and she had been wearing expensive shoes. Somehow she didn't seem to belong with him, and he wondered if she was a runaway. But if so, the trip was much more than she had bargained for, and he was sorry for her, as he stared at Malcolm.

'Hasn't told me what?' Malcolm looked confused, and with good reason.

'About the last time she went to Europe?' In sobbing tones, she had told the doctor, and confessed that she couldn't stay on the ship now. It was too terrible, and what if they sank? She was half crazed as she clung to him, and he had already decided to keep her sedated. And if the American agreed, he was going to put her in the ship's infirmary and keep her there under the vigil of his nurse until they reached England.

'I don't know anything about it.' Malcolm looked annoyed.

'You don't know that she sailed on the *Titanic*?' If they were married, she certainly had shared very little with her husband, but now he looked impressed.

'She couldn't have been more than a tiny child then.' Malcolm looked doubtful.

'She was six, and she lost her parents, and her sister's fiancé went down with them.' Malcolm nodded to himself, thinking that that explained a lot about Edwina. He had never wondered either why there were no parents watching over her, but only George and the ever vigilant older sister. He had simply thought they were around somewhere. In truth, he had never really thought about it, and didn't care, and Alexis had never volunteered her story.

And now the doctor went on, 'She was separated from them that night, and she was taken off the ship against her will in the last lifeboat. She didn't find her family again until they were on the ship that rescued them. I believe it was the *Carpathia*.' He frowned as he recalled. He had been the ship's surgeon on the *Frankfurt* then, and they had taken some of the *Titanic*'s last distress calls. 'May I suggest,' he said pointedly, 'that we keep your wife sedated for the remainder of the trip. I'm afraid she will not be able to tolerate it otherwise, and she appears, well . . . very fragile . . .' Malcolm sighed as he sat back and listened to him. This was all he needed, a hysterical girl on a ship whose family had gone down on the *Titanic* . . . and how the hell would he get her back to the States when they were ready to go back? Maybe it would have to be George's problem by then, or Edwina's, if she showed up, but now he knew that they wouldn't. He was safe from all of them, until he was ready to deal with them on his own terms. And by then, Alexis would be totally his, and they would have to deal with him. Forever.

'That's fine.' Malcolm agreed to the doctor's plan. It even left him free to play a little, if he chose to.

'May I have your permission to move her, sir?'

'Of course.' Malcolm smiled, saluted smartly, and went up to the bar, while the doctor, the nurse, and a stewardess removed the heavily sedated Alexis from Malcolm's cabin.

She slept the rest of the trip, waking only long enough for them to sedate her again. She remembered vaguely that she was on a ship, and more than once she screamed in the darkness for her mother. But her mother never came. There was only a woman in a white dress, speaking words she didn't understand, and she wondered if the ship had sunk, and she was in another place . . . and maybe now she would find her mother at last . . . or was it only Edwina?

35

Edwina had a hard time boarding the ship too, and there was no German doctor to keep her sedated. She boarded the *Paris* in first class, with the small bag she had brought with her from California. She had no evening clothes with her at all, but she knew she wouldn't need any. Her only goal was to reach London and bring Alexis back. She had read her ridiculous letter, outlining their plans, and insisting that she was happy with Malcolm. But Edwina didn't care how happy she was. She was seventeen years old, and she was not going to let her run off with that rotter. It made her sorry now that she had ever taken her to Hollywood at all, or let her make so much as one movie. There weren't going to be any more movies now. There was going to be their quiet life in San Francisco, once she got rid of Malcolm Stone. And if she was very lucky, no one at home would ever know what had happened in New York or that they had even gone there. She was prepared to tell whatever lies she had to now, to protect her younger sister. And getting her back was the only thing that got Edwina on the ship, as her legs trembled beneath her.

She was shown to her cabin by a stewardess, and she closed her eyes and sank onto a chair, trying not to remember the last ship she'd been on, or who she had been with, and what had happened after they set sail.

'May I get you anything, madame?' The steward for her corridor was very attentive, and looking very pale, she shook her head with a wan smile. 'Perhaps if madame went up on deck, she might feel a little better?' He was very solicitous and very French and she only smiled and shook her head, and thanked him.

'I'm afraid I don't really think so.' And as they pulled out of New York Harbor a little while later, she found herself thinking of Helen and George on their honeymoon. She had told Fannie and Teddy once again when she called that if George called, they were not to tell him anything, except that everything was fine and she and Alexis were out. She knew that he would be busy with Helen anyway, and he wasn't likely to call very often. But the children knew where she was and that she had gone to London. But neither of them realized what a terrible strain it was for Edwina. Both of them had been so young when their parents died, that at two and four they had scarcely retained any memories of the *Titanic* at all. But for Alexis on the *Bremen* it was close to unbearable, and for Edwina on the *Paris*, it was extremely painful as well.

She took dinner in her room the first night, and scarcely ate anything, as the steward observed with disappointment. He was having trouble understanding what ailed her. He had assumed she was seasick, but he wasn't entirely sure she was. She never left her cabin, she kept her curtains drawn, and whenever he brought her a tray, she looked dreadful and terribly pale. But she looked more like someone suffering from grief or a terrible trauma.

'Madame is sad today?' he asked with fatherly concern, as she smiled up at him from something she'd been writing. She had been writing a letter to Alexis about everything she thought of her wild flight and her outrageous affair with Malcolm. And she was planning to give it to her when she saw her. At least it kept her mind

327

occupied while she tried not to think about where she was. She was a young woman, but a very serious one, he decided. And on the second day, the steward wondered if perhaps she was a writer. He urged her to go outside again then. It was a beautiful October day, the sun was high in the sky, and it broke his heart to see her so unhappy and pale. He wondered also if she was traveling to Europe to escape from a broken love affair. And finally, after he had nagged her again, when he brought her luncheon tray, she laughed and stood up, looking around the room she had hidden in for almost two days, and agreed to go up on deck for a walk. But she was shaking all over again as she put on her coat, and walked slowly up to the Promenade Deck.

She tried not to think about the similarities and differences as she walked slowly around the Promenade Deck of the *Paris*. There were lifeboats hanging everywhere, and she tried not to look at them as well, but if she looked beyond them, she was looking out to sea, and that was upsetting too. There was nowhere she could go to hide from her memories here, and although it had been so long ago, it was all too fresh, and all too difficult to hide from. There were moments when she had to remind herself that she wasn't on the *Titanic*.

And as she walked back in from the Promenade Deck, she could hear the strains of music from the tea dance, and suddenly tears filled her eyes as she remembered dancing one afternoon with Charles, while her parents smiled as they stood by and watched them. She wanted to run from the memory now, and she started to hurry away without watching where she was going, and in a moment, as she wheeled away, she collided with a man and literally fell into his arms as she tried to escape the sound of the familiar music.

'Oh . . . oh . . .' She could hardly keep her balance as he reached out and caught her with a single powerful hand.

'I'm terribly sorry . . . are you alright?' She looked up suddenly into the face of a tall, handsome blond man somewhere in his late thirties. He was beautifully dressed and impeccably tailored, in a hat, and a coat with a handsome beaver collar.

'I . . . yes . . . I'm sorry . . .' She had knocked two books and a newspaper right out of his hands, and it was comforting, she thought suddenly, to see him carrying such ordinary pastimes. Sometimes just the thought of being on a ship made her want to put on her life vest.

'Are you quite sure you're alright?' he asked again. She looked very pale with her stark black hair, and he was afraid to let her arm go for fear that she might faint. She looked as though she was badly shaken.

'No, really I'm fine.' She smiled faintly then, and he felt a little better and let her arm go. He was wearing gloves, and she looked up then and noticed how warm his smile was. 'I'm sorry, that was clumsy of me. I was thinking of something else.'

A man probably, he assumed incorrectly. But a woman who looked like that was seldom alone, or not for long anyway. 'No harm done. Were you going in for tea?' he inquired politely, but he seemed in no hurry to leave her.

'No, actually I was going down to my cabin.' He looked disappointed as she left, and when she reached her stateroom, the steward congratulated her for finally getting out and getting some air. And she laughed at his fatherly devotion. 'It was very nice. You were right,' she admitted, and accepted his offer of a pot of tea. He brought it with a plate of cinnamon toast a few minutes later.

'You must go out again. The only cure for sorrow is sunshine and fresh air, and nice people and good music.'

'Do I look sad then?' She was intrigued by his observations. She hadn't been sad as much as frightened. But she had to admit, she was sad too, it was just that being here on the ship brought back too many memories that were all too painful. 'I'm alright. Really.'

'You look much better!' he approved, but he was disappointed when, that evening, she asked for dinner to be served in her cabin.

'We have such a beautiful dining salon, madame. Won't you eat dinner there?' He didn't mind serving her, but he was so proud of the ship that it always hurt him when people didn't take full advantage of all its luxuries and comforts.

'I didn't bring anything to wear, I'm afraid.'

'It's of no importance. A beautiful woman can go anywhere in a plain black dress.' And he had seen the black wool dress she had worn only that morning.

'Not tonight. Perhaps tomorrow.' He obliged her by bringing her filet mignon with asparagus hollandaise, and *pommes soufflées* made for her especially by the chef, or so he claimed, but as with the other meals he'd brought in the past two days, she ate very little.

'Madame is never hungry,' he mourned as he took the tray away, but that evening when he came to turn her bed down, he was pleased to find that for once she was not in her cabin. She had thought about it for a long time, and finally decided to go out again and get some air before she went to bed. She stayed away from the rail, and walked slowly along the Promenade, keeping her eyes down, for fear of what she would see if she looked far out into the ocean. Perhaps a lifeboat, or a ghost . . . or an iceberg . . . She was trying not to think of it as she walked along, and a moment later she collided with a pair of elegant black patent leather men's evening shoes, and looked up to see the handsome blond man in the coat with the beaver collar.

'Oh, no! . . .' she laughed, looking truly embarrassed. She had knocked something out of his hands again, and this time he laughed too.

'We seem to have something of a problem. Are you alright again?' She was, of course, and she was blushing and feeling more than a little foolish.

'I wasn't watching where I was going. Again!' She smiled.

'Nor was I,' he confessed. 'I was looking far out to sea . . . it's beautiful, isn't it?' He glanced in that direction again, but Edwina did not. She just stood there, watching him, and thinking that he was very much like Charles in his manner. He was tall and handsome and aristocratic, and yet he was blond and not dark, and considerably older than Charles when they'd been on the *Titanic*. The man looked back at her then, with a friendly smile, and seemed to have no inclination to keep walking. 'Would you care to join me?' He crooked his arm for her to slip her hand into it, and she was looking for a polite way to decline after crashing into him for the second time, and she couldn't think of a single reason.

'I was . . . I'm actually . . . a little tired . . . I was going to . . .'

'Retire? So was I in a little while, but perhaps a walk will do us both good. Clears the head . . . and the eyes . . .' he teased as she slipped a hand into his arm without thinking. She followed him slowly around the deck and wasn't sure what to say to him. She wasn't used to talking to strangers, just to children, and to friends at home she'd known all her life, and George's Hollywood friends, who, to her, were a bit less impressive because most of them were so silly.

'Are you from New York?' He was talking mainly to himself, as Edwina was too nervous to speak to him at first, but it didn't seem to bother him as they walked along in the cool night air, with the moonlight overhead. And walking along with this handsome stranger, she felt more than a little foolish. She didn't know what to say to him, but he didn't seem to notice.

'No, I'm not,' she almost whispered in the darkness. 'I'm actually from San Francisco.'

'I see . . . going to London to visit friends . . . or Paris?'

'London.' To snatch my sister out of the arms of the bastard who ran off with her even though she's only seventeen years old and he's probably fifty. 'Just for a few days.'

'It's quite a trip for just a few days' stay. You must like traveling on ships.' He chatted on smoothly as they walked, and eventually stopped at two deck chairs. 'Would you like to sit down?' She did, still not knowing why, but he was so easy to be with that somehow it was easier just to follow along. She sat down in the deck chair next to him, and he put a blanket across her legs, and then turned to look at her again. 'I'm sorry . . . I've totally forgotten to introduce myself.' He held out a hand to her with a warm smile, 'I'm Patrick Sparks-Kelly, from London.'

She shook his hand properly and settled back in the chair beside him. 'I'm Edwina Winfield.'

'Miss?' he asked straightforwardly, and she nodded with a smile, not sure why it made a difference. But when she nodded, he raised an eyebrow. 'Aha! More mysterious than ever. People have been talking about you, you know.' He looked greatly intrigued and Edwina laughed again. He was funny and nice and she liked him.

'They have not!'

'I assure you, they have. Two ladies told me today that there is a beautiful young woman who walks around the Promenade and won't speak to anyone, and she takes all her meals in her cabin.'

'It must be someone else,' she said, still smiling at him, sure he had made it up.

'Well, do you walk around the Promenade Deck alone? Yes, you do. I know, because I've seen you myself, and,' he added jovially, 'been run into several times by this very same beautiful young woman. Do you take your meals in the dining saloon?' He turned to her questioningly, and she laughed again as she shook her head.

'No, I don't. Well . . . not yet . . . but . . .'

'Ah, you see! Then I'm right. You are indeed the mystery woman everyone is curious about. And I must tell you right now, people are imagining all kinds of exotic stories. One has you as a beautiful young widow, on your way to Europe to mourn, another has you as a dramatic divorcee, yet another has you as someone very famous. I'll grant you that no one has, as yet, figured out who, but undoubtedly someone we all know and love, such as, for instance,' he thought for a moment as he narrowed his eyes and looked at her closely, 'could it be Theda Bara?' She burst out laughing at the suggestion, and he smiled too.

'You have a wonderful imagination, Mr Sparks-Kelly.'

'The name sounds ridiculously complicated, doesn't it? Particularly when spoken in an American accent. Please call me Patrick. And as for your identity, I'm afraid you'll just have to tell us the truth, and admit which movie star you are before everyone in first class goes mad trying to guess. I'll have to admit, I've tried to guess all day myself, and I'm quite at a standstill.'

333

'I'm afraid everyone is going to be very disappointed, it's just me, traveling to Europe to meet my sister.' She made it sound a little more innocent than it was, but it was just as well, and he looked interested in even that.

'And you're only going to stay for a few days? How sad for us.' He smiled, and she thought, as she looked at him, that he was really very handsome. But it was a purely clinical observation, which came from meeting so many movie stars with her brother. 'How interesting that you're not married, though.' He made it sound like a fascinating job, and somehow he amused her. 'Americans are so good about that sort of thing. Somehow, they do that with style. English girls all panic that they'll never marry by the time they're twelve, and if they're not married in their first season out, their families bury them alive in the back garden.' She laughed aloud at the thought, and had never considered her single state as either a virtue or a preference. In her case, it had been a fact of circumstance, and an obligation.

'I don't know that being single is such an American skill. Maybe we're not as easy to marry as Englishwomen. Englishwomen are much better behaved. They don't argue as much.' She smiled, and then thought of her aunt Liz and uncle Rupert. 'I had an aunt who was married to an Englishman.'

'Oh, really, who?' He acted as though he should have known them, and perhaps he did, she realized.

'Lord and Lady Hickham, Rupert Hickham, he died several years ago, and so did she, actually. They never had any children.'

He thought for a moment and then nodded. 'I believe I know who he is . . . or was . . . I think actually that my father knew him. Rather a difficult sort, if that isn't too rude.' She laughed at the understatement, and realized that he did know exactly who Rupert was, if he remembered that about him.

'It's not rude at all, but quite accurate. And poor Aunt Liz was afraid of her own shadow. He terrified her into submission. We went to see them at Havermoor . . .' She had been about to say 'eleven years ago,' and then suddenly realized that she didn't want to say it. 'A long time ago.' Her voice was suddenly sad and husky. 'I haven't been back to England since.'

'And when was that?' He looked interested and seemed not to notice her discomfort.

'Eleven years ago.'

'That's a long time.' He was watching her face, wondering what had happened then, as she nodded. A terrible shadow had crossed her face, as he pretended not to notice.

'Yes, it is.' And then she stood up, as though she had to get away again. She was tired of running from the past, and tired of dealing with the present. 'I suppose I'll turn in. It was nice speaking to you, Mr Sparks-Kelly.'

'Patrick,' he corrected. 'May I walk you to your cabin, or may I waylay you briefly for a drink in the lounge? It's actually very pretty, if you haven't yet seen it.' But the last thing she wanted to do was tour the ship, sit in the lounge, get to know the people, it was all too reminiscent of their crossing on the ship that had gone down. She never wanted to see another ship again, and she was only on this one because of Alexis.

'I don't think so, but thank you very much.' She shook his hand and walked away from him then. But when she got downstairs, she found that she couldn't bear to go into her cabin either. It was all too oppressive, too familiar, too awful, and she couldn't bear the thought of going to sleep and living with her dreams, and her memories and her nightmares. She walked back out on deck then, just outside where her cabin was, and stood at the rail, thinking of what might have been, and how it had ended. She was so lost in her own thoughts that she didn't hear the footsteps, and all she heard was the gentle voice as he stood right behind her.

'Whatever it is, Miss Winfield, it can't be as bad as all that . . . I'm sorry.' He touched her arm and she didn't turn around. 'I don't mean to intrude, but you looked so sad when you left that I was worried.'

She turned to look at him then, her hair blowing in the breeze, her eyes bright, and he could see that there were tears on her cheeks in the moonlight. 'I seem to spend all my time on this ship telling people I'm alright.' She tried to smile, but she couldn't quite pull it off as she wiped her eyes and he watched her.

'And have you convinced anyone?' His voice was warm and kind, and she almost wished she hadn't met him. There was no point. He had his own life, and she had hers, and she was only here to bring back Alexis.

'No.' She smiled at him. 'I don't think I have convinced anyone.'

'Then I'm afraid you'll have to try harder.' And then, with the kindest voice she'd ever heard, he asked a difficult question. 'Has something really awful happened to you?' He couldn't bear watching the suffering in her eyes, and she had looked that way since they'd left New York Harbor.

'Not lately.' She wanted to be honest with him, without going into all the details. 'And I'm usually not this maudlin.' She smiled and wiped away the tears with a graceful hand as she took a deep breath of the sea air and tried to look more cheerful. 'I just don't like ships very much.'

'For any particular reason? Do you get seasick?'

'Not really.' She was vague with him. 'I just don't feel well on ships anymore . . . there are too many . . .' She stopped at the word *memories*, and then decided to throw caution to the winds. She didn't know who he was, but for that moment in time, he was her friend, and she knew she liked him. 'I was on the *Titanic* when it went down,' she explained quietly. 'And I lost my parents and the man I was going to marry.' She didn't cry this time, and for a moment Patrick was stunned into silence.

'My God.' There were tears in his eyes now. 'I don't know what to say . . . except that you're very brave to be on the ship now. It must be awful for you. Is this the first time you've sailed since?' It explained why she was so strained and pale, and why she so seldom came out of her cabin, as she nodded.

'Yes, and it isn't easy. I swore I'd never get on a ship again. But I had to come over to bring back my sister.'

'Was she on it too?' He was fascinated now. He had known of people who had been on the ship and gone down, but he had never met any of the survivors.

'We thought we had lost her. She was lost when we were getting into the lifeboats, or we thought she was. Actually, she'd gone back to the cabin for her doll. She was six years old then.' She smiled sadly. 'The ship went down on her birthday. Anyway, we found her on the rescue ship, she was hysterical, and she's never been . . . well, she's a difficult child because of what she's been through.'

'Did you have any other family?' He was interested in everything, but most of all in her. She was, after all, what they had thought her, a beautiful, mysterious young woman.

'I had three brothers, and two sisters and we all

337

survived. Only my parents, and . . . my fiancé . . . went down. He was English too.' She smiled at the memory as Patrick Sparks-Kelly watched her. 'His name was Charles Fitzgerald.' Her voice grew husky again as she said his name, and for an instant she instinctively felt for the engagement ring on her finger. But she hadn't worn it in years. She had offered to return it to his family, but Lady Fitzgerald had insisted that she keep it. But Patrick was staring at her now in amazement.

'My God . . .' He looked as though he'd seen a ghost, as his eyes met Edwina's.

'I remember hearing about you . . . an American girl . . . from San Francisco . . . that was . . . oh, God, ten or twelve years ago. I was just married myself about then.' And then he explained what he was saying. 'Charles was my second cousin.'

They stood in silence for a moment, thinking about him, and Edwina smiled again. It was a strange world, and it was odd that they should meet now, so long after he was gone.

'That was a terrible thing. Only son . . . favorite child . . . terrible . . .' He thought about it and it all came back to him, he even remembered hearing about Edwina. 'His parents mourned him for years.'

'So did I,' she whispered.

'And you never married?'

She shook her head, and then smiled quietly at him. 'I was too busy after that. I had the other children to bring up. I was twenty then, and most of them were still quite small. My brother Phillip was sixteen and he tried very hard to be a father to them, but it must have been hard for him to be so young and have so much on his shoulders. And he went away to college a year later, in 1913. And George was twelve, Alexis six, my little sister Fannie was four, and the baby was barely two. They kept me amused for a few years.' She grinned and he looked at her in amazement.

'And you did all that . . . alone?' He was stunned. She was quite something.

'More or less. I managed. I did my best, and sometimes I threw my hands up in despair, but we've all survived it.' . . . except for Phillip.

'And what happened to them now? Where are they all?'

She smiled as she thought of them, suddenly missing the two younger ones she had left in San Francisco. 'My oldest brother, Phillip, died in the war six years ago. And my brother George is the family hero. He dropped out of Harvard when Phillip died, and he came home, and eventually went to Hollywood and has been a big success there.'

'As an actor?' Patrick looked intrigued. They sounded like an interesting group, certainly much more so than his own family in England.

But Edwina shook her head as she explained. 'No, he's a studio head now. And he's awfully good at it. They've made some fairly major movies. And he just got married a few weeks ago.' She smiled. 'And then there's Alexis. The one I told you about. I'm meeting her in London,' but she didn't explain why. 'And Fannie, who is our homebody, she's fifteen. And the baby, Teddy, is thirteen now.' She finished her account of them with a look of pride that touched him deeply.

'And you've managed them all single-handed. Bravo. I don't know how you've done it.'

'I just did. Day by day. No one asked if I wanted to. It was something that had to be done, and I loved them all . . .' And then, in a gentle voice, 'I did it for them . . . and for my mother . . . She stayed on the ship to find

Alexis. And then . . . when they wouldn't let the men into the lifeboats, she chose to stay on with my father.'

The thought of it horrified him as he thought of the children leaving the sinking ship in a lifeboat with only Edwina, and now she stared out to sea unhappily, remembering the night that would haunt her forever. 'I think at first they must have thought there would be another lifeboat. No one ever really understood how few there were, or how dire the situation was. No one ever told us that we *had* to get off right then. The band just played on, and there were no sirens, no bells, just a lot of people milling around, thinking they had lots of time, and those precious few lifeboats going down. Maybe she thought she'd go later, or stay with him until other ships came . . .' But then, she turned to look at him, this stranger who had almost been her cousin, and she told him the truth she had hidden from herself for eleven years, and he reached out and took her hand as she said it. 'For a long time, I hated her for what she'd done . . . not leaving me the children . . . but choosing to die with him, for loving him more than she did us . . . for letting her love for him kill her. I think it frightened me for a long time . . . it made me feel so guilty for leaving Charles, as though I should have stayed with him, too, just because she stayed with Papa.' There were tears rolling down Edwina's cheeks now. 'But I didn't . . . I left in the first one, with the children . . . I took them off and let Mama and Papa and Charles die, while we were all safe in the lifeboat.' Just saying it released her from a burden of guilt she had carried for almost a dozen years, and as she spoke the words, she let herself drift into his arms and he held her.

'You couldn't have known what would happen then. You didn't know any more than they did . . . they thought

340

they would all come in another lifeboat, or that they would still be on the ship later and they wouldn't go down.' It was exactly what she had thought.

'I never knew I was saying good-bye to them,' she sobbed. 'I hardly even kissed Charles . . . and then I never saw him again.' She cried in the night air as Patrick held her.

'You couldn't have done anything more. You did everything right . . . it was just rotten luck that it happened at all. But you weren't to blame because you survived and they didn't.'

'But why did she stay with him?' Edwina asked him as though he knew, but he could only guess, just as she had.

'Maybe she loved him too much to live on without him. That happens sometimes. Some women feel that way. Perhaps she couldn't face it, and she knew you were there to take her place with the children.'

'But it wasn't fair to the children, or to me . . . and I had to live on without Charles.' She sounded angry now as she spoke her innermost feelings for the first time. 'Sometimes I hated her because I had survived and she hadn't. Why did I have to live with the pain? Why did I have to live without him? Why did I have to . . .' She couldn't go on, and it didn't matter now. They were all gone, and Edwina had lived through it. She had devoted her life to loving Charles and them and bringing up her parents' children, but it hadn't been easy for her, and as Patrick listened to her cry, he knew it.

'Life is so unfair sometimes.' He wanted to cry with her, but he knew it wouldn't help anything. He was only very flattered that she had talked to him. And he knew from the way she spoke that it was probably the first time she had admitted most of it, particularly her resentment of her mother for choosing to die with her father.

'I'm sorry.' She looked up at him finally. 'I shouldn't have told you all this.' She wiped the tears from her cheeks again, and he handed her a beautiful linen handkerchief with his crest embroidered on it, and she accepted it gratefully. 'I don't usually talk about all this.'

'I assumed that.' And then he smiled down at her again. 'I wish we had met twelve years ago, and then perhaps I'd have stolen you from Charles, and you would have led a much happier life, and so would I. You'd have kept me from marrying someone I shouldn't. Actually,' he smiled as he went on, 'I married a first cousin of Charles's, on his mother's side. A very "handsome girl", as my mother said, but I'm afraid I never realized until too late that she didn't love me.'

'Are you still married to her?' Edwina looked at him as she asked, and blew her nose again. The thought of having married Patrick instead was an intriguing one, and she was sorry again that she'd never met him until their crossing on the *Paris*.

'I am,' he said stoically. 'We have three fine sons, and we speak to each other approximately once every two months, between trips, and over breakfast. I'm afraid my wife is . . . ahh . . . not overly fond of gentlemen, and she's far happier with her lady friends, her female relatives, and her horses.' Edwina thought he had just said something rather important to her, but she was too embarrassed to ask him to elaborate, so she didn't. Suffice it to say that he was married to a woman he didn't love, and who didn't love him, and perhaps what the 'lady friends' meant was unimportant. But in fact Patrick had said what she thought he had. The only amazing thing was that in a very few attempts, they had actually managed to have three children, and that was unlikely to happen again, as the attempt was no longer made, nor desired by either party.

'Would you ever divorce her?' Edwina asked quietly, but Patrick slowly shook his head.

'No, for a number of reasons, among them my sons. And I'm afraid my parents would never survive it. No one in our family has ever divorced, you see. And to complicate matters further, thanks to a French grandmother, I am that rarest of all birds, a British Catholic. I'm afraid that Philippa and I are bound for life, which leaves things rather lonely for me, if not for her, and a rather grim prospect for the next forty or fifty years.' He spoke matter-of-factly, but underneath it, Edwina could hear the loneliness and see it in his eyes as he described his marriage.

'Why don't you leave her then? You can't live like that for the rest of your life.' It was amazing. They were strangers and they were sharing their innermost secrets. But those things often happened on shipboard.

'I have no choice,' Patrick said quietly, referring to his wife again. 'Just as you didn't when you were faced with bringing up your brothers and sisters. *Noblesse oblige*, as my grandmother would have said. Some things are a matter of duty as well as love. And this is mine. And the boys are wonderful, they're growing up a bit now, and, of course, they're all away at school. Richard was the last to go last year, at seven. It frees me up quite a bit now. Actually, I don't have to be at home at all, and most of the time I'm not.' He smiled a boyish smile at Edwina. 'I spend a great deal of time in New York. I go to Paris on business whenever possible. I have my father's lands to keep up. I have friends in Berlin and Rome . . . you see, it's not as bad as all that.' But Edwina was honest with him, as she stood close to him and he kept his arm around her.

'It sounds very empty and very sad.' She didn't mince words with him, and he looked down at her honestly.

'You're right. It is. But it's all I have, Edwina, and I make the best of it. Just as you do. It's not a life, but it's my life. Just as yours is. Look what you've done, you've spent a whole lifetime mourning a man who's been gone for a dozen years. A man you loved when you were twenty. Think of it . . . think of him. Did you really know him? Do you know who he is, who he was, if he would ever have made you happy? You had a right to so much more than that, so did I, but simple fact is, we didn't get it. So you make the best of it, surrounded by the brothers and sisters you love, and I do the same with my children. I have no right to more than that, I'm a married man. But you're not, and when you get off this ship, you ought to go find someone, someone you love, maybe even someone Charles would have liked, and marry him and have children of your own. I can't do that anymore, but you can. Edwina, don't waste it.'

'Don't be foolish.' She laughed at him, but he had said wise words to her, whether or not she knew it. 'Do you know how old I am? I'm thirty-two years old. I'm much too old for that. My life is already half over.'

'So is mine. And I'm thirty-nine. But do you know what? If I had another chance, a chance to love someone, to be happy, to have children again, I would jump at it in a minute.' And as he said that, he looked down at her, and before she could answer him again, he kissed her. He kissed her as she hadn't been kissed since Charles had died, and she couldn't even remember having been kissed that way then, and for an instant what Patrick had just said crossed her mind. Was he right? Was Charles only a distant memory from her childhood? Had she changed so much? Would she have outgrown him? Did she really even remember? It was impossible to know now, and there was no doubt in her mind that she had loved him.

344

But perhaps she had carried him for too long. Perhaps the time to let him go had come at last. And suddenly, as she kissed Patrick back, all else faded from her mind, as they held each other like two drowning people.

It was a long time before he let her go again, and they stood there holding each other close as he kissed her again, and then he looked down at her and told her something she had a right to know from the first. And he knew he had to tell her.

'Edwina, no matter what happens between us, I can't marry you. I want you to know that now, before you fall in love with me, and I with you. No matter how much I come to love you one day, I am a dead man. I will stay married to my dying day. And I don't want to destroy your life too. I'll tell you right now that if you let me love you, I will set you free . . . for your sake, and for mine . . . I won't hold on to you, and I won't let you hold on either. Do you understand?'

'I do,' she said huskily, grateful for his honesty, but she had sensed from the beginning that he was that kind of person. It was why she had let herself talk to him, and why she already knew she loved him. It was absurd, she scarcely knew him, yet she knew she loved him.

'I won't let you do what you did with Charles . . . carry the memory for years . . . I want to love you, and send you on your way, a whole and happy person. And if you do come to love me one day, you'll marry someone else and do what I told you.'

'You worry too much.' She smiled. 'You can't foresee everything. What if Philippa dies one day, or leaves you, or decides to move away somewhere?'

'I won't build my life on that, or let you do it either. Remember, my love, I will set you free one day . . . like a little bird . . . to fly back home from where you've come, far across the ocean.' But as he said the words, it made her lonely for him before anything began and she clung to him and whispered softly,

'Not yet . . . please . . .'

'No . . . not yet . . .' he whispered back, and then like a memory in a distant dream, he ruffled her hair with his lips, and whispered again, '. . . I love you . . .' Strangers though they were, their confessions, and the link of Charles, had brought them together.

36

It was the sort of thing that only happened in books, or one of George's movies. They met, they fell in love, and they existed suspended between two worlds, as Edwina discovered a life she'd never had, or had forgotten about in the past eleven years. They talked, they laughed, they walked for hours around the ship, and gradually she lost her terror that they would sink at any moment. He made sure to be with her at lifeboat drill, although in point of fact he belonged at another station. But the purser didn't object. And from the distance, other passengers watched them with warm smiles and envious looks and silent cheering from the sidelines. They were discreet as they sought private spots and hideaways just to talk and kiss and hold hands. It was what they had both missed for so long, although Edwina suspected that Patrick had had it from time to time, although he claimed that he had never loved anyone since he got married, and she believed him.

'What were you like as a child?' he asked, wanting to know everything, every detail, every smallest bit about her.

'I don't know,' she smiled happily up at him, 'I don't think I've ever thought about it. Happy, I guess. We had a pretty ordinary life, until they died. Before that, I went to school, I fought with Phillip over our toys . . . I used to love to help Mama in the garden . . . in fact,' she remembered now, 'when she first died . . . after we came home, I used to talk to her out there, clipping her rosebushes, and pulling weeds, and sometimes I'd get pretty angry. I wanted to know why she had done what she did, what made her stay with him when she had all these children that I felt she had deserted.'

'And did you ever get any answers?' He smiled down at her, as she shook her head.

'No, but I always felt better afterward.'

'Then it must have been a good thing. I like gardening, too, when I get the chance. Although it's not considered very manly.' They talked about everything, their childhood friends, their favorite sports, and most-beloved authors. He liked the serious, classical stuff, and she liked popular authors like F. Scott Fitzgerald and John Dos Passos. They both liked poetry, and sunsets, and moonlight and dancing. And she told him with tears in her eyes how proud she was of George and what he had done, and how much she liked Helen. She even told him about giving Helen the veil she had been meant to wear for Charles, and that time Patrick cried as he listened.

'I wish you'd have worn it for me.'

'So do I,' she whispered as she wiped the tear off his cheek, and that night, the day after they'd met, they went dancing. She bemoaned the fact that she didn't have a single decent dress, but miraculously, he had a stewardess find her one for the evening. It fit perfectly and had a label from Chanel, and all night she expected some irate first-class passenger to tear it off her back, but none appeared and they had a wonderful time circling the floor in the first-class lounge. Everything was perfect.

And the ship didn't sink, but it arrived too soon. It seemed like only moments before they reached Cherbourg and then Southampton.

'What do we do now?' she asked mournfully. They had discussed it a hundred times, and in her head she had rehearsed leaving him, but she found that now she couldn't bring herself to do it.

He repeated it all for her again, 'You find Alexis, and we have lunch or dinner in London to celebrate, and then you go home again and begin a happy life and find a nice man to marry.' She snorted as he said the words.

'And how was it you suggested I do that again? I put an ad in the San Francisco paper?'

'No, you stop looking like a grieving widow, and you go out in the world, and in ten minutes there will be a dozen men at your front gate, mark my words.'

'That's nonsense.' And it wasn't what she wanted. She wanted Patrick.

She had long since confessed why she had come to London at all, and he had been irate at her description of the errant Malcolm. And he had already volunteered to help find the girl. Together they were going to comb the small hotels, and he had several in mind where actors stayed. He suspected that it might not be very difficult to find them. He was going to go to his office that day, settle some affairs, and meet her later that afternoon to begin their search, but as much as she wanted to find Alexis again, she didn't want to leave him, even for a moment. After being together almost every hour of the day for three days, it was going to seem strange now being without him. The only time they had left each other had been at night, by silent agreement. They had kissed and hugged and held hands, but he didn't want to take advantage of her and then leave her. And in a way she agreed with him, and yet in a way she wished that things were different. It was ridiculous, really. Her seventeen-year-old sister was having a wild affair, and she was returning to the United States, a virgin spinster. She laughed at the thought and Patrick smiled at her, seeing something in her eyes.

'What are you up to, you bad girl?'

'I was just thinking how incongruous it is, that Alexis is off misbehaving with that deadbeat, and I am being very circumspect. I'm not sure I like the scenario at all!' They both laughed, but had they wanted it to be different, it would have been. It had just been too soon, for both of them, and they didn't want to cheapen what they had. What they had, they both knew, was very rare and very special.

He took the boat train to London with her, and they sat quietly in the same compartment and talked, while he explained that Philippa didn't know or care that he was arriving that day, and he suspected she would be away anyway, probably at some important horse trials in Scotland.

He checked her into Claridge's then, and promised to be back at five, it was not yet noon by then. And she immediately sent a telegram to the children, telling them where she was, and that all was well, and requesting that they wire her if they had news of Alexis. And she could only assume that they were fine, or in the next day or so they would wire her at Claridge's, to tell her their problems.

She went to Harrods quickly then, and bought more dresses in less time than she had ever done in her life, got her hair done nearby, and took a cab back to the hotel, laden with hatboxes and dresses, and her new hairdo. And when Patrick arrived at five, he found her elegant and smiling, and excited to see him.

'Good heavens,' he grinned, 'what have you been up to all afternoon?' But he had been busy too. He had bought her a rare copy of Elizabeth Barrett Browning, and had she been more familiar with London shops, she would have known that the box he pulled out of his pocket came from Wartski's. She gasped at first when he handed it to her, and she was afraid to open it, but at last she did, and for a long moment, she fell silent as she stared at his gift. It was a narrow diamond bracelet, and the legend was that it had been given to Queen Victoria by Prince Albert. It was rare that items like that came up for sale at all, but for special customers, they sometimes offered one or two very special items. It was the sort of thing she could wear all the time, and she knew as she put it on her arm, that it would stay there for a long, long time, in memory of Patrick.

He had also brought her a bottle of champagne, but after only one drink, they both decided that it was time to start looking for Alexis. He had hired a car and driver just for that and they began their search of every hotel in Soho. And at eight o'clock as they tried 'just one more,' Edwina walked in with a photograph, as they had for the last two hours, and Patrick slipped a five-pound note to the desk clerk.

'Have you seen this girl?' she asked, showing a small photograph that she had carried for years in her wallet. 'She's traveling with a man named Malcolm Stone, a tall, good-looking man of, say, forty-five or fifty.' The desk clerk looked at Edwina, then Patrick, and then at the bill in his hand, and finally this one nodded and looked up at them again.

'Yeah, they're here. What's she done? Stolen something off yer? They're American, you know.' He apparently hadn't noticed Edwina's accent, and as the money had come from him, he addressed himself to Patrick.

'Are they here now?'

'Nah, they left yesterday. They only been here a few days. I can look up exactly when they came, if you want to know. She's a right pretty girl she is, got a headful of yeller hair.' Edwina could feel her heart pound to know that she had come this far and was now this close to Alexis, and a tiny part of her was almost sorry to find her so soon. Now it meant she had to go home, and leave Patrick. 'They went to Paris for a few days, least that's what he said. Gave up the room for two weeks, but they said they'd be back again. They will too. He left a suitcase.' Patrick glanced at Edwina, and as she nodded imperceptibly he slipped the boy another bill and asked to see the suitcase. There were assorted men's clothes in it when they opened it, but right on top there was a white suit. It was the one she'd been wearing when she left Los Angeles, and the hat was all but ruined, but Edwina knew it immediately as Alexis's.

'That's it!' Her eyes shone with tears as she touched it, wondering what had happened to her since she left. 'That's hers, Patrick. That's what she was wearing the day she disappeared in Los Angeles, the day after George's wedding.' It seemed a lifetime ago now, and in a way it was. It had been more than two weeks, and in that time Alexis's whole life had changed, she knew, as she looked up at Patrick.

'What do you want to do now?' he asked softly as the desk clerk went back to the front desk to answer a phone.

'I don't know. He said they'd be gone for two weeks.'

'Why don't we go to dinner and discuss it.' That sounded fine to her, and before they left, the desk clerk asked if he should say that they'd been there, but Edwina was quick to answer.

'No. Don't say anything.' Another pound note assured his silence. And she and Patrick walked outside to the waiting car, and drove back to Claridge's for dinner.

They went back up to her room, and Patrick was quick to ask if she wanted to follow them to Paris, but it seemed like a wild-goose chase to her. They didn't know where they'd gone, or why, and the suitcase told her that they'd be back again. 'I think we just have to wait.' But now they had two weeks at their disposal.

'Is there anything special you want to do here?' he asked. There was one thing, but there was time for that, and she was going to ask Patrick about it later.

'Not really.' She smiled. But he already had an idea. It was something he had wanted to do for years. There was a place he had always longed to go back to in Ireland. He hadn't been there since he was a boy, and it had always seemed like the most romantic place in the world to him, and as Edwina listened to him tell her about it over dinner, she knew that all she wanted to do now was go there.

'Can you do that?' she asked cautiously, and he grinned, feeling like a wild young boy again. She made him feel young and happy and alive, just as he did for her. She felt like a girl again, only now she knew what she'd missed. And suddenly, everything was ten times as romantic.

'Let's do it, Edwina,' he whispered to her as he leaned across the corner of the table to kiss her.

And in the morning, it was done. She called Fannie and Teddy to let them know she was alright. And then Patrick picked her up, and they took a train, a ferry across the Irish Sea, and then hired a car and drove to Cashel, where by nightfall they stood in front of the Rock of Cashel. It was a sober, enormous, imposing place, and the fields beyond it were covered with gorse and heather, and even at this time of year she thought she'd never seen anything as green, as they walked for miles at sunset. And at last they stood in the circle of each other's arms as he kissed her.

'You've come a long, long way to be with me,' he said

in the cool evening air as the sun went down over the lake behind them.

'It's as though it was meant to be, isn't it?'

'It was,' he promised her, in the gentle brogue of County Tipperary, and then in his own voice again, 'I will always remember this day, Edwina, until I'm very, very old, and on the day I die, I will remember this moment.' He kissed her again, and they walked slowly back to their hotel, and upstairs to their room, and she knew at that moment that she had been born for him, that this was meant to be. He had rented a single room for them, and they both knew why. They had so little time, so much to share, so much to learn, and as Patrick gently peeled her dress away and lifted her onto the bed, she knew that he had so much to teach her.

She lay beside him until the dawn, as he drank her in, and she knew that her wedding day had come, the only one she'd ever had, not the one she had been meant to have with Charles, but the only life she would ever have, these brief, sweet, precious two weeks with Patrick.

37

The moments sped by on angel's wings as Patrick and Edwina roamed across the hills, rowed on the little lake, picked wildflowers, and took photographs of everything, and spent the nights in each other's arms deep in their bed, and it seemed as though in the blink of an eye, it was over. They traveled back to London silently, anxious not to get there. In the end, they had stolen two extra days, but they both knew they had to get back, and Edwina had to find Alexis. She felt foolish about it at times. By now she suspected the girl didn't want to be found, and her letter to Edwina in New York had reiterated that they were married. And there were even moments when Edwina envied her, because perhaps she had everything she wanted. Although it was hard for Edwina to imagine Malcolm Stone as a pleasant man, there was always the unfortunate possibility that Alexis really loved him. She still didn't know what she was going to say to George when she got back, if anything. But right now she wasn't thinking of Alexis or George. She was only thinking of Patrick. She slipped her hand into his, and wished that an entire lifetime could be theirs, but they both knew it could never be. He had told her that from the first, and she had to go back to the States to live the life she had left there. But for one shining moment, the dream had been theirs, and she knew they would always cherish it as something rare and precious. As they walked back into Alexis's hotel, the diamond bracelet shone on her arm, in memory of the days they'd shared, the love they'd spawned, the moments they would treasure.

Patrick asked for Malcolm Stone this time, and this time a different desk clerk told them they were in, and with a quick slip of the hand Patrick told him not to ring, and he looked at Edwina.

'Do you want to come up with me, or shall I see him first?'

'I'd better come up with you,' she whispered, 'or you'll frighten Alexis.' Although admittedly by now, it was difficult thinking of anything that could frighten her, after the life she must have led for the past four weeks. It had been nearly a month since she'd run away. And George was due back home again in a few weeks. She was going to have to get her home quickly if she was going to do it quietly at all, and she followed Patrick up the stairs to the room number they'd been given. And with trembling hands, Edwina waited while Patrick knocked on the door, as they both wondered what they'd find there.

Patrick looked at her, smiled to buck her up, and then knocked loudly, and less than half a minute later, a tall, handsome man with bare feet and a cigar pulled the door open. He had a whiskey bottle in one hand, and beyond him a pretty girl in a satin slip stood watching them. And it was only an instant later that Edwina realized the pretty girl was her sister. The long mane of blond hair had been bobbed and then marcelled, and she was wearing pale white powder and rouge and lots of kohl and lipstick. But even beneath the mask she wore, Patrick saw that Edwina had been right, the child was a beauty.

She began to cry the minute she saw them, and Malcolm bowed low and invited them in, amused that the virgin sister had brought a hero.

'My, my, a family visit so soon.' He looked at Edwina

356

with sarcasm warmed by Irish whiskey. 'I had no idea you'd be kind enough to visit us in London, Miss Winfield.' For an instant, Patrick had the same urge George had had when he'd floored him in Rosarita months before, but he restrained himself and for the moment, said nothing.

Edwina looked solemnly at her sister, and Patrick saw the softness disappear. She was suddenly stern and almost imposing. 'Alexis, please be good enough to pack your things.' And then she looked at Malcolm Stone with contempt. He reeked of booze and cheap cigars, and she shuddered at the life of total degradation her sister must have led with him. But Alexis hadn't moved since she and Patrick had entered.

'Are you planning to take my wife somewhere?' he mocked as he asked Edwina.

'Your "wife" happens to be a seventeen-year-old girl, and unless you plan to answer to charges of kidnapping and rape, I suggest that you let her come home with me, Mr Stone,' Edwina said coolly.

'This is not California, Miss Winfield. This is England. And she is my wife. You have no say here.'

Edwina looked at him as though he did not exist, and then directly past him at her sister. 'Alexis, are you coming?'

'I . . . Edwina, do I have to? I love him.' The words struck her sister like a fist, and Patrick sensed it only because he knew her, but there was no sign of it, and he found himself admiring her even more for her strength with this obviously wicked child and disgusting profligate she'd run off with. However upset Edwina may have been, she showed nothing but dignified restraint as she spoke to her sister.

'Is this how you wish to live?' She spoke softly to her,

looking around the room, leaving nothing out, the open toilet, their clothes on the floor, the empty whiskey bottles, the dead cigars, and finally, she glanced at Malcolm. 'Is this what you've always wanted?' It would have shamed anyone, particularly a seventeen-year-old girl. Even Patrick was embarrassed by her tone, and secretly, so was Malcolm. 'Is this your dream, Alexis? What happened to the rest of it? Where is the movie star . . . the home . . . where is all the love you've had? Is this what you've turned it into?' Alexis started to whimper and turned away, and in her heart, Edwina knew what she'd done, and it hurt her to realize it. It was no accident that she had done this the day after George's wedding. She was looking for the father she had lost . . . just as she had tried to run away when Phillip left for Harvard . . . she needed men, a man, anyone. But what Alexis really wanted was not a lover or a husband, or just any man, but a daddy. And it almost made Edwina cry as she looked sadly at her sister.

'Edwina . . .' Alexis began to cry. 'I'm so sorry . . .' It hadn't been anything she had expected. She had thought it would be glamorous and fun running off with Malcolm, but for weeks now she had known the truth. He was only using her in every way he could, and it was dismal and depressing. Even Paris had been grim. He had been drunk all the time, and more than once she knew he had gone off with other girls, but at least then she knew he'd leave her alone. She didn't want anything to do with him, and yet in some part of her, she always wanted him to love her. And when he called her 'baby', she would have done anything for him, and he knew it.

'Get dressed,' Edwina said quietly, as Patrick watched, full of admiration for her.

'Miss Winfield, you may *not* take my wife.' Malcolm

358

took a step toward Edwina then and wove a little as he tried to look menacing, and out of the corner of her eye, she saw Patrick approach, but she held a hand out to stop him. She had an idea, and she wasn't leaving until she knew the truth. He wasn't the sort of man to marry anyone, let alone a child of seventeen like Alexis.

'Do you have proof of your marriage to my sister, sir?' she asked politely. 'You can't expect me to believe it if I don't see proof. And by the way . . .' She turned to Alexis then, as the girl was dressing. She was putting on a red satin thing that made Edwina cringe, but she was only glad to see her putting her clothes on. 'By the way, Alexis, how did you get into England and France without a passport, or did you get one in New York?' Edwina spoke very coolly, and Alexis gave her the answer.

'Malcolm told them I'd lost my passport. And I was so sick they didn't want to upset me.'

'Sick, on the ship?' Edwina asked, sympathetically. She knew how traumatic the trip must have been, and was surprised she'd gone at all.

'They kept me drugged the whole time I was on the *Bremen*.' She said it innocently as she put her shoes on.

'Drugged?' Edwina's eyebrows shot straight up as she looked at Malcolm. 'And do you plan to return to the States, Mr Stone, *ever*? . . . drugged . . . kidnapped . . . raped . . . a girl of seventeen . . . a minor . . . what an interesting tale that will make in court.'

'Will it?' Malcolm slowly came to life. 'Do you really think your brother and his fancy Hollywood bride are going to want to spread that around? Just exactly what do you think that's going to do to her reputation? No, Miss Winfield, he won't go to court, and neither will you, nor will Alexis. He's going to give me work, that's what he's going to do, for his brother-in-law. Or if he doesn't want

359

to give me work, maybe he'd just like to give me money.' He laughed, as Edwina listened in horror, and then she looked at Alexis and knew the truth. She was crying as she listened in shame to the man she'd run away with. She had known, suspected all along, that he didn't love her, but now there was no hiding from it at all after what he'd just said to Edwina.

'Alexis, did you marry him?' Edwina looked her straight in the eye. 'Did you? Tell me the truth. I want to know. And after what you just heard, you should tell me, for George's sake and your own.' But Alexis was already shaking her head, much to Edwina and Patrick's relief, and crying softly, as Malcolm swore, furious with himself for putting it off. But he had never thought they'd come for her all the way to England.

'At first he said we did and I was too drunk to remember it. And then he admitted we didn't. But we were supposed to get married in Paris, and he was always too drunk to do it,' Alexis cried, and Edwina almost laughed with joy as she glanced at Patrick.

'You can't take her,' Stone tried to bluff his way through. 'She's my common-law wife. I won't let you take her.' And then he had another thought. 'Besides,' he said hopefully, seeing gold slipping through his fingers, 'what if she's pregnant?'

'I'm not,' Alexis answered instantly, much to Edwina's relief. At least that much was sure. And Alexis went to stand next to Edwina then, and looked sadly at Malcolm.

'You never loved me, did you? I never was your little girl . . .'

'Sure you were.' He looked embarrassed in front of all of them, and glanced at Alexis again. 'We could still get married, you know. You don't have to go with them, unless you want to.'

But Edwina left no misapprehension in either of them as she looked at him and then at her sister. 'I will remove her physically, if I have to.'

'You can't do that.' Malcolm took a step toward her again, and then suddenly looked at Patrick as though for the first time. 'And who's he anyway?'

Edwina had been about to answer him when Patrick cut her off and looked menacingly at Malcolm. 'I am a magistrate. And if you say one more word, or detain this child any further, we shall put you in jail and hasten to deport you from the country.' But as Patrick said the words, for the first time, Malcolm Stone looked truly deflated. He watched as Patrick opened the door, and Edwina walked her out. And Alexis only looked back once over her shoulder. A moment later they were all downstairs again, and the nightmare was ended, as Edwina thanked God that Alexis had never married him, and prayed that she would get her back to San Francisco without anyone ever knowing what had happened. And as for Alexis's movie career, she could kiss that good-bye. From now on, Edwina promised herself, Alexis was going to stay home with Fannie and learn to make bread and oatmeal cookies. But what made her saddest of all was knowing that no matter how much love Edwina had given her over the years, it had never been enough, and she had sold herself in her futile search for a daddy.

She said as much to Patrick later that night, once Alexis was in Edwina's bed at Claridges. There had been a long tearful scene, hysterical apologies, and Alexis begging Edwina for forgiveness. None of which had been necessary, as Edwina held her in her arms and they both cried, and at last she had fallen asleep, and Edwina had come back outside into the living room, to talk to Patrick.

'How is she?' He looked worried, it had been a long

evening for all of them, but they had come out of it a lot better off than Patrick had expected. The girl was basically fine, and Malcolm Stone had been surprisingly easy to dispose of.

'She's asleep, thank God,' Edwina answered with a sigh as she sat down, and he poured her a glass of champagne. 'What a night.'

'What a dreadful character he was. Do you think he'll come back to haunt you?' She had wondered about it herself, but there was little she could do about it now, other than tell George and have him blacklisted, but she wasn't anxious to do that either.

'I don't know. I hope not. It doesn't exactly make him look like a prince either. Thank God he was too lazy to marry her. We could have had it annulled, of course, but it would have complicated everything, and I'm sure then it would have ended up in the papers.'

'And now?'

'With luck, I can sneak her back into the country, and no one will know. Do you suppose I can get a passport for her here?'

'I'll talk to the embassy for you tomorrow.' He knew the American ambassador well, and hopefully he could get a passport for her, without too many questions. As Malcolm Stone had done, he was just going to say she lost it, while traveling with her sister.

'Would you do something else for me too?' She had wanted to ask him that ever since she had discovered that Charles was his cousin. 'Will you call Lady Fitzgerald for me? I know she must be rather old by now.' She hadn't been young eleven years before. 'But if she's willing to, I'd like to see her.'

He was quiet for a moment and then he nodded.

'I need to say good-bye to her,' she said softly. She had

never had the chance to do that before. And most of all, she had needed to say good-bye to Charles, and Patrick had finally helped her do that.

'I'll call her tomorrow too.' And then regretfully, he kissed her good-bye. 'I'll see you in the morning.'

'I love you,' she whispered, and he smiled and pulled her close to him again.

'I love you too.' But they both knew now that the end was near. If she was going to get Alexis home quietly, she'd have to go soon. And Edwina hated the thought of leaving Patrick.

38

The next morning, Alexis got a dreadful fright when
Patrick appeared. She opened the door to him and then
went running to find Edwina.

'The magistrate is here again!' she whispered in urgent
tones, and Edwina went to see what he wanted. But she
exploded into gales of laughter when she saw him.

'That's not the magistrate,' she laughed, 'that's Patrick
Sparks-Kelly, my friend.' And then she added by way of
explanation to Alexis, and because she felt she had to
justify knowing him so well, 'He's Charles's cousin.'

'But I thought . . . you said . . .' Alexis looked like a
child again, the makeup washed off, the hair as simply
combed as Edwina could get it. She had done some awful
things to it in Paris. And now Alexis smiled, looking clean
and beautiful again as Edwina explained that Patrick had
only pretended to be a magistrate to frighten Malcolm.

'Just in case your friend gave us trouble,' he explained.
And then he told Edwina all she had to do was pick the
passport up at Number 4 Grosvenor Gardens and then he
told her quietly that Lady Fitzgerald was expecting them
at eleven.

'Was she surprised to hear from me?' Edwina didn't
want to provide too great a shock. She had calculated that
she would be well into her seventies by then.

But Patrick shook his head. 'I think she was more
surprised that I knew you.'

'How did you explain that?' She looked at him

worriedly. They had so much to hide, even from Alexis.

'I just told her we met on the ship.' He smiled. 'A happy coincidence . . . for me . . .'

'Do you think it will upset her too much to see me?' she asked worriedly, and he shook his head again.

'Not at all. I think she made her peace with it a long time ago, far more than you did.'

And when they met later that morning, Edwina realized that it was true. Lady Fitzgerald welcomed her openly, and sat and talked with Edwina for a long time, while Patrick and Alexis strolled in her splendid gardens.

'I always hoped you'd marry someday,' she said sadly, looking at Edwina. She had been such a pretty young girl, and she still was. It seemed a waste to her to learn that she'd never married. 'But I suppose you couldn't with all the children to raise. How terrible that your mother went down with your father. It was an awful thing . . . so many lives . . . such waste and all because the company was too foolish to carry enough lifeboats . . . the captain too stubborn to slow his ship in the face of icebergs . . . the radio on the nearest ship shut off . . . it used to trouble me terribly, and in the end I had to decide that it was fate that Charles didn't survive it. You see, my dear, that is destiny. You must be grateful to be alive, and enjoy every moment.'

Edwina smiled at her, fighting back tears again, remembering the first time they'd met, with Charles, and the wedding veil she'd sent when it was completed, even though he was gone by then, and Edwina would never wear it. She thanked her again and Lady Fitzgerald explained why she'd sent it.

'I felt wrong keeping it. And even though I knew it would upset you at the time, I thought that you should have it.'

'My sister-in-law wore it last month, and she looked beautiful.' She promised to send a photograph and the old woman smiled, looking tired. Her husband had died the year before and she herself was not in the best of health, but it had warmed her heart to see Edwina.

'Your younger sister is a very pretty girl, my dear, not unlike you at her age, except that of course her hair is so much lighter.'

'I hope I wasn't quite as foolish as she is.' Edwina smiled, flattered by the compliment of being even remotely compared to Alexis.

'You weren't foolish at all. And you've been very brave since then . . . very brave . . . perhaps now you will be lucky as well, and find someone who loves you. You've hung on to him for all these years, haven't you?' She had sensed that about Edwina the moment they had started to talk, and with tears brimming in her eyes, Edwina nodded. 'You must let him go now,' she whispered, gently kissing Edwina's cheek, and for an instant she was so deeply reminded of Charles that she almost couldn't bear it. 'He's happy now, wherever he is, as your parents are. Now you must be happy, too, Edwina. All three of them would want that.'

'I've been happy,' she protested, blowing her nose in the handkerchief she still had from Patrick, and she wondered briefly if Lady Fitzgerald saw it. But she was too old to notice details like that, or to care whose handkerchief Edwina carried. 'I've been happy with the children for all these years.'

'That's not enough,' Charles's mother scolded, 'and you know it. Will you come back to England sometime?' she asked as they stood up and walked slowly out into the garden. Edwina felt drained, but she was glad she had come, and she knew that what Lady Fitzgerald said was true. They would have wanted her to be happy again. She couldn't hide anymore. She had learned that with Patrick. And now she was going to have to say good-bye to him too. Her life seemed to be full of painful good-byes at the moment.

She kissed Lady Fitzgerald good-bye at noon, and she felt lighter and happier when she did than she had in a long time, and she talked about her to Patrick over lunch, and said what a nice woman she was. And he agreed, as did Alexis.

He took them to lunch at the Ritz, and afterward they booked their passage on the *Olympic* and then went to pick up Alexis's passport. They were fortunate, they were told. The *Olympic* was leaving the following morning, and Edwina suddenly felt a wave of panic wash over her at the thought of leaving Patrick. She glanced quickly at him and he nodded his head, and she booked two adjoining first-class staterooms for herself and Alexis.

But Alexis had grown up a great deal in the past few weeks, and she made a point of leaving them alone that night and claiming to be utterly exhausted.

'You don't suppose she's sneaking off again, do you?' Patrick asked her worriedly as he left to take Edwina to the Embassy Club for dinner.

But Edwina laughed at him, and assured him that this time she felt sure Alexis had learned her lesson.

And once again, the evening went too quickly and all too soon they were back at Claridge's again, and there was no way to share the tenderness that they had had in Ireland. She wanted to make love to him again, but they both knew that it was just as well that they didn't.

'How am I going to say good-bye to you, Patrick? I've only just found you.' It had taken her eleven years to say goodbye to Charles, and now she had to let his cousin go in a single moment. 'Will you come to Southampton with us tomorrow?' But he shook his head sadly.

'That would be too hard for both of us, wouldn't it? And it might be unsettling for Alexis.'

'I think she knows anyway.'

'Then you are both going home with dark secrets.' He kissed her gently then, and they both knew that nothing they had shared had been anything but light and beautiful, and in some hidden, secret way, Edwina knew that he had freed her.

'Will I see you again?' she asked as he left her outside Claridge's.

'Perhaps. If you come back. Or I go there. I've never been to California.' And she doubted that he ever would. It was exactly what he had said from the first, they both had to let go, to let each other fly free forever. She felt the gift from him on her arm, where it always would be, and his touch on her heart, but the rest would be gone, a distant, happy memory he had given her for a few weeks, to free her from the bonds that had chained her for so long. 'I love you,' he whispered just before he left her. 'I love you desperately . . . and I always will . . . and I will smile each time I think of you . . . I will smile, as you should, each time I think of Ireland.' He kissed her then one last time, as she cried, and he left in his car without looking back. She stood for a long, long time, crying and then slowly, she walked back into Claridge's, knowing how much she had loved him.

39

They left at eight o'clock the next day, for Southampton, as they had done years before, but this time, just the two of them, two sisters, two friends, two survivors. They were quiet as they drove away, and Alexis suspected there was a lot on Edwina's mind. And for a long time, Edwina only sat staring out the window.

They boarded the *Olympic* on time, and still feeling nervous about being on a ship at all, the two women went to their staterooms. And then Edwina surprised Alexis by saying that she was going on deck to watch them sail. She went alone, as her younger sister had no desire to see it.

And she stood on deck, as the huge ship slipped its moorings, and just as she left the dock and moved away, Edwina saw him there. It was as though she had known that he would be there. Patrick stood on the dock, waving solemnly, watching her, and she blew him a kiss as she cried, and touched her heart. And he touched his. And she saw him wave as long as she could, until the ship was far, far away, but Edwina knew she would always remember Patrick.

It was a long time before she went back downstairs, and she found Alexis asleep on her bed. For both of them, the trip had been exhausting.

They had their lifeboat drill that day, and all Edwina could think of now was Patrick, not Charles . . . their walks around the deck, their endless hours of talking, his going to the lifeboat drill with her . . . the night they danced, she in the borrowed dress . . . it made her smile thinking of it all, and as she looked overhead she saw a bird flying past and was reminded of what he had told her. No matter what happened between them, he was going to set her free to find her way home. They had their own lives, their own worlds, and there was no way that they could ever be together. But at thirty-two she had loved and been loved by two men and she felt strangely grown up as they steamed home, and even Alexis saw it.

'You fell in love with him, didn't you?' Alexis asked on the second day, and for a long time Edwina stared out to sea and didn't answer.

'He was a cousin of Charles's.' But that still didn't answer the question, and Alexis knew it. But she knew now also, and had learned at great price, that some questions are better left unanswered.

'Do you think George will know, about Malcolm, I mean?' She looked genuinely scared, and Edwina thought about it carefully.

'Maybe not, if you're very discreet, and the children don't tell him.'

'And if they do, or someone else does?'

'What do you really think he can do?' Edwina asked, addressing her as an adult for the first time. 'He can't do anything. Whatever harm that was done, was done to you, in your heart, your soul, whatever part of you that truly matters. If you can make your peace with that, then you've won. You've learned some hard lessons, and put them behind you. All that really matters is what you got out of it. The rest is just noise.' Alexis smiled in relief, and Edwina patted her hand as Alexis leaned over and kissed her.

'Thank you for getting me out of it.' The truth was, it had done them both good. Edwina had learned some valuable lessons too, and she was grateful.

'Anytime.' She smiled and then lay back on her deck chair, eyes closed, and then opened them rapidly again. 'Well, not exactly "anytime". Let's not do that again, thank you.'

'Yeah, let's not.' Alexis laughed.

They kept to their cabins most of the time, read, played cards, slept, talked, and got to know each other better as adults. Alexis claimed that she was serious about a movie career, and Edwina told her she thought she should wait until she was at least eighteen and could handle it a little better. And Alexis agreed. Her experience with Malcolm Stone had frightened her about the kind of men she'd meet, and she said she always wanted Edwina there with her from now on, for protection.

'You'll be able to handle it next time.' But Alexis was no longer so sure, and she talked about how lucky Fannie was, wanting nothing more than a home and children one day, and nothing more exciting in her life than making dinner for her husband. 'Big challenges aren't for everyone,' Edwina said. 'Just a rare few. And the people outside those magic circles never really understand it.'

They made a few friends on the way home, and were both relieved when they docked in New York. Some bad experiences die hard, and they both knew that that one would always be difficult for them. And as they stepped off the ship, Edwina still missed Patrick. He had sent her flowers on the ship with only 'I love you, P.' on the card, and those he sent to the hotel in New York said, *Je t'aime . . . Adieu*, and she stood looking at them for a moment, touched the bracelet on her arm, and put the card in her wallet.

They stayed in New York for only one night, called Fannie and Teddy, only to learn that George had called twice and Fannie had rather ingeniously told him both times that Alexis was out, and Edwina had terrible laryngitis. Sam Horowitz had called too, and she had told him the same thing, and other than that, 'the coast was clear', and the children were thrilled that all was well with Alexis. She spoke to them herself, and they all cried, or at least the girls did. And four days later, they were home, amid jubilant hugs and kisses and tears and Alexis swore she would never leave them again, not even to go to Hollywood, and Edwina laughed as she heard her.

'I'll make you eat those words one day,' she teased, just as the phone rang. It was George. They had gotten back to Hollywood that day, after a glorious honeymoon, and when she talked to Helen afterward, she whispered to Edwina on the phone that she thought she might be pregnant.

'You are? How wonderful!' And she was surprised at herself when she felt a pang of envy. Helen was ten years younger, had just returned from her honeymoon, and had a husband who adored her, unlike Edwina, who was alone again, and back to taking care of the children.

And he got back on the phone when Helen was through to ask solicitously, 'How's your throat, by the way?'

'Fine. Why?' And then she remembered Fannie's story. 'Oh . . . perfect now . . . but what a dreadful cold that was. I was afraid it was going to turn into a bad case of flu, or pneumonia or something, but it never did.'

'I'm glad. I had the oddest dream about you one night.' He didn't tell her that he'd imagined her on a ship, he knew it would have upset her too much, but it had unnerved him so much that he'd woken Helen. And Helen was convinced that was the night she'd gotten pregnant.

'Anyway, I'm glad you're alright. When are you coming down to see us?'

The very thought of going anywhere again filled Edwina with dread. She had just come back from halfway around the world, but of course he didn't know it. 'Are you coming home for Thanksgiving?' she asked, but George had another idea.

'Sam was thinking that we could take turns. He could do it at his place this year, and you could do it next year.' He had promised Helen he would put it to Edwina that way, but he had also warned her that if it upset his sister not to host Thanksgiving herself as she always did, they would have to go to San Francisco.

And at her end, Edwina thought about it for what seemed like a long time, and then slowly she nodded. 'Okay . . . that might be fun for a change. Even though poor Fannie wanted to do her special turkey.'

'She can do it at Sam's,' George suggested with a smile, patting Helen's still flat tummy. 'Helen wants to help with the cooking too, don't you, dear?' he teased, as she groaned. Helen didn't know one end of the kitchen from the other.

'I guess that's why Sam called,' Edwina said pensively, she hadn't even had time to return his call yet.

'Probably,' George assumed. 'Well, we'll see you in a few weeks then.'

She told the children they were going to Los Angeles for Thanksgiving, to start a new tradition with Helen and George and Sam, and everyone seemed pleased, even Alexis.

'I thought you were never going to let me out of this house again.' They had grown closer since their big adventure, but the others seemed not to mind. Teddy and Fannie were almost like twins, and they were happy to have

Edwina and Alexis home again, and it was odd, Edwina thought to herself as she went to bed that night, everyone seemed suddenly grown up now. And as she drifted off to sleep, she couldn't help thinking of Patrick. It all seemed like a dream now, the ships, the trains, the trip to Ireland, the incident with Malcolm and Alexis, the diamond bracelet, the champagne, the poetry, the visit to Lady Fitzgerald. There was so much to think about that Edwina felt as though she were still sorting it out in her head when they went down to Los Angeles for Thanksgiving.

Helen and George looked well, and by then Helen had confirmed to everyone that she was pregnant. Sam was ecstatic over it, and put in a request for a grandson. And Fannie made her 'special' turkey for everyone and asked Helen if she could come to Hollywood for a few months and help her with the baby. The idea took Helen by surprise, but it was due in June, and Fannie was going to be out of school for summer vacation.

'And what am I supposed to do all summer while you change diapers, Fan?' Teddy complained, but George was quick to intervene.

'I thought you might like to work as a grip at the studio next summer.' He had been meaning to suggest it anyway, and Teddy was almost hysterical with joy as they ate the pumpkin pie Fannie had baked. She was a remarkable cook and Sam complimented her on everything, which touched Edwina's heart. He was sweet to all of them, as though they were his family now, too, and that meant a lot to her. And she tried to thank him for it later, when Alexis was talking to George about a new film, and Fannie and Helen and Teddy were playing cards, and she and Sam decided to take a walk in the garden.

'Thank you for being so good to them. It means a lot to me,' she smiled.

'You've given up your life for them for a long time. But they do you proud.' He looked down at her with wise eyes and a gentle smile. 'What are you going to do when they grow up, Edwina?'

'Same thing you do now, with Helen.' In her eyes they were of the same generation, but in truth, they weren't. She was thirty-two years old, and Sam Horowitz was fifty-seven. 'You wait for grandchildren. I wait for nieces and nephews. Same thing really.' She smiled gently, and he shook his head.

'No, it isn't.' He spoke quietly in the night air, as they walked, exercising off their dinner, but she felt very comfortable with him, as though they had always been old friends and could say anything to each other. She liked Helen's father, she always had, as much as she liked Helen. 'I had a whole life a long time ago, with a woman I loved, and who hurt me very badly. You've had much too little in your life, except a bunch of kids you love and give everything you have to give to. But when do you get yours? When is it your turn? What happens when they're gone? That's what I meant . . . nieces and nephews aren't enough . . . you need a lot more than that. You should be having kids of your own.' He sounded serious and she almost laughed at him.

'Why is everyone saying that to me these days?' Patrick . . . Lady Fitzgerald . . . now Sam . . . 'Hey, I raised five children as though they were mine. Don't you suppose I've done enough?'

'Maybe. But it's not the same. At least I don't think so.'

'I think it is.' She sounded serious with him. 'I've loved those five children as though they were mine.' She hesitated before she went on. 'I almost think I loved them more than my mother did.' . . . She didn't love them enough to stay alive for them, to leave her husband for

375

them . . . but as Edwina thought of it now, after talking about it with Patrick, after all these years, she was no longer angry. And then she decided to ask Sam something about what he had said, since they were being so open with each other. 'Why did you say that your wife had hurt you so badly? I thought she'd died.'

'She did.' He looked soberly at his young friend with the wise heart and kind eyes. 'She was running off with another man when she was killed in a train wreck. Helen was only nine months old, and she doesn't know that.' For a moment, Edwina was stunned into silence.

'That must have been awful for you,' she said, impressed at his never having told his daughter. He was a kind and decent man, which was only a small part of why she liked him. She had admired and respected him from the first, and she valued his friendship.

'It was awful. And I was angry for a long time,' Sam went on. 'I kept it all inside until it almost ate me up. But one day, I just decided it was too much trouble to carry around anymore, so I gave it up. She left me Helen, and maybe that was enough. In fact, now I know it was.' But Edwina thought that it was sad to think he had never remarried. That had been twenty-one years before, and it was a long time to be lonely. She knew he went out with some of the most important actresses in Hollywood from time to time, but she had never heard of him being seriously involved with anyone, and neither had George. Sam Horowitz lived for his business, and his daughter. And then, he stunned Edwina with his next question. 'How was Europe, by the way?' She stopped walking and turned to look at him in amazement.

'What makes you think I was in Europe?' Fannie had said that when he called she told him the same laryngitis story she had told her brother.

'I called a couple of times to see how you were. You were so sweet to Helen on her wedding day, you were like a mother to her, and I wanted to thank you. And little Fannie just lied her little tail off, about how you had this terrible cold, and just couldn't talk, and had this dreadful laryngitis,' he did a perfect imitation of Fannie, and Edwina laughed as she looked at his strongly chiseled face and his white hair shining in the moonlight, and she realized as she had before that he was actually very handsome. 'Anyway, I figured something was wrong, so I did a little careful checking around, and discovered that not only had Malcolm Stone disappeared out of town, but so had Miss Alexis. And then I figured out where you'd gone. I thought of coming after you at one point, but then I decided that if you needed me, you'd call, or at least I hoped you would have. I like to think that we're friends.' He looked at her cautiously. 'I was actually a little disappointed that you didn't call me.' And then he looked down at her very gently. 'You got on a ship all by yourself, didn't you?' She had, but she hadn't stayed that way for long. 'That took a lot of guts,' he continued, as she nodded. 'And you found her. Where was she?'

'In London.' Edwina smiled, thinking of the scene when they'd found them, and 'the magistrate', Patrick.

'She was with Stone?'

Edwina hesitated and then nodded. 'But George doesn't know, and I promised her I wouldn't tell him.' She looked worriedly up at Sam, and he shook his head with a rueful expression. She was still impressed that he had known and hadn't told anyone. Sam was smart, and discreet, and incredibly caring.

'It's not up to me to tell either my son-in-law or my partner what his sister's been up to. As long as you have it in control, I respect that. Where is Stone now, by the way?'

'I think he stayed there. I don't think he'll be in a hurry to come back to Hollywood. He's too afraid of George.'

'Smart man. I think your brother would kill him if he knew. My late wife taught me a few tricks I could have lived without, which is why I suspected Alexis had left town, but she seems to be behaving herself now.'

'She is, and she wants to come back to Hollywood in the spring when she turns eighteen, to do another picture. I think maybe George will let her by then, if she still wants to.' But Edwina was sure she would. All she talked about was her career as an actress.

'And you?' he asked pointedly. 'What are you going to do now?' His eyes met hers and they held for a long time. There were many things he wanted to ask her, things he wanted to tell her about himself, things he wanted to know about her.

'I don't know, Sam.' She sighed. But she seemed happy. 'I'll do whatever they need me to do, go along, stay at home, whatever . . .' She wasn't worried about it just then. She had been following them around for eleven years and she had nothing else to do. Besides, she loved them, but Sam was getting at something else, something he wasn't sure how to broach with Edwina. Something he had been thinking about for a long time, but he didn't know where to start, and for the first time in a long time he was frightened.

They stopped walking and he looked down at her again. Her face was shining up at him in the moonlight, her eyes blue as steel, and her skin stark white in sharp contrast to the dark hair. 'What about you, Edwina? When do you get yours? They all have their lives, they're almost gone and you haven't even noticed. Do you know when I realized Helen was gone? The day she married George. All of a sudden, I stood there and handed her over to him. I built an empire for her, and suddenly she was gone. But do you know what else I found out that day, while you were fussing over her, and straightening her veil . . . the veil you would have worn, if your fiancé hadn't gone down with your parents . . . I discovered that I built the empire for myself, too, and there is no one to share it with now. After all these years, and all this work, and all that love I poured out on Helen, and her mother before her . . . suddenly, I'm alone. Sure, there will be grandchildren one day, and Helen is still around, but it's not the same. There is no one to hold my hand, to be there for me, no one to care about me . . . and no one I care about, except my only daughter. I watched you that day,' he said gently, as he took her hand in his much larger one, his face close to hers, and she saw what she'd liked in him right from the beginning. The gentleness, the strength, the kindness, and wisdom. He was the kind of person her father had been, someone you could laugh with and talk to, someone you instinctively loved. He was natural and real, and for a moment she almost thought she loved him. And as she struggled with the thought, he smiled at her. 'Do you know what I want? I want to be there for you, to hold your hand, to hold you when you cry and laugh with you when you're having fun. I want to be there for you, Edwina. And I'd like you to be there for me when I need you. We have a right to that, you and I.' He smiled at her almost sadly then. 'And we've never had it.'

She was silent for a long time, not sure what to say to him. He wasn't Patrick or Charles, he wasn't young, but neither was she, and she knew that in an odd way she loved him. He was the man she had wanted for years and never really known it. A man she could care for and respect, and love. A man she could spend the rest of her life with. And then suddenly, for an instant, she understood something else. She knew she would stand beside him through anything, in thick and thin, for better or worse until . . . and so it had been with her mother. She had gone down with Bert, because there had been no greater love . . . no greater love than she'd had for him . . . or than Edwina had had for their children . . . or than she and Sam would have one day for each other, or perhaps even their children.

Edwina knew suddenly that one day they would have the same kind of love her parents had had. The kind of love you build, and you cherish, and you take good care of. The kind of love you live for . . . and are even willing to die for. Theirs was a quiet thing, but she sensed that beneath the bond that had already formed was the solid rock you could build a life on.

'I don't know what to say . . .' She smiled up at him, almost shyly. She had never thought of anything like that with him. She had only thought of him as Helen's father . . . but then she remembered how she had turned to him when Alexis had disappeared, how he had been there, and how she had known that if she really needed him, she could call him. He was her friend before he was anything else, and she liked that about him. The truth was, she liked everything about him. 'What do you suppose Helen would think?' . . . and George . . . and the others . . . but she suspected they'd be pleased, just as he did.

'I think she'd think I was damn lucky, and so would I.' He held her hand tightly in his own. 'Edwina . . . don't say anything if it's too soon. I just want to know if it's possible for you, or if you think I'm crazy.' He looked at her hesitantly, almost like a boy, and she laughed as she was suddenly reminded of the children.

'I think we're both crazy, Sam, but I think I like it.' She moved closer to him, and he smiled, and then he turned, pulled her close, and held her tight as he kissed her.

THE END

MIRROR IMAGE
by Danielle Steel

A novel that explores one of life's most powerful and mysterious relationships – the bond between identical twins.

To look at one was to see the other. For the family, even the girls' own father, it was a constant guessing game. For strangers, the surprise was overwhelming. And between twins Olivia and Victoria their bond was mysterious, marvellous, and often playful – a secret realm only they inhabited.

Olivia, born eleven minutes before her sister, was shy and serious, while free-spirited Victoria wanted to change the world, and embraced the women's suffrage movement. Then in 1914, the girls' twenty-first year, Victoria's life was about to become a public scandal, and handsome lawyer Charles Dawson was brought in to save her reputation. In an act of deception that only Olivia and Victoria could manage their lives were changed forever as one of the twins left for the battlefields of France, and the other moved into a marriage she longed for but thought she could not have.

From Manhattan society to the trenches of war-torn France, *Mirror Image* moves elegantly and dramatically through a rich and troubled era. With startling insight, Danielle Steel explores women's choices: between home and adventure, between the love for family and the passion for a cause, between sacrifice and desire, against a vivid backdrop of a world at war.

o 552 14134 8

THE KLONE AND I
by Danielle Steel

Finding the perfect mate in an imperfect world . . .

Stephanie had a rat of a husband. But after thirteen years of marriage and two kids, she was devastated when he left her for a younger woman. Suddenly, Stephanie was alone, and after trying to find a little romance on New York's wild singles circuit, she was reconciled to raising her kids alone – until a spur-of-the-moment trip to Paris changed everything. On the Left Bank she met Peter Baker, a marvellously handsome high-tech entrepreneur. He seemed just too perfect, but to Stephanie's amazement he contacted her when they returned to New York – and Stephanie embarked upon a bizarre and hilarious adventure beyond her wildest dreams.

Shy, serious Peter, chairman of a bionic enterprise, was supposed to be away on business. But instead, he's standing at her door, wearing day-glo satin and rhinestones. Naturally, Stephanie thinks this is a joke, until she discovers – this isn't Peter, but his double! Calling himself Paul Klone, this wild, uninhibited creature isn't remotely like Peter except for his identically sexy good looks.

An uproarious novel which explores the outrageous triangle between Stephanie, Peter . . . and The Klone.

0 552 14637 4

A LIST OF OTHER DANIELLE STEEL TITLES AVAILABLE FROM CORGI BOOKS AND BANTAM PRESS

THE PRICES SHOWN BELOW WERE CORRECT AT THE TIME OF GOING TO PRESS. HOWEVER TRANSWORLD PUBLISHERS RESERVE THE RIGHT TO SHOW NEW RETAIL PRICES ON COVERS WHICH MAY DIFFER FROM THOSE PREVIOUSLY ADVERTISED IN THE TEXT OR ELSEWHERE.

☐	13525 9	**HEARTBEAT**	£5.99
☐	13522 4	**DADDY**	£5.99
☐	13524 0	**MESSAGE FROM NAM**	£5.99
☐	13745 6	**JEWELS**	£5.99
☐	13746 4	**MIXED BLESSINGS**	£5.99
☐	13526 7	**VANISHED**	£5.99
☐	13747 2	**ACCIDENT**	£5.99
☐	14245 X	**THE GIFT**	£5.99
☐	13748 0	**WINGS**	£5.99
☐	13749 9	**LIGHTNING**	£5.99
☐	14378 2	**FIVE DAYS IN PARIS**	£5.99
☐	14131 3	**MALICE**	£5.99
☐	14132 1	**SILENT HONOUR**	£5.99
☐	14133 X	**THE RANCH**	£5.99
☐	14507 6	**SPECIAL DELIVERY**	£5.99
☐	14504 1	**THE GHOST**	£5.99
☐	14502 5	**THE LONG ROAD HOME**	£5.99
☐	14637 4	**THE KLONE AND I**	£5.99
☐	14134 8	**MIRROR IMAGE**	£5.99
☐	54654 2	**HIS BRIGHT LIGHT:** The story of my son, Nick Traina	£5.99
☐	04070 8	**BITTERSWEET (Hardback)**	£16.99*
☐	04075 9	**GRANNY DAN (Hardback)**	£9.99*
☐	04072 4	**IRRESISTIBLE FORCES (Hardback)**	£16.99*

* including VAT

All Transworld titles are available by post from:

Book Service By Post, P.O. Box 29, Douglas, Isle of Man IM99 1BQ

Credit cards accepted. Please telephone 01624 675137, fax 01624 670923, Internet http://www.bookpost.co.uk or e-mail: bookshop@enterprise.net for details.

Free postage and packing in the UK. Overseas customers allow £1 per book (paperbacks) and £3 per book (hardbacks).